BOUGHT BY THE ALPHA

THE ALPHA KING'S BREEDER BOOK ONE

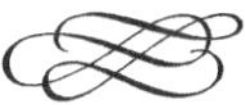

BELLA MOONDRAGON

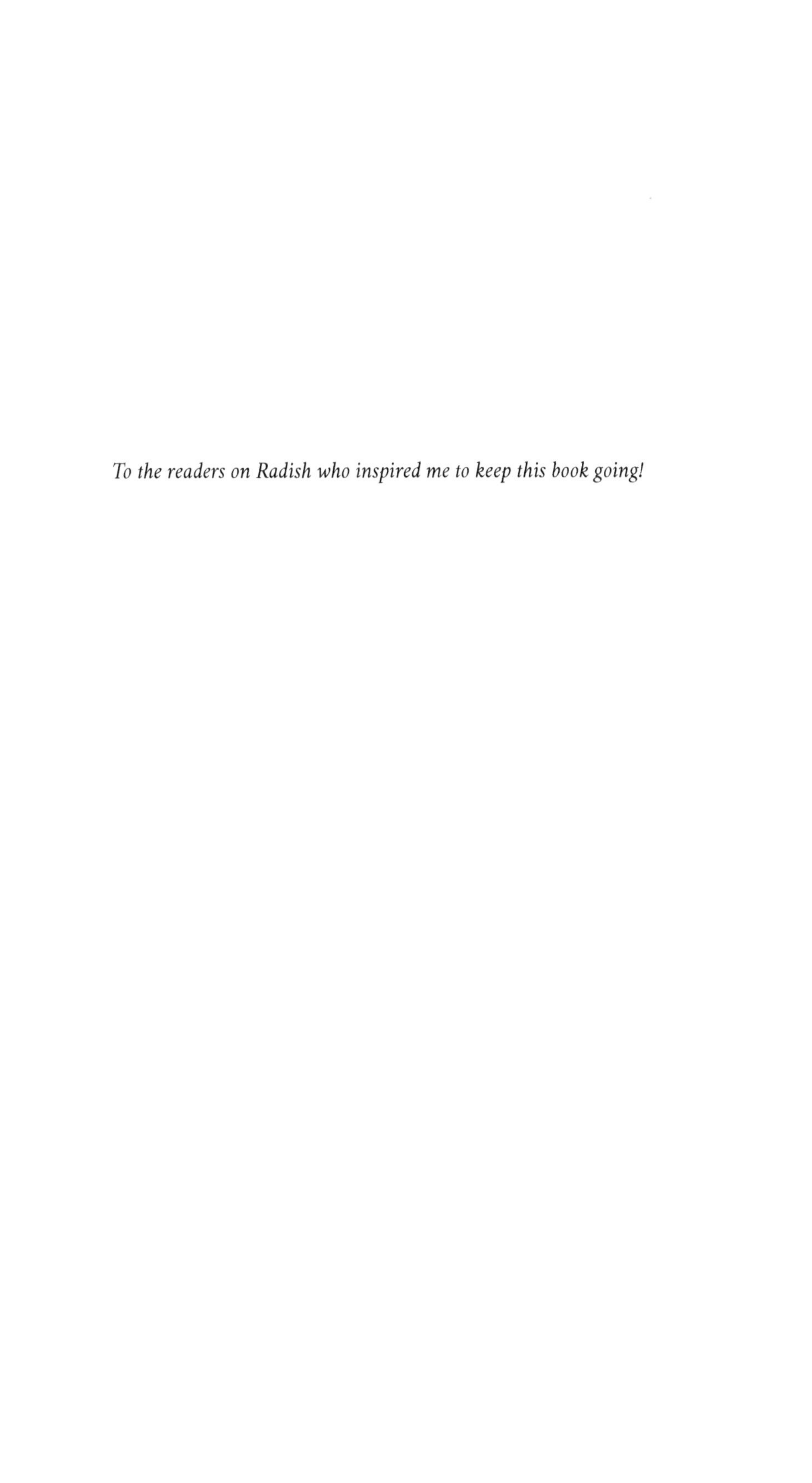

To the readers on Radish who inspired me to keep this book going!

CONTENTS

WHEN IT RAINS, IT POURS

Isla

RAIN POUNDS my back as I follow Alpha Ernest up the wide marble steps to a home I never expect to see in real life. I look around quickly, but he is walking fast, and I don't have much time to see the outside of the mansion. I only know it resembles a castle. The dreary sky seems fitting, considering my bleak outlook.

Likewise, this castle is fitting for an Alpha King.

Under the wide porch, there is a bit of shelter from the wind. I pull my thin cloak around my shoulders. When Alpha Ernest's fist pounds on the door, I jump. Everything about this day is unexpected and has me on edge.

The door opens a bit and a man with a thin, long nose gapes out at us. He is wearing a butler's suit, and I relax only slightly.

Not that I expected the cruel king to open his own door, but I am thankful not to be faced with him right away.

"Greetings! Greetings!" Alpha Ernest says in his jovial, exceedingly loud voice. He laughs in the back of his throat, his gruff tone as raspy as the thunder in the distance. "It is I, Alpha Ernest of Willow pack! His Majesty is expecting me."

The butler looks him over and then his eyes fall on me for a moment as if he isn't sure whether or not the rotund, sweaty man in the white shirt with the sleeves rolled up to his elbows could possibly be an actual Alpha. The detail of Omegas that are hanging out in the car that brought us the two hours make it more convincing.

"Come in," the butler says, pulling the heavy wooden door open.

"Thank you, thank you," my Alpha says, and I follow him inside, absently wondering why he must say everything twice.

My happiness at being let in from the rain only lasts a moment as I follow along behind the two men who walk quickly down a long corridor. The inside of the house doesn't resemble the castle in the sense that the floors are not made of stone—they are wood—and the walls are covered in drywall. But it is a huge building, and it is lavishly decorated with fine furnishings, all kinds of pieces of art from paintings to sculptures to ancient vases, and I try to keep up with our guide while my eyes roam over objects that are worth a hundred times more than what my parents make in a year—a thousand times more.

The sale of just one of these objects would have been plenty to pay off my parents' debts. If I'd had just one painting to sell, I wouldn't be here now.

I can't think of that at the moment. My fate is sealed. I grasp my small bag in my hands and struggle to keep up. It doesn't help that I haven't eaten much of anything in the past week. I feel lightheaded.

We turn down a few corridors, and it's clear to me that we are now in the part of the building that is for work instead of show. Artwork still hangs on the walls, but it's not as elaborate. The doors we are passing seem to be offices, not libraries or parlors.

"Wait here," the butler says, pausing outside of a closed door. He knocks, and I hear a low gravelly voice call him in.

I feel my heart begin to thump in my chest. I'm still not quite clear what Alpha Ernest has in mind for me. When I came to him for help earlier in the day, he asked me a few personal questions, a smile split his face, and then he told me to go home and pack all of my most prized possessions. He said to tell my family goodbye, if I was serious about paying off my family's debts, and to be back in his office in one hour.

Then, we'd gotten in the car and driven here. I hadn't asked any questions other than for him to put it in writing.

"John and Constance Moon are no longer in debt to Alpha Ernest Rock if their daughter, Isla Moon, follows through with the agreement made with said Alpha on this day…." Dated, signed by both parties, and here I am.

Still not sure what that agreement is.

Alpha Ernest goes inside of the office, and I am tempted to strain to see inside, too, but I don't. I've never seen him before, the Alpha King, the head of all of the Alphas and all of the territories in our region, for thousands and thousands of miles. I've heard lots of stories about him, though.

Presently, I am hoping that most of them are not true.

I would like to see his face, to know if the rumors of his attractiveness are accurate.

But I'd rather not see him at all, if I had a choice. Word of his cruelty precedes him, and it is said that he is just as brutal as he is handsome.

"You may sit," the butler says, gesturing to a chair near the door that has closed behind Alpha Ernest.

I nod, but I am not capable of thanking him verbally right now, not when my teeth are near chattering with fear.

I sit down, still grasping my bag in my hands. I wish I had put on more than the thin cloak my mother had given me last winter. Cloaks were cheaper than coats, so that's what I had.

I wouldn't hide the trembling that was beginning to ravage my body, though.

Doing my best to ignore the shaking, I tried to focus in on the faint voices I could hear coming from behind the thick wooden door. I didn't expect to be able to hear because the door looked sturdy, but Alpha Ernest is loud.

And Alpha Maddox…. Well, he just sounded agitated.

"Thank you for seeing me on such short notice," Alpha Ernest was saying.

When Alpha Maddox replied, it was harder to hear. He wasn't as loud. "I don't know why you're here unless it's to pay me the money you owe me." At least, that's what I think he is saying.

"Unfortunately, sir, I don't have the money—not exactly," the other man replies. I hear Alpha Maddox grumble in response. "But I have something else to offer you instead. Something better."

"Something better than the one and a half million dollars you owe me?"

My heart catches in my throat and I nearly choke. One and a half million dollars? Did I hear that correctly? What in the world could Alpha Ernest have that is worth that kind of money?

"Oh, yes!" Alpha Ernest says. "Please, sir, hear me out. I have a bargain for you. One that will allow me to settle our debt and help you with a certain… problem you have."

Problem? What problem could Alpha Maddox possibly have—other than the fact that he might have killed all of the people that he wanted to yell at.

I sit with my feet flat on the floor, my eyes focusing on the eggshell wall across from me, listening, not believing what I am hearing.

"Ernest," Alpha Maddox says, "you are the last person on earth I would turn to to help me solve a problem, not that I even know what you're referring to."

"Let me enlighten you, sir, if you don't mind?"

Alpha Maddox growls again. If he says anything else, I don't hear it.

Alpha Ernest continues. "You have just turned twenty-nine last month, yes?" I assume Alpha Maddox confirms this because my pack Alpha continues. "Everyone knows that the Alpha King is expected to have an heir by the age of thirty."

"Alpha Ernest—" the king says.

"Give me only a few moments of your time, Alpha" Ernest says, and I can imagine his hands up in front of him. "You need someone who can bear you a child, someone with no complicated relationship involved, someone who is beautiful, with good, healthy genes. A strapping mother who has born many children and proven herself to be from good stock."

With every word he speaks, my heart leaps higher into my throat, even though my brain still doesn't want to compute what he is saying.

"What are you proposing, Ernest?" Alpha Maddox says. "I don't have any problem picking up women. You know that, don't you?"

"Yes, yes, of course!" Alpha Ernest says. "But women at court are complicated. They have expectations. I know you don't intend to marry again. So… what you need is a willing, compliant, beautiful girl who is eager to spread her legs to earn money, bear you a child—or two or three—and then fade away. And I have just the girl for you."

I take a deep breath and hold it. Surely, Alpha Maddox will not agree to this. Why would he agree to this?

Why have I agreed to this?

Did I agree to this?

"Let me see if I understand you correctly, Alpha Ernest," I hear Alpha Maddox say, and I can't tell if he's angry, offended… or intrigued. "Are you proposing I take some girl you've brought with you into my home for the sole purpose of having a child?"

"That's right, Your Majesty," Ernest says. "I'm proposing you take on… a breeder."

THE PROPOSAL

Maddox

I HEAR the word come out of Alpha Ernest's mouth, watch his gums flap as his fat cheeks shift into a smile, his greasy mustache dancing as he tips his head up and blinks at me.

He's like a shady used car salesman, trying to convince me to take something I don't want or need.

Something that's broken and doesn't even work correctly—something that will never serve its intended purpose.

What he doesn't know is that I've already been considering finding a breeder for the last few months. I just haven't had the time to try to find a woman who would fit the requirements.

Everything he's said is true. I certainly don't ever want to marry again, no matter what. Even thinking about my wife makes my heart tighten up and my eyes begin to water. I have to immediately push her beautiful face from my mind. No, I will not ever take another bride.

That means, in order to have an heir, I have to find a woman who'd be willing to carry my child knowing that there are no strings attached.

That simply cannot happen with any of the women at court. They all want something more.

They all want me.

Finding a woman from one of the other pack lands has always been a possibility, and I've had a few Alphas mention their daughters from time to time, but I've never wanted to put a loyal Alpha in a position where I'd be using their daughter in such a manner. Whoever carries my child will essentially be unable to ever marry and have a normal life.

What other man would ever want her? Even if she found her fated mate, he'd know that she'd been with me, the Alpha King, and he'd never, ever be able to live up to those standards.

She'd live the rest of her life by herself, discarded and alone.

Who would want that?

Apparently, Alpha Ernest has found someone who won't mind. I need to know more.

"Who is the girl?" I ask, trying not to sound too interested, like I am humoring him. It isn't too hard for me. My reputation for being abundantly cruel isn't completely unfounded.

"Her name is Isla Moon, Alpha Maddox. She is a member of my pack. Today, she came in and asked if I had any odd jobs she could do to pay off the debt she owes me, and I offered her this one. She accepted."

He is holding something back. I can tell by the way his eyes are wide, the way he shrugs his shoulders as he speaks. There has to be more to Isla's story than this. "Why does she owe you money?" I ask him.

He only shrugs. "Family debt. I'm not sure."

I study his face. He is lying. He knows exactly what it is. I wonder if the girl has been manipulated to be here of if she came of her own free will. Had she heard about the handsome, mysterious Alpha King and wanted to take advantage of the opportunity to spend some time in his castle and frequent his bed?

I also want to make sure she isn't some prostitute who is going to make me sick. "Has she been… inspected?"

"No," he says. "But that's not necessary. The girl is a virgin."

I scoffed. "How do you know that?"

"I've known her for her entire life," he says quickly. "My pack is small. I know everyone. Of course, if you are worried, you can send your physicians in to see. If I am lying, I would gladly pay you twice what I owe you, sir. I would never deceive you about such a thing." I raise my eyebrows. He realizes he slipped up. "I would never deceive you about anything."

Somehow, I doubt that. "What does she look like?" I ask.

"She's beautiful," he tells me. "She's outside the door."

I shake my head. I don't want to see her yet.

"She's a small girl, about this tall." He raises his hand to show me she's about five foot two or so. "She has long, blonde hair that is curly, and her eyes are wide and blue. Her skin is smooth like porcelain and bright. She's a bit skinny, I think, but she has large breasts and curvy hips."

I close my eyes and slowly shake my head at his crassness. It shouldn't surprise me. I wonder if the girl can hear us. "Is she intelligent?" I don't want my heir to be an idiot.

"Oh, yes. She did very well in school. Top of her class. She went to college for a couple of years but had to drop out for… some reason." Again, he is holding back. He knows why. "She's a sweet girl. You will enjoy her." He winks at me, and I know he means sexually.

It makes my skin crawl because I know he wishes that he could enjoy her.

I don't know why the girl has decided to come with him here, but I won't be sending her back home with him, not today anyway.

I have a lot to do today, including a dinner party with an Alpha from a distant region. I decide I will keep her and possibly speak to her for a bit before I determine what to do. While it does sound like her services may be the solution to my problems, I'm not sure I'm ready for all of these complications.

"How old is she?" I ask him.

"Twenty, I think," he says.

Twenty. She is young. When I was twenty, my father was still alive. I wasn't even the Alpha King yet.

It seems like a very long time ago.

The image of my wife's face flutters in front of my mind, and my mouth wants to move of its own accord.

"Rebecca…."

I don't say her name. I've learned not to. It makes people question my sanity, and since they already do that enough over my alleged viciousness, there's no reason to have them think I'm seeing ghosts as well.

If there's one thing they don't need to worry about it's me seeing Rebecca. I've looked everywhere for her and have never seen her, not even once.

Rarely even in my dreams.

"What do you say, Alpha Maddox? Why don't we make this agreement? Take the girl. Enjoy her. If she gets pregnant and gives you an heir in the next year, my debts are erased. If she does not… I will find another way to repay you… plus interest."

Alpha Ernest extends his hand to me. I take a deep breath and look at his palm, not sure whether I should shake his hand or not.

Do I want to take the girl and keep her as a breeder—or send her back home with this man, possibly to her family, or possibly to become some sort of sex slave to him?

∼

Isla

. . .

"This way. Keep up, and don't touch anything."

I follow along behind the tall, middle-aged, blonde woman in a suit as she walks very quickly through the castle. She's wearing a pair of gray slacks and a black jacket, the shirt beneath with a white collar that's buttoned up to her chin. Her hair is in a tight bun, and she has her nose in the air. She seems very proper, and I don't think she's very nice.

I keep thinking about that word. Breeder. What does it mean? Why am I here?

I do my best to keep up, but she's walking so fast, and I have no idea where we are going or why we are going there. I didn't hear much of the conversation between Alpha Ernest and Alpha Maddox. Once Alpha Ernest offered to sell me to Alpha Maddox to get rid of his debts, they began to negotiate much quieter, and I don't know what's happening now.

I walk through narrow halls, through larger openings that have pieces of artwork like vases and paintings, and even some suits of armor. Everything is regal and expensive as it had been before, and I wouldn't touch anything even if she hadn't told me to because I am afraid I might break something.

Everything here looks like it is worth more than my family makes in a year.

"I have no idea why Mr. Thompson, the butler, has asked me to show you to this room," the woman says as I follow along, carrying my bag in front of me and trying to keep up. "But apparently, the king has asked him to. I, personally, think it must be a mistake, judging by how you're dressed."

My eyes immediately drop down to see what I am wearing, and I remember that I didn't have much time to get ready to come on this journey. I am still wearing a black skirt and white blouse I had put on for work that morning under my black cloak. My shoes are old tennis shoes that have a hole in one toe, and because they are wet from the rain, they squeak a little. I'm sure she loves that.

"I asked him if he meant for me to show you to the maids' quarters, but he said no. I was to show you to this suite. Whatever in heaven's name the king has in mind for you, it's none of my business, but perhaps he's got it in his head that you're from Alpha Jordan's pack, Maple pack, though none of them have arrived yet. I'll set him straight in a bit."

"Yes, ma'am," I say, trying to be polite.

She stops and spins around, her dark eyes like daggers. "I am the head of the staff here at Castle Blackthorn. You will address me as Mrs. Worsthingshorethinshire. Do you understand me?"

I stare at her for a long moment, wondering why she would address a guest in such a way. Her eyes are wild, and I imagine a maid would get a slap across the face for such an offense. I'm not even sure how to answer since I'm quite certain I cannot repeat back that name.

I most certainly will not say, "Yes, ma'am."

So instead, I nod my head. "Beg your pardon," I say.

She continues to stare at me for what seems like a minute or two before she says, "I beg your pardon, Mrs. Worsthingshorethinshire."

I clear my throat and say, "I beg your pardon Mrs. Worsthingshurtinshirthenshire."

She takes a deep breath and blows it out slowly. "Worsthingshorethinshire. It's not that difficult!"

I am afraid she's going to make me try to say it again, but she doesn't. Instead, she spins around and starts walking once more, and I follow, feeling sorry for the maids who have to answer to her and attempting to practice her name as I go.

I do not like her at all, this Mrs. Worsthingstirshorethinsire… or whatever her name is.

And I just want to go home.

"Your room, for now, is just down the hall from the king's room. But don't expect it to stay that way. Because, as I said, I believe there has been a mistake."

We round a corner quickly, and I run into a table. The contents, a silver bowl and a vase, clatter, and she turns around and comes at me. "Be careful!" she shouts.

"I'm so sorry!" I say, praying that nothing falls.

She rights the bowl and steadies the vase, shaking her head as she does so. "I told you not to touch anything. If that happens again, you're going to wish you never stepped foot in this castle! I don't care who you are or why you're here, young lady! In my castle, under my watch, there are consequences for breaking rules!"

I take a step backward, feeling myself shrink a bit with each shout. I know I must try to say her name again as she towers over me, her face red with rage.

"Yes, Mrs. Worthersthershirhirethire."

"That's not even close!" she screams in my face. "You're incorrigible, aren't you! It's no wonder someone brought you here and left you!"

I wonder how she knows that, but I say nothing, only watch the veins in her neck protrude.

I have seen that before, right before my boss at the flour mill would hit me because I dropped a bag or before my boss at the diner would beat me for accidentally spilling a tray of food. I'm not clumsy, but I'm not that strong. Eventually, after working eighteen or nineteen hours, I would grow tired, and things would slip.

I am afraid she's going to hit me now, but she doesn't. She only walks a few more steps before she produces a key and unlocks a door.

We walk inside what must be an antechamber because there's another door. This room is mostly empty. Just a little sitting area and a table with another vase on it. It's quaint and pretty.

She props the main door open with a doorstop and then continues. "These are your rooms, for now," she says, leading me to the other door.

As she pushes the other door open, I step aside and bump the table, slightly, with my hip. I think nothing of it, though, because these are my rooms.

Until I feel pain radiating through the side of my face and am knocked off my feet, falling to the floor as my bag goes flying free from my hands so that I can try to catch myself.

"I told you not to touch anything!" she screams at me.

Shocked, I sit there on the floor for a moment, trying to grasp what has just happened. Did she just hit me for bumping a table in my own chambers?

Am I not supposed to sleep in the bed the king has appointed for me?

Or sit on any chairs?

Before I can react, she reaches down and grabs me by the collar of my cloak, yanking me to my feet. She is so much bigger than me, and stronger. She is shaking me as she screams, "Who do you think you are, coming in here and messing things up? You little tramp? She slaps me again, and this time, I manage to get my arm up to partially block it, but I still feel her hand make contact with my cheek. Over and over again, she swings at me, and it's all I can do to keep her from knocking me down again.

Until I hear a commanding voice shout, "What on earth are you doing?"

WHY AM I HERE?

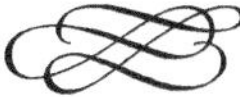

Isla

THE HEAD MAID lets go of me when we hear a male voice demanding to know what she is doing.

She turns to address him as I cover my face, pain radiating through my cheeks and nose.

"Beta Seth," she begins, "this girl was being careless with the king's belongings and disrespectful to me. I was simply teaching her a lesson, the same way I would teach any new servant a lesson, sir."

I wipe a bit of blood from my upper lip with the back of my hand and turn to see a handsome man walk into the room. He is tall with dark blond hair and wide shoulders. His green eyes are focused on the other woman in the room, and his intense stare has her rigid stance wavering.

"How dare you?" he demands. "You were asked to show Miss Isla to her room, Mrs. Worsthingshorethinshire. No one asked you to teach her anything. I can't imagine she did anything careless. What could she have possibly done? I didn't see anything broken between here and the king's offices."

I watch as the woman's throat moves viciously as she swallows. "Well, she bumped a table in the hall and then again in here and…"

"In her own room? So what?" He seems to be getting angrier by the moment, and as he takes another step toward her, Mrs. Whateverhernameisshire bumps into the table. "I suppose now that you've bumped the table, we should teach you a lesson, hmm?"

I notice then that there are two other men with him. Both of them are dressed in guards' uniforms. They are large, muscular men as well, and as Beta Seth raises a hand, they step forward.

"Oh, no, Beta, please," she says. "I didn't mean to."

"Well, I'm sure Miss Isla didn't mean to either. But you took it upon yourself to slap her until her face is bleeding. So… I think Daniel and Stephen shall do the same to you." He snaps his fingers and moves aside.

I watch as one of the large men grabs her by the collar and the other begins to slap her across the face. It only takes a few smacks for her nose and lip to start bleeding. She begins to cry, begging them to stop.

"Please," I say, my eyes wide. "Please, don't." I reach out to touch the Beta's shirt sleeve, but I fall short of actually grabbing it. "Can that be enough, please?"

He turns and looks at me while the other two continue to slap her, taking turns now. He snaps his fingers and they stop, letting her go in the process, and she falls to the ground. "You think she's had enough, Miss Isla?"

I nod. I wouldn't have wanted them to slap her anyway. Even though she is an awful person, and she hurt me, I don't like to watch others suffer.

He studies my face for a moment before one side of his mouth pulls up into a grin. "You are… different," he assesses, and I don't know if that's good or bad. "Daniel, take Mrs. Worsthingshorethinshire to her chamber to gather her things. She'll be departing the castle now."

"Yes, Beta Seth," Daniel says, and he hauls the woman up off the ground by her shirt collar as she begs to keep her job.

"You're firing her?" I ask.

"Yes," he answers as if it is the most obvious thing in the world. "You haven't even seen your room yet. Here we are."

I feel bad for the woman, even if she was a witch, but we have moved on, and as Beta Seth opens the door to my room, I can't believe my eyes.

"This is… my room?" I ask.

"That's right," he tells me. "King Maddox wanted the best room for you."

I stand in the doorway for a moment and take it all in.

To my left, there's a large, cherry wood dresser with a beautiful mirror and a bench where I can sit and do my hair and makeup, if I had any makeup. Just down from there is a plush blue chair that looks cozy and inviting. A large window with drapes the same shade as the chair is next to it, and there's a matching one on the other side of the bed.

The bed is massive, big enough for at least three people. It is a four-poster bed in the same cherry wood as the dresser, and the bedding matches the rest of the fabrics in the room. The mattress looks so plush and divine, I can't wait to try it out. I've been sleeping on a thin piece of foam for so long, I can't remember what a real mattress feels like.

Next to the second window, there's a door, which stands ajar, and I can see that inside is a bathroom, and a clawfoot tub looks so inviting, I want to jump right in. The tile on the floor is black and white checkered, and it looks very sleek and polished inside the en suite bathroom.

There's a large fireplace, though it isn't lit at the moment. The mantel has some beautiful blue vases and over it is a cottage scene that I imagine I could stare at for hours.

Near the fireplace stands a larger armoire that matches the other furniture, and there's another door that I imagine is a closet.

In the corner to my left is a round table in the same cherry wood finish with four chairs, upholstered in the same blue.

The carpet is beige, but there's a large throw rug that has beige and blue woven through it.

"Well?" Beta Seth asks as I stand there gaping at all of this.

"I think that Mrs. Worthershtirshirehover was right," I say, noting that he is chuckling at my butchering of her name.

"What did Mrs. Worsthingshorethinshire say, dare I ask?" Beta Seth questions.

"She told me that she thought there's been some mistake and that I'm actually supposed to be shown to the maid's quarters. Beta Seth, sir," I begin, bowing my head in respect, "I went to my Alpha to borrow money to repay a debt, and he brought me here to repay a debt he owes to the king. I believe I should be working to pay that debt off. Shouldn't I be in the maids' quarters to do that?"

Beta Seth's smile fades. "No one told you then?" he asks me.

My eyebrows raise, and I feel my heart begin to thunder in my chest as I try to guess what his words are supposed to mean. "No one told me… what?" I ask.

"No one told you what your duties shall be… in order to pay off the debt?"

I shake my head. "No, sir. No one has told me."

He clears his throat. "I don't really want to be the one to tell you, but if it isn't going to be King Maddox himself, then I suppose it's going to be me."

"Please, sir. You've been so kind. I'd like to hear it from you, if you don't mind."

He nods, and I brace myself to hear what he has to say. I have no idea what it could possibly be. None at all.

"You're going to repay your debts by becoming the Alpha King's Breeder."

I nod—but I'm still lost, and I don't know how to tell him.

WHAT AM I DOING?

Maddox

I NEED to prepare for my meeting with Alpha Jordan's pack before the formal dinner we'll be having. We have many points to discuss, and I need to be on top of my game to make sure that I don't get swindled on any of them.

After all, Alpha Jordan is one of my strongest allies, but he's also quite shrewd and nearly twice my age.

It would be quite easy for him to take advantage of me if I'm not paying close attention.

But I can't get my mind off the girl, and that's irritating.

I've sworn not to ever take another Luna, so there's no need for me to even let that thought cross my mind. It's not that.

I just wonder… what is she doing here? And am I crazy for even letting Alpha Ernest's ridiculous suggestion enter my thoughts?

Breeder….

I had been thinking about it before, though. It used to be common practice, a long time ago, back when Lunas had trouble conceiving male heirs and Alphas wanted to make sure that they had a strong son to put on the throne or to rule the pack after them.

Just because I hadn't heard of anyone doing it in decades didn't mean it wasn't a good idea.

Still… the girl….

I'd only caught a glimpse of her as she'd gone down the hallway, and she hadn't seen me at all. I hadn't even seen her face.

Alpha Ernest had said she was beautiful, but that didn't mean anything. Beauty was in the eye of the beholder.

Beyond that, I had a reputation for being a cold, cruel man on the battlefield.

Could I also be one in the bedroom?

People spoke of me as if I had a harem of women that I used and abused, but the truth of the matter was I hadn't slept with many women at all since my wife had died. When I did, they knew that there were no feelings involved.

"Rebecca...."

Her name rolled from my lips so easily, even though I wished it wouldn't. Even when I wished her memory would fade to the back of my mind and simply become a part of my subconscious.

A knock on my door brought me out of my thoughts.

"Seth," I said, seeing my Beta walk into the office. He knew he could walk in any time I wasn't with someone else. "Did you check on our... new guest?"

"I did. She's... a tiny thing. Sweet—a bit odd, perhaps."

"Odd?"

He shrugged. "It's hard to describe. You'll have to meet her. She's quite lovely, though. At any rate, it isn't her I came by to tell you about."

With my elbows on my desk, I leaned toward him. "What is it then?"

"It's Mrs. Worsthingshorethinshire." Seth let out a lamentable sigh as he sat down in a chair across from me. "I'm afraid I've had to let her go."

"Let her go?" I repeat. "But she's the head of the house staff, the head of the maids anyway. Whatever for?"

"Well, when I walked into the room, she had slapped the girl, Miss Isla, so hard, she'd knocked her across the room, and when I asked Mrs. Worsthing-shorethinshire why, she said it was because the girl had knocked into a table in her own room. Naturally, I couldn't let that be tolerated. It's not the first time I've heard of Mrs. Worsthingshorethinshire doing something so cruel."

I can only stare at him for a moment, hardly believing my ears. "And I have the reputation for being brutal."

He nodded. "I was so infuriated at the sight, I had my men give her a taste of her own medicine." He looks down at the floor, a bit embarrassed, I think. "Maybe I shouldn't have, but I thought she deserved it."

"No, don't beat yourself up about it," I say, trying to crack a joke, but Seth doesn't seem to think I am funny right now. "You did the right thing. How is the girl?"

"I left her in her rooms. I have sent for Poppy. I think she's the right maid to take care of her. I will also have some dinner sent to her and a wardrobe. I assume you will be in to see her... eventually?"

I shrug. "I don't know what my plans are, Seth. This breeder business… it's probably not for me. Especially if she is as you say she is… tiny and frail."

"Well, she is tiny, but I don't think she is frail. And she is quite lovely. There's something about her that's quite striking—and before you say it—no pun intended." He gives me a look that says he likes me better when I'm not trying to be funny.

"Is that what's odd about her then? The striking part?" I ask, putting my strange sense of humor aside.

"No," he says. "I think what's odd was that she just took it, like she's used to being knocked around. And that sort of seemed sad to me. That someone so young should be so used to being hit so hard."

I can only shrug at that. Empathy is not my strong suit. "Thanks for letting me know," I say. "Alpha Jordan will be here soon, and I need to prepare."

"All right," Seth gets up and heads out of the room, and I go back to my notes about my meeting with Alpha Jordan, but I cannot concentrate at all.

All I can think about is the girl.

POPPY

Isla

I sɪᴛ on the bed in my new room, not sure what to do, grasping my bag. I look around, but I'm not sure what to do.

Why am I here?

If I touch anything else, will someone come flying out of the closet and slap me again?

Beta Seth has assured me that this is my room, and I can do whatever I want, but I am still hesitant. I can't help but think that this is all a huge mistake.

Mrs. Worchestshire or whatever her name was had mentioned that she thought I was meant to go to the maids' quarters, and while Beta Seth said that wasn't right, I can't help but think maybe someone will come and take me there soon.

If I get too comfortable in here, I will just have to go.

And this is the nicest room I've ever seen.

I haven't been sitting here too long when there is a knock at the door.

I look up, and a girl with brown hair and wide hazel eyes is staring at me, just her head sticking in the door. "Hello, Miss," she says. "May I come in?"

"Yes, of course," I say, starting to get up.

"Oh, no, don't get up!" she insists, flying into the room like a flurry, a small, contained tornado. "I'm Poppy, Miss Isla," she says with a small bow of her head. "How do you do?"

I hesitate to respond because I'm not used to being addressed this way, but then I say, "I'm f-fine, thank you."

"Good! Beta Seth sent me to take care of you. I will be your personal maid. So… what can I do to assist you, miss?" she asks standing at attention with her hands folded in front of her.

I don't know how to respond to her because I have never had anyone bring me anything in my life, not since I was a child and needed my mother's help. "I don't know," I admit to her. "Do… do you know why I'm here?" The last part is a whisper.

Poppy laughs, and it sounds a bit like a melody. "No, miss, I'm afraid not. But don't fret. I'm sure there's a good reason, if you don't know. Now, let's see…. Food is on its way from the kitchen. A meal should be arriving shortly. Is that your bag?"

I look down at the pathetic bag I'm clutching in my hands, my knuckles white, and I nod.

"May I?" she asks, extending a hand.

I don't want to let go of it, but I do. She takes the bag from me, and looks through it.

"All right," she says. "We have plenty of clothes in the castle. We keep them in case guests forget their bags. Or so they say." She takes my things over to the armoire and begins to put them away. "Although, I have to say, I think it's also in case they are robbed on their way to the castle. You know there are plenty of rogues out there. And some Alphas who can't seem to remember who is king." She shakes her head, and I am surprised. I didn't know that there were any Alphas who would rise up against the Alpha King.

"At any rate, I will go and get you more clothing. You should have a regal wardrobe. I will get what I can, but we will see that you have everything that you need. Beta Seth said that you are to be treated as the finest ladies in the castle."

My eyes bulge. "He did?"

"Yes, he did. Now, what size are you?"

I have no idea. I shake my head. "My mother makes my clothes."

"Well, do you mind standing up?"

I manage to slide off the bed, and she looks me up and down.

"Tiny thing, aren't you!" Poppy proclaims.

She is rather thin herself, but she is much taller than me. My hands are trembling a bit, and I don't know what to do with myself. I've only been here a few hours, and I already miss my family.

"What happened to your face?" she asked, staring at the spot where that woman hit me.

I can only shake my head. I don't want to tell her.

"Oh! That's why they hauled Mrs. W. out of here by her hair, isn't it?"

"By her hair?" I ask, my eyes wide. I can hardly believe it.

"Yes! She deserved it anyway, awful witch! She treated everyone like that." Poppy shook her head. "Well, it's good she's gone. Now, why don't I go draw you a hot bath so you can soak? You've had a long day. Then, I'll go get you something proper to wear, and you can eat something and lie down."

"All right," I mutter, even though I'm fairly certain the king himself will be in soon to tell me it's time for me to go home—or go to the maids' quarters.

Poppy goes into the bathroom, and soon enough I hear water running and smell roses. She comes back a moment later with a big grin on her face. "Do you need any help getting undressed?"

"No, thank you," I say. I can't imagine needing help with that.

Rich people are… strange.

"All right. Do you need anything else before I go?"

"No, thank you."

She smiles at me and says, "I'll be back soon."

"Thank you, Poppy," I say before she goes.

She nods and then heads for the door, and I can't help but think that we might be friends—if I stay here.

Even if I do end up being a maid.

ALPHA JORDAN

Maddox

"Alpha Jordan?" I say, eyeing the man across from me and wondering what he's doing in my office when we are meant to have dinner in less than two hours. "What is it that you need?"

He looks at me and a small chuckle escapes his lips as he rubs his chin with a fist. He's at least twenty-five years my senior, maybe more, and it's easy to tell. His hair is gray, his face is wrinkled, and he looks worn—tired.

Will I look like that in a couple of decades?

Being an Alpha takes its toll.

Being an Alpha King is worse.

"Thank you for seeing me, Alpha Maddox," he begins, withdrawing his hand from his mouth. "I do appreciate you letting us stay here for a few nights. Traveling all the way through the kingdom is tiresome."

"Of course," I say, folding my hands on my desk. He still hasn't answered my question. I am a patient man until I am not.

He clears his throat. "I guess I should get straight to the point, then?" he says, that rumbling chuckle back.

I wait, not needing to say that he most certainly should do just that.

"A few of the Alphas have been speaking about the… conflict that is going on now. The problems we've been having."

"I know all about that," I say, not wanting to get into it right now. "What have you been discussing?"

"Well, only that… with the instability in the kingdom and the unrest, it would be best for the people if they had something to celebrate, something to… cheer them up and stay focused on that is more positive."

I continue to look at him, my forehead wrinkled. I am trying to figure out where he is going with this, but I don't want to attempt to guess because if it is where I think it might be… I might leap over my desk and cause bodily harm to the man.

"What are you getting at?" I finally ask him.

He shifts his weight in his chair. It creaks under the strain as if it also wants to protest whatever it is he's about to say to me. "You need an heir."

It is exactly what I thought he was going to say, and exactly what he should have never let come out of his mouth.

Keeping my face stoic, I glower at the man.

"I have a beautiful daughter who is a few years younger than you. She has gone through her first few heats. She is ripe for breeding. She could give you an heir, Your Majesty. It would be good for the kingdom. Zabrina would make a wonderful Luna." He takes a deep breath as if he is satisfied that he has gotten the message out.

The air settles around us, and I lean back in my chair, remembering what Seth always tells me about thinking before I react.

The man is introducing the idea of his daughter to me in similar language to the way Alpha Ernest mentioned the girl he brought me, though there was no talk of her heats. I suppose that's only because he had no way of knowing.

He had told me the girl was a virgin, though.

Alpha Jordan had not made any mention of that for his daughter.…

I shake my head. "Alpha Jordan, I thought I had made it clear that I didn't intend to marry again. Your daughter deserves to find her mate and—"

"She's found him," he says, interrupting me.

Waiting, I stare at him, anticipating he'll tell me more.

"It was the son of a Beta from a neighboring kingdom. She met him at a ball. The mate bond was not strong, but it was there. She rejected him, and he left." Alpha Jordan shrugs like this is of no consequence.

"But everyone knows rejecting one's mate has consequences," I remind him.

"I believe that the consequence was that our territory was attacked shortly thereafter, but we were victorious. Nothing else has happened. Zabrina is fine."

"And she's had no physical pain from the rejection?" This goes against everything I've ever heard.

"No, not that I've heard her complain of," he says nonchalantly.

"Strange." I have to wonder if perhaps this man wasn't actually her mate. Losing my mate has caused me nothing but torturous heartache.

And the only way it will ever end is if the Moon Goddess grants me another mate….

"Nevertheless, I don't intend to take another Luna, Alpha Jordan," I tell him dismissively.

"But what about an heir?" he asks. "Our kingdom must have an heir, Alpha Maddox."

"I am aware," I tell him, my tone sharp. "Why don't you let me handle that for myself, Alpha Jordan?"

His face turns a bit pink as I put him in his place, but then, he feels it is necessary to tell me, "Of course, but… know that the other Alphas are discussing the situation. There's… chatter."

I clear my throat and lean forward in my chair a bit, looking into his eyes. "I hope that those Alphas who are speaking against me understand that there will be consequences for traitorous behavior."

I see his eyes widen slightly. "Oh, yes, sir. No, nothing like that. We are all loyal to you, sir. Only… concerned. That's all."

I nod, but I don't trust him.

I'm not sure I trust any of them.

"Thank you, Alpha Jordan. I appreciate your concern, and I'm sure your daughter is a lovely person, but I am not looking for another Luna. Rebecca was my Luna and that's how it will remain."

He adjusts his tie and cannot look at me as he says, "Yes, of course, Alpha Maddox. But if you change your mind—"

"I won't." I stand, and he does as well. He offers his hand, and I shake it before showing him to the door.

Once he is gone, I go to the cabinet and pour myself a drink. Downing it, I refill my glass. I need to go get ready for dinner soon. I am so tired of hearing about how we need an heir, as if I don't know that.

The whisky burns my tongue as it goes down. Maybe Alpha Ernest isn't such a fool after all.

MAN, OH, MAN

Isla

I SIT on the edge of the bed for a few minutes after Poppy leaves, contemplating what to do. She's turned the bathtub on, so I know I have to go into the bathroom eventually or else the tub will overflow.

I want to take a bath. It sounds luxurious. I can't remember the last time I did anything like that for myself. For the last few years, everything I've done has been for my family.

But… the idea of taking my clothes off and soaking in the tub in this amazing room seems frightening and foolish.

All of this has to be a mistake, and when they find out about it, shouldn't I at least be dressed?

Still, if I take a quick bath, maybe I can be in and out before Poppy returns. If there's one thing I've learned about this castle it's that it is huge.

Setting my bag down on the chest at the end of the bed, I head into the bathroom and take my clothes off, hanging my wet, dirty clothes on a hook on the door, embarrassed by my old underwear and bra that doesn't really fit me correctly. I decide to leave the door open a crack so I can hear if Poppy comes back in.

I turn the bathtub off and notice there are hair clips on the sink, so I grab a few. I want to wash my hair, but then I plan to clip it up out of the way so I can be sure to wash well.

The moment my feet touch the warm water, I feel a soothing sensation ripple through my body. I'm not sure what Poppy put in this water, but it feels amazing. I sink into it and my whole body relaxes. Not only does it smell wonderful—like roses and lavender—but it wraps around my body like a warm blanket.

I may never get out of this tub.

Remembering I was going to try to hurry, I sink down and wash my hair, using the bottles of floral smelling shampoos and conditioners on the side of the tub, I scrub my hair and my scalp before clipping my hair up out of the way and using the body wash and a soft sponge to wash myself off. Once I'm sure I'm clean from head to toe, I sink back into the water, telling myself I'm just going to soak for a minute and then I'll get out.

I must've dozed off because when I open my eyes later, the water is a bit cooler, and I realize I'd been asleep.

But then I also realize that what had woken me was the sound of the door opening in my bedroom.

I sit up quickly, remembering that I had that robe but not remembering exactly where it is. I see a pile of towels nearby.

"Poppy, is that you?" I call, praying it is just the housekeeper coming back with the clothes she'd gone to find for me.

"No."

I get my answer when a deep, rumbling voice answers my question. I inhale sharply and hold it for a second. There is a man in my room—and I am naked.

Quickly, I get out of the tub, drying off as best I can. At least my hair is dry. I am frantic, and clearly, I am not thinking straight. I wrap the towel around myself, thanking the Moon Goddess that it's so huge that it will wrap all the way around me and then some, and then walk out to see who he is.

I stick my head out first, and he is just standing there, his hands on his hips, near my bed.

He is gorgeous. My breath catches in my throat, and I stand there, wide-eyed, glad he's not looking directly at me while I fight to get control of my racing heart.

He's tall, at least six foot four, with dark brown hair and eyes that glow like emeralds. His broad shoulders are ripped beneath the white button-down shirt he's wearing, and he looks to be nothing but lean muscle. Visions of what lies beneath his clothing come to mind, but I can't let them linger because I am aware that I am still naked.

His eyes land on me then, and they widen slightly, as if he's just realized he's interrupting my bath. Since he is clearly someone important, I rush out, holding my towel tight. "I'm sorry, sir," I say. "Poppy is getting me something acceptable to wear, but if I'm in the wrong room...."

"No, no," he says. "You're not." He looks me up and down, but he doesn't let his eyes dawdle on the part of me that's covered with the towel like some men would do.

I expect him to say more, but when he doesn't, I just stand there for a moment before I realize. "I… have a robe."

He nods. "Good."

I assume that means I should get it, so I rush back into the bathroom and see where Poppy has placed it. I drop the towel and put the robe on, tying it tightly and running back out through the partially ajar door.

When I'm back in the bedroom, I still don't know what to say to him, and he seems to be a man of few words.

"I wanted to see if you were all right," he finally says, his voice a low rumble that makes my body tingle.

"Oh, yes. I'm well, thank you," I say, wondering if perhaps he works for Beta Seth. Perhaps Beta Seth couldn't come.

He nods. "I heard about Mrs. Worsthingshorethinshire striking you."

"Yes, sir," I say, my hand going to my face. Is he here to investigate that incident? I withdraw my hand and clench the robe closed.

"She won't bother you again." His hands are shoved deep into his pockets, and he seems very sure of himself.

I can't help but feel bad about the entire situation. "Thank you," I say, but I still feel bad for her.

He picks up on that. "Are you bothered by her being let go?"

"Oh, uh… it's just… she was fired because of me." My eyes are glued to the ground near his expensive leather loafers.

"No," he corrects me. "She was fired for striking a guest in the face. That's completely unacceptable."

He has a point. "Yes, sir," I say. I lift my head a bit and look him in the face, and I can't help but notice his eyes are scrutinizing me now. I wish I knew what he was thinking. We are so far apart. I want to be closer to him. I want to breathe him in and wrap his scent around me. If I were closer, perhaps his hand might accidentally brush my skin….

"Well, I should go. I just wanted to check on you. If you need anything, I'm sure Poppy will get it for you."

"Yes, sir," I say. "Thank you." I manage to smile at him, but I am not very confident, not that I doubt Poppy, but I still don't know why I am there.

He takes a step backward, toward the door, but before he can turn to go, the door comes flying open, and Poppy bursts through. "I'm back!" she announces. "And boy have I got some beautiful outfits for you! You're never going to—Oh! Your Majesty!" Immediately she drops the dresses on a chair by the door and bows low to the ground.

Confusion washes over me as he shakes his head and turns to walk out. "You can get up, Poppy," he says as she lifts her head.

"You know my name?" Poppy asks.

"Yes, of course I know your name, Poppy. Everyone knows your name." He opens the door to walk out.

She says, "Thank you, Alpha King Maddox."

And the world starts to go black as I feel like I'm going to pass out.

ENCHANTING

Maddox

I NEED AIR.

I need to think.

I need to get away from… that woman.

It's a good thing that Poppy came into the room when she did, or else… I'm not sure what might've happened, but it might've gotten heated very quickly.

I walk down the hallway the short distance to my own rooms, dragging my hand down my face as I go. I know I shouldn't have even stopped there on my way to my room to get ready for my dinner with the visiting Alpha, but curiosity got the better of me.

The urge to see her for myself overwhelmed me, so I made a stop.

Part of me is very glad that I did, but the other part of me wishes that I had just let it be….

I had no idea she was going to be in the bathtub when I walked in.

Then, she'd scurried out, dripping wet, her pale skin glistening with water droplets, the scent of rosewater enticing me to step closer.

Her hair, golden curls, pulled up on top of her head in the back, were damp and not secured all the way. Ringlets framed her beautiful face as she stood there, wide-eyed, her sapphire eyes staring at me, trying to determine what I was doing there.

Her luscious lips, slightly parted, were so plump and perfect, I could imagine what they must taste like. I wanted to step across the room and take her bottom lip between my teeth. I could have lifted her tiny body up onto the bed, the towel sliding onto the floor as my hands wandered all over her body.

She had no idea that when she went into the bathroom to put on that robe she'd left the door slightly ajar, and in the mirror, I'd seen her perfect backside reflected in the mirror, the curve of her breast, her erect nipple….

I pulled the door open to my room, my erection straining against my pants and headed straight for my shower, turning the water to cold. I knew I'd be thinking about the girl, Isla, all through dinner.

If the Alpha's daughter, whatever the fuck her name was, threw herself at me again, I might have to take her up on the offer only to get rid of the enormous hard on I've got growing in my pants just thinking about her.

I've got to get her off my mind.

Undressing, I jump into the shower and let the cold water wash away the stiffness in my groin. I try to think about the work I need to do, the conversations that need to be had with Alpha Jordan and others. If I think about work, maybe I won't think about the girl.

I should be used to not thinking about women I don't want to think about.

Flashes of Rebecca's beautiful face flicker before my eyes, and I push them away as I have been doing for years.

Ever since that fateful night.

Since then, I've been with lots of women, mostly to drown the pain of losing her, but none of them have meant a thing to me. I definitely haven't had any issues with getting them off my mind.

Isla's bright blue eyes come to mind, and I have to wonder if she just might be different.

I turn the water so that it's a tad colder and stand beneath it a bit longer before I finally get out and get dressed for dinner.

When I'm dressed in a suit with a jade green tie that's nearly the color of my eyes, my hair is styled, and I'm ready to go, I take a moment to stand in front of the mirror and wonder why I even have these formal dinners.

"Why can't we just retire these dinners and make them a thing of the past?" I ask myself aloud. I hate them so much….

But visitors to the castle like them, so we continue to have them.

And we, theoretically, get a lot of work done at them….

A knock at the door alerts me that Seth is there to collect me. I grumble a bit before I say, "Yeah," and he sticks his head in.

"Ready?" he calls.

"No," I say.

He looks around my room. "Why don't you ever turn on a lamp?" he asks.

Rather than answering the question, I reply, "Why don't you ever mind your own business?" and walk to the door.

We head down the hall together, past Isla's room, and I take a deep breath as we go.

I smell rosewater, and my pants begin to tighten.

It seems I can't do anything to escape the allure of the woman, no matter what I do. I will just have to keep my mind on something else.

In the dining room, most of the guests are waiting for us to arrive so that we can be seated. It is my duty to be the last to get there.

Before we take our seats, Alpha Jordan comes over, two women accompanied him.

"Alpha Maddox, you remember my wife, Luna Elaine?"

"Yes, of course." I force a smile at the older brunette on his left arm. "Good evening," I say to her.

"Good evening, Your Majesty," she says to me. "Thank you for inviting us."

I nod, and since Seth is standing right next to me, I manage to say, "Thank you for coming."

"And this is our daughter, Zabrina." He turns and gestures to a young woman on his right.

The blonde who steps forward is tall and thin, with far too much makeup on. Her bright purple dress is very sparkly, and she has on large earrings that match. When she smiles and bats her eyelashes, I feel like I must be looking at the fakest, most spoiled Alpha's daughter in all the land.

"Hello," I say as she offers me her hand, but not to shake... to kiss.

"Hello, Your Majesty," she says as I stare at the back of her fingers.

I do not feel like pressing her hand to my lips, but an image of Isla's mouth comes to mind. That... I'd like to press to my lips.... I take Zabrina's thin hand and twist it, giving it a good shake before I let it go. Her eyes widen as she is shocked at my behavior, but I am the king, and I'll do as I wish.

"Shall we be seated?" Seth says, stifling a laugh.

"Yes, let's do." I walk to my seat, and everyone else does as well. I wait for everyone else, and we pull our chairs out and sit down.

I am ready to get this dinner over with. Unfortunately, there will just be another one tomorrow.

THAT'S WHAT I'M DOING HERE!

Isla

"Miss Isla? Miss Isla, are you all right?"

The sound of Poppy's voice has my eyes flying open, and I realize I haven't quite blacked out, but I have come close. I blink a few times and note she has her arms around me, and I have one arm on the bed. "I'm fine," I tell her, blinking my eyes as I try to clear my head. "I'm fine." I try to push myself up onto the mattress but find myself floundering, unable to get my limbs to cooperate.

"Here, lie down for a moment. I'll get you some water." She begins to lift me up onto the bed, which is so tall, it's nearly waist-high on me.

"I can manage," I assure her, and she lets me go. Somehow, I manage to climb up onto the bed, and Poppy heads into the bathroom, muttering under her breath that it's taking far too long for them to bring my food.

I sit there for a moment, staring at the door that King Maddox has just left through. My cheeks heat just thinking about him.

That was the king!

I feel like such a fool. I should've known that it was the king I was speaking to, but then, I've never seen him before.

How was I supposed to know?

"Here you go, sweetie," she says, handing me the glass. I take it and sip it, but I'm still in shock. I barely get out a thanks. I hold the glass to my lips for a

35

few minutes, willing the water to go down. "How long was he in here?" she asks me.

"Not long," I tell her. "Just a few moments." I set the glass aside and force some deep breaths down my throat.

I need to get a grip on this situation. Of course, I would meet the king eventually. I am just shocked that he was able to come in here and speak to me without me even realizing that it was him.

"What were you talking about? Not that it's my business." Poppy gives me a small smile, and I feel like I need to tell her everything.

But I don't know what to say so I just tell her, "Nothing. He just wanted to make sure that I was okay, after that woman hit me." I still couldn't believe the king himself would come by to check on me—a lowly servant. I figure I would see him from afar, as obviously Poppy has at some point. But to have him in my chambers? Up close and personal? That seems impossible to believe.

"That was awfully kind of him," Poppy says. She goes back to the pile of clothing and begins to straighten it up. Some of it fell on the floor when she saw the king and dropped to her knees. Maybe I was supposed to do the same. Should I have immediately dropped to the floor? That would've been difficult in the little I am wearing. Did I even bow my head? I don't even remember.

A knock at the far door interrupts Poppy, and she goes out to it, leaving me alone with my thoughts for a moment. The king just saw me wearing only a towel with my hair up and a bare face. I'm sure he wouldn't expect anything more of a servant, but still... it's embarrassing. I can only imagine what he must be thinking of me. He probably thought I looked hideous. I'm sure I won't ever see him again, not after that.

"Here you go—finally!" Poppy says, setting down a plate with some dinner on it. I can't see what it is, but it smells good. "Come and eat, sweetie, while I figure out what you should put on. I doubt you'll have any more visitors tonight, but one never knows."

I am starving. I can't remember the last time I ate a full meal, so even though I feel a bit odd eating in front of her, I get down off the bed and go over to eat.

It's chicken and mashed potatoes with gravy and a roll. To drink, there's a small bottle of champagne.

"This is for me?" I ask her. "Are you sure?"

"I'm sure," she says. "That's what they're having at dinner. They just fixed a plate for you."

I stare at her for a moment, flabbergasted. Servants at the castle eat really, really well. I sit down and begin to eat, trying to control myself. I didn't even see the chocolate cake at first. I can't believe all of this food is for me.

Poppy finishes hanging up the clothes, and as she does so, she talks about King Maddox. "He's so handsome. He has women from all over the kingdom throwing themselves at him all of the time, of course. And he doesn't like it. You know, he's sworn never to take another Luna."

"Yes, that's what I've heard," I say.

"Luna Rebecca was the love of his life, his true mate. He loved her so much. Some people say they've never seen anyone so much in love with their mate. He's even said that if the Moon Goddess gives him another mate, he would reject her. That's what I've heard anyway. It's not like I converse much with him."

I don't have much to say to that. He did say he knew who she was, after all. I only smile at her and keep eating, trying to remember to chew and not scarf it down.

"But… he is lonely and sad, I think, and he's too young for all that. I hope, one day, he meets a beautiful young woman who will make him forget all of his sadness." She smiles at me with a twinkle in her eye, and I think she's trying to imply something, but I don't know what it might be.

I am nearly finished eating now. I haven't drank the champagne because I don't really drink alcohol, and I'm so lightheaded from nearly fainting, it's probably not a good idea. I take a few bites of my cake and say, "Well, I hope he finds someone. He seems like a nice man."

She chuckles. "Yes, I hope you do."

I look up at her, not understanding what she means. The way she said that implies that I may have had an ulterior motive in what I said, and I most certainly do not. "What do you mean?"

"I mean… it's only natural that someone in your position would want him to find… someone to make him happy. I think you should put this on when you're done." She smiles and sets out a pajama set for me on the bed. I have no idea what time it is, but if the king is eating dinner, maybe it is time to get ready for bed. I think those dinners usually start late.

I finish eating and take another sip of my water before I ask, "What do you mean, someone in my position?" I get up and walk over to the bed where she has laid the pajamas as she goes to the table to get the tray I'm finished with ready to set out for the other servants to pick up.

The pajamas are very nice. I have no idea what's happening or why I am here, but I still think there's been some sort of a mistake.

Poppy gathers up the tray and opens the door as she says. "You know, someone in your position. Someone like you will obviously grow attached to him. I know I would." She makes a face at me, wide-eyed, and smiles before she goes out.

I am lost and wait for her to come back in. "Attached to him?" I ask as she reenters the room.

"Of course. Or… is this not your first time doing this sort of thing? Forgive me. I didn't know. I just assumed…."

"What sort of thing?" I ask. She must know more about why I'm here than I do. Sitting up straighter on the bed, I ask, "Poppy, do you know why I'm here—what my job at the castle is?"

"Why, of course, I do," she says with a shrug. "Everyone does!"

"Everyone does?" I ask. Apparently, everyone does but me.

"Yes, of course! It's been the talk of the entire staff since your arrival. I have to say, there are quite a few women who are jealous of you! If I'm completely honest, I'm one of them." She laughs and covers her mouth. "I hope that doesn't offend you. I'm sure it's not as easy a job as everyone thinks."

I am still quite confused, so I look her in the eye and finally ask "And what is that exactly? What job is it that I'll be doing?" I ask her.

She scoffs and says, "You just want to hear me say it, dear? Fine! I don't mind. Everyone knows it. You're the Alpha king's breeder. You're going to have his baby."

TRUTH AND RUMORS

Isla

I need to sit down. I find a way to sit on the bed, struggling to catch my breath, the pajamas I was getting ready to put on forgotten on the bed next to me since I've heard Poppy's words. That's what breeder means??

Poppy is looking at me from across the bedroom, a puzzled expression on her face.

"You... didn't know?" she asks me. "How is it that you didn't know? How did you get here?"

"I..." I feel my face flush as I lean back against the pillows, trying to process everything.

How is this possible?

That's what Alpha Ernest sold me to Alpha Maddox to do?

To be his breeder?

"I'm so sorry," Poppy says, coming over and resting her hand on my leg. "I just assumed that you either had done this before or had taken it upon yourself to make this into your career. I had no idea you had no idea, dear. And don't think that I was judging you because of it! I mean... who wouldn't want to be a breeder for Alpha Maddox?" She smiles at me and waggles her eyebrows, and I know that she's trying to make me laugh, but it's not working.

I want to bury my face in my hands and cry.

I think of my poor mother back home and how hard she's worked for all of her children, how my dad saved when I was little to be able to afford to bring us all to a new land to start over after political insurrection made us flee his homeland.

How I've spent so many hours slaving away at so many jobs over the last two years trying to erase this debt that just keeps mounting because of my brother… through absolutely no fault of his own, bless his soul.

And this is where I end up.

My mom would be so disappointed in me. When my parents find out that this is what I'm doing, that this is what Alpha Ernest has traded me off to do… they will disown me.

No, they are too sweet for that, but they will be so disappointed in me, they will never be able to look me in the eye again.

Tears begin to stream down my face. I can't help it. Poppy wraps her arm around me. "I am so sorry, sweetie. You know, Alpha King Maddox is scary on the outside, but I bet if you tell him your situation, that you didn't know, I bet he will let you go. I'm sure, however, you got here, he'll reverse it."

I think about her words for about five seconds and then shake my head. "I can't do that," I say, sitting up and wiping my eyes on the back of my hand. Poppy grabs a tissue for me from the nightstand. "Thank you."

I dry my face and try to get myself under control before I tell her, "My Alpha brought me here. My family owes him a lot of money. I went to him this morning to see if there was any work I could do to pay off our debt, and he brought me here. If I go back now, he will not be fulfilling his promise to Alpha Maddox, and I won't be fulfilling my promise to him. So… my family will either still owe him money, or he'll make me become some sort of sex slave to him." The thought of servicing Alpha Ernest makes my blood run cold.

"I take it that your Alpha is not as… fetching as the king?" Poppy asks, and I nearly throw up all of the food I just ate.

I make a face and shake my head, and she laughs, which makes me laugh.

"Well, of all of the jobs to have, honey, it could be worse. I mean… at least he looks like a god and not like your Alpha," she says with a shrug."

I want to think that that's true, and it is, but still… the idea of Alpha Maddox on top of me, of my naked body underneath his as he enters me…. No, I can't let my mind go there. I spit out, "I'm a virgin."

"Oh," she says, her eyes wide. She opens her mouth, closes it, and then says, "Oh," again. "I guess… that's why you're worth so much, perhaps?"

"I don't know," I tell her. "My mother told me a bit. I have a lot of brothers and sisters, so I know how it all works. But… that doesn't mean I'm comfortable with it."

"How old are you, sweetie?" Poppy asks.

"Twenty," I tell her. "Just barely. My birthday was a few weeks ago."

She smiles. "I'm twenty-three, and I've been with two different men. Neither of them was my mate. I haven't found him yet. It's okay, though. It can be fun. Well, it depends on the man. Anyway, I'm sure, with the king… it'll be pretty amazing."

I can only stare at her. "But… what about having a baby? And giving birth? And then what? I suppose he'll hire a nanny or something, and I'll leave here. I'll go back to my pack, and I'll never see my baby again?"

Poppy sits down near my feet and lets out a sigh. "Yes, I do think that's how it normally works. I don't have a lot of experience with breeders, but I do know of another maid who used to work at Alpha Samuel's estate in his pack lands, and he had a few breeders. Each one had a child, and every time, he'd send them away." She looks at me, a sad expression in her eyes. "Maybe knowing it ahead of time will help you to keep from getting too attached."

"Maybe," I say, but I doubt it. I don't think I can carry a baby for nine months and not love it completely.

But then… I don't think I can make love to a man and not love him either.

"Why doesn't he just find another Luna?" I ask. "I know what you said about him loving his first wife and mate so much that he swears he'll never have another wife, but I can't imagine what could've possibly happened to Luna Rebecca that has made him decide he'd never fall in love again."

Poppy makes a face, and I'm not sure what it means. "No one knows for sure what happened to her," she says, her voice a whisper.

I look around. No one is here, so I don't know why she is whispering. I shrug. "Well, it couldn't be so awful that he thinks he should be forced to live the rest of his life alone. If he is a good man, as you say, then he shouldn't have a breeder. He should find a worthy woman, an Alpha's daughter, and marry again. He deserves a second chance at happiness."

Poppy shrugs. "Perhaps, but not if the rumors are true…"

"Rumors?" I ask. "What rumors?"

"About what happened to Luna Rebecca," she says, still whispering.

I am getting tired of playing guessing games. "And what, exactly, is that?" I ask her.

Poppy clears her throat and says, "That he killed her."

∼

MADDOX

"THIS HAM IS DELIGHTFUL. I absolutely love the flavor. Did your chef prepare it especially for me, Alpha?"

The sound of the insipid girl seated across from me blathering on about ham is making me want to tear off all of my clothes and shift right here on the table. I want to let my wolf run free, to grunt and growl and howl at the moon, and if my sharp claws and long fangs should happen to make contact with her pasty white skin and make a tear or two, well, sometimes these things cannot be helped….

"Alpha King Maddox?" she repeats, as if I'm not answering her because I somehow managed to not hear her. "Did your chef make this lovely ham with me in mind?"

"Yes," I say. "Yes, he did. He somehow knew that you would love it, even though he's never met you before."

Seth's foot taps mine beneath the table. It is the closest thing to a warning my Beta will give me since I am the king, after all. It isn't as if he feels he can get away with mashing his heel into my toes or something of that nature.

Zabrina thinks I am being silly, I guess, because she giggles behind her hand. "He is a wonderful guesser then because it's just divine."

I say nothing in response, and she takes a drink of her wine, draining it. Her glass isn't empty for more than two seconds before her entire disposition changes and she angrily snaps her finger at the servant standing behind her, a woman she's brought with her for the express purpose of waiting on her, and the woman springs into action to pour her more.

"That's more like it, Maud," she says, her tone showing her irritation. "The ham might be flavorful, but that doesn't mean I won't get thirsty."

The servant girl says nothing, only falls back into her place, near the wall. I can't help but look at her, standing there, her eyes downcast. She can't be more than fourteen, maybe fifteen. She looks terrified, and I have to wonder if Zabrina is the type of woman who would strike her servant if she didn't do what she wanted.

I believe she is.

The servant isn't the only woman Zabrina has brought with her. She has also brought along three friends. She calls them her ladies, and they are just as annoying as she is. I have no idea what their names are. She introduced them earlier, but I wasn't paying attention. All I know is, between the four of them, I'm bound to be irritated to no end if Alpha Jordan intends to stay in the castle more than a night or two.

He has only asked to stay here on his way through the area on business, but now that I know his true intention, I have a feeling he will have some sort of calamity befall him.

Something will be wrong with one of his vehicles. One of his drivers will fall ill. He will suddenly lose all sense of direction and have no idea where he was going….

He will be forced to stay in the castle until I say I will marry his daughter.

He will be forced to stay here until the day after never then because that simply will not happen.

Though it's obvious that the other Alphas are growing weary of my excuse, that I simply will not marry again after what happened with Rebecca, it will have to appease them because it's the truth.

I will not take another bride.

If I am to have an heir… it will have to come another way.

My mind returns to the girl.

The soft round mound of her breast. Her erect nipple. The way her bottom moved as she reached for her robe.

I let my mind get away from me for a moment and imagine myself following her into the bathroom, coming up behind her to cup her breasts. She leans back into me as my mouth comes down on her neck. She moans my name softly as my teeth nip at the tender flesh of her shoulder, my tongue tracing up to her ear.

My hands caress her full breasts, my thumbs working her nipples, plucking and pulling as her groans get louder, her arousal stronger. I smell it in the air around us. Her open mouth against my cheek as she hunts for my mouth, longing to taste me, moans with desperation.

I slide a hand down her flat belly, pressing her against my erection as I spread her legs and slip a finger between her dripping wet thighs. She's already in spasm when my finger enters her. I feel her muscles tense around me as her arm comes up to loop around my neck. She begs me to take her, to bend her over right there and press my cock inside of her so deep that I stretch her completely and fill her fuller than she's ever been before—

"Alpha?"

Seth's voice has me blinking and I realize I've completely lost track of the conversation around me. My dick is so hard beneath the table, it may as well have five legs. I won't be getting up anytime soon. "Yes?" I ask.

"Are you all right, sir?" he asks me.

"I'm sorry. I have a lot on my mind," I tell him. "With… the situation with the… attacks."

Seth arches an eyebrow, and I know he doesn't believe me, but Alpha Jordan says, "It is an abysmal situation that is certain. You know, I heard twenty-five civilians were killed last week alone?" He launches into a discussion of what he has heard about attacks in his own territory.

I want to ask him if he thinks that it has anything to do with his daughter rejecting her mate, but I don't bother.

We've already had that discussion today, and it fell on deaf ears.

It doesn't take too long before the talk of war had deflated my erection, and I decide it is time to leave the table before it returns. If my mind returns to the girl again before I can make it back to my room, I might be there all night.

"Well, I say," setting my napkin aside, "I will take my leave."

"But…" Zabrina says, a wide-eyed disappointed look on her face, "I thought we might go for a walk in the garden, Your Majesty."

"Not tonight," I tell her. Not any night, I want to add but don't. "The rest of you are free to stay and enjoy the musicians in the great hall, but I have had a long day and will be retiring for the evening. Beta Seth will be happy to entertain you."

Seth is never happy to do so, but he knows it is part of his duties. "Yes, of course," he says. "Let's finish our dessert first, shall we?"

I haven't even made it through the final course, but I don't care. I'm the king, and I shall do as I please.

My shoes echo down the hall as I head toward my room. Most of the lights are off now, and the pieces of artwork cast strange shadows. It's times like this when I sometimes wonder, if Rebecca is still here, might I see a glimpse of her?

But I never do….

I reach the girl's door first, and even though I intend to keep walking, I find myself stopping outside of the door. I wonder if she is still awake. I wonder if she is lying there, thinking about what her duties are supposed to be, now that she is here. Is she frightened? Is she excited?

Has she thought at all about me the way I've been thinking about her?

Under normal circumstances, I would think of course she has. I am the Alpha King. Any woman would be lucky to have the opportunity to be bedded by me.

But there's something different about Isla. Something unique.

I lift my hand and rest it on the door, wanting to go in. I just want to see her, or so I tell myself.

But it's too soon.

She is young and vulnerable, and I don't want to scare her.

Everyone says I am ruthless and terrifying.

Perhaps that is true, but I don't need to be that way to her.

Not yet anyway.

I make myself keep walking. I may ravish her—but tonight it will have to be in my dreams.

THINKING

Isla

I LIE AWAKE FOR HOURS, staring at the ceiling, pondering what it is that Poppy has told me about the Alpha King. It's hard to believe it could possibly be true.

Yet, how can I doubt it?

Back home, I never knew much about him. I had too much to worry about to ever spend much time thinking about the Alpha King. Whenever anyone mentioned King Maddox, it was always in one of two contexts—how unbelievably good looking he was.

Or how unbelievably cruel he was.

Now… Poppy has revealed to me that everyone in the castle believes he is responsible for the death of his mate, Luna Rebecca, the woman everyone says is the sweetest, kindest, gentlest soul any of them had ever met.

How is that possible?

I don't know, but as I lay here on my back, staring at the ceiling, I have to wonder… will a similar fate befall me?

I'm to be his breeder.

What will that entail exactly?

A shudder begins at the top of my neck and travels down my spine. I know the gist of it. I understand that it will be my job to lay with the king, to spread my legs for him, to pleasure him.

He is an attractive man, and I'd be lying if I said that I didn't find myself experiencing sensations I never had before when he was in my room earlier.

Even though I had no idea who he was, just being in his presence made my muscles clench in ways they never had before.

I felt a tightening in my core that I never had until that moment.

My hand slides down between my legs just thinking of it now, and I'm glad I'm alone, lying in this massive bed with these plush, comfortable blankets. I press my fingers against the outside of my most sensitive area, hoping that doing so will make the ache I'm feeling go away.

It doesn't seem to help. Just thinking about the king makes my flesh bead up with a sheen of sweat. I need to push the blankets down away from my face so I can breathe.

I wonder what it would feel like if it was his hand on me and if these pajamas were not in the way.

This certainly isn't making the ache go away….

"Knock it off, Isla," I whisper to myself. "You're just making it worse."

I try rolling over and remind myself that I'm in a strange place, away from my family, and I have no idea when I might see them again.

That's enough to make the ache dissipate. I miss my parents and my brothers so much. How I wish that I could've stayed at home and paid off my parents' debt from there.

Alpha Ernest should've been more straightforward with me.

But now, the damage was done, and here I am.

I hope that Alpha Maddox will allow me to go home for a visit soon. I imagine my mother's face. I hope she's not crying. I miss her so much, and I know she has to miss me, too.

Taking a deep breath, I close my eyes and try to go to sleep. Otherwise, I might start to cry.

Since it's been such a long day, I am exhausted, and I am just about to doze off when I get the sensation that someone is standing outside my door. Not the one right across the room from me, but the other one, the outer door.

It's so far away from me, I really shouldn't be able to tell, but I get the idea that someone is there just the same.

And I know who it is.

I hold my breath, not moving at all, as I wonder what might happen if he enters the room.

It's too soon, isn't it? This is my first night here. Surely, he won't come in and want me to have sex with him on my very first night in the castle, will he?

Won't he at least give me one night to get settled?

It's not as if I'm so beautiful that just catching one glimpse of me earlier will leave him so intrigued he won't be able to forget about me.

He's the king! He can have any woman he wants. Is he in that big of a hurry to make an heir?

After a moment, I get the feeling that he has moved on, and I allow myself to breathe again.

A wave of relief washes over me, and I thank the Moon Goddess that I won't be called upon to service the king tonight.

"What a relief," I whisper. "I'm so glad that didn't happen."

At least, that's what I'm trying to convince myself.

The ache is back between my legs, and something tells me, when I fall asleep tonight, I won't be dreaming about my family.

I'll be dreaming of the Alpha King—and he'll be on top of me.

～

MADDOX

I WAKE up the next morning with a hard cock and the memory of a very vivid dream about Isla.

This girl is affecting me in ways I never would've thought imaginable, and I don't know why. It isn't as if I've never seen an attractive woman's naked ass before.

Still, I have to take another cold shower before I can go to the office, and my hand was already sticky from my dirty thoughts of her the night before when I couldn't fall asleep.

As I pass her room on my way to the office, I hear someone moving around behind the door and imagine it must be her.

The urge to burst in and go to her floods my mind. She belongs to me, after all. I can take her anytime I want to.

I could never force a woman to do anything against her will, though. I might be brutal on the battlefield, but not in the bedroom.

Well, not like that anyway.

I keep my feet moving. Temptation is high, but I will persevere.

In the office, I start working and manage to get through several reports before Seth is knocking on my door. I sigh and tell him to come in, knowing it's him because of the way he knocks. It's always the same every morning.

He walks in looking like hell, and I have to wonder how long he stayed up entertaining our guests. "Good morning," he says because it's expected, not because he means it.

"Seth," I say, trying not to laugh. "What the hell happened to you?"

He shakes his head. "Zabrina happened to me, Alpha. That woman doesn't know how to... shut up."

A chuckle erupts from my mouth. "I'm sorry," I tell him. But I'm not really.

He shakes his head and sits down across from me to give me an update.

47

"We've heard that there are more attacks happening along the borders of Duster pack and Pine Tree pack. Alpha Hayes seems to think he can infiltrate Alpha Bhamers territory and just take it."

I stare at him for a moment. Alpha Hayes of Duster pack is one of the bigger threats to the peace of our kingdom. I don't like it when one Alpha attacks another, but in this case, I know why he's doing it. Alpha Hayes wants to prove he's capable of being the greatest leader in the kingdom.

Greater than me.

He's not the only Alpha who has this affliction, but he's one of the more serious ones. And it doesn't hurt that he has five strapping sons, so if he were to become king, there'd be no question that the bloodline would continue.

I am meant to have a child by now…. If I don't have one soon, the Alphas will be able to rebel against me and see it as justified.

Thirty is the cut-off, and I'm almost there….

"Anything else?" I ask Seth as if his announcement isn't surprising or troubling to me.

He raises his eyebrows. "No, that's all. Except Alpha Jordan spent a great deal of time last night trying to get me to speak to you on behalf of his daughter."

I roll my eyes. "I'm not interested in Zabrina."

"I know you're not," he says. "But… if you're not planning on using the girl you purchased—"

"I didn't purchase her," I correct him, feeling anger begin to bubble up inside of me. "I merely accepted her in exchange for a debt."

"Isn't that the same thing?" he asks.

Narrowing my eyes, I tell him, "No, it's not."

He shrugs. "Anyway… you know you only have ten months left before you turn thirty."

"I am aware of when my birthday is, Seth."

"So, you need to do something, Alpha. Or else, we'll have even more problems on our hands."

He's right, but I don't want to talk about it. "Go down to the military barracks and tell Commander Taylor to send a detail to Duster. I want to keep an eye on that situation and make sure that it doesn't escalate out of control."

He seems surprised at my dismissal of his comments without a remark. "Yes, sir," he says. "But Zabrina wants you to have dinner with her again tonight… alone."

"And Zabrina can want whatever she'd like," I tell him.

"You may as well give her a try. If you don't, he'll just keep asking and complaining. Why don't you have dinner with her, and if you don't like her, you can tell Alpha Jordan it wasn't a match?"

The thought of having to sit through a dinner date with Zabrina makes bile rise up in the back of my throat.

But, as usual, Seth has a point. "Fine," I tell him, shaking my head. "Arrange it. But you'd better think of a way to get me out of there quickly."

I can tell he's fighting a smile. "Yes, sir," he says getting up to leave the room.

I watch him go and then swear under my breath. This is the last thing in the world I want to do.

Having a baby with Isla would make things much easier, but I don't even know why she's here. I could go speak to her, but that would be dangerous.

I return my attention to my work, hoping to lose myself in what needs to be done. But my mind keeps flickering back to her. The soft curve of her breast, the tight muscles of her bottom....

I'm in trouble.

THE NEXT LUNA?

Isla

"Good morning, dear," Poppy says, pulling the curtains in front of the window open. I squint at the bright light and try to wake myself up. It took me forever to fall asleep last night, and now that I am awake, I feel like I've been hit by a bus. My head is throbbing, and all I can think about is the dirty dreams I had about the king last night.

I mutter, "Good morning," and manage to get my eyes to open as I sit up.

"Your breakfast is on the way. Would you like to take a shower while we are waiting? I will get your outfit ready for the day. I'm not sure what the king's plans are, but we have permission to go outside. I can show you the gardens." Poppy smiles at me in an encouraging manner, and I find myself growing a little excited to get outside of this room.

"I think that would be lovely," I tell her.

"Good," she says. "I'll go warm the shower."

Before I can protest, she is off and in the other room turning on the water. I can manage. I've never had anyone do anything like this for me before, and I'm not sure what to think about it now.

But I can't stop her from doing her job. We all have a job around here, apparently. I would love to change jobs with her. She has already told me that she would like to be the king's breeder.

I certainly don't want this job.

But it's mine, and there's nothing I can do about it now.

I make my way into the bathroom, and as Poppy hums a song out in the bedroom, I go about taking a shower, making sure to wash better than I ever have before. I also inspect my body for any unsightly hairs. I have no idea exactly what the king might expect of me, but I don't want to be embarrassed if he should see me naked.

The idea of the king seeing me naked has my face flushing. I wonder if I will get a chance to tell him I've never been with a man before, or if he will even care. Perhaps he won't treat me any differently than he has any of the other women he's been with, and he will hurt me in the process.

I try not to worry about it. I suppose that it's just part of the job, and nothing he does to me will last forever.

When I'm done with my shower, I get out and dry off, getting as much water out of my hair as possible. I stare at myself in the mirror. There are all kinds of cosmetics and lotions, perfumes and powders on the dresser. I don't usually wear much makeup, and I'm not even sure that I'm skilled enough to put it on, but I feel like I need to do something. I can't let the king see me with nothing on my face again.

"Are you all right?" Poppy shouts through the closed door to me.

"Yes," I tell her. "I am just trying to decide how to do my makeup."

"Can I come in?" she asks me.

"Of course," I tell her.

She comes in and says, "I can help with that, if you want."

My ears perk up. "Really?" I ask her. "I'm not very good at it."

"Sure!" she says, coming over to me. "No problem." She directs me to sit down on a stool, and then she starts working on my face, talking as she goes. "With your coloring, you should wear brown eye shadow. It'll make your blue eyes pop. And red lipstick will look lovely with your coloring, especially with your light hair." I sit still and let her do her thing, and when I look at myself in the mirror, I can hardly believe I'm looking at myself.

"Wow...." I mumble.

She laughs. "Pretty good, huh? Of course, you're already beautiful. I just made your eyes pop."

"Thank you so much, Poppy!" I tell her. I think about hugging her, but I don't know her that well yet.

"No problem!" she declares. "Now, let's get you dressed."

She's laid out a blue dress for me, and while I don't need her help putting my clothes on, when she volunteers to style my hair and pick out my shoes and jewelry, I let her. When she's done, I hardly recognize myself.

Half of my hair is pulled up on top of my head in a silver clip that matches my earrings, necklace, and bangle bracelets. The rest is falling down my back in loose curls. My shoes are silver sandals that match the rest of my accessories perfectly.

I am beginning to feel like a princess!

But then, I remember, I'm just the Alpha King's breeder. Not his romantic interest. No matter how beautiful I may look or feel, I am still just little ol' Isla Moon from Willow pack. No one important….

"Let's go outside and get some fresh air," Poppy suggests. I nod and force myself out of the stupor I've fallen into.

We walk down the winding halls, me following behind Poppy because I have no idea where we are going, and eventually, we make it to a door that leads outside. I'm glad I didn't bump into anything along the way this time. Not that Poppy would hit me.

Guards stand at the door, but they don't blink as we approach, and Poppy pulls the barrier open. We step outside into fresh air and sunshine.

Immediately, I feel better. I'm so glad that the rain from the day before has passed.

"The garden is this way," she tells me, and I follow along behind her as we make our way over to a huge section of velvety green grass with little walking trails that are lined by thousands and thousands of flowers of every color and variety. The scent is magnificent, and I can't help but stop to smell each kind, from red roses to orange marigolds.

We walk along, taking in the beautiful scenery and smelling the flowers, chatting about how lovely everything is, including the fountains and statues we find around every bend. I can't help but smile. It's such a beautiful day with birds chirping in the trees and hardly a cloud in the sky.

And then… we realize we are not alone.

"Who are you?" a female voice snarls at me from behind a large oleander bush.

I arch an eyebrow at her, not sure who she may be either, but it seems clear she's someone important. She is dressed in a long red gown, her light hair pulled up on top of her head. A thousand jewels adorn her neck and ears. Her arms tinkle when they move, she's wearing so many bracelets.

On either side of her stand two beautiful dark-haired women with the same evil glare in their eyes as the three of them take measure of me and Poppy.

"I… I'm no one," I stammer, looking down at the ground. I don't want to offend her, since clearly she is a guest of the king or lives here.

"You must be someone," she says, her hand on her hip as she steps around the bush. "Only a few important people have access to the king's garden."

"I… I…"

"She's Isla," Poppy says. "She's a very important guest of the king."

"Are you speaking to me, servant girl?" the woman barks back. "I don't need to hear an explanation from the likes of you!"

I don't know who this woman is, but I don't appreciate the way she's speaking to Poppy. "She's simply answering your question," I say, finally meeting her gaze. "I am Isla. And I am a guest of the king. That's really all there is to it."

"A guest? From where?" she asks me. "Are you an Alpha's daughter?"

I almost laugh. "No," I tell her. "I'm not. I'm from Willow pack. I arrived yesterday. May I ask who you are?"

"No, you may not!" she says, taking a few hasty steps toward me until she's right in front of me, nearly toe to toe. Her two friends come along. "Just know that I am the most special guest of the king of all of his guests, and one day, you will be calling me Luna!" With that, she tugs on her skirt and flips around, the dress flying up like a cape. The other two women glare at me for a moment before they all three turn and leave.

I stand there staring after her for a long moment, wondering who in the world she was and what she meant about becoming the Luna.

Is Alpha King Maddox engaged?

"What a bitch!" Poppy exclaims. "I hate that woman already!"

I can't say the same because I don't know her at all, and while she wasn't nice to me, I don't usually judge people so quickly. "Who is she? Do you know?" I ask.

"I do," Poppy says, folding her arms and narrowing her gaze in the direction the three women left. "That was Zabrina from Elm pack," she tells me. "Her father is Alpha Jordan. They also arrived yesterday. They're allegedly here for some meetings with the king about the threats of war, but it seems to me that perhaps Alpha Jordan has something else in mind."

I shake my head. I can't bear to think about Alpha Maddox marrying someone like Zabrina. I may not be head over heels in love with the idea of being his breeder, but I can't allow myself to think about him being with that woman either.

Or any other woman, for that matter.

After the dreams I had about him the night before, the thought of him so much as kissing another woman makes my heart drop to my stomach.

"Well," Poppy says, "I guess she's in for a rude awakening."

"Why is that?" I ask. "She's beautiful. Maybe he'll fall in love with her."

Poppy scoffs. "Nope. It won't happen. King Maddox will never marry her, no matter how beautiful she is."

"How do you know?" I ask, finally turning to look at my companion.

"Simple," she says with a shrug. "After Luna Rebecca died, he said he'd never marry anyone again. So that means he can't marry her."

I stare at her for a moment before I nod and look away.

I'm glad that he won't be marrying Zabrina. But I can't help but think, if he's never going to marry anyone again, that also means he won't be marrying me.

While it is a farfetched dream for me to even consider Alpha King Maddox might fall in love with the likes of me, it was a dream I had considered.

Until that moment.

Now, I knew for sure, all I would ever be was his breeder.

And nothing more.

HE'S CLAIMING ME

Maddox

SITTING across the small table on the balcony near the dining room from Zabrina, I try to be polite, but it's difficult. She will not stop talking, and I couldn't care less about what she has to say.

"So then, I told Daddy that I really wanted the shoes in silver and gold. Because you never know what color will look best, you know?"

I nod. No, I don't know. And I don't care. I really, really don't give a flying fuck.

"So he bought them, even though they cost ten thousand dollars for each pair. But then… it's just money." She giggles and takes a drink of her champagne. "You know what I mean, of course?"

I smile. I do know what she means, but then, I also try not to waste money. I have an entire kingdom to think of, not just myself.

Picking up my knife, I slice through my steak, watching the pink juice spill all over my plate. For a moment, I contemplate what it would look like to run the knife across her jugular, watching a different kind of juice, a dark crimson juice, pour out.

I set the knife aside and remind myself I'm not on a battlefield. Sometimes, when you've seen everything I have, it's difficult to remember….

My mind flickers to Rebecca, and I have to push the memory away. She certainly knew the secret darkness that haunted me since I returned from the war in the east….

"You should drink some more of your champagne," Zabrina says, her eyes on my half-finished glass. "You know, it's a special bottle I brought with me from our pack lands. You'll love it."

I smile at her and raise my glass to my lips. I usually like champagne, and she's right to say that her pack is known for their wonderful champagnes and wines. But something about this particular glass tastes off. I can't quite put my finger on it. When her lady-in-waiting brought it to me, I was anxious to taste it and finished my wine to have a sip, but now… I wish I hadn't. It's bitter, and I don't know why….

But I don't want to be rude, so I take another drink. Maybe I should just finish it off so I can have some more wine. But knowing Zabrina, she'll insist on a refill.

I set my glass down, nearly empty, and Zabrina's eyes twinkle. "Do you like it?"

"Sure," I tell her, and she looks pleased.

Eventually, the staff brings out dessert, and I am overjoyed to know that this is the last course. As soon as it is finished, I will dismiss myself and get out of here. I've done my duty as a host.

"So…" Zabrina says, "I was thinking, after dinner, we could go for a stroll in the garden."

"The garden?" I repeat. "Tonight?"

"Yes, I was there earlier today, and it's so beautiful. I'd love to have you join me for a moonlit stroll."

In my mind's eye, I see Isla's face. If she was the one asking, I'd be tempted to take her up on the offer. I imagine her smiling face as she looks up at me, the silvery moon playing off her golden curls. I feel a twitch in my pants just imagining it.

"Not tonight," I tell Zabrina. Suddenly, all I can think about is Isla. Did she have a good day? Is she beginning to relax now that she's been here a night and day? Or is she still terrified? I could tell when I met her the day before she was frightened. She shouldn't be. I will take very good care of her….

"You really should finish your champagne," Zabrina says, slicing into her pie.

Reluctantly, I lift the glass and finish off the drink. Setting it down, I am tempted to sarcastically ask her if she's satisfied. I don't, though. I only smile at her.

She smiles back, and I swear I see something wicked in her grin.

I take another bite of my chocolate cake, but I hardly taste it. My mind is still on Isla. I imagine she is lying in her bed now, naked, touching herself… running her hands along those curves, up the side of her breasts, along her round bottom, to her wet, aching core. She plunges three fingers in and cries out, whispering my name.

Under the table, my dick springs to life. I feel like a man about to peel his skin off.

"Are you all right?" Zabrina asks, still smiling at me.

"Actually, no," I tell her, setting my napkin on the table. "I'm not feeling well. I'm afraid you'll have to excuse me."

Her face falls. "What? But… our stroll…."

"Not tonight," I tell her. "I'm sorry, Zabrina, I truly am, but I must go."

"But—"

I don't wait to listen to her protest anymore. I have never felt this way before in my entire life. Though I've certainly been turned on before, the urgency I feel inside of me is all-encompassing. I fly up from the table and shoot out the door and down the hall as fast as my three legs can carry me.

As I speed down the hall toward Isla's room, I am reminded that occasionally Rebecca would get me in such a frenzy, I'd have trouble controlling myself in public. She was so beautiful, such a graceful dancer, and her intoxicating floral perfume would drive me mad. I'd want to take her into a hallway bathroom and ravage her on the sink during a dinner party. I never did.

Even in all of those times with my wife that I had trouble controlling myself, never once did I feel the earnestness I feel right now. My cock is so hard, I feel like my suit pants are about to be torn to shreds much like they are when we don't strip before we shift.

I am almost to her door now, and I can't contain myself. I know that I'm liable to scare her, and with my heart pounding in my chest and my dick ready to spring out of my pants, I'll likely hurt her if I can't find a way to control myself, but in my mind, she's lying in there, spread wide open, waiting for me, her hand stroking her pulsing pussy.

No, I need her. I need her now.

I won't be able to control myself.

The door is no barrier to me, even if it's locked, and I don't even bother to knock.

❧

Isla

Lying on the bed for the second night in a row, I look up at the ceiling and try to wrap my mind around where I am, why I'm here, and how I'm going to manage this new assignment I've been given.

It's not easy. I've never been with a man before, and I'm terrified of what it will be like to spend my first night with the king.

I would like to think that all of those rumors about him being cruel have more to do with the battlefield than the bedroom, but I have no way of knowing.

Poppy mentioned earlier that there's an herbal medicine I can take to help me get over the struggle of following my instincts and giving in to the king in the bedroom. She told me that it will help me with my inhibitions.

She also said it tastes bitter so it's best to swallow it in a capsule, which I am also leery of. I often choke on pills. So she suggested we dissolve in a drink. She said it would still be bitter, but not too bad.

I will think on it. I would hate to have my first experience tainted by any sort of drug, even if it's herbal.

She called it red wolf's blood, but she said it comes from a plant, and it's just called that because of the plant it comes from, some form of ginger.

I don't know much about plants; I'll have to take her word for it.

Still staring up at the ceiling, my mind goes back to the woman I met in the garden, the one that said she will be the next Luna.

Who is she? Why is she here? And why in the world can't she be the one to have the king's baby, then, if she's truly set to marry him?

Poppy said she's just blowing hot air, that the king isn't engaged to marry anyone, and she must just be wishfully thinking aloud.

I'm not so sure.

The woman was beautiful, likely an Alpha's daughter.

I am no one. Why would anyone want me to carry their child?

If the king decides he doesn't want me after all, I won't be surprised. He may come in to bed me, take one look at my thin little body, and turn around and leave the room.

Thinking about King Maddox coming into my room to bed me has my mind going to all different sorts of places, though. Once again, I find my heart racing as my hands slide over my body. I want to imagine that he is touching me. Inhaling deeply, I think I smell his cologne.

Then… I realize I do smell his cologne.

That is just before my bedroom door opens.

I sit up, my eyes piercing through the darkness of my room. A sliver of moonlight leaks in through the curtains, and I can see him.

King Maddox is in my room. He's wearing a pair of suit pants and dropping his tie on the floor as he unbuttons his white shirt, his shoes and socks left somewhere along the way.

His eyes are practically glowing in the near darkness as he stares at me, and I can tell by the way his nostrils are flaring and the bulge in his pants exactly what he wants.

My dreams of a moment ago are about to become a reality.

But he seems too aroused, I am afraid.

What if he hurts me?

"Your Majesty?" I ask quietly, but he doesn't respond, not verbally. He rips his shirt off and tosses it on the floor, revealing his perfectly sculpted chest muscles, which ripple in the moonlight as he climbs onto the bed.

Inhaling deeply, I hold my breath, the scent of his woodsy cologne coating my lungs, my eyes focused on his face. The look in his eyes makes me think he's not thinking clearly. His pupils are wide, and his eyes are moving slightly, shifting back and forth.

He pulls the blankets down off my body, revealing the thin light pink nightgown I am wearing. That and a pair of silk panties is all I have on, and I feel my nipples harden as the cold air of the room hits them.

Or maybe it's because of the way he is looking at me....

His mouth crashes down on mine, drawing all of the air out of my lungs, and as he lifts a hand to my breast, I don't know if I should rip myself away, scream, and try to run, or if I should simply lay back and enjoy it.

After all, I do belong to him, don't I? And his hand feels so good as his thumb rubs against my erect nipple through my nightgown.

But... I'm also terrified. I don't know what to do—I'm not sure I'm ready for this.

He tastes of wine and something else... something bitter... and as he releases my mouth, his eyes shine down on me, and I know it doesn't matter whether I'm ready or not.

He's claiming me.

HOT IN HERE

Isla

Alpha King Maddox is on top of me, and even though I'm terrified, the more he touches me, the more I want to be touched.

His warm mouth latches on to mine, his tongue probing deeper and deeper. The taste of wine and something else, something bitter, glides over my tongue as his twirls around mine. I am afraid to touch him, so my fingers intertwine with the bedsheets as I try to stabilize myself. He's kissing me so deeply, I'm growing dizzy and breathless.

Finally, he releases my mouth, and his lips slide over my neck. I find myself arching my back, leaning into him, the ache between my legs growing with every touch of his fingers against the thin fabric of my nightdress as he continues to thumb my erect nipple.

I can feel his erection against my belly, and the urge to spread my legs for him is undeniable, but I can't at the moment because of the way he is lying on top of me. He is a mass of muscle, heavy and solid, and I couldn't free myself if I tried.

Not that I want to try. The more that he licks, sucks, and nips at my neck, the more clouded my thinking becomes. I remind myself that this is exactly why I am here. I am his breeder, after all. He owns me. He can take me any time that he wants to.

While I don't understand his urgency tonight, it's not my place to question the king.

The Alpha's hand slides down my stomach as he lifts himself slightly off me. His hand glides beneath my nightgown, leaving a steaming trail across the flesh of my stomach. I find myself whimpering slightly, and then, his hand is on the outside of my panties. I'm so wet, he has to know that my body is longing for his. He presses against the outside, his fingers spreading me even with the barrier of cloth between us. I wish he would slide his fingers around the thin garment and touch my bare skin again, but for now, him pressing against me, stroking up and down, feels so good, I find myself grinding against him.

He nips at my ear. "Do you like that, little flower?"

I moan an answer as his other hand slides my nightgown down off my shoulder so that my breast is exposed. When his mouth comes down around my nipple, I lift a hand for the first time and press it against the back of his head. His tongue laps at my sensitive skin as he sucks. I hold him there, my fear fading as pleasure takes over.

I feel his finger slip around the silk of my panties, and then he is exploring my folds, sliding around in my wetness, teasing me by touching the entrance to my pulsing core but not coming in.

He lifts his head and finds my mouth again as he presses one finger inside me, just up to the first knuckle, not far at all. It stings a little, but the pleasure far outweighs the pain, and I want more. I want more than just his finger. His hard cock continues to rub against me, hitting my thigh as he kisses me deeper and deeper.

And then… there's a knock on my door.

Maddox groans into my mouth, clearly displeased. We ignore it, and he continues to kiss me. My hand is resting on his back, and all I feel beneath my palm is a wall of rippling muscle.

The knock continues until I hear Beta Seth's voice. "Sir, I know you don't want to be interrupted, but it's very important."

Maddox lifts his mouth away from mine. "Not now, Seth!"

"But sir… I need to tell you something immediately!"

The king lifts his head and rests it on my shoulder, withdrawing his hand from my wet pussy. "Just a moment, darling," he says to me, and I begin to wonder if he even remembers my name.

He steps away from me, leaving me exposed to the coldness of being without him. I pull my blanket back up over me, panting, wondering if this has all been a dream.

I can't hear what they are saying right outside of my bedroom door, but I do hear Maddox ask, "What the fuck?" loudly, and I know that whatever his Beta has told him, it isn't good. A moment later, I hear another knock at the door.

"Yes?" My voice cracks with nervousness as I keep the blanket tucked beneath my chin.

"It's Seth. Can I come in?"

"Yes," I say again.

He steps inside, but his eyes are not focused on me, and I can tell he is as embarrassed as I am. "I beg your pardon, Miss Isla, but I need to gather the king's clothing. He has an emergency to tend to."

"All right." What more can I say? I can feel the heat reddening my cheeks, and it has nothing to do with passion. I am so embarrassed. Seth knows what we were doing, and even though I know that that's why I'm here, it's still difficult to get past the idea that the entire castle will know that the king and I are having sex.

Well... we will be. Eventually. I suppose.

He picks up the items Maddox left on the ground and then turns to go, only telling me, "Goodnight," as he pulls the door closed.

"Goodnight," I whisper, but it doesn't matter that he's too far away to hear me because he wasn't waiting for me to speak.

I sink into the bed, making sure my clothing is righted. My heart is heavy as I wonder whether it was something I had done wrong. Perhaps King Maddox had used the mind-link to ask Seth to come and get him away from me.

I roll over and close my eyes, hoping to fall asleep, but with every breath, I inhale the scent of the king, and I wish he was still here with me. Even though I was frightened to give myself to him, I am his to claim.

At least, if he had done it, everything would be over. Now, I am here, alone, wondering what is wrong with King Maddox that he had to leave, wondering what is wrong with me that he didn't stay.

～

MADDOX

"WHATEVER THE FUCK you interrupted me for, it had better be good, Seth," I say as I follow my Beta down the hallway to my office.

"I told you, Alpha," he says, giving me a minute to button my shirt. I've scrapped the tie and my socks, but at least I have my pants and shirt on, as well as my shoes, "one of the kitchen maids found something in your glass when she was doing the dishes after dinner."

"I know. It's wine!" I practically growl.

Seth only shakes his head. "No, that's not it. Just come to your office, and I'll show you."

That's what he said to lure me out of Isla's room, and now, my balls are so blue, I can hardly think straight. What the hell is the matter with him? I was about to get it on with that beautiful girl, and she was actually into it—which wouldn't be surprising, except she's a virgin, and you just never know how they'll act.

We walk into my office, and I see a familiar wine glass on the desk. At the bottom of it, there are some crystals of something, some kind of powder.

Now, I get what he's so uptight about.

"What the hell is it?" I ask him, wondering if someone has tried to poison me. Was someone trying to take my life?

"We're not positive, but I asked the healer to come in and look at it before I went to get you, and both of us think it's probably red wolf's blood." Seth picks up the glass and sniffs it before putting it down.

"That makes sense," I say, not needing to smell it myself. I have already tasted it. I distinctly remember thinking there was something bitter in my glass at dinner. Red wolf's blood is bitter tasting.

It is also a powerful aphrodisiac.

I sink into my chair behind my desk and rest my heaad in my palm. No wonder I was so eager to go jump that poor girl's bones.

I'd been drugged.…

She probably thinks I'm some sort of a horny monster.

"So… the wine came from Zabrina," I tell him. "She has to be responsible for this." She must've thought she could seduce me. All I can do is shake my head.

"Zabrina?" he repeats. "Did you see her put anything into it?"

I stare at Seth like he is an idiot. "No," I tell him. "She wouldn't have done it in front of me. She had a maid bring it in."

"Right," he says. "I guess we need to speak to that maid."

"I guess so." I look at him expectantly, and he picks up the phone on my desk, calling the kitchen to find out if anyone there knows who she was. Once he has a name, he calls security to go get her and bring her into the office.

It takes about fifteen minutes before the girl is located. I wasn't paying too much attention to her at dinner, but I recognize her. Besides, the fact that she's crying makes it obvious. "Sit," Seth tells her as two guards walk her in. She's still in her maid outfit, and she's wiping at the tears on her cheeks.

"What's your name?" I ask her, not losing my cool because I know it's not her fault, that she likely had no choice but to do as she was ordered. Still… if it had been poison, or if I'd been allergic to it, I'd be dead at her hands.

"Alva," she says. "Please, sir—"

"Hush, Alva," I tell her. "No need for all of that. Tell me what you put in my drink."

"I don't know," she said, bursting into tears again. "I only put in what I was told to!"

"And who told you to?" Seth asks.

She is too busy crying to answer, and before she can speak, my office doors fly open, without so much as a knock.

"What in the world is going on?" Zabrina asks, bursting into the room in a pink silk robe. Her father is right behind her. He is dressed at least. Alpha Jordan looks confused, but Zabrina just looks angry.

"What's going on is that someone put something in the Alpha King's wine at dinner, and we're trying to get to the bottom of it!" Seth exclaims.

"Well, you can't think Zabrina had anything to do with it!" Alpha Jordan says.

"Did we say she did?" I ask him, tipping my head to the side to watch his reaction carefully.

"No, but you think her maid did," he says, gesturing at the crying girl in the chair.

"The wine came from you, and was served by your girl," Seth countered, looking at Zabrina.

"So what? The glass isn't mine, and for all I know, one of the pack floozies His Majesty has hanging around did it. Like that pathetic little blonde girl I saw in the garden today!" Zabrina had her hands on her hips like this was her office, and I was the intruder.

Had she run into Isla in the garden? Was that what this was about? Was Zabrina trying to get to me before I could get to anyone else?

"Listen," I say, too tired and too pissed off to argue, "I know that your girl put the substance in my drink. I just need to know if you ordered her to do it or not."

"Of course, she didn't!" Alpha Jordan says, but Zabrina's face tells me everything I need to know.

Still, she says, "No, I did not, and I will not take the wrap for her."

"Very well," I say. "Then the two of you may leave."

Alpha Jordan looks like he wants to say more, but it's Zabrina who speaks. "You pathetic little whore," she says to the shaking girl in the chair. The two of them exit as Alva continues to cry.

"Sh-she made me," she manages to get out.

"Of course, she did," I say. "Nevertheless, you could've told me the situation. You could've let me know what was happening."

She nods. "I'm so sorry, my King."

"Yes, well, perhaps a few days in solitary confinement will make you think twice next time." I gesture for Seth to take her away, and his eyes widen. He thinks I'm being unfair. But I don't have a reputation for being a cruel king because I am kindhearted and fair.

The girl cries louder as Seth helps her up and walks her out to the guards who are waiting outside of the door. He tells them what to do with her, and her wailing echoes off down the hallway.

He returns to me as I stare at a note on my desk. It's not important, and I'm not even looking at it, not really. I just want him to leave.

"Sir?" he says.

"What, Beta?" I ask him, not looking up.

"You know you're punishing the wrong party. Won't this teach Zabrina that what she's done is all right?"

"Don't worry about Zabrina," I tell him. "I have something else planned for her."

He knows better than to question me, and at the moment, that's a good thing because I haven't quite worked all the details out yet, but Zabrina will pay for what she's done to me.

One way or another.

TALKS WITH THE KING

Isla

I AM SITTING at my table in my room, eating lunch, trying to get what happened the night before out of my head while Poppy talks about life at the castle and hangs up new clothes she's gotten for me in my closet. I try to pay attention to her, but mostly I am lost in thought as I eat my salad.

At least I have enough to eat while I am here. I don't know how long I'll be at the castle, but that's something.

"Really, though, Mrs. W. was the worst. You know, she wasn't ever even married? They always call the heads of house staffs missus even if they've never been touched by a man. Really, what man would want to touch her? I mean other than to knock the shit out of her like Beta Seth did." She laughs, and I laugh, too, even though I wasn't really listening to what she said.

Once her words catch up to me, I stop laughing. I didn't like it when the Beta had that woman beaten in front of me, even if it was on my behalf.

She continues on, and I try to listen, but I am thinking about King Maddox again. Why was he in my room? Why was he pulled out so quickly?

Why didn't he come back?

Would he come back?

My question was answered by a knock on the door—even though that wasn't quite what I had in mind. He wasn't going to proposition me in the middle of the day—was he?

Somehow, I knew it was him. Rather than jumping up and preparing myself, bowing or something, I sat there with my fork hanging over my bowl while Poppy goes to open the door, still talking about nothing.

"Yes?" she says as she opens it. As soon as she sees who it is, her eyes widen, and she drops her head, bending at the waist. "Your Majesty!"

"Hi, Poppy," he says, clearly annoyed. "Can you give us a moment, please?"

"Of course," she says, standing back up. He has to clear his throat for her to leave the room. What she thought he meant before, who knows?

He turns to look at me, his eyes piercing through me, and that's when I realize I'm just sitting there with my fork in my hand, looking at the king.

I quickly drop my fork and leap to my feet, but he stops me.

"No, no, no, Isla, that's okay," he says, waving his hands in front of me. "You don't have to do all of that. Especially not when it's just me in here."

I look at him for a long moment before I sit back down, unsure of myself. I don't know what to say so I just sit there... quiet.

"I... uh... just wanted to check on you," he begins. "After last night." His face is a little red, though I'm not sure why.

Why would he be embarrassed? He's the king. He can do whatever he likes.

"I'm fine," I tell him.

"Good. I just... I wanted you to know that someone slipped something into my drink last night. I don't usually act like that."

I stare at him a moment, and then it all comes together, and I realize that's why he was attracted to me last night. He was drugged. It makes perfect sense.

What other reason could someone like him possibly have for being with me?

I feel my cheeks redden and I drop my eyes so I'm staring at his knees. "Okay," is all I can get out.

"I mean... I hardly know you, and even though I understand what it is that your Alpha brought you here for... I'm not that kind of a man. Usually."

I think I am getting what he's trying to say. He's apologize for scaring me, for leaping on top of me the way that he did. But I'm still unclear if that means he might do it again one day—once he gets to know me.

"Yes, Your Majesty," is all I can say.

"So... if you... uh... I mean... I would like to get to know you better. If... that's all right with you." He stands there, staring at me, with his hands in his pockets, and I can't imagine why a king would be nervous to say something like that to me.

"Certainly," I tell him.

He looks at me for a few moments before he says, "I'm asking you, Isla, if you are interested in getting to know me. As a person. Not as a king that owns you."

I am shocked and in awe. Why? Why would he even care what I want? He doesn't have to worry about my thoughts or feelings. He's the king! He can do whatever he wants.

Perhaps there is more to the terrible, cruel King Maddox everyone has always told me about that hurts others and does nothing to help his people.

No, this doesn't sound like the same person at all.

"Yes, of course," I tell him.

He nods a few times before he says. "Very well," and then he takes a few steps backward toward the door. "I'll speak to you soon."

I nod. "Yes, Your Majesty."

He opens the door and disappears so quickly, it's difficult for me to even follow his form out with my eyes.

Just like that, he's gone.

So strange….

And yet, I can't help but feel a little giddy that I'll be getting to spend more time with him soon. I understand that he's the king and I am no one, and perhaps he is just trying to be nice to me before he uses me for the reason that I have been sold to him, but still… being in the same room with him makes my heart palpitate. Now, I know I will get to spend even more time with him.

I suddenly realize I have no idea how to talk to someone like him…. Maybe this isn't such a good thing after all.

Still… I want to see him again, and I am hopeful that I will get to.

A few moments later, Poppy bursts through the door. "Well? What did he say? What did he want? Is he making plans to ravish you later this evening?"

My eyes widen, and I can feel my cheeks heating up again. "Uh… no," I tell her. "But he did ask if he could come and talk to me soon."

Poppy's face falls. "Talk to you? About what? Why would he want to do that? You don't even talk! No offense."

I shrug. "None taken." I don't point out that she doesn't give me a chance to talk. "I don't know what he wants to talk about," I admit. "I guess I'll find out." I go back about eating my salad, and I can tell that it's killing her that I don't have more to say.

Oh, well. Let her stew.

I smile to myself as she goes back to hanging up clothes and talking.

I begin to daydream about sitting on a couch near King Maddox and talking about our favorite books or all the places he's visited, and I can't help but let my smile widen.

Maybe being the king's Breeder isn't so bad after all.

～

MADDOX

. . .

BACK IN MY OFFICE, my mind is on Isla, even as Seth goes over all of the information I will need for the meetings I have later. I know I should pay attention to him, but I can't.

She hadn't seemed angry at me, and I couldn't understand why.

Most women would be shocked that a strange man had burst into their room with plans to ravish them, but not Isla.

Not that she'd seemed too eager to have me claim her the night before, either. She was clearly nervous last night, but perhaps there was a chance she found herself responding to me, despite the fact that we hardly knew one another....

"Alpha?" Seth says, clearing his throat. "You're not listening to a word I'm saying are you?"

I chuckle. "I'm trying to," I tell him. "But you're boring me to tears. How's the maid we locked up? Did you do as I said with her?"

"Put her in the nicest jail cell we had available and make sure she has everything she needs? Yes, I did. But Alpha Jordan is asking to have her released, saying he'll send her back to his pack. He says this whole thing seems to have been a mistake, and he doesn't want her to be punished for it."

I scoff. "A mistake? He knows, and I know, that it was no mistake. It was his daughter."

"I am sure he probably does, but he's not going to stand by and watch her be punished either. What do you intend to do about Zabrina?"

I can't help the smile that pulls up the corners of my mouth. "I'm still trying to decide. But whatever it is, it will be fun."

He shakes his head at me. "Just be careful. Alpha Jordan is powerful."

"Last night, you were ready for me to punish Zabrina!" I remind him. "Now, you want me to be careful not to offend her father?"

"I've thought about it," he says with a shrug. "You weren't physically harmed, thank the Moon Goddess. Neither was the girl."

"Her name is Isla," I remind him.

"Yes, of course. I know her name," he says. "She's fine. You're fine. Perhaps… let's just be thankful for that and let it go."

My eyes lock on my Beta's face for a long moment. "Are you getting soft on me, Seth?" I ask him.

He clears his throat and looks away, and I realize there's something he's not telling me.

"What is it?" I demand.

He shakes his head slightly. "Nothing. Just some rumors."

"What kind of rumors?" I lean forward in my chair, my forearms resting on my desk. With all of the other mindless garbage he's told me, I don't understand why he can't tell me the important information he has, like what he's hinting at now.

"I've been told that some of Alpha Jordan's allies have been speaking about the possibility of combining their forces to take over some of the smaller packs near them. My understanding is that the only reason they haven't done so is because of their allegiance to Jordan. Not you. If you were to do something to make him angry, there's a chance he might step back and let them do as they will."

I understand now why Seth was hesitant to tell me that. I feel the weight of it in the pit of my stomach. The idea that Jordan could potentially be more important to some of the other Alphas than I am angers me.

So does the possibility that Jordan knew this information but didn't share it with me—and he might stand by and do nothing while more vulnerable packs are taken over. We were discussing how vile it is that some of the stronger packs are doing that on the other side of the kingdom just a few days ago, but he said nothing of this.

"I want names," I told Seth.

He opens his mouth to say something, but I can tell by his expression it's going to be him disagreeing with me.

"Now."

Seth nods and picks up a pad of paper and a pen from my desk, knowing it's better for me if he writes this sort of thing down.

When he's finished, I take it and see the names of four Alphas whose packs are relatively large and one small one—Green pack, led by Alpha Ben.

"Thank you," I tell him, putting the note in my desk.

"What are you going to do?" Seth asks, clicking my pen quickly, which grates on my last nerve.

"Stop them," I tell him.

He nods. "Yes, but how."

I don't want to tell him I don't know yet, so I say, "Decisively."

Seth's head rocks back and forth, and he stops his line of questioning. We move on to other matters, and my mind slips back to Isla.

I need a stress reliever in the worst way possible, but I want to get to know the girl before I take her.

Having an heir would help calm much of this madness, I know. The Alphas are in an uproar because they see an opportunity, but once I have a child, it will be more difficult for them to try to claim my throne.

So... I need Isla more than ever to fulfill her duties.

Yet, I want Isla more than ever to fulfill my desires.

I hope the girl and I can get to know one another soon because I don't know how much longer I can keep myself out of her room at night.

A DATE?

Isla

THE DAYS PASS SLOWLY, and for a few, I don't see King Maddox at all. I am beginning to think he has forgotten about my existence. I wonder how long it might take for him to realize he has a guest in his castle—or am I a prisoner—sitting in a room, withering away?

Of course, Poppy brings me food and keeps me company quite often. Sometimes I am alone. I have books and the window. I like to look outside at the gardens. Sometimes, a gardener will be out there working, making the plants beautiful.

Some might think it is boring, and to some extent it is, but it's nice not to have to work all the time.

I miss my family so terribly, though. I wish I could call them or otherwise receive word of how they are doing. I have no way of knowing what Alpha Earnest told them. For all I know, my parents might think I am dead.

Thinking of my mother missing me, of her assuming the worst, makes my heart heavy.

I sleep a lot, too. I find myself nodding off in the chair by the window with a book or I climb into the plush bed and let my head sink into the fluffy pillows.

I sleep so that I can dream.

I dream so that there's a small chance I might get to see King Maddox.

In my dreams, we are a couple. He cares about me, not just as his breeder, but as a person. He smiles and holds my hand. We laugh and spend time together in the garden.

Sometimes, we make love, and it is always so soul-shattering that when I wake up after such dreams, I find my body clenching and spasming in places I didn't know existed before I came here. My face is always flushed, and a thin layer of sweat always glistens on my skin.

Thankfully, Poppy hasn't walked in right after one of my dreams has ended—yet. I suppose I can always just tell her I was having a nightmare and had to run....

The more I dream about King Maddox, the more I know that I am not doing him justice. When I get to know him in real life, if I get to know him, he will probably be nothing like in my dreams, and that will be disappointing.

But right now, dreams are all I have.

Dreams at night, and daydreams.

I do plenty of that, too, imagining what it would be like to spend time with the king. I can't think about my family without getting teary-eyed, so I spend my time thinking about him....

I am sitting on my bed with a book in my hand one afternoon several days past when King Maddox stopped by my room to see if I would be willing to get to know him when there is a knock on my door. Poppy is straightening the room, something she does often, even though there's no reason for it.

She crosses to answer the door, and I feel a fluttering in my gut.

What if it's him?

My hair is pulled back in a braid, and I am wearing an outfit for lounging, linen pants and a blouse, both in shades of gray. It's not the best outfit I have, but it's comfortable, and I don't look bad.

I hold my breath as Poppy opens the door.

It's Seth.

I let my breath out. "Hello, Poppy," he says as she bows to the Beta. "May I speak to Miss Isla, please?"

"Of course, sir," she says. He comes into the room and stops at the end of the bed, smiling at me. I start to get up, but he signals for me to stay. Turning toward the door, he says, "That will be all, Poppy."

I know that she is supposed to leave so he can speak to me alone, but she never seems to remember that until she's asked.

Poppy goes out and closes the door behind her.

"How are you?" Beta Seth asks me.

I nod. "Well, thank you. And you, sir?"

He smiles at me, a slight chuckle under his breath. I'm not sure why. "I'm well, thank you. I have a note for you." He withdraws a paper from the inside pocket of his jacket and hands it to me.

I stare at the paper, noticing my name is written on the outside. It is sealed with a red sticker so that no one can open it without me knowing.

"Thank you," I say, staring at my name. The slant of the writing makes me think it is a male's handwriting, but I don't recognize it.

Could the note be from… King Maddox?

"Go ahead and open it," Seth prompts me.

"Of course," I tell him, blinking away my daze. I break the seal and unfold the paper.

The message isn't long. I glance down the length of the paper quickly before I read:

DEAR ISLA,

If you are available, I would like to have dinner with you tonight.

--M

THAT'S IT. That's all it says.

If I am available?

"Well?" Seth asks me. "Are you free?"

"I will have to check my calendar," I say with a small smile.

He laughs. It's sad that we both know I have nothing else going on.

"Yes, I'm free. I would be delighted to have dinner with the king," I tell him, my stomach twisting as a spray of butterflies launches, trying to work their way out through my throat.

"Good," he says, still smiling. "He will be pleased. Be ready at seven o'clock, please."

"Yes, sir," I tell him.

He shakes his head slightly. "There's no need for you to call me sir, Isla. You're not a servant here."

"But aren't I?" I ask, giving him a pointed look. "I might not be a maid, but I am a servant, I believe."

Seth takes a moment before he says, "In a way, we are all servants, here to do what our king and the kingdom require. But, no, you should not think of yourself as a servant. You are a guest of the king."

"Yes, sir… I mean… Beta Seth," I correct, feeling heat rise in my cheeks.

He chuckles at me again. Clearly, my awkwardness amuses him. I wonder if I will amuse the king as well. "See you later, Miss Isla." He bows his head to me, and I give him a similar nod before he turns and walks out the door.

Keeping King Maddox's note in my hand, I take a deep breath. I am going to dinner with the king, and I have a note from him… in my hand.

Only a few seconds after Beta Seth leaves the room, Poppy comes bounding in. "Well?" she asks me, a broad smile on her face. "What did he want?"

"He, uh… I uh… I'm having dinner with… with… with—King Maddox." I don't usually have so much trouble speaking, but this time, it's all too unreal for me to comprehend, so my mouth seems uncooperative.

"What?" Poppy squeals and jumps up and down, clapping her hands. "When?"

"Tonight," I tell her.

"What time?" she asks, impatiently.

"Seven," I tell her.

Poppy's face melts, and her eyes widen in horror. "Seven?" she screeches. "But… it's past five now!"

I am confused. My forehead crinkles as I look at her. "And??"

"And—it will take a few hours for you to get ready!" she exclaims.

"Why?" I ask her. "My clothes are here, my makeup is here, everything is here."

She is shaking her head. "No, honey! You'll need a good soak. You'll need to make sure you don't have a hair on your body, and you'll have to make sure your makeup and hair are on point!"

"No hair?" I ask her.

"No hair! Except for your eyebrows, eyelashes, and your head, of course. Now, come on!" She grabs my arm and hauls me off the bed to the bathroom.

I don't know what to say as she turns the bathtub on and gets the bath ready, dropping in salts and bath bombs and other fragrances. I am under the impression King Maddox and I are just going to dinner. I don't expect there will be anything more tonight. He said he wanted to get to know me.

He didn't say anything about s-e-x.

Does he expect that to happen tonight??

Clearly, Poppy thinks so. She is going to a lot of trouble to make sure I am perfect in every way.

"Do you know how to shave… down there?" she asks me, holding up a razor.

I stare at her for a minute. "Why is that necessary?" I want to know.

"You need to be neat and tidy! The king may want to… taste you!"

I feel my face catch on fire as she thrusts the razor at me again.

"I think I can manage," I tell her. I've never had a reason to shave… down there before. But it's not exactly a wild jungle either.

She gives me a skeptical look, like she is afraid I will mess this up and leave the king revolted by my hairy mound.

"You can go, Poppy," I tell her.

"But—"

"I can manage," I tell her, gesturing toward the door.

Muttering under her breath, she says, "I hope you don't mess this up."

"Your faith in me is overwhelming," I say sarcastically as she goes out the door. I lock it.

I can manage a bath, washing my hair, shaving... places... by myself. I will need her help with my makeup and making sure I have the right dress. But I can do this.

I think....

Stripping off my clothes, I get into the bathtub and pour in some bubbles. I like bubbles. Once I am concealed in my cloudy white sanctuary, I begin to shave my legs. I shave my armpits. I contemplate Poppy's advice and sigh.

She's probably right.... I shave... down there.

Something tells me this is not going to be comfortable in a day or two....

Satisfied that the king will not be revolted, I wash my hair and let the conditioner sit for a bit before I rinse that off, too.

I am about to get out of the tub when Poppy bangs on the door. "Are you about done?"

I mumble, "Give me a minute..." before I tell her, "yes."

Getting out of the tub, I wrap myself up in a towel and unlock the door. Poppy bursts in, a whirlwind of action as she goes about getting the rest of me ready.

She dries my hair, curls it, styles it, and then moves on to my makeup, taking her time and making everything careful.

Then... I go out to see she's laid out a beautiful sapphire blue gown that will make my eyes sparkle, as well as lacy, satiny undergarments. I get dressed, putting on silver heels and diamond jewelry. When I am all ready, she leads me to the floor-length mirror.

I look like a princess. I feel like one, too.

"You're so gorgeous!" Poppy has tears in her eyes as she stands behind me, admiring me in the mirror.

"Thank you," I tell her. I turn to hug her. "I couldn't have done this without you."

"I know," she says, patting my back, and I stifle a laugh.

Poppy... so humble.

A knock at the door has both of us jumping. My eyes travel to the clock. It's seven—right on the dot.

I know that it's King Maddox at the door because of the way my stomach is reacting to him, and I can smell his spicy cologne as notes of it waft in on the breeze. I swallow hard.

"You're going to do great," she says to me. "Did you shave?"

"Shh!" Her voice is loud and carries. I nod as she giggles and goes to open the door.

She bows low as she pulls the door open and steps aside, and I see Maddox standing there in a suit, looking so delicious, I want to taste him, too.

80

DATE WITH THE BREEDER

Maddox

This is a mistake....

I can't help but think perhaps I should not have arranged to take Isla out on a date. After all, I haven't dated anyone in… years. Not since Rebecca and I were first introduced. That was almost ten years ago.

At the time, we'd just discovered we were fated mates, and I was so excited to get to know her. She was gorgeous, and I wanted so very much to touch her in every way possible.

But Rebecca was a lady, and she had a reputation to maintain. I had to bide my time with her, waiting until we were engaged before we ever even kissed.

We married a few months after we established our mated bond. After that… everything changed.

Rebecca was a wild woman in the bedroom, completely uninhibited in every way. The woman I had been dating and the creature I encountered in the bedroom seemed like polar opposites, and I was shocked with all of the positions and kinky toys she wanted to try.

Personally, I preferred two or three positions that Rebecca thought were boring. But… I did what she wanted, not wanting to be teased for being too "vanilla."

It was Rebecca's cravings that eventually led to her demise….

Something told me, Isla would be different. But I had no way of knowing for sure.

The other night, when I had been drugged, I had pounced on her, and she'd responded favorably.

Perhaps my little virgin Breeder would be different in the bedroom as well.

Straightening my tie, I reminded myself that I wasn't wooing Isla. She wasn't a woman I was dating so that I could decide whether or not I wanted to marry her.

She was simply a girl I was getting to know before I ravished her and eventually impregnated her, assuming all went as planned.

I hadn't even sent her to the pack healer's office yet to make sure she was even capable of carrying my child. Nor had I checked Alpha Earnest's claim that Isla was a virgin. I would find that out for myself soon enough. What she'd done before she got here was none of my business, so long as she wasn't diseased. A simple blood test would reveal that much, so I should probably get that done.

I just didn't want to make her nervous when it was clear she was already frightened to be here.

So… this date was for what? To calm her nerves? To make her think I am a nice guy? To see if we are compatible?

I didn't know for sure, but after I invaded her room and left her trembling beneath me, I felt I owed her a few niceties.

"You look handsome," Beta Seth says from my living room area as I walk out.

I grumble at him. "If only you were the girl I am trying to impress."

He chuckles. "What's not to like?"

I shrug. "I don't know what the hell I'm doing, Seth." I would never admit that to anyone else. "What if she falls in love with me, and it turns out I can't stand her?"

He laughs louder. "I don't think that's possible. Isla is a lovely, sweet girl. I know the kind of girl you like, and she fits the description."

From what he's saying, she's not so much like Rebecca. Even when we just first started dating, before I knew what kind of an animal she was in the bedroom, I wouldn't have used the word "sweet" to describe her. Rebecca had biting wit and was always thinking of something clever to say.

Isla only spoke when spoken to from what I could tell. She was timid and quiet. I couldn't imagine she had a lick of quick wit to exchange in banter with me.

I was about to find out.

"Good luck," Beta Seth says as I head out the door. I turn and smile at him and then go to Isla's room, which is just down the hall.

I've requested we have our dinner served in a private dining room over-looking the rose garden, one where we are less likely to have someone walk in on us. Zabrina was the type of woman who would hunt me down just to try to drive me crazy.

I'd be happy when she left the castle…

A sharp knock on the door, and I hear scurrying on the other side. My stomach twists a bit. I am nervous, and I don't know why. It's just a servant girl I'm taking out to dinner, after all—isn't it?

Visions of her naked bottom fill my mind, the way she felt beneath my body, the taste of her tongue in my mouth….

"Your Majesty!" Poppy says, bowing low as she opens the door.

I wish I could send her away sometimes, too. "Hello, Poppy," I say, but my eyes aren't on the maid.

They are on the maiden.

Isla is standing near her bed wearing a sapphire blue dress that makes her eyes twinkle. She is gorgeous, and I can't even hear what Poppy is popping off about as I walk into the room.

Suddenly, I feel like I should've brought a gift—flowers, jewelry, half my kingdom….

"Hello, Isla," I say to her.

She dips her head. "Hello, Your Majesty," she says, looking up at me through her long eyelashes.

"Shall we?" I offer her my arm, and she comes forward, slipping her slender arm through mine, and I lead her to the door.

"Have a good time!" Poppy shouts, as if she is Isla's mother.

The scent of vanilla and roses wafts through the air. She smells lovely, almost edible.

We walk down the hallway to the stairs, and I attempt to make small talk. "How have you been?" I ask her.

"I've been well," she says, "thank you. How have you been, sir?"

I sigh. "We've talked about this, Isla." I chuckle a bit. "You can call me Maddox."

"Beg your pardon, si—uhm… Maddox."

The way my name comes out of her mouth makes my groin tighten, though I can tell she is hesitant to use my first name. She's so damn polite, she just can't seem to take my word for it that I'm not offended by her lack of formality.

"I've been busy," I admit as we climb the stairs. I hold her hand, rather than her arm, making sure she doesn't slip in her heels. She takes her time, gripping the railing on the other side. I can tell she's not used to walking in this sort of a get-up—heels and a gown. She looks natural enough in it, because she's so beautiful, but clearly, her family is not of the social status that would generally get invited to the sort of affairs where one would be required to dress this elegantly on a regular basis.

"I'm sorry you've had so much to do," she says. I look at her, and she smiles shyly at me.

"It's always the case," I assure her, and she nods. I think I see her smile falter a bit. Perhaps she doesn't like the idea that I might not always have enough time for her.

That was Rebecca's biggest complaint.

That and she wanted it so hard, I would have to be a jackhammer to completely satisfy her....

We arrive at the dining room and I open the door for her. Isla thanks me and walks in, her eyes lighting up at the beautiful space.

It's quaint, only one table presently, with carved wooden accents on the walls and a painted ceiling depicting a lovely ball from a few centuries ago. The floor is walnut, the same wood as the carvings and the wainscoting, and as I pull out a chair for her, I see her eyes widen as she continues to look around the room.

Soft violin music plays in the background. I had considered having live musicians, but I don't want anyone else nearby. The candlelight flickers as I pull out my seat across from her, watching her take it all in.

"Do you like it here?" I ask her.

"It's beautiful," she says, smiling, her cheeks pinking.

"Out the window, there's a lovely view of the rose garden." I pull the drapes back so she can see.

Isla gasps. "That garden is so beautiful! The one out my window is as well, but this one...."

"This is the prize garden of the castle," I assure her. "The garden out your window, the Luna's Garden, isn't quite as well maintained." It is full of Rebecca's favorite flowers, but since I never go there, the gardeners do not spend as much time as they used to... before.

"I just love gardens," Isla says, beaming at me.

I make a note to be sure to bring her flowers the next time I take Isla out on a date.

The staff steps in quickly and brings the first course. I know she is confused about the forks, so I make a point of saying, "Let's see, oh yes, it's this little one on the outside," so that she doesn't need to feel embarrassed.

As we eat, we talk about our lives. She doesn't have much to say. I ask her about her family, and she says, "Honestly, I miss them so much, it's hard to talk about them."

"I'm so sorry," I say. "Perhaps you would like to call them tomorrow?"

Her eyes light up, but then she shakes her head. "My parents can't afford a phone."

"There must be some way to speak to them," I assure her.

She shakes her head, "Not that I know of."

I will figure that much out. "Do you have siblings?" I know what Earnest has told me, but there's no way to know for sure that what he's said is true.

"I have five younger brothers and two older sisters," she tells me. She smiles when she mentions them.

"What are their names?" I ask her as the first-course ends and the second one begins.

"My sisters are Kenna and Brandy. They're married and live in other packs. My brothers are Christopher, Jeremy, Benjamin, Ryan, and Blake," she says.

"And you're close with all of your brothers?"

"I am," she says. "I don't see my sisters much, but my brothers and I have always been close. Especially Ben…." Her voice fades a bit. My brow furrows with concern. She shakes her head, and I decide she just must miss him the most. "Anyway, I'm not sure what they would think of all of this."

"What do you mean?" I ask her.

She shrugs. "Well, my parents have very high moral standards. They feel that a woman should only have relations with her fated mate and then only after marriage. So…." She shrugs again, and I understand.

"You are afraid they would be disappointed in you?"

She nods.

"Well, they should be glad that you've paid off their debts," I remind her.

"I hope so, but there's no way to know for sure if Alpha Earnest actually forgave their debt." She purses her lips together and averts her eyes, looking out the window.

"What do you mean?" I spear a piece of meat with my fork but wait for her to speak before I begin to chew.

"Well, it's just… Alpha Earnest is not always a man of his word, and I am not completely convinced that he didn't just take whatever relief he was given but not pass it along to my family."

"So, it's your family that owes the debt to him, not you. Is that correct?"

"Yes," she tells me.

It really doesn't seem fair that she's the one here, paying off a debt that isn't her own.

Perhaps, I should send her home….

Can I even do that at this point?

I can't imagine letting her go.

Besides, technically speaking, a father can do whatever he'd like to repay a debt whether it belongs to one of his children or himself. It seems like an archaic law, but that's the way it is.

Yet, I find myself saying, "Well, after a few weeks, if you are terribly unhappy here, perhaps I can let you go."

Her eyes widen as she looks up at me. I hope she will say that she is perfectly happy here, but all she says is, "Thank you."

I nod and we go on about finishing our meal. We talk about other things. She asks about my family, and I tell her I don't have one. My parents are dead, and I have no siblings, just a few distant cousins. Isla is saddened about this, telling me that having a close family is so important to her.

I love to listen to her speak. Her voice is so sweet and soft, almost like a melody. She is intoxicating in every way.

When we are done with our dessert, I stand and offer her my hand. "Would you like to dance?" I ask her.

Isla's eyes flicker from my face to my hand and then back again before she swallows hard and says, "No."

WILL YOU SLEEP WITH ME?

Isla

"WOULD YOU LIKE TO DANCE?" the king had asked me.

I'd looked from his intoxicating eyes to his outstretched hand, and my first thoughts had been of my two left feet.

Even back home, when I was dancing at school dances with boys of little consequence, I was the most ungraceful person in the building.

He is a king and has likely danced with all sorts of beautiful, graceful women over the years.

I would make a fool of myself!

So I said, "No."

I see his face falter slightly and inhale deeply, wishing I had the words to explain.

"I, uh… don't know how," I stammer.

"Oh," he says, grinning at me. "I see. Well, that's no problem, Isla."

I love the way my name sounds when it rings from his lips. Like I am an unexplored territory in paradise….

"It isn't a problem?" I ask him, feeling my cheeks redden.

He shakes his head and reaches for my hand, gently guiding me from my chair. "I can lead you."

"Oh, but I…."

He cuts me off. "Don't worry. It's just the two of us."

I don't tell him that is precisely what I am worried about.

Not to mention, that's not exactly true. There are servants bustling in and out of the room. But I suppose, to the king, they are no one.

He leads me away from the table, keeping my left hand in his right while he wraps his arm around me and places his other hand on the small of my back. In this dress, that is bare skin, and the feel of his palm against my flesh makes warmth radiate throughout my body, pooling in my core.

He smells like the air after a rainstorm, and I can't breathe him in deeply enough.

With a reassuring smile, he begins to move me slowly around what has become our dance floor. The room isn't large, so we don't have a lot of room, but it is enough for just the two of us.

"There," he says, his voice a soft whisper near my ear. "It's not so bad, is it?"

I don't know what to say. No, it's not bad. It's fine. In fact, it's lovely. He moves so agilely, it is as if he was born to the sound of music. Perhaps he was. I don't even fear tripping with his arms around me.

I find myself leaning into him, wanting to get closer, as if being pressed against him isn't quite close enough. I can't see his face now because he's taller than me, and my head is nearly on his shoulder, but I know him well enough already to envision the expression in his eyes.

"Some say that making love is a lot like dancing," he says in that breathy voice, and I feel a flutter deep within me. Visions of the dreams I've had of him flash before my eyes, the two of us tangled in the bedsheets, my fingers clawing for a grip as he thrusts into me, deep and fast, over and over again.

I say nothing, only make a noise in the back of my throat that is meant to be an agreement, or an inquiry that he should say more.

He does. "It's the give and take, the rhythm, the two bodies moving so fluidly together."

I can see that. Sometimes, at school dances, teachers had to break couples apart who had forgotten they were in the gymnasium at school, not the bedroom.

We are not doing that particular kind of dance with the grinding and the gyrating, but as he moves me, as my body glides along with his, I understand exactly what King Maddox is talking about.

I lower my head to his shoulder, overwhelmed by his presence. I have never known anyone like him before. Not only does his magnetism command the room, one glance from him makes my body react in ways it never has before. Even now, I can feel myself growing damp beneath my silk panties, and I wonder if he can smell my arousal with his heightened wolf senses.

Even though I am pressed tightly against him, I cannot say whether or not he has any sort of attraction to me at the moment. If his body is physically responding to mine, it is subtle beneath his jacket and suit pants.

I long to know.... Was it just the drug the other night or is it possible he might actually be curious about me?

He can have any woman he wants, and so many are more beautiful and poised than I. Yet, I am the one in his arms right now. I am the one he has chosen to spend his time with.

It can't just be because of his investment in me... can it?

"Isla." My name is a moan as it escapes his lips, and I feel a trembling in my lower extremities. The warmth of his lips sends tingles radiating throughout the flesh of my neck as he carefully places kisses beneath my ear and down to the spot where my shoulder disappears beneath the gown.

If he truly wants me... he can take me now. I would gladly surrender myself to him. I am like a flower petal in his strong hand, waiting to be caressed... or crushed.

Maddox lifts his face to look into my eyes. His eyelids are hooded as if he is just as intoxicated as I am.

He reaches up and runs his hand along my cheek, his thumb strumming my cheekbone. I close my eyes and lean into his hand.

"Tonight, I planned only to get to know you, beautiful," he says, and I open my eyes to look into his. "I want you to know that I am worthy of your trust. That I understand that it wasn't your choice to be here or to give yourself to me."

I nod, feeling my insides crumble. He is letting me down gently. He has no intentions of fulfilling the fantasies I have had about him these past few days.

"But..." He pauses, taking a deep breath and letting it out slowly, the scent of the brandy he had with dessert filling my lungs. It makes me want to plunge my tongue between his perfect pink lips. "I am fascinated with you, Isla. I will not force you to come back to my room like I forced you to dance." A crooked grin slides into place on his handsome face, and I smile back at him, thinking it's true, he did force me to dance. "But I must invite you. Do you think... you might want to accompany me back to my room? At any point, if you change your mind, I'll make sure you get safely back to your own chambers."

If all of this has been a ploy, a way to make me think that I have decided to be his breeder, rather than simply being a servant purchased for a purpose, then he is the most sincere actor I have ever met.

I truly feel that he is offering me a choice.

The ache from between my legs tells me I only have one answer that will satisfy my growing need. "Yes," I say, barely recognizing my own heady voice.

His eyebrows arch slightly. "You're certain?"

I bite my bottom lip and nod.

His smile widens and he lowers his head, softly brushing his lips against mine. I rise up on my tiptoes, wanting more.

He accommodates me, making a second pass and lingering. He kisses me several times, as he had when his lips were exploring my neck. When his tongue glides along my lower lip, I open my mouth and let him in. The rough surface of his tongue as it taps against mine has me threading my fingers through his hair and leaning into him. He tastes like cool mountain water, and he is the only thing that can extinguish the flame flickering inside of me.

Maddox attempts to pull back away from me, and I groan a protest before I realize what I have done. He smiles at me and smooths his palm against my cheek again.

"If we stand here and kiss all night, we'll never make it back to my room," he reminds me.

I feel my face flush again, but I am incapable of a verbal reply.

With my fingers wrapped around his, we turn and head for the door. As we make our way down the hall, past the priceless works of art and the interesting historical displays, I say nothing. I concentrate on keeping the air in my lungs and my head from spinning.

Is this actually about to happen? Is the Alpha King about to claim my virginity?

My mind slips to an unhealthy place as, for a moment, I imagine his teeth sinking into my neck as he marks me, making me his own. I know that it will never happen, that I am not meant to be the next Luna, only the woman who will carry his child. Still… I cannot help but think of how perfect it would be if the two of us could truly be in love, and I could be the wife that makes him happy for the rest of his years.

Thinking of marrying him makes me remember that he has been married before.

Queen Rebecca.

She died….

Some say he killed her.

I can't imagine that's the case. He's so kind, so thoughtful.

No, I won't believe it.

We turn the corner, and I recognize the hallway. The king's chambers are up on the right. Just one more corner and a bit of a hallway, and we'll be there. I bite down on my lip again, the butterflies in my stomach taking flight in a flurry of wings.

He pauses before we get to the last hallway. Looking at me, he says, "Isla, sweetheart, are you still sure?"

I nod. "Yes, King Maddox. I'm sure." I am surprised by my own confidence, but it gets a smile from him.

We round the corner, my heart beating out of my chest, my face beginning to ache from smiling so widely.

And then… we both come to a halt as we take in the view in front of us.

"Oh, thank the Moon Goddess!" the woman in front of us says. "Your Majesty, help!"

I freeze, covering my mouth with both hands as I stare at her.

It's hard to recognize her, considering the state she's currently in, but I know who she is.

It's Zabrina, Alpha Jordan of Elm Pack's daughter.

She is standing there with her hands wide, wearing a fancy light yellow dress, her hair pinned up, as if she'd gone somewhere nice tonight.

But now… her dress is ruined, and she looks… like a nightmare.

"Please, help!" she says again as Maddox steps forward.

"What in the world happened, Zabrina?" he asks.

Then, he asks the same question I've been wanting to know since we first saw her.

"And why the hell are you covered in blood?"

ANOTHER DEATH IN THE CASTLE

Maddox

"ZABRINA, why are you all covered in blood?" I ask again as I stare at Alpha Jordan's daughter. Her yellow dress is covered in the red, sticky substance, as are her hands. It's smeared all the way up her arms and even on her chin. "Are you injured?"

She shakes her head, "No, King Maddox. It's not me... it's... the maid!"

I let out a sigh of relief that it's not Zabrina who is bleeding profusely, not because I care so much about her but because I don't want to have to explain to Alpha Jordan or any of his friends that his daughter was grievously injured while she was in my home.

I've already sent for help using the mind-link, and as I hear footsteps approaching from behind me, I know that it's Seth.

Reluctantly, I turn to Isla. She is even more pale than usual, and her bottom lip is trembling as her sapphire eyes stare in abject horror at the bloody monster in front of us.

I really fucking hate Zabrina right now. "Isla, dear, I'm going to have to let Beta Seth walk you back to your room. I'm so sorry."

"No, it's all right," she says. "I just hope... everyone is okay."

"Me as well," I tell her. I long to lean down and kiss her lips, but in the mental state she is in right now, I think it's best to hold off.

Turning to Seth, I say, "Come back directly."

He nods and takes Isla's arm. I am tempted to watch her go, but I have a problem to handle. Judging by the amount of blood we are dealing with, it is a big one.

Two guards approach from either end of the hallway, also coming from my call. I don't want to conduct this interview alone. Witnesses are a good thing to have when speaking to someone you think might possibly have committed a heinous crime.

"What happened with the maid?" I ask her.

Zabrina's arms flop about as she talks, and she sounds frantic, but I know she isn't. For one thing, she isn't sweating at all, and her eyes are not dilated.

"I went down to visit her in her cell," she tells me. "I felt so bad for her, you know? I have known the woman for so long, and I have become friends with her over the years." She locks eyes with me, and without blinking says, "We're very good friends, despite her station."

I nod. "Go on."

"Well, I was thinking, perhaps she didn't do this, poison you that is, because there's a good chance someone else slipped into the castle and poisoned the wine. After all, there are many people who might want to dispose of you, Your Majesty."

I do not take this moment to point out that it was an aphrodisiac I was slipped, not a poison.

Unless my enemies would like me to fuck to death, I'm guessing it wasn't their doing....

"So I went to speak to her," Zabrina continues. "As she was eating the steak I brought to her, I asked her if she had done it, and she started to cry. She said her father told her to do it, that he was an assassin ordered by an enemy Alpha to kill you."

"What Alpha?" I ask, taking careful mental note of everything she is saying.

She shrugs. "That's the thing. She didn't say, and then, as I was telling her that I would have to tell you of her vicious plan, despite the fact that she and I have come to be such good friends, she grabbed the steak knife and sliced her own throat! She cut clean through her jugular! It was... horrendous."

"That explains all of the blood," I murmur.

"Yes! It was spurting everywhere, and I... well, I tried to make the bleeding stop." Zabrina holds her hands out as if I might be able to see from all of the blood how much effort she put forth.

"But it was fruitless?" I ask her. "Alice died anyway?"

"That's right!" she says with a firm nod, and I try to hide a revealing smile. "I cried out to the guards to fetch a healer, and they did, but by the time they returned, my beloved Alice was dead." Fake tears stream down Zabrina's cheeks as she shakes her shoulders, a loud sobbing sound emitting from her mouth.

I give her a moment to finish her elaborate portrayal of a woman who has just lost her best friend. When she seems to have herself pulled together, I ask, "Then what did you do?"

"Why… I came looking for you, of course. I thought you should hear from me, not only that Alice was dead, but that she was the one who had tried to harm you. So you see, it wasn't me. It was her… the corrupt maid. The woman I had trusted to take care of my every need for years. I'm so sorry, Your Majesty." She takes a few steps toward me, but I put my hands up and back away.

The last thing I want is for that innocently spilled blood to get all over my suit.

"May I ask why you thought it necessary to take a steak knife into the dungeon?" I ask her. "Also… wasn't your maid friend in solitary confinement?" I believe that had been my order.

Zabrina's shoulders raise and drop. "I just wanted her to have a nice meal. The guards allowed me to go in and see her."

That was something I was going to have to take care of. I had no doubt the beautiful Alpha's daughter had used her ability to beguile men to sneak her way in. Picnic basket and all….

What I was going to do about Zabrina now, I wasn't sure, but I would have to be decisive. I knew every word that came out of her mouth was a lie—save the fact that the poor maid had bled out like a sieve; of that I had no doubt.

"Where is your father?" I ask her.

Again, she shrugs. "Likely in his room. Why do you ask?"

I study her face for a moment, trying to determine what to do. Alpha Jordan is powerful. He has many powerful friends, and he is quite influential when it comes to the old guard, the gentlemen who have been Alphas since before my father passed away.

Angering Alpha Jordan is a risky endeavor. If I do so, I can easily anger several large packs at once.

Yet, I can't let this woman stand here before me and lie about what happened when I know damn good and well that she is the one who used that knife to slice through the maid's neck.

Why would she do a thing? Simply put, she was afraid that the maid would convince me of what I already knew to be true—it was Zabrina who slipped the drugs into my glass--or at the very least, her order that caused the maid to do so.

I decide to hold my cards for now. Seth is back. I can hear him approaching behind me again and know the cadence of his footsteps well enough that I don't have to turn to look at him to know it's him.

My mind flashes with images of Isla. I should be in my chambers with her right now, kissing her, exploring her body with mine.

Instead, I am standing her gaping at a bloody nightmare.

"Go get cleaned up," I tell Zabrina. "We will speak of this tomorrow."

She nods. "Yes, Your Majesty. I think... a good sleep will help to ease my troubled mind. Perhaps... you could pay me a visit later? I could... take comfort in your arms."

She is propositioning me now? When she is covered in the blood of the woman whose neck I have no doubt she slashed? And she's just seen me walking down the hall with Isla?

"Not tonight," I tell her, managing a sympathetic smile. Again, there's no reason to alarm her at the moment.

Her bottom lip protrudes in disappointment. "Perhaps you'd be more inclined if I wasn't covered in the blood of the woman whose life I tried to save," she says. "You know... some would count me as a hero for even trying."

I press my lips together for a moment, choosing my words carefully, before I say, "It takes a special kind of person to do what you've done."

Zabrina's face lights up. "Thank you, Your Majesty," she says, totally missing what I am saying to her. "I like to think so." She bows her head to me and then heads off to her room, and I notice bloody footsteps all down the hallway.

"What the hell happened?" Seth asks me.

"She killed that poor, innocent maid," I tell him.

Seth's eyes widen and then narrow again. "The one I told you not to punish?"

I glare at him. "Well, she wasn't completely innocent. She is the one who put the substance in my drink. But yes. Her."

"How do you know Zabrina is the one that killed her?" Seth asks me.

"It's simple enough," I reply. I look from one guard to the other to see how closely they were paying attention to our conversation, but they both look at a loss.

Sighing, I take a few steps, pressing a hand to my forehead. "Zabrina claims that she took the maid dinner because they were nearly best friends, and she felt sorry for her. First of all, that's suspicious because when we first discovered that I had been given something in my drink, Zabrina said the maid acted alone. I seriously doubt she would've just decided that she was mistaken."

"True," Seth says, "but that hardly seems like enough evidence to accuse Zabrina of murder. After all, she could've just felt bad for the woman, someone she knew, and wanted her to have something to eat."

"Does that sound like Zabrina to you?" I ask, giving him a dry look.

"Well, no," Seth admits. "But we hardly know her. Perhaps we haven't gotten a good impression of her. Maybe she's been nervous around you and hasn't acted quite like herself."

I can't help the chuckle that escapes my lips. "I somehow doubt that. At any rate, I have further proof that she slashed that girl's neck."

"And what proof is that?" he asks me.

I inhale sharply and blow it out through my nose, going back over the conversation. "Zabrina claimed to have been best friends with the girl. I asked her if she sought medical attention for the maid, for Alice, and she said she did, that she'd sent for a pack healer." I shrug. "So you see, Seth... that's how I know she's lying."

His forehead knits together. "I'm not following. What is it in what you've just said that proves she was lying?"

"I asked her about Alice several times," I tell him. "Her alleged best friend. She never once corrected me."

"Corrected you?" Seth asks.

"Yes, Beta Seth. Don't you remember?" He stares at me blankly. Finally, I put him out of his misery and fill him in on what he's missing. "The maid's name is Alva."

MY WOLF SMELLS A RAT

Isla

THAT WAS CERTAINLY NOT what I was expecting!

After a lovely dinner and dancing with the handsome king, he had invited me back to his room so that we could get to know one another better.

I had fully expected this to be the night when I began to fulfill my duties.

Now, I am back in my own bedroom, sitting on the edge of the bed, staring at the mirror above the dresser across from me, trying to process what I've just seen.

What the hell happened to Zabrina?

All I know is that she said something about the maid. But I don't know what she's talking about.

From the looks of all of that blood, I'm imagining that someone had to have been hurt pretty badly.

Poppy opens the door between our rooms and walks out slowly, peeking around the door like she's afraid the king is in here and she's interrupting something.

"Hi," I say to her in a solemn voice. I'm not sure why I'm so upset. It's not as if I wanted to breed with the king anyway. I need to remember that. The longer I can put that off, the better I'll be.

Right?

"Well?" Poppy says, her eyes wide. "Did you… have fun?" She wiggles her eyebrows at me, and I know that she is implying something.

"I had fun," I said with a shrug. "But... we didn't have fun, if that's what you mean."

She laughs, and I don't know what to say. "But did you have fun?"

"Yes," I tell her. "We had fun, but then something happened, and he had to bring me back here. Well, Beta Seth had to bring me back here."

Poppy comes over to the bed and sinks down next to me. "Why?" she asks, and it is as if we are just two girlfriends, not a maid and the woman she is helping. It's still difficult for me to think of myself as anyone important, but I do kind of find it odd that Poppy is having the same problem.

Still, she has asked a question, one I should probably try to answer. Somehow.

"Well, we were headed... down the hallway when we saw Zabrina, and she was having a problem." I purposely left out the part where we were going back to King Maddox's room to do... whatever we were going to do.

Poppy's eyes widen. "A problem? Like what? Keeping herself out of other people's business? Avoiding interrupting people? Trying not to sabotage another woman's date?"

I want to laugh at her because I know she's in a tizzy, but when I tell her what happened, or at least, what I saw of what happened, I know she will lose her mind.

"No, she was covered in blood," I explain.

Poppy's eyes widen. "Blood?"

"Yes."

"Covered?"

"Yes."

"Covered... in blood?"

I look back and forth from one side of the room to the other a few times. "That's right."

"Wait!" Poppy leans forward and puts both of her hands on my knees. "Zabrina was in the hallway... covered in blood?"

"This is what I am telling you." I can only stare at her.

She stares back for several seconds before she gasps loudly and covers her mouth with both of her hands.

It makes me jump a bit.

"Miss Isla!" she shouts. "Why in the world was Zabrina covered with blood?"

"I'm not sure," I admit. "But she said something about a maid. Now, I don't know if it was the same maid that was accused of slipping something into the king's drink or not—"

"Well, it would have to be!" Poppy leaps up off the bed, pacing back and forth. "This is... unbelievable!"

The only reason I know much at all about the maid is because Poppy has a very good ear for gossip and comes back often to tell me everything. King Maddox didn't tell me nearly as much about the situation with Zabrina's hired girl as Poppy found out from the rest of the staff.

Not that I necessarily trust everything Poppy tells me. I am fairly certain that the maid who works in the office in the dungeon doesn't really have three eyes, a hump on her back the size of a camel, and a total of fourteen toes.

But then... we are shifters. Perhaps she got mixed up coming back to her human form....

"This is unbelievable!" Poppy declares again.

"I heard you the first time," I tell her.

"I need to go find out what has happened." She is already headed to the door without me saying it's okay if she goes.

"It's okay if you go," I call after her.

"Really! I wonder if Trudy and Anastasia know about this!" She is out the door before I can answer.

That doesn't stop me from responding. "If they don't, I'm sure they will soon enough."

Trudy is the maid who cleans Beta Seth's room, I am told, and Anastasia is responsible for King Maddox's room. They didn't like Poppy until recently because she was a simple housemaid, but now that she is taking care of someone "important" like they are, she is in their inner circle.

If I have done nothing else since I arrived at the castle, I have at the very least elevated Poppy's social standing.

Perhaps that makes missing my family and being put into the situation where I am supposed to carry the king's child all worth it?

Somehow... I don't think so.

I decide to prepare for bed. It has been a long day, and I am tired.

I go to my dresser and pull out a pink silky nightgown that looks comfortable and the matching panties that go with it. In the bathroom, it takes me several minutes to get out of the dress since the zipper is nearly unreachable, but after some contorting, I finally manage to get it down.

By now, I am exhausted. I finish all of my bathroom rituals—now that I belong to the king, I have to take better care of my skin, Poppy says—and then go to bed.

And all I can see is Zabrina's bloody hands and the way the crimson liquid covered her dress.

I don't know what happened to the maid, but it can't have been good.

In the back of my mind, I have to wonder... is Zabrina capable of killing someone?

How badly would she have to hate someone to slash them up with a knife?

I suppose a person would have to hate another person an awful lot to do such a thing to them.

That makes me wonder… how much does Zabrina hate me?

My breath catches in my throat, and I feel a nervous tension growing in my stomach.

I don't know how much Zabrina hates me.

But I can imagine… it's quite a lot.

~

Maddox

"Why in the world did you let her down here in the first place?" I ask the guard who was on duty when Alva died. I have been questioning him for about ten minutes and haven't really gotten anywhere. It is as if the last few hours are all a blur to him.

He is crying. "I don't know, Your Majesty," he says between sobs. "I messed up. I messed up so bad!" He bursts into another fit of tears, and I look at Seth, shaking my head.

We are in the office in the dungeon, a place that the head jailor usually does his work in, though he's gone home hours ago now. He only works during the day. At night, it's our rule to have one guard per prisoner and then two near the bottom of the stairs leading to the dungeon and two at the top.

All five of these guards should've been able to stop Zabrina, but the other four said she had a convincing story that she'd gotten permission from me to visit her maid.

This one has said the same thing, but he is the last protection the prisoner had, so I'm not sure why he would think I had changed my mind and it was okay for her to have a visitor.

He could've used the mind-link to ask me but did not.

My wolf is restless; he smells a rat.

"Larry, for the love of the Moon Goddess," Seth says, handing the man a tissue from a box on top of the desk, "you've got to stop crying so we can get this over with. No one is saying you're in trouble yet, but if you don't stop blubbering and answer the damn questions, Alpha King Maddox is going to throw you in the cell you were watching!"

That gets Larry's attention. His eyes widen. "The one with the blood all over?"

I sigh. "Yes, that one." Shaking my head, I look at Seth again. We've had the blood cleaned up. Grunda, the dungeon maid, wasn't too happy to get out of bed to do it, but she hobbled out anyway. Poor old dear… such a fright, what with her unsightly wart in the middle of her forehead, her hump... and all of those extra toes. But she's a good worker.

Larry breathes in deeply and finds a way to control his tears. "She said that she had your permission."

"You've told me that," I remind him. "But why did you believe her?"

"She was very convincing," he says. Then, he clears his throat and says, "And... well... she has... boobs."

My forehead crinkles. "What's that now?"

"Boobs!" he shouts. "She has them! And they're big and bouncy, and well, when she leaned over to tell me that she had your permission to go in, I saw... most of them."

"The way you say that, it sounds like she has more than two." Seth is staring at him the same way that I am.

"No, no, just two... big, round, juicy ones, with hard nip—"

"All right!" I say. "So she flashed you? That's how she won you over?"

He shrugs. "I was... distracted. And she promised me dessert. I didn't know if she meant food from the basket or... something else."

I inhale deeply, hold it for a few counts, and let it go. "Larry, she is the daughter of an Alpha, and you are a prison guard in the dungeon of a castle. Did you honestly think that she was interested in you?" Larry is not a bad-looking young man, I suppose, but he's not strikingly handsome, and I know Zabrina. She would never want to have anything to do with Larry romantically.

All he can say is, "But... boobs."

"So a woman is dead because you haven't seen a pair of tits up close recently?" Seth blurts out.

That sends Larry into a fit of crying again, and I am done. "All right," I say. "I will leave your complete punishment for breaking protocol to Reginald when he returns to duty in the morning. In the meantime, Beta Seth please escort Larry to one of the holding cells."

"You're locking me up?" he shouts, sniffling back more tears.

"For the time being, yes," I say. "All of the guards that were on duty and fucked this up are locked up." I stand.

"But King Maddox!" Larry begins.

Tired and irritated that my night has gone so awry, I say, "Don't bother, Larry. I have my reputation for a reason."

He shuts up very quickly when he remembers all of the rumors he has heard about my cruelty.

Most of them aren't completely true....

I check the time on my watch and head upstairs. It's past 1:00 in the morning now that I've spoken to all of these people, and it's far too late for me to call on Isla. Disappointment settles around me.

I was looking forward to getting to know her even better.

The memory of touching her skin while we were dancing, of kissing her neck, floods me with want, and I feel myself begin to stiffen up despite the gory scenes I've seen tonight.

I head down the hallway, back to my quarters, deciding I can figure out more regarding the maid tomorrow. But for now... it's clear to me that Alva did not slit her own neck.

And since there were only two other people present, it was either Larry— or Zabrina.

He is locked up, and her room is heavily guarded. I have told her it is for her own safety, but that's not the case.

I hope she doesn't find a way to beguile those guards and get out of her room.

I've seen enough blood for one night.

Besides, I can't think of anyone else Zabrina hates enough to kill.

MY DEAD BODY

Maddox

I run down the hallway, frantic, my eyes wide with terror as I pray to the Moon Goddess above that my own stupidity hasn't cost me again.

How could I have been so stupid? To have gone back to my room thinking that there was no one else Zabrina would want to kill!

Once again, I feel like my own idiocy has cost me dearly.

I can only pray that the girl is all right, and the Moon Goddess and I haven't exactly been on speaking terms these last few years since Rebecca's... untimely death.

My shoes slide on the slick floor in the hallway as I try to round the corner, and as I lose traction, I look down to see that it's not just the shiny marble surface that has made me lose control, the floor is wet as well,

Smears of red paint the floor like an angry finger painter, a child who was allowed to stay up too late before visiting the art center, perhaps one that had far too much sugar.

The red streams around the corner into the next hallway as well, making my footing even more precarious.

Nevertheless, I can't slow down, so I fight the out-of-control thinking and keep running, trying to comprehend how my room got so far away from my target.

I thought the Luna suite was only a few doors away....

Shaking my head, I run on, noticing a mist in the castle, its wispy gray fingers dancing around me as I continue to run.

Has someone left a window open?

Has someone left all of the windows open?

The fog continues to swirl and twirl, but I can still see the red beneath my feet as I chase the endless hallway.

"Is everything all right, sir?" Walter, one of my butlers says, stepping out from the wall, a silver tray in his hand as he blocks my way.

Coming to a screeching halt, I stop just before I collide with him and the steaming pot of coffee he holds.

"Walter! Get out of the way!" I shout at him, intending to step around him.

Moving to block my way again, Walter says, "Perhaps a cup of coffee would hit the spot about now, aye, Alpha?"

Despite the hot liquid, I push him aside, ignoring his shouts from contact with the coffee as it splashes out to scald him.

I am in a hurry, damnit!

At the end of the hall, I turn left, thinking this can't be right.

Where the hell is the Luna Suit?

Fog circles me, and even more blood covers the floor now.

As I come around the corner, I run into a small table holding a vase. The antique bobs back and forth for a moment, threatening to fall to the floor. I reach out and grab it, righting it and the table.

"What do you think you're doing!"

Mrs. Worsthingshorethinshire stands beside me, her hands on her hips, an ugly scowl on her face.

"That's a priceless piece that dates back three centuries!" she continues.

"Didn't I fire you?" I ask.

Her hand comes around and smacks me right in the side of my head, sending me reeling into the vase which falls to the floor and shatters into a thousand pieces.

"Now look what you've done!" she shrieks. "The king will have your head for that!"

"I am the king!" I remind her.

"Don't you talk back to me—"

I give her a shove, and she flies across the hallway into the wall, sliding down and resting in a pool of blood.

Rather than wasting any more time on a horrid woman I thought I had fired, I begin to run again. The hallway never seems to end, and the blood is so thick now, it's coating my shoes and splashing up every time I pick up my feet.

"There you are, King Maddox!" Alpha Jordan is standing in front of me wearing a brown lounging coat, smoking a pipe. "I thought we should discuss how wonderful it is that you've agreed to marry my daughter."

"Marry your daughter?" I ask. I don't slow down to speak to him, so he begins to run backward with no effort whatsoever.

When did Alpha Jordan become such an athlete?

"That's right," he says, "and she's bloody well looking forward to it!" His laughter rings out through the hall, sounding menacing in the fog.

"No!" I tell him, hitting him in the side with my elbow. He gasps and then disappears behind me in the fog bank.

"Maddox, what are you doing?"

I look over to see Seth jogging alongside me wearing gray sweats and a matching headband. He looks ridiculous, but at least he's not running backward.

"I have to save her!" I shout.

"You should be in bed. It's late," my Beta advises.

'Where the fuck is the Luna suite?" I ask him.

"It's right there, stupid!" he says. "Man, how would you survive without me?"

I don't answer him. I see the door now, and I'm almost there. I pick up speed and only stop sprinting when I reach the door.

What if it's locked?

My hand connects with the golden knob, and when I twist, it opens. I breathe a sigh of relief.

But then... as I walk into the antechamber, I see that the blood is spread throughout this room as well, staining the floor the same crimson color as the hallways.

Am I too late?

The door to the bedroom is ajar. With a deep breath, I move forward, my heart pounding against my ribcage as my breath reverberates out of my mouth so loudly, I think I could wake the dead.

A push on the open door causes it to squeal, and I poke my head inside.

The fog in the room is thick, but as I narrow my gaze, the scene before me comes into focus. As if my own realization has cleared the mist, the room clears, and I see a woman standing there, next to the bed, the knife in her hand nearly a foot long. The silver blade catches the light of the moon streaming through the window.

On the bed, I see nothing but a sea of red and pieces of flesh. It reminds me of some of the worst scenes I've ever witnessed on the battlefield, the bloody meat, chewed-up flesh, pools of blood associated with the grizzliest, most merciful kinds of death.

Her body is chopped to bits, but her face is untouched, except for her eyes.

Those are missing... but the rest of her lovely features are all intact, her mouth hanging open as if she were trying to scream for help....

Scream for me.

Her blonde curls are pink in the moonlight as the sticky liquid coats them.

"Isla!" I scream my hands covering my face in grief.

Next to her, the woman with the knife begins to giggle, her laughter a high-pitched tinkle, like the sound a bell makes, the same noise I imagine a gleeful fairy would make.

I recognize that laugh… but it's not the loud cackle Zabrina makes when she is amused.

No, this sound is far more familiar to me, and as she turns her head to look at me, I realize it's not Zabrina standing over Isla's bed with the murder weapon in her blood-soaked hand.

As our eyes meet, mine widen, the shock and devastation I felt at entering the room morphing into confusion and disbelief.

"What's the matter, darling?" Rebecca asks me. "Did you think I'd really let you find love again?" Her laughter is so loud this time, I have to cover my ears. I feel the sound as a vibration in my brain.

"Rebecca…." I murmur.

She continues to laugh. "You marry again? Over my dead body!"

Gasping for air, I sit up, my hand to my chest. My eyes dart around the room, and I see I am in my bedroom. It's night, and I am beneath the covers, wearing my pajamas.

My lungs burning, I suck in a few more deep breaths as I try to still the madness inside of me. Even though I am aware now that it was all a dream, images of the macabre scene I've just discovered still fill my mind.

Looking around the room again, I confirm I am alone. Rebecca is not here. Isla's body is not mutilated and on display across the room.

I raise a hand to my forehead and collapse back onto the pillow. "It was just a dream," I tell myself. "Just a stupid, stupid nightmare."

My experience with such disturbances is profound; since Rebecca's death, I've had more bad dreams than good.

Still… most of the time they are not so gory. And she is usually the victim… not the killer.

What is my subconscious trying to tell me?

I am not sure I want to know.

I do need to know something else, though.

Once my pulse has slowed down, I swing my legs out of bed and slide my feet into my slippers, grabbing my robe off the back of a nearby chair and pushing my arms into it. I tie it in place over my blue pajamas and take a sip of water from the glass on the nightstand before I head off down the hallway.

Thankfully, when I step outside of my room, the floor isn't red, and there is no fog to greet me either.

It only takes a moment to reach Isla's room. I am surprised to see two guards posted there. One of them is a man I'd seen earlier in the hallway, one of the soldiers who'd been there when I'd first spoken to Zabrina.

"Good evening," I say to him and the other one. "You're one of the new recruits, aren't you?"

"Yes, Alpha King Maddox, sir," he says. "I'm Private Wylie, sir." He makes the sign of respect to me by hitting his left shoulder with his right hand.

"Thank you for your service," I tell him. Turning to the other young man, I say, "Thank you as well, Private Parker." The other man, one I've had on staff for a few years, makes the sign of respect as well.

"Who stationed the two of you here?" I ask. It hadn't even crossed my mind that Isla could be in trouble until I'd fallen asleep. I am glad someone had considered the possibility that our potential, and likely, murderess, Zabrina, might be unhappy with the woman I have been paying so much attention to.

"Beta Seth, sir," Private Wylie tells me.

I smile. "I imagined as much. I would like to go in and see Miss Isla," I explain.

"Yes, sir," Private Wylie says. "The door is locked, but Commander Jones gave me a key."

I have a key to every room in the castle, but I hadn't thought to bring it with me. It is lucky that Private Wylie has one.

He unlocked the door to the antechamber, and I thank him before stepping inside. I imagine Isla has started locking the door after my last intrusion.

I wonder what she will think of this one….

Quietly, I push the door to her bedroom open, expecting her to be fast asleep. But she is sitting up in bed, staring at me, her eyes wide in the moonlight.

"Isla?" I whisper. "It's Maddox."

"I know," she says, swallowing hard.

Was she afraid of me?

"I just… wanted to make sure you were okay," I explain.

"I'm… f-fine." Her voice broke, and I knew that wasn't the case.

Taking a few steps closer to her, I say, "You have nothing to be afraid of."

She nods. "I know… but I had a bad dream."

I don't want to tell her that I'd had one, too. But I feel an ache in my heart that she has also experienced that. "Do you want to talk about it?"

"Not now," she said. "But would you… would you stay here? Please? For a while?"

"Of course," I move to her quickly, pulled by an unseen force, and sit down next to her on the bed. Cupping her cheek, I stroke her smooth skin. "You're safe, Isla. I'm here."

A small smile parts her lips as she leans her head against my chest. I pull her close and kiss the top of her head.

If anyone ever tries to hurt Isla… it will be over MY dead body.

TASTING ISLA

Isla

KING MADDOX IS LYING in my bed… with his arms around me. He is holding me like I am something of high value to him, something precious, and for the first time in my life, I start to think maybe I am more than just the daughter of well-meaning parents who had misfortunes and could never quite make ends meet.

Maybe I have some worth to me after all.

I drift off and have pleasant dreams the rest of the night, mostly about him, this amazing man who has me tucked away against his chest, cradling me in my sleep.

In the morning light, I awake, thinking at first he is likely gone, but he's not. His firm chest is still beneath my head, and when I lean up to look at him, his eyes are wide and looking into mine.

"Good morning, Isla," he says. "Did you sleep well the rest of the night?"

"Yes, I did, thank you," I tell him, still trying to figure out whether I am awake or caught up in a dream again.

Why is the king still in my bed?

"That's good to hear." He runs his hand along my cheek, caressing me, like he did last night. It makes my face heat, and I can feel my skin tingle all the way down my neck, to my spine.

"H-how did you sleep?" I ask him.

"Wonderful," he says with a smile. "That was the best sleep I've gotten in a long time."

I can't help but grin at him. I'm glad to hear that. If he told me I was snoring or talking in my sleep, that would be embarrassing.

"I have a meeting in about an hour," he explains.

"Oh, I'm sorry." I start to move away from him, but he holds me tight.

"It's okay." He brushes his hand through my hair. "I have a little time."

I had thought I was what was preventing him from leaving before—because I am still lying on top of him, and he didn't want to disturb me.

But in his eyes, I see a hint of something I saw last night, when we were headed to his room, before the bloody incident with Zabrina.

Maddox pulls me to him, and his mouth presses against mine. I am aware of my stale breath, but he doesn't seem to care as his tongue taps against my lips, begging me to open.

I do, and he slides inside of my mouth. He tastes like mint, which makes me a bit jealous, but after he kisses me for a few moments, my mouth begins to taste fresh, too, and I find myself responding.

My hands roam along his chest. I wish he didn't have this shirt on. I want to feel his skin against my palms. I want to run my fingers along the muscles of his chest and abdomen.

The king rolls me onto my back, and he is hovering over me, the kisses becoming deeper now. I am reminded of the first time he was on top of me and how I was both scared and mesmerized. He moves his mouth to my ear and nips at my lobe, his hand caressing my breast through my nightgown.

I didn't think I'd be having sex with the king for the first time in broad daylight, and I begin to wonder about my body. What if he thinks I am too skinny? My ribs are still showing a bit....

His mouth is on my neck and I feel heat radiating from between my legs. I no longer care about anything but the feel of him on top of me.

His hand slides down my side and tugs my nightgown up around my waist, and I wonder what in the world he is doing.

Especially when he slips down, kissing my stomach along the way.

He lifts his head, and I open my eyes to see what he is doing. He is only smiling at me, and I give him a questioning look before he hooks his thumbs through my wet panties and pulls them down.

My eyes widen—I can't believe this is happening!

I find myself lifting my hips to help him slide them off, and then he untangles them from my feet and tosses them on the floor. My heart is pounding in my chest.

Will he be taking off his pants next?

He doesn't, though. Instead, he drops back down so that his mouth is on my stomach, and then, his hand is between my legs, and his fingers are brushing against me, stroking my hot flesh between my folds. A slow moan exits my mouth. His touch feels so good, and I want more of it—more of him.

His mouth wanders lower until I feel his lips on my mound. 'What is he doing?' I ask myself. Surely, he's not—

I get my answer when I feel the touch of his rough tongue near my opening. I gasp. The Alpha King is licking me—there?

I try not to move. He's the king. He can do whatever he wants. Why he wants to do this, I don't know, but... I didn't even know people do this!

Do people do this?

From the way he is doing it, I have to think this is not his first time. He seems to know exactly what he's doing. He drags his tongue along my slit, and I can no longer keep still. My hand shoots out, and I thread my fingers through his hair, letting my body respond to his touch.

It feels so good, especially when his tongue touches my nub, I find myself crying out in pleasure.

He takes his time, swirling his tongue around, hitting me in all of the right places. He pulls me in between his lips and sucks, and I feel myself clenching and releasing as if trying to pull his tongue inside of me, deep inside of me, into my core, which is beginning to ache for him.

Maddox releases me but goes back to licking me, more frantically now, like an animal lapping up milk. A sensation like I've never felt before fills my body, centralizing around my lower abdomen, and I feel like I am on the precipice of a large mountain, about to tumble over the edge.

I am waiting... the sensation lingering... the pressure building... my muscles tightening... my lungs burning.

And then... I fall over the edge, and I feel the pull of gravity sucking me down as my entire body contracts, pulling me up so that I am almost sitting. I can't breathe—I can't scream. My mouth is frozen open, my eyes clenched shut, my hand grasping Maddox's hair as I attempt to signal to him that my body cannot take much more.

It feels so good, it's frightening, and I can't imagine what might happen next if he doesn't release me and let me breathe.

I quake a few times before I'm finally able to suck in a breath. "Goddess!" I shout. "Maddox—please! Please!"

He lifts his head, and now that he's no longer touching me there, I feel a release as my muscles slowly relax.

I inhale deeply, filling my lungs with his scent and the sweet oxygen they've been craving.

He is chuckling. It is a low rumble... like thunder.

I crack my eyes open and see him sitting on his knees between my still open legs. I want to close them, but they are no longer taking directions from me.

Maddox is certainly their ruler now.

"Are you all right?" he asks me.

I don't know how to answer that or if words will even come out, so I just lift a hand and drop it back onto the mattress.

He thinks this is hilarious and breaks out into a roar of laughter before he moves so that he is lying beside me, his head on my pillow.

I turn slightly to face him and smell my scent all over his face. He kisses my cheek. "That was delicious," he says to me. "You taste… like a dream."

I want to make sure he doesn't mean a nightmare, but I don't have to ask. The smile on his face tells me he doesn't.

I smile at him, but I can't speak yet.

Maddox leans up and kisses my forehead. "I have to go. I will see you later."

I don't want him to leave, but I also know my body needs to recover from that.

If the man can do that with his tongue, what the hell can he do with his cock?

Still not moving, I watch as he puts on his robe and slippers. He comes around the bed and pulls the blanket up over my exposed body. Leaning down next to my ear, he whispers, "You're so beautiful, Isla. Why don't you go back to sleep for a little while? That way… you'll have more energy for later."

My head rocks back and forth. I agree. Sleep does sound good. He presses his lips to my forehead and walks away. I hear the door open and close again a moment later.

Will his staff smell me on his face? Even after he takes a shower? I can't help but wonder….

I close my eyes, thinking I'll go back to sleep for an hour or two. It sounds as if he intends to come back later, and I'm guessing we will have sex then.

After all, he can't impregnate me with his tongue—can he?

MADDOX

I PRACTICALLY SKIP back to my room, the smile on my face wide as the scent of Isla's tantalizing pussy still lingers on my face.

I'll have to take a shower before I head to my office, but I don't want to wash her fragrance away. I've never tasted any woman quite as sweet as Isla. Her untouched cunt was so fresh, so ripe, it reminded me of eating fruit just picked from the vine.

She seemed to have enjoyed it, I think, as I go into my room, heading for the bathroom. I can imagine she was a little surprised at first, having never done anything like that before. It's been a while since I've seen a woman have an orgasm like that one. And technically, her cherry is still in place, so that was a virgin orgasm.

Later, I will claim her completely and watch her writhe beneath me as I send more shockwaves of pleasure through her system.

A nap will help with that. She will need her strength. I intend to take her more than once, though I will have to try to keep in mind that she is a virgin, and I don't want to ruin her perfect pussy.

I step into the shower and let the warm water wash over me, still smelling her and thinking about her gorgeous body. I want to see her rump up close, in my face as I dive into her from behind. I want to cup her full breasts in my hands and squeeze her nipples until she sings like she just did with my tongue buried deep inside of her.

My cock is so hard right now, I have to take care of it myself. That's not a bad thing, though. Jacking off before I have sex always helps me to last longer. Besides, all I'll have to do is think about her for a moment, and I'll be hard again.

Or sniff my fingers where, no matter how hard I scrub, her scent lingers on.

After my shower, I dress and head to the office, a wide smile still lighting my face.

When Seth sees me, his forehead wrinkles. "Why are you so happy?" he asks me.

I shrug. "Just… had a good morning, that's all." My stomach rumbles, and I realize I haven't eaten anything yet. Well, not any *food* anyway.

"Are you hungry?" he asks, clearly hearing my stomach complaining.

"Yeah, can you go grab me something to eat?" I ask him. He makes that face he always makes when I ask him to do something "beneath" him. "Or have someone else do it? Also, I need a phone number."

"What phone number?" Seth asks me as we arrive at my office. I open the door, but he hangs back since he will have to go get someone to bring me breakfast.

I remember that Isla said her parents didn't have a phone. "I need to figure out a way to get a hold of Isla's parents without Alpha Ernest knowing."

"So you want their phone number?" he asks, confusion all over his face.

I shake my head. "They don't have one. Figure out a way to get ahold of the Moons."

"Yes, sir," he says, his tone laced with annoyance. I laugh because he hates it when I give him impossibly hard tasks.

But he'll get it done. He always does. I walk into my office and sit down. A moment later, there's a knock at my door. I sigh. "Yeah?"

"Alpha? Do you have a moment?"

It's Alpha Jordan. And he looks pissed.

BUSINESS AS USUAL

Maddox

"ALPHA JORDAN," I say as the other Alpha comes into my office. "What can I help you with?"

His eyes are narrowed as he says, "I want to speak to you about what happened with my darling daughter, Zabrina, last night."

I nod. "Yes, I'm glad you came by. I think it's a good idea for us to talk about it as well."

"You do understand how close she was to being killed yesterday, don't you?" he asks me as he sits down in a chair across from me, his forehead wrinkled with concern.

I stare at him for a long moment, not sure how to respond to that. "She almost died?" I repeat. "I'm not sure I understand what you mean."

"That woman—the maid—whatever the hell her name is… she could've killed my Zabrina. What if she would've stabbed my daughter instead of killing herself? I find it horrific to think that your guards in the dungeon are of such poor quality that they can't even prevent a prisoner from getting access to a knife!"

When he is finished, I take a moment, trying to process what he has said to me.

Is he serious? Could he be joking?

He's dead serious, and I have to come up with a way to respond to this bullshit.

Clearing my throat, I say, "Alpha Jordan, you do understand that it was your daughter who took the knife into the cell, don't you?"

"Yes, obviously, I know that," he says, and I see I've irritated him further. "She shouldn't have been allowed to do that! That's my point!"

"Well, of course, she wasn't allowed to do it, Alpha Jordan. She simply did it anyway. She managed to charm the guards into letting her in with her picnic basket, which contained a knife."

"And they should've been smart enough not to do that!" he replies with his hands spread wide. "My daughter didn't have any idea that what she was doing was dangerous. She didn't know this woman would turn out to be some sort of a psychopath!"

I'm not sure what to say to this. A knock on the door alerts me that Beta Seth is back with my breakfast. He pokes his head inside of the office but gestures at me, wanting to know if he should leave.

The smell of bacon and fresh biscuits has my mouth watering, so wave him into the room. He sets it down on my desk and greets Alpha Jordan.

Jordan glares at him. "I see you're too busy to address my concern at the moment," he says to me.

"I'm not too busy, Alpha Jordan. I'm just surprised that you are concerned that your daughter might've been harmed when she was the one who brought the knife into the room, not to mention... she had an awful lot of blood on her hands." I hope he will get what I am saying without me having to spell it out for him.

"Of course, she had blood on her hands! She tried to save that wretched woman's life! Surely, you're not implying that you think Zabrina hurt that woman?" His eyes are wide and his chubby face is stretched as he gapes at me.

I am saying exactly that, but I know if I try to explain that to Jordan right now, he will further lose his shit. "I'm saying... the investigation is ongoing. That's what I'm saying."

He shakes his head. "Really, Alpha Maddox, I can't believe what I am hearing. If you think my daughter had anything to do with that, you're crazy!" He stands and heads for the door. "We should've never stopped here!" Spinning around, he points at me, "I tried to help you! I tried to make a match for you with a beautiful woman, the daughter of a powerful Alpha all of the other Alphas respect—me! But you're too out of touch with the rest of the kingdom to even see that!"

I ignore his rant and say, "Jordan, if you're sorry you stopped here, perhaps you should get going."

"Oh, I will!" he says. "I'll be out of here in a week or less, you just wait!"

"A week?" Beta Seth says, and I nudge him with my elbow, hoping he'll just stay out of it.

"Yes, a week!" Alpha Jordan shouts, opening the door to go. He stops, though, and turns back. "If you do anything to my daughter before we leave, believe me, you will regret it!"

"Goodbye, Jordan," I say, and he walks out into the hallway, slamming the door behind him.

I pick up the silver platter my breakfast is on and move it in front of me, thankful to finally get to eat.

"Are you really going to let him leave and take her with him?" Seth asks me.

My mouth is full of delicious bacon, so I can't answer right away. I finally get out, "I'm not sure yet, Seth. I need to do some further investigating into the situation. Right now, my major proof that she is a murderer is that she forgot the girl's name."

"And she brought the knife into the cell with her, and there's no reason for the maid to have killed herself when you basically told her she wasn't really in trouble," he spells out for me.

I shrug. "True, but we know nothing about this girl. For all we know, she had some issues before that made her want to claim her own life."

He shakes his head. "I guarantee Zabrina did this because she didn't want to get in trouble for drugging you."

"That may well be," I agree, "but I need proof, and none of the guards saw anything that will help us."

"If we let her go, she'll think that she can kill people and get away with it." Seth folds his arms and paces slightly next to my desk.

His words distract me, though. After Rebecca died, everyone said the same thing about me, that I had killed her and gotten away with it.

In a way… that was true….

But I didn't really get away with anything because I was a prisoner in my own mind every moment of every day because of what had happened to her.

"Maddox?" Seth says. "Did you hear me?"

I hadn't heard him. "Sorry—what was that?"

"I said… I tried to get a hold of the Moons, but every number I called in Willow pack says they don't have a phone, and they live so far away from everyone with a phone, there's really no way of getting in touch with them except for to call the Alpha and set up a meeting with them."

I let out a sigh, chewing a bite of eggs that are light and fluffy, just like I like them.

Calling Alpha Ernest will defeat the purpose. No, I need to meet with them without him knowing my plans.

It's a two-hour drive—each way.

I sigh and look at the clock. I don't have time to go today. I have too many meetings and urgent work that has to be done today. "Tomorrow," I tell him.

"What's that?" Seth asks me.

"I'll go visit them tomorrow. Make it happen, Seth."

He sighs. "You're going to drive to Willow pack tomorrow?"

I nod. "That's right."

"And are you planning on taking Isla with you?"

I shake my head. I know she'd love to see her family, but I don't want her to know what I'm up to. "Not this time."

"Fine…" he says. "I'll clear your schedule tomorrow. What time do you want to leave?"

"Eight," I say, thinking that's usually the time I try to get into the office. But then I think about what I have planned for later tonight, and I change my mind. "Make it ten."

"Ten," he says as a note to himself. "All right. And what are you going to do there, exactly?"

"I want to make sure that Alpha Ernest forgave the debt the Moons owed him."

"And if he didn't?" Seth asks me.

I look up at him, wiping my mouth on a napkin. Setting it aside, I say, "He will not like what happens to him if he didn't."

∼

Isla

I wake up to the sound of Poppy moving around my room. Blinking a few times, I try to remember back to what happened earlier. Maddox's smiling face flashes before my eyes, and I suddenly remember what happened earlier.

"You're awake!" Poppy says. "Sorry if I woke you, but I thought you might be hungry. Have you eaten today?"

"Eaten?" I repeat. "No, I haven't eaten." I've been eaten… I haven't eaten anything myself.

Poppy stares at me as her eyebrows slowly knit together. "Is everything all right?" she asks me.

"I'm fine," I tell her, remembering that I did not put my panties back on after Maddox left, and I have no idea where they are. I look down at the floor, but I don't see them. My face heats even more.

"I put them in the hamper," she says. "Believe me… you wouldn't want to put those back on."

I swallow hard, not bothering to ask her what she means.

She must think I'm some sort of sexual deviant who can't help but take her panties off and touch herself.

"Well, I can go get you something to eat if you'd like to go take a shower. Any idea what you'd like to wear today?"

Has she let it go? Poppy? She's not going to ask me why I'm not wearing any underwear?

"Uh… I don't know what I want to wear," I tell her.

"I'll lay something out for you," she says with a smile. "Should I include panties, or are you just not wearing those anymore?" She snorts and then starts laughing.

I narrow my eyes at her. "Stop that, Poppy," I insist. "Yes, I will be wearing underwear!"

"All right. I just wanted to make sure. You do you, girlfriend."

I shake my head. "Poppy… you don't know what you're talking about, so please stop."

She stares at me for a long moment, and I realize I have said too much. "Did… did the king come in here last night?"

I take a deep breath and shrug. "I don't want to discuss it, Poppy."

"Oh, my Goddess!" she declares. "Did you two… I mean, it doesn't smell like sex in here, but—"

"Poppy!" I duck down and hide my face with my hands. How can she be so blunt? "We didn't have sex, okay. Just… some other stuff."

She giggles like a schoolgirl and jumps up and down. I just want her to go. I'm not getting up until she's out of my room.

Eventually, she catches her breath. "Aren't you going to tell me about it?"

"No!" I shout. "I'm not going to tell anyone about it. Now, please go get me something to eat while I take a shower."

"Okay, okay," she says, looking wounded that I won't dish everything with her. "I'll go. But… I think you should tell me. I'm your only friend now, you know."

Sighing, I tell her, "Maybe later."

She has to be satisfied with that, so she accepts it and walks out the door, and I know she will get it out of me later.

She's wrong—she's not my only friend here; she's my only friend anywhere.

Once she leaves, I get up and head to the bathroom, noticing how odd it feels down there now that I've had part of another person in there. Maybe it wasn't his cock, but it was still a part of him, and every time I think about how good it felt to have the Alpha King licking me, I feel my heart race and my breath catch in my throat.

Later, I think he'll come back, and he'll finally claim me once and for all.

I turn the water on and take off what I have left on before stepping inside of the shower. I'll make sure everything is sparkling clean for him, in case he wants to explore other parts of my body.

My knees weaken just thinking about it.

I had been so frightened to come here, so terrified to become Maddox's breeder, but now that I'm here, I can't imagine ever being anywhere else.

And I can't imagine ever being with anyone else.

I'm definitely falling for him.

Falling hard.

MADDOX MAKES HER COME

Isla

I RECEIVED A NOTE FROM MADDOX, written by his own hand, that he'd be by to get me for dinner at 7:00.

Now, it's 6:55, and I am watching the clock, wondering if it's possible for the hands to actually move backward.

It seems to be taking forever for him to arrive!

I am pacing back and forth at the end of my bed, the long red dress I am wearing swishing back and forth. It's not exactly a gown, but it's fancier than most of the dresses I have in my wardrobe.

I want to look nice for him, especially tonight.

Is there a chance this will be the night he will claim me?

My heart races as I think about it. I sure hope so.

"You're going to wear the carpet out," Poppy says, her nose in a book. She's hardly spoken to me today, and she hasn't done a lick of work either. She's upset that I didn't tell her what happened between Maddox and me last night. I keep thinking she'll get over it, but so far, what I've learned about Poppy is that it takes a lot for her to get past things.

I don't respond to her, though. I am holding the note Maddox scent in my hands, my eyes tracing every stroke of his writing as I go back and forth, back and forth.

At 6:59, I pause, my nose in the air. I smell him…. The scent of his cologne tinges the air. I know he is nearby.

"He'll probably be late," Poppy says. "It's not even—"

Her remark is cut off by a knock on my door. I smile at her, lay the note on my bed, and bound over to get it myself, even though Poppy is closer. She puts her book down and stands out of respect.

Maddox looks amazing. He's not wearing a tie, but he has on a dark gray suit jacket over his white button-down, and I can see a tuft of his chest hair sticking out. I want to wrap it around my finger.

"Hi," he says, smiling at me.

"Hi," I say back, sounding like a teenage girl.

He extends a bouquet of pink roses. "Do you like pink?" he asks me. "I was going to get red, but I thought that might be… a bit too… forward."

Because red means love, and he's not sure he loves me yet? Well, of course, he shouldn't be because he's not supposed to love me ever. He's just supposed to make a baby with me.

And yet, he's brought me flowers, so I must mean more to him than just any old breeder, right?

I take the flowers and bring them to my nose, breathing in deeply. "I love them," I tell him. "Thank you so much." No one has ever brought me flowers before except for my father. He stopped and picked some wildflowers once for my birthday. It was the only thing he could afford. I'd kept those flowers and pressed them. In fact, I had them with me now in a book in my nightstand drawer.

"I'm so glad," he says. "Poppy, can you get a vase?"

"Of course," she says, bowing her head. She takes the flowers from me, and Maddox offers his hand.

"Shall we?"

I don't answer with words, only giggle, and he leads me from the room, out to the hall, and around all of those precious works of art that one must never touch.

"I thought we could dine in the garden this evening, if that's all right with you?" he says as we go to an exterior door.

"That sounds… beautiful," I say. I am wondering if there will be enough light, but as he takes me to the spot where he already has a table and chairs set up, I can see that the trees around the table are decorated with thousands of tiny twinkling lights.

I stop to cover my mouth with my free hand, not wanting to let go of his. "It's… gorgeous!" I say.

He smiles. "I'm glad you like it. I thought it would be… romantic." He shrugs. "I'm not usually very good at this sort of thing, but I thought lights, flowers, music, and a nice meal might be a good way to impress you."

"Impress me?" I ask him, my eyes widening. "You impress me enough just by being you, Alpha."

I see a shift in his countenance as he absorbs my compliment. "Thank you, Isla," he says in a humble tone. "That's… kind of you."

"It's true," I assure him. "But this!" I turn back to the scene in front of me where waiters are setting the table. "This is like something out of a dream!"

With a chuckle, he leads me over and pulls out my chair for me. I hear soft violin music and see the musician standing in the background between some of the trees.

"I thought live music might be better this time," he explains.

I don't care what kind of music we listen to. As long as I'm with him, that's all that matters.

The servants bring us Italian this time—salad, lasagna, breadsticks, red wine, and for dessert, tiramisu, something I've never tried before. I can't even remember the last time I had lasagna. My mom tends to make a lot of soups and stews because she can get the ingredients for those dishes cheaply, and they last a long time.

"Do you like it?" Maddox asks me as we eat.

"I love it," I tell him. "This is the best thing I've put in my mouth for a long time."

He smirks at me, and I raise my eyebrows, wondering what I've said. He replies, "I can't say the same. I had something pretty delicious in my mouth earlier today."

My face turns the same crimson shade as my dress. It takes me a moment to realize that he is talking about tasting… me, and I can't help the rush of blood to my cheeks.

He looks serious, though, and I am speechless.

After a moment, Maddox chuckles and says, "Sorry, Isla. I didn't mean to embarrass you."

"No, it's okay," I tell him, and I mean it. I tear a breadstick in half and dip one of the ends in red sauce. "It's just… uh… different for me. But it's not embarrassing." How can I be embarrassed that the king spent his morning… between my legs?

We finish eating, and I linger with tiramisu in my mouth even though my stomach is full. It tastes so good, though, I don't want to stop eating it, even with King Maddox finished, not really touching his dessert, and smiling at me from across the table.

I wonder if he will want to dance again.

Finally, unable to put another bite in my mouth, I lay my fork down.

"Are you done, beautiful?" he asks me.

My face heats again, and I can only nod, afraid if I open my mouth something other than words will come out.

He stands and comes around the table, offering me his hand. I take it, and he pulls me to my feet.

Without another word, he leads me back inside. He's already asked me, the night before, if I will go back to his room with him, so I don't feel that he needs to ask again. And ultimately, he paid for me, so he can do what he wants.

We make it down the hallway this time, no bloody Alpha's daughters popping out to spook us, and we go inside of his chambers. His living room is bigger than my house back in Willow pack. He has a kitchen area, a dining room, and then we go through another door to his bedroom.

The bed is massive—I think four people can fit in it. I wonder if he's ever had more than one woman in the bed with him, but push those thoughts away and classify them as "not my business."

His furniture is dark wood, his comforter black, and everything about the room seems intimidating, except for the man standing behind me, breathing in my hair.

I lean back into him, letting his mouth come down on my neck.

We've been so close to this a few times now, and though I was nervous, maybe even afraid, the first time he came into my room, and I thought he was going to claim me, tonight, I am not afraid at all.

I am electrified—ready to let him claim me in every way imaginable.

As he kisses a trail down my neck, his hands come around to my chest, and he pulls the strap of my gown down.

I'm not wearing a bra....

I don't need one in this gown.

When he sees that, he gasps, and immediately his fingers move to my nipple, which is already hard just from his presence.

But he has a way of making it even harder as he tugs and works it, rubbing it between his expert fingers. I groan and lean back, feeling that ache between my legs grow.

Maddox slides my other arm out of the strap, and my slinky gown falls to the ground, pooling around my sandals. I work my feet out of them as his other hand begins to work my breast. I press myself into him, my eyes closed so I can savor every sensation.

He's hard. I can feel his massive erection against my back. I can't help but rub against him. I want him to feel as good as I do, better even.

A grunt reverberates in his throat. I turn my head, and his lips encapsulate mine, his tongue snaking around mine. One hand slides down my stomach, and when he touches my wet panties, I suck in a deep breath and spread my legs.

His finger slides around the fabric, and he begins to explore my folds. As my breath leaves my lungs, I began to move my hips, wanting more.

"You like that?" he whispers in my ear.

"Y-yes." My voice is a stuttering whisper as I try to get a response out of my mouth.

His fingers continue to search my most intimate area, and when he slips a finger inside of me, I gasp and take hold of his wrist.

He works his finger back and forth, much the same way as he did with his tongue that morning, and it feels so good, I feel my legs growing weak.

Without a word, Maddox withdraws his hand, lifts me off the ground, and carries me to the bed, depositing me so that my head is against the pillows.

I can hardly open my eyes. Even without his finger inside of me, I still feel like my body is on fire.

He stands next to the bed and begins to undress, and my hand roams my breasts as I watch him. His body is magnificent. The rippling muscles of his abdomen and chest flex as he bends and moves to take his pants off, and I am mesmerized by his physique.

Maddox looks up and sees me watching him and smiles. When he drops his pants, he takes his underwear down, too, and his penis springs free.

His cock is huge, rock hard, and pointing directly at me. I bite my bottom lip as he crawls over toward me, hooking his thumbs around my panties and pulling them off.

"You're not frightened, are you?" he asks as he positions himself between my legs.

I spread them wide for him and shake my head. "No, I'm not frightened."

His mouth crashes down on mine, and I lift a hand to the back of his head. I feel his erection against my wet pussy, and I want him so bad, I'm already beginning to throb.

"I'll try not to hurt you," he whispers in a sultry voice, "but it might sting a bit."

I'm still not scared. I want him inside of me.

All of him.

I wrap my arms around his muscular back and splay my fingers. As the tip of his shaft pushes inside of me, I lift my hips. My head tips back, and my fingernails dig into him.

"Oh, Goddess," Maddox says on an exhale. "You're so tight. You feel… so good, Isla."

I can't speak as both pain and anticipation take over, and when he uses his hips to thrust the rest of the way inside of me, a sharp pain radiates out from between my legs.

But then, his mouth is on mine again, his teeth pulling on my bottom lip as he kisses me over and over again, his tongue twirling with mine.

His hips start to move, and I move with him, lifting and grinding and doing my best to make him feel as unbelievable as I feel.

Maddox knows exactly where to touch me. His hands run the length of me, stopping and caressing all of my most sensitive areas, and within moments, I find myself panting and moaning, my voice sounding so high and ethereal, I hardly recognize it. My body feels so good, it's like every fiber of my being is slowly catching fire with the heat of this passion he has ignited within me, and all I want is to feel this way forever.

When my muscles begin to spasm around his shaft, I can't help but cry out, "Oh, Goddess, Maddox!" before the muscles in my core tighten, my toes curl, and my mouth drops open in a silent scream of bliss.

With his hips continuing to thrust, I am frozen that way for so long, my mind goes blank, and all I am aware of is this amazing man and the waves of pleasure washing over me, like an ocean pounding the surface at high tide. I can't breathe, but I don't need oxygen anymore, as long as I have him.

After what seems like hours, Maddox finally grunts a few times and releases himself into me. Warmth spreads throughout my abdomen, and while I'm sad that it's over, I can finally take my first full breath in several minutes.

Covered with perspiration, he lowers his head to mine and kisses me softly before he rests his head on my shoulder. He's still inside me, though I can feel he's no longer nearly as hard.

I wrap my arms around him, holding him there, next to my heart. I never want this to end. Though I haven't known him that long, I am certain I am already falling for him.

Maddox's eyelashes brush my cheek as he blinks a few times, obviously tired. "Thank you, Isla," he says in a deep, husky voice.

I don't know what to say. I don't feel like I've done anything, but I reply, "Thank you... Maddox." He smiles up at me, and then rolls onto the other pillow.

My body feels cold without him on top of me, but it's only for a moment before he pulls me over against his chest and wraps me up in his strong arms, and the rest of the world fades away.

A FLUTTER

Maddox

THE SUN IS up as I blink my eyes and check the time. I've woken just before my alarm is set to go off, so I quietly switch it so that it will not sound. There's no reason to wake the beautiful woman sleeping next to me.

Rolling back toward her, I take her in. Her eyes are closed tightly, and her long lashes flutter every once in a while. Perhaps she is dreaming. I hope that her dreams are sweet.

I hope that I am in them.

She's curled up with one hand under her chin, reminding me of a cherub, of a precious angel, and as I listen to the sounds of her soft inhales, I remember how good it felt to finally be inside of her the night before.

We'd made love for the first time, and she had made me feel sensations I hadn't experienced in years. The countless faceless women I'd been with since my wife passed all faded away as I remembered what it was like to meld into another person, to give and take with them, not just to receive pleasure but to gift it to my partner as well.

All I can think about as I remember what needs to be done that day is that the world will seem much colder once I slip from this bed.

I don't want to leave Isla.

With a heavy sigh, I pull myself from the bed, my gaze lingering on her face for as long as possible before I must turn and go into the restroom.

As I go about my business, I think about how strange it is that I've become attached to her so quickly. She's such a sweet, innocent little thing, so very different than Rebecca ever was. Yet, that hasn't stopped me from being attracted to her, from wanting her, from longing for her when she's not around.

I haven't figured out just yet whether or not this is just a sexual infatuation or there's a chance it might be more. But if it is more… I know that will be a problem.

When I said I'd never take another Luna, I meant it. Having feelings for this girl won't change that.

Sure, if she becomes pregnant with my heir, that will be helpful in appeasing the distant Alphas who think that I need to be replaced on the throne because I can't promise longevity and stability.

But Isla bearing my child doesn't mean that she will be my Luna—and it doesn't mean I can let her stay here forever either.

I need to get all of this sorted out.

For now, however, I have another task to take care of.

I shower quietly, the early rays of the sun streaming in through the frosted bathroom window. I don't want to wake her. She looked so peaceful when I awoke, I thought she should just stay there in my bed for as long as she wants.

When I'm done, I dress and walk out to see she's still asleep, so I write her a note and leave it on the nightstand where she will see it when she wakes.

My plan is that this trip will only take a few hours, and then I'll be back. While it will mean more work for me to finish later, which will take time away from Isla, at least I will have an answer to the nagging question I need a response to.

Did Alpha Ernest forgive the debt to Isla's parents?

Beta Seth meets me in the hallway, handing me a protein shake in a tumbler I can take with me. "You're always thinking, Seth," I say.

"Well, I remember how hungry you were yesterday, and I figured we didn't need a repeat today." He smirks at me, and I feel like telling him Isla and I hadn't even had sex yet when I was famished the day before, but I realize it's no one's business. So I keep the comment to myself.

"While I'm away, keep an eye on Zabrina," I tell him. "Make sure she stays away from Isla."

"Of course," he tells me, and he has never let me down once in all of the years that he's been my Beta, so I have no reason to think he will now.

"Be certain those guards stay posted outside of Isla's room, too. I don't want her to have to worry about anything while I'm away." I turn and look him in the eye so he understands how serious I am.

"Are you going to be gone for a few hours or a few weeks?" Seth asks me, chuckling under his breath. I narrow my eyes at him, and he stops laughing.

I know he was just teasing, but I can't laugh about Isla's safety. It's not as if I've had particularly good luck with the women I love staying safe.

Did the word love just spring to mind?

It was way too early for that.

Care about—the women I care about.

As we approach the exit where I have arranged for my driver to meet me, I see that guard who has been stationed outside of Isla's room coming back inside. It takes me a moment to remember his name, but then it comes to me.

"Oh, good morning, Private Wylie," I say. "How are you today?"

"Good, Alpha King Maddox," he says, making the sign of respect. As he hits his chest with his fist, I notice a smudge of something black on his hand. It looks like grease, which I think is odd.

"What have you been up to?" I ask him.

His eyes widen slightly and he says, "Oh, uh… just out for a run, sir. I like to… shift before the sun comes up and take a run before duty begins. Unless, of course, I've been on the night shift, which I wasn't last night."

He seems nervous. Perhaps he's just not used to talking to someone of my stature. But then, the other night, he'd seemed confident.

"Were you running by the garage?" I ask him. The garage that houses all of my personal cars, as well as many of the vehicles that belong to the kingdom and the military transport vehicles isn't too far from where we are standing.

"The garage?" he asks, his forehead crinkling. "Wh-why would you…."

"You have grease on your hand," Seth points out. "Maybe you stepped in it, got it on your paw, now it's on your hand." Seth shrugs, and I wish my Beta didn't always have to be so explanatory of everything.

"Right!" Private Wylie says, turning his hand over to look at it. "I guess that's what those big buildings over there are. Ha, ha…." He lets out a nervous laugh. "I wasn't paying that much attention, I guess. I tend to get a little lost when I'm running."

"Same," Beta Seth says.

I shake my head. It would make sense that he would step in some spilled oil or something and not realize it. All kinds of vehicles come and go from that garage.

Private Wylie makes the sign of respect again, careful not to smudge his clothes, and then he heads down the hallway, and Seth opens the door for me. I am about to tell him to keep an eye on that kid when my driver, Godfried, interrupts.

"Car's all ready for you, sir," he says, saluting me the same way everyone else does.

"Thank you, Godfried," I tell the older gentleman who has been my driver since I became king. He was my father's driver before that. He's old enough to be my grandfather, I reckon.

"Don't worry about us," Seth insists. "Everything will be fine here."

I nod, sure he's right. I'm not leaving that long. It's not as if I'm always here. I leave for various occasions frequently. Meetings, social events, even to take a military detail out into the pack lands when I have to squash a potential uprising.

Nevertheless, a heaviness settles over me as I carry my protein shake to the car. Godfried opens the door for me, and I slide into the back across from two of my commanders.

"Good morning, King Maddox," Lionel, the older of the two says.

"Good morning, sir," Helena says with a nod.

I manage a smile at them. "Good morning. Thank you both for accompanying me on such short notice." As much as I can handle myself in any situation, it never hurts to have a bit of muscle along with me, just in case it's needed, and these two are a couple of the strongest warriors I have.

"Of course, sir," they both chime as Godfried starts the car.

As we pull away from the castle, I look back at my home through the window, thinking I'm acting silly. I'm just going to Willow pack, and it's only about a hundred miles away. I'll be back before dinner.

Yet, that sense of foreboding from earlier is still situated in my chest cavity, and I can't help but think something bad is going to happen while I'm away.

Out of the corner of my eye, I see a flicker of movement in the top right corner of the building, and my eyes move to look more closely at the window there. The drapes seem to be stirring, just barely. I narrow my gaze—that's impossible. I swear I see the outline of a woman standing there for just a moment, but then she's gone, and I am left with my mouth hanging open because that room has been locked up for years.

It's not possible for someone to be in there unless they've managed to steal the key.

I check my pockets, and the only key that still exists is on my keychain, where it always is.

So… no one could've been standing there. It had to have been my imagination.

"Are you all right, King Maddox?" Lionel asks me. "You look troubled."

Blinking a few times, I turn to face him. "No, no, I'm fine." When I turn away, only the turrets of the castle are visible because we've traveled so far.

It had to have been my eyes messing with me. That's the only explanation. I didn't see anyone. I didn't see anything.

How else could I explain why the curtains would be moving and the figure of a woman would be standing in an empty room?

Rebecca's room.

LOCKED UP

Isla

Sitting in the chair in my room next to the window, I read the note again, 'Had to go on a quick business trip. Be back soon. Stay safe, M.'

I had found it on the desk this morning—in Maddox's room. I wish it said more. I wish I knew where he had gone and exactly when he'd be back.

But I wasn't in any position to ask those sorts of questions. I was just his breeder after all, and even though I felt a connection to the king, that didn't mean that I was nearly as important to him as I wished I could be.

"You're not planning on sitting there all day moping, are you?" Poppy asks as she comes back into the room after delivering my breakfast tray back to the kitchen. "You have to live your life, girl!"

I can't help but grin at her and shake my head. She has such a unique way of putting things. "No, but, I miss him, that's all."

She shook her head slightly at me. "How lucky are you to be in a position to know what to miss!" she exclaims.

"Did you see Beta Seth?" I decide that changing the subject is better than replying to her comment.

"No, I didn't see him. He is very busy handling all of the duties King Maddox usually takes care of, so I couldn't ask him where the king has gone to. Sorry, dear." She makes a frowny face at me.

"It's okay," I assure her. I had been hoping she'd be able to get some answers to my questions from Beta Seth, but I'm really not too surprised that he hasn't answered her.

"Now, I did see Mrs. Dixon, the new head of the staff, and while she's not quite as awful as Mrs. Worsthingshorethinshire was, they were good friends before Mrs. W. got tossed out on her ear, thanks to you. So… she shouted at me to get back to work, and I did."

"I'm sorry she yelled at you," I tell her. I can't imagine anyone being as awful as Mrs. Werthingtonhamshire, or whatever her name was, but it seems like people in that position let power go to their heads.

"It's all right," she says with a wave of her hand. She opens the armoire across the room, turning the key that's always just left in the lock, and pulling the door open. "She was second in command before, so it's not the first time she's gotten on to me, but she's usually a little nicer."

She takes out a pink floral patterned day dress and swirls it around, showing it to me.

"That looks fine," I say with a shrug. I have no thoughts about what I should wear today.

"I was thinking we should go to the village," Poppy suggests. "It'll give you something to do to take your mind off things."

"The village?" I ask. "Oh, Poppy, I don't know."

"Why not?" she asks. "We can pretend to be little girls and go to all of the best shops—the dress shop, the toy shop… the candy shop!" She twirls around, like she's a little girl who's had too much candy, and I can't help but laugh. She bumps into the armoire, and I hear the key fall out of the door.

Ignoring it, Poppy brings my dress over and lays it on the bed. "I can't wear this, though. Do you mind if I go change?"

"Have I agreed to go?" I ask her.

She laughs. "Of course you have. I'll be back in a few minutes. I'd just borrow something of yours, but I think we know my waist is a few inches wider than yours."

"Poppy?" I call, but she's gone, and I realize that means I'm going to the village.

I get up to go put my dress on and bend over to pick up the key while I'm at it. As I'm standing back up, I hit my head on the open door.

"Ouch!" It smarts, and for a moment, I feel dizzy. I rest my hand on the shelf, laying the key down so that I can steady myself by holding onto the shelf.

I press my other hand to the top of my head, hoping it's not bleeding. When I pull my hand away, it's not bloody, thank goodness, but it does hurt.

Perhaps I can't get away with dressing myself after all.

Irritated, I move away from the armoire and take my time getting dressed because of the pain in my skull.

By the time I have the dress on, I feel better. I go into the bathroom to put on a little makeup.

"Are you about ready?" Poppy calls as she comes back into the room.

"Yeah, just a minute," I say, finishing up my lip gloss. I know if I tell her I hit my head, she'll be concerned, so I decide to keep it to myself.

"Here are your shoes." She hands me a pair of brown sandals from the armoire. I take them just as she closes the door.

"Wait!" I tell her, realizing the key is inside. "The key!"

"What about it?" she asks, turning to look at the furniture. "Where is it?"

"It fell on the floor before," I tell her, and she immediately starts searching the ground with her eyes. "No, it's not there anymore."

"What?" she asks, her forehead crinkled. "Where is it?"

"It's in the armoire!" I exclaim. "I picked it up, but then I hit my head, and I set it down."

"You set the key to the armoire... inside of the locked armoire?" she asks me.

"It wasn't locked then!" I tell her.

"Well, technically, it was locked. It just wasn't closed." Poppy rattles the doors—they are locked.

"Dang it!" I declare, sitting down on my bed. "Now what?"

"Oh, don't worry about it," she says, waving her hand. "Mrs. Dixon is a pro at picking locks. We'll get her to come and open it later."

I stare at her for a moment. "Mrs. Dixon? The new head of staff who is awfully mean to everyone now?"

She shrugs. "She's not as mean as Mrs. Worsthingshorethinshire. Besides, she'll have an excuse to come in here and see your room. She's so nosy. She always wants to see everyone's room. Also, she's easy to bribe. We can get her some sweets at the candy store, and that'll be enough for her to want to help you. The woman is portly and will do anything for a good bar of chocolate or a handful of sour candies." She giggles, and I feel a little better.

Except I have no money. "What are we going to buy these gifts with?" I ask her.

Poppy narrows her eyes at me and shakes her head. "Really, Isla... it's as if you've never even opened your own belongings." She walks over to a handbag that is on the dresser. It's been there since I moved into the room.

Opening it up, she pulls out a wallet, and from one of the slots, she pulls out a credit card. It's black with the crest of the royal family on it. "You belong to the king now, so you have access to some of his money, silly girl."

My mouth drops open. I had no idea that was in there.

She puts it away, and I finish putting on my shoes. It's then I finally get a chance to say, "By the way, Poppy, you look really cute in that dress. Green is a good color on you."

She spins around again, the exact motion that got us into this predicament to begin with, and I laugh. She looks so different out of her maid's uniform. She's adorable.

"Are you ready?" she asks me.

My head still stings a little bit, but I am ready. At least now I have a reason to go to the village—to get Mrs. Dixon a gift.

I wonder if I might be able to get Maddox something while I'm there. But doesn't it seem strange to buy him something with what's technically his own money?

"I'm ready," I tell her, carefully standing up. She smiles and takes my arm, and we walk out of the room like two friends going out on the town—not like a breeder and her assigned chambermaid.

In the hall, I see the two guards who have been standing outside of my room most of the time since the death of the other maid. I smile at them intending to just go on by, but one of them steps in front of me.

"Excuse me, Miss Isla," he says. "Where are you going?"

"Oh, we're just going to the village," I say.

"It's fine, Private Wylie" Poppy chimes in. "She can go if she wants to. She's not a prisoner here!"

"No, of course, she's not," he says with a little laugh. "But I think it would be safer if Private Parker and I went with you. We were instructed to keep an eye on you while King Maddox is gone."

"We don't need you two hanging around, ruining our girls' day!" Poppy declares, her tone a little rude.

"King Maddox personally asked me to keep an eye on you when he left this morning," Private Wylie insists, looking at me. "If something were to happen to you, well, I would never forgive myself. I'd be letting you down, the king down, everyone."

He had a point, and I didn't see the harm in letting them come along. "Can you just sort of hang back, so we at least think we're alone?" I ask him.

A smirk pulls up the corner of his mouth, and I realize he's actually good-looking, though not nearly as striking as Maddox. "Of course, my lady. Whatever you wish."

Poppy groans, but we start walking again, and our two uniformed guards come along with us, staying about ten feet behind us, at least for now.

As we pass down the hallway, I see Zabrina coming toward us, along with some of her friends from her pack that came along with her. I avert my eyes. The last conversation the two of us had was ugly, and the last time I saw her, she was covered in blood.

"Look, it's the king's whore and the girl who cleans her toilet!" Zabrina jokes.

I feel my face flushing, but I say nothing. I yank on Poppy's arm to remind her to be quiet.

So I'm shocked when I hear a male voice say, "Leave Miss Isla be, Miss Zabrina."

I turn to see Private Wylie glaring at Zabrina. She makes a wide-eyed face, as if she is shocked but says nothing more and heads on down the hall.

I am impressed. "Thank you, Private Wylie," I say.

"Of course, my lady," he says. "I would do anything for you."

I smile at him and turn around, feeling my cheeks turning pink again.

Who was this guy, anyway?

MRS. OVER-THE-MOON

Maddox

THE DRIVE to Willow pack is uneventful, once we've gotten away from the castle. I use the time in the back of the car to get some work done on my phone, the best I can anyway, on the bumpy roads. Godfried is a skilled driver, but we need to look into doing something to get these roads repaved. They are full of potholes.

Eventually, I see the main village in Willow pack up ahead in the distance. The forest opens up as the road leads into town. Factories fill the sky with gray smoke along the far northern side of the town, giving the air a slightly dirty look that smells of burning chemicals and plastic products. I need to do something about that, too. I'm certain there are better ways to make the products created here, but Alpha Ernest is a cheap man, and I am certain he will not willingly spend his own money to bring anything into the current century without some prodding by me.

Depending upon how this meeting goes, it might not matter. Ernest may not have a say in anything having to do with Willow pack for much longer.

"Do you have the address, Godfried?" I ask my driver, my eyes searching out the window at the street signs as we make our way through the residential part of town. Many of the homes here are mid-sized and look fairly nice. I am wondering if one of these houses might belong to Isla's parents.

"I do, sir," Godfried says. "It's 1302 Ash Street."

"Ash Street," I mutter. "I wonder if that's over by the factories…." Is it named that because the houses are often covered with debris from the factories?

We find Ash Street toward the end of the town, and here, the houses are different. They no longer look like middle-class family homes. Rather, they are all run down and dilapidated. Most are small, with pieces of siding missing, and some even have tarps over the roofs.

We find 1302 and I stare for a moment at what looks like a two-bedroom home, at least a hundred years old, with a sagging porch and white paint so dingy, the house looks gray. The yard is neatly trimmed, but small, and there are cracks running through the walkway that leads up to the house.

"This is it, sir," Godfried says. "Do you want us all to come with you?"

"Not for this part of my journey," I assure them. "Possibly later… if there's a later." I hope to meet with Mr. and Mrs. Moon to find out that they have been treated fairly and there's no reason for me to even carry out the second part of my plan.

I get out of the car and walk up the front step, keeping my eyes on the cracks so as not to trip. It's still early in the day, and the street is quiet. Somewhere in the distance, I hear a dog barking, but other than the sound of traffic a few blocks over, the world is silent. The air is heavy with unshed rain, and I can tell it's going to be a muggy day.

I knock on the door, absently wondering if they have air conditioning in their home and thinking they probably don't. Will anyone even answer, or are the parents at work, the children at school? It's not quite summer yet, so school is likely still in session.

The door opens and a woman who looks like an older, more tired version of Isla is looking back at me, her blue eyes wide. Her hair is up in a messy bun, and she's wearing a pair of faded jeans with a rip in the knee that look to be a couple of sizes too big for her thin frame. Her light blue T-shirt is stained, the emblem faded, and she looks nervous to see me standing here.

"Hi," I say, offering her a smile. "Are you… Mrs. Moon?" Isla has told me that her two older sisters no longer live here, so this has to be her mother.

"Yes, I'm Constance Moon," she says, her tone friendly enough but still wary. "Can I help you, sir?"

She doesn't recognize me. Maybe that's for the better. Her eyes go past me to the car, and her brows knit together. She's confused.

"I believe so," I say. "Is your husband home?"

She shakes her head. "He's at work… at the auto garage down the block." She gestures with the top of her head, and my eyes follow in that direction, but I don't see the place she means.

"That's too bad. I was hoping to speak to both of you. But that's all right. If you don't mind, I'd like to have a moment of your time, Mrs. Moon, to discuss the debt you owed to Alpha Ernest."

Her face falls. She looks down at the porch, her eyes closed for a moment, and I can tell I've upset her. I open my mouth to try to make her feel better, but before I can, she starts crying. "I'm so sorry, sir. We're doing everything we can to pay him back. Our daughter was helping us… but she's missing, and until we find her, we don't know what we can do. The Alpha said—"

I cut her off. "Missing? Isla?"

She has tears in her eyes and begins to nod. "The Alpha said that she told him she was going to another pack in search of work, but… it's not like Isla to disappear like that. She was paying a good portion of our bills, and without her…. And I've missed a lot of work while I've been searching for her. But I can't find her." She begins to sob, covering her face with both hands, and I want to wring Alpha Ernest's neck.

"Mrs. Moon, I know where Isla is," I tell her. "She's safe."

Her hands drop, and she's staring at me through her tears. "You know where my daughter is? Please, don't hurt her!" she says. "We're doing everything we can to pay back the money Alpha Ernest loaned us for our son's medical bills. Please!" She has her hands folded together as if she is praying and begging me at the same time.

"I assure you, it isn't my intention to hurt Isla. In fact, I'll do everything in my power to make sure that no harm ever befalls her. She's very important to me."

A look of relief washes over her face. "Oh, thank you, sir," she says. "Would you like to come in?"

Rather than standing on the front porch, I decide this is a good idea, so I follow her into their humble living room. The furniture is old and worn, but it's clear Mrs. Moon has tried to make a home for her family here. The décor is pleasant, though modest. Simple items—framed pictures from magazines, jars holding wildflowers. It's quaint but lovely.

On the wall, I do see a picture I recognize. A family photo with a smiling girl with long blonde curls and sparkling eyes. She was beautiful even when she wasn't yet ten years old.

We sit down on the couch, and I have to move over slightly because of a coil that's poking my leg, but I don't let on.

"You say you know where Isla is?" she asks before she adds, "oh, do you want a drink?"

"I'm fine, thank you," I tell her. "Yes, she's fine. She's… working at the castle."

Her mouth drops open. "Working? At the castle? Our Isla?"

"That's right," I tell her. "And she's doing a fine job."

A little screech of joy comes out of her mouth. "Oh, that's amazing! What is she doing?"

I feel my cheeks begin to pink, and I decide maybe now isn't the time for her to know that. "Oh, well, she's a member of the king's staff," I stammer. "She's… a wonderful… servant."

Her smile brightens. "Her father will be so proud of her! We always taught her the importance of handling everything correctly in the bedroom!"

I lift an eyebrow, not sure I understand. "You… what?"

"You know, keep the bed made at all times. No clothes tossed on the floor… that sort of thing. She is a maid, right?"

I want to say she's not a maid… anymore. "Uhm, I, uh… the nature of her duties is something she may want to discuss with you herself. You see, in exchange for Isla being hired to work at the castle, your Alpha was supposed to forgive all of your debts."

She stares at me, her mouth consisting of two saucers and a gaping hole where her features should be.

"Mrs. Moon? Are you well?" If she doesn't blink soon, I will have to wave my hand in front of her face.

Eventually, she says, "Oh, yes. Yes. I… uh… that information was not relayed to us, sir."

"I was afraid of that," I reply. "And how much money have you paid to Alpha Ernest since Isla has been away?"

"A thousand dollars," she says. "We usually pay him two hundred dollars a week, but he demanded more saying he had more expenses. We didn't really have it. We had to stop giving Ben his medicine because we couldn't afford it. That's a parent's worst nightmare."

"Ben?" I repeated. I remembered Isla's siblings' names, and I remembered when she spoke of Ben, she said his name differently than the others.

Mrs. Moon nods. "Yes, he's very ill. That's why we are in so much debt. He has had three operations on his heart, but he needs another."

"Operations?" I repeat. "But those should be free. The pack has healthcare—"

"Not for people who weren't born here," she says, shaking her head. "My husband and I were born overseas. So we don't qualify."

I stare at her for a moment. "Says who?" I ask.

"The hospital. They told us that we weren't covered. It's always been that way since he started having his operations six years ago."

It's no wonder she looks so exhausted.

That's how she amassed such a huge amount of debt. And that's why Isla has been working so hard her whole life.

And that's why she was willing to take a job as my breeder….

"Mrs. Moon, whoever told you that at the hospital has been misinformed. In the kingdom of Crescent Falls, we do not distinguish between our citizens. All people who live as members of our packs are covered when it comes to medical care."

Her forehead crinkles in confusion. "But we even went to the Alpha because we thought that information was wrong. He said he'd let us pay it off at fifty percent interest."

"Fifty percent interest?" I repeat, and she nods her head. "That's insane!"

"We couldn't get a loan anywhere else because by then we'd spent all of our money on other medical treatments. We'd even sold our home and rented this place. It's been… a nightmare. But I have eight children. I had to do what I had to do."

"I understand," I tell her. "Listen, Mrs. Moon, you don't need to worry about this anymore. I will handle it. Consider your debt paid. I will speak to the people at the hospital and make sure they understand that Ben Moon's treatment is fully covered from now on, as is anything else your family needs. As for Alpha Ernest…." Anger boils up inside of me. The man had taken advantage of my kindness. He is going to pay. "I will handle him as well."

Once again, tears sprang to her eyes. "You can do all of that?" she asks me.

I nod. "That's right. I can."

"Oh, I don't know how to thank you enough!" She shoots out of her chair and flings herself at me, hugging me tightly. I am taken aback at first but then hug her. "Thank you so much, sir!"

"It's nothing," I tell her as she backs away. I stand. "Also, this is from Isla." I reach into my pocket and pull out an envelope. In it, there's twenty thousand dollars, but she won't know that right away. "It's just part of her earnings. There will be more."

She takes the envelope from me and sees how thick it is. "Isla is earning this kind of money? As a maid?"

I shrug. "Isla is very good at her job."

She shakes her head slowly. "She must be!"

I head to the door, and she follows. "Sir, do you think we can speak to her soon?"

"Of course. In fact, you should use some of that money to install a phone. Then, just call the castle, and you'll be able to speak to her any time you'd like."

"Oh, that's a wonderful idea," she says.

"And I'll make sure you see her soon, as well." I can imagine bringing Isla back to visit her folks. Maybe she can help them find a new house.

In the back of my mind, I realize, she may want to stay here if she comes back, and I know, considering the circumstances, if she does want to leave… I have to let her. Otherwise, I really am the horrible person everyone says I am.

"Who should I ask for when I call?" she says as I open the front door to leave.

"You can ask for Isla," I tell her.

"Great," she says. "And… if they ask me on whose authority I am calling, can I give them your name, sir?"

I hesitate because I had almost managed to do all of this without telling her who I was. I could lie and give her the name of one of my assistants. But then… Isla will tell her eventually who I am. "Yes, of course," I finally say.

"Thank you, sir. And what is your name?"

I clear my throat and let out a deep breath. "Maddox."

Mrs. Moon nearly drops the envelope in her hands as she stammers, "Wh-what? Did you say… Ma-Ma-Maddox? As in… Alpha King Maddox?"

I pat her on the shoulder. "Have a nice day, Mrs. Moon." I turn and walk away, heading briskly for the car before she has a conniption.

It's better if that happens out of my line of sight.

I get in the car and see that Lionel and Helena are laughing. "She nearly fainted," he says.

I shrug. "I have that effect on people sometimes. Godfried, take me to the Alpha's mansion."

"Yes, sir," he says, and I settle into the mindset of a vigilante.

Alpha Ernest is about to find out what happens when you cross the Alpha King.

LINKED TO THE KING

Isla

THE VILLAGE IS EXACTLY how I've imagined it in my mind, though it is also nothing like my hometown. The main village for Willow pack is called Ernestown. It was changed a few years ago when Alpha Ernest became Alpha. Before that, it was just called Willow Village. I guess our Alpha wants everyone to know who the boss is in our pack lands....

Our village is rundown and full of factories. The sky is always hazy, and it's hard to see the blue through all of the gray that hangs over the city from the chemicals filling the sky from the various plants that make all kinds of cheap goods to ship to other parts of the kingdom. Most of the people who live in our town are either middle class or poor, like my family, and it's rare to see a car because most of us can't afford them, let alone other luxuries.

But here in the heart of the kingdom, the village, called Wolfcrest, is lively and full of color. The buildings are all freshly painted in vibrant hues, and there are plants and flowers everywhere. The sky above us is a bright azure blue, and the road is well maintained. The sidewalks are made of cobblestone, but they are smooth, and as the four of us walk along, I can't help but smile.

"This is so quaint!" I tell Poppy.

"I know. I thought you'd like it. There are all kinds of shops for us to go into. We can buy some new clothes if you want or some jewelry!"

"I have plenty of that stuff," I remind her. "But I would like to get a gift for King Maddox."

Poppy turns to look at me, and her eyes bulge slightly. "A gift? For the king?" she clarifies. "Why?"

I am taken aback. "What do you mean? I care about him, so I'd like to get him a gift. To thank him for his kindness."

Poppy's grin widens. "Does someone have a little crush on the king?"

I feel my face flush and look around. The two guards are several steps behind us. Private Parker is pretending not to listen, staring out at the road while Private Wylie is smiling mischievously at me. I know he's eavesdropping.

"Listen, Poppy," I say, turning back to my maid—or friend—or whatever she is, "I would just like to get the king a gift, that's all."

"All right," she says with a shrug. "But what in the world do you get a man who has everything he could possibly ever want or need?"

It's a good question, and I don't have an answer for her, but I have a feeling that I will recognize the best gift when I see it.

"We need to get that chocolate for Mrs. Dixon, too," she reminds me.

"Oh, yes, that's right." I don't want to forget to get her a gift so she'll come down and unlock my armoire. "We should probably get that last, though, in case it's a warm spring day. I don't want the chocolate to melt while we are walking around." It isn't hot yet, but it is humid, and the sky shows no promise of rain, which is good. Getting soaked again would remind me of the day I'd arrived here, and I don't want to remember that because it will make me miss my family too much.

"Let's go in here," Poppy suggests, and she grabbed my hand, tugging me into a jewelry store.

I'd just told her I didn't need any jewelry, but I went with her because she was strong and had a good grip on me.

The door chimes as we walk in, and an older gentleman behind the counter greets us. He has only a bit of gray hair left around the edges and peers at us through wire-rimmed spectacles.

"Hello, young ladies... gentlemen.... What can I help you with today?" he asks.

"Oh, we're just looking, thank you," I say.

Poppy is more vocal. "Do you have anything fit for a king?" She snickers under her breath with the question.

"Fit for a king?" he repeats, his eyebrows arched behind his glasses. "As in... the king? King Maddox?"

"That's right," Poppy says. "My friend here wants to get the king a gift." She giggles and hides her mouth behind her hand. I glare at her.

The shopkeeper only smiles back, though. He doesn't laugh. "I actually do have something," he says, "something very rare and precious that I think the king would like very much."

"Is it another woman?" Poppy jokes, cracking herself up. "Because I don't think Isla wants to get him any competition."

"Poppy!" I stare at her, wide-eyed. She's becoming obnoxious, which shouldn't surprise me, because she's like that a lot back at the castle, but I didn't expect it from her in public.

"No, it's not another woman," he says, scratching his head. "I'll show you. Give me one moment, please."

He leaves, ducking through a swinging door behind the counter, and I try to concentrate on looking at the fine jewelry locked in glass cases. I do see some pretty items, but I don't want to spend money that doesn't really belong to me on anything I don't need.

Poppy looks at everything, gasping and pointing out the prettiest pieces, in her opinion, to me. I agree they are lovely. I think about buying her a pair of earrings she really likes, but she needs to be nice or else I won't do it. She's settled down a bit now.

The man comes back with a small black velvet box in his hands.

"Do you expect her to ask the king to marry her or something?" Obnoxious Poppy is back, and she is laughing at her own ridiculous joke. I hear a male clear his voice behind me and turn to see Private Wylie is as annoyed with her as I am. He won't say anything, though. That's not why he's here. Still, he is glaring at the back of her head like he wants to thump her.

I am beginning to like this guy.

"No, it's not a ring," the shopkeeper says as if he doesn't understand that Poppy is trying to be funny. "It's a pair of cufflinks."

He opens the box to reveal two gold wolf cufflinks, each of them with gems for eyes. One has green emerald eyes, and the other has red rubies. They are gorgeous.

And… for some reason… they seem slightly familiar to me, though I have no idea why.

"They're stunning," I tell him. "Do you think he has any like this?" I ask Poppy. Is it possible I've seen these before—on Maddox?

"No, I've never seen anything like these before, and I always pay attention to what King Maddox is wearing."

I raise an eyebrow at her.

"What?" Poppy asks, shrugging.

"And you say I'm asking him to marry me."

That gets a laugh out of the guards behind us.

I turn back to look at the wolves. They are both howling at the moon, and in their 3D shape, they look almost lifelike, the craftsmanship is so good. They are about half an inch tall, and the quality of the piece that went on the other end to hold them in place is solid as well, so I know they can't come unhooked.

"Where did you get them?" I ask the kind, old gentleman.

"They came from a distant land," he tells me. "A few months ago, a trader came in, said she'd been to the castle in a pack way across the ocean, where there'd been a revolution several years ago. The castle was abandoned and boarded up. She managed to sneak in somehow, and she got these as well as a few other pieces."

"So they're stolen goods?" Poppy asks him.

He gave her an incredulous look. "I didn't steal them," he replies. "I paid good money for them. Besides, my understanding is that the king of that kingdom and his family were killed a good fifteen or twenty years ago. I don't suppose he'll be needing them now."

I stare at him for a few moments, thinking that's the saddest story I've ever heard. "What pack was it?" I ask him.

"Uh… I can't remember the name of it. Something weird. They had a big revolution. Lots of people died. Others fled. The king's ability to rule came into question because he was fated to a maid or some other worker in the castle. That made the pack elders question how he could be a legitimate heir to the throne. Why would the Moon Goddess match an Alpha with a maid? So… it started a big kerfuffle, and he ended up being killed. Her, too, I guess. And by then they had a few kids. I'm not sure of the details. But if that trader comes back in, I can ask her."

"That would be interesting to hear about," I tell him. The idea of children being killed because their mother was a maid caused an ache to develop in my heart.

"Anyway," he continued, "these are certainly fit for a king."

"Yes, they are," I agree. "How much do you want for them?"

"Well…" he began, rubbing his chin with his hand as he thought it over, "considering what I paid for them… I think I could let them go for two thousand."

"Two thousand?" I repeat. That's a lot of money. More money than I've seen in one place—ever. I would have to work for five or six months back home to make that kind of money.

"That's pocket change," Poppy whispers, and I know what she means. King Maddox has shoes in his closet that he's never worn that cost more than that, I imagine.

"All right," I tell him. I hand over the card from my wallet, and he smiles as he rings them up. I'll have to make sure that nothing happens to them before I can give them to him. It's not as if I can just lock them up, not when people like Mrs. Dixon can get through any lock, apparently.

He hands me the card back and puts the cufflinks in a little bag. I thank him and drop it into my purse. But just before we go, I say, "Give me those earrings, too, please," pointing out the ones Poppy really likes.

We do the process all over again, and he hands me the earrings. She has a questioning look on her face, and I hand them over.

Poppy squeals. "Really?" she asks.

"Yes, but stop being such a pest," I tell her. She wraps her arms around me and squeezes me so tightly, I think my head might pop off.

"Let's go get the candy!" Poppy exclaims as we walk out of the shop, and I smile and go along with her. Why not? I can use some candy. The sky still doesn't look like rain, but it's not too hot, so maybe it won't melt.

We walk along beside each other, and Poppy holds my hand, like we are good friends. And maybe we are.

As long as she stops teasing me about Maddox....

I sure hope he likes his gift, and I hope that he can tell me where they came from. I feel bad for that poor king and his family, but in the back of my mind, I have to wonder....

If that king could be fated to marry a maid, could King Maddox be fated to marry someone of lesser status, too?

Like... a breeder?

ALPHA ERNEST GETS WHAT HE DESERVES

Maddox

THE ALPHA'S mansion is completely on the other side of town from where the Moon family resides. It takes about six minutes to get there by car. I notice there's really not a lot of traffic here, and many of the driveways have no cars in them either.

I am beginning to think that Willow pack is not as wealthy as some of the other packs in the kingdom, and if many of the citizens have been treated similarly to the Moons, then I suppose I know why.

Ernest's house is palatial. It's a Victorian-style home with a huge wrap-around porch, gingerbread cutouts along the overhang, and lots of grand windows. It's painted a pristine white, as if Alpha Ernest is pure somehow. That notion almost makes me laugh.

I assume he is here and not off in an office somewhere. I believe I heard that he no longer went to the office anymore a few years back.

The house isn't gated, but there are plenty of guards standing around. When the car pulls up out front, I tell Helena and Lionel, "I intend to handle this myself, but be on the ready."

"Yes, sir," they both say. "Shall we get out?"

I look at the number of guards in the yard. Theoretically, they answer to me before they answer to Alpha Ernest, but with all of the strife going on within many of the packs these days, I won't bank on that.

"That's probably a good idea," I tell them. Godfried shuts the car off, and the three of them get out with me, though they hang back. Godfried is a driver firstly, but all of the people who work at the castle have some sort of training in fighting, just in case.

I walk up the pathway toward the front door, and immediately, two guards step in front of me. I notice that they have guns. That is absolutely against protocol. All honorable wolves fight without weapons.

"Where do you think you're going?" one of them asks, folding his arms across his chest. He is muscular, but not as big as I am. Of course, the gun evens things out quite a bit.

"To see Alpha Ernest," I tell them.

"Do you have an appointment?" the other one, slightly shorter than the first, asks. "'Cause the Alpha don't see nobody without an appointment, son." They snicker at one another, and I slowly shake my head.

"He'll see me," I tell them. "Now, get the fuck out of my way unless you want the imprint of my insignia ring on your ugly ass forehead."

Their eyes widen as they exchange glances and then start laughing again. "You think you can take both of us? Or are you going to call upon your friends back there to help you?" the first one asks.

"Yeah, that chick looks really tough," his idiotic friend chimes in.

"I don't need them," I say. "But I'm going to go ahead and warn you right now, if you two buffoons don't get the fuck out of my way, you're going to be sorry."

As they begin to laugh again, another guard comes over in a hurry. "Guys!" he says. "Th-th-that's the Alpha King!" He bows his head in respect, and the other two laugh louder.

"Sure it is, Stanley," the first guard says. "Why the fuck would the Alpha King be here? In Ernestville?"

"Ernestville?" I repeat. "When the fuck did Ernest change the name of this village to Ernestville?"

"See!" the second guard chimes in. "The Alpha King would know that."

"Look at his ring!" Stanley insists.

"You're about to see it up close and personal, I say, raising my hand and drawing it back in a fist.

It's then that they see the ring. "Holy hell," the first guard stammers. "We... we're so sorry, sir." He drops his head and steps aside, but the other one is still confused.

"He's not the fucking Alpha K—"

That's as much as he gets out before my fist connects with his jaw. His eyes roll back in his head, and he drops to the ground.

"Now, gentlemen," I say loud enough for all of the guards in the yard, and there are about ten of them, to hear me, "your Alpha and I are going to have words. If you wish to not be lying on your back in the yard like this poor bastard, I suggest you remember who your loyalty should lie with—and that would be me."

"Yes, Alpha King Maddox!" every single one of them chimes as they make the sign of respect by hitting their left shoulder with their right hand and bowing their heads to me.

I step over the guard who is lying on the ground in front of me, not caring that I smashed his hand in doing so, and head up the walkway.

When I get to the house, I pound loudly on the door and wait.

A few moments later, a thin man who looks to be about my age opens the door. "Yes?" he asks.

"Hi, I need to see Alpha Ernest," I say to him, shaking my hand out a little. The adrenaline is leaving me, and it's beginning to sting a little.

"Oh, he... uh... he's sleeping," the man, who seems to be his butler, I guess... explains.

I look at my watch. It's nearly 11:00 in the morning. "Still?" I ask.

"Yes, sir," he replies. "He was up late last night... seeing to... pack matters." He makes a face at me, and I am confused as to what that means, but then I doubt it's true anyway.

"Well, go wake him," I tell the butler, or whoever he is, as I step inside. "It's important."

I'm not sure if he recognizes me or not, but he is obedient, at least. "Yes, sir." He hurries upstairs, leaving me standing in the foyer.

I look around the house. It's grandly decorated with all kinds of important pieces of art and expensive furniture—but it's a wreck. Empty bottles of liquor and beer cans, food wrappers, and stray clothing litter the floor and every surface of the furniture.

I can only assume that Alpha Ernest had a party the night before. Maybe every night. And by the number of bras I see on the ground, I'm guessing there were several women involved.

Was it... an orgy?

I am thankful that I don't have time to ponder that for long as I hear Ernest's voice from the top of the staircase.

"Whoever the hell it is, Billy, tell him to get the fuck out!" he yells.

I decide it is time to use the mind-link. "I don't think that's in your best interest, Ernest," I tell him.

"Oh, shit," he replies. "King Maddox? I had no idea you were coming today."

"Surprise," I mind-link back.

A moment later, Ernest is coming down the stairs, tying his robe. I get a flash of what's beneath it—nothing—and my stomach turns. Ernest is a fat, floppy, small-dicked bastard.

"Well, isn't this a surprise!" he says, coming into the foyer. "Billy! Why didn't you offer our guest a seat and a drink?"

"Sorry, sir," Billy says, looking sheepish. "Alpha King, sir, would you like—"

"I'm fine, Billy," I assure him. "This won't take long. Where's your Beta, Ernest?" I ask.

"Miguel? Who the fuck knows?" Ernest says. "He's worthless."

I have known Miguel for a long time, and I know that's not the case. "Billy, go find Miguel," I tell him.

"Yes, sir," he says and heads out the door.

I could've used the mind-link to contact Miguel, but I'd rather have my "discussion" with Ernest alone, not in front of Billy.

"What seems to be the problem, sir?" Ernest asks me, clearly able to tell by my attitude that I'm bothered. "Is it the girl? Did she lie to me? Was she not a virgin after all?"

"This isn't about the girl," I tell him, irritated as hell that he'd just assume I'd found fault with Isla. "Not directly, anyway."

"Then what is it, sir?" Ernest asks, but I can tell by the dots of perspiration springing up along his forehead that he's nervous. He probably already suspects I'm on to him.

"This is about her family," I tell him. "Did you forgive their loan?"

"Why… yes! Of course, I did!" he says with a rich chuckle. "As soon as I got back to Ernestvi—uh, Willow Village, I told them that all was forgiven."

"I know that you changed the name of the town, Ernest," I tell him, though this is new information to me. "And I also know you're lying about the Moons."

"What? No! It's true. Not a penny more owed or paid to me since you took the girl. I keep my promises! I am a trustworthy man!" He chuckles again, but it just makes me want to punch him harder.

"So, you're saying if I went to the Moons' residence right now, they'd tell me all is forgiven?" I fold my arms across my chest, wondering if I should stretch a little before I start punching.

"Yes, you could. Except… I believe they are out of town. I think they decided to take a well-deserved vacation now that they can save a little money."

"They're not home?" I repeat, clarifying. Is that what he's really telling me?

"I'm afraid not." He shrugs, shaking his head.

"Oh, I see," I say, nodding along. "So… when I stopped at their house a bit ago, that wasn't really Constance Moon I spoke to, but someone impersonating her?"

He can see that he's caught in another lie, so he starts to stammer. "Oh, uh… well… maybe they are back."

"Or maybe you're a fucking liar!" I scream at him. "And maybe you didn't forgive their fucking loan at all! And maybe you've continued to collect payments from them even though you know you shouldn't be!" I am livid now, thoughts of Isla crying, everything she's been through because of this man, making my anger boil over. If he hadn't made the hospitals lie to their patients just to collect money I was already providing to him from the crown's coffers to cover medical expenses, the Moons would've never been in this situation to begin with, and Isla wouldn't have had to work herself half-to-death!

"No, sir, I—"

I don't give him a chance to get the words out. My fist strikes him in the right eye first, knocking him backward. He shouts out in pain, raising his hands to cover his injured orb. But I'm not done yet. No, I plan to take my time beating the shit out of this asshole.

I hit him again. This time, it's a left jab, right to the nose. Blood spurts out, missing me but spraying the floor. Ernest screams in agony. I raise a knee to his gullet, making him double over in pain as I slam my fist into his jaw.

Over and over, I hit him, thinking of Isla and her family the entire time. When I am finally done, he is on his knees, blood pouring from his nose and busted lips, both eyes swollen. "This is your last day as Alpha, Ernest. You're done!"

"But, sir!" He spits a mouthful of blood on the floor. "Please! Give me another chance!"

"The fuck I will!" I tell him.

I turn to see Miguel standing behind me, his eyes wide.

"Beta Miguel, take this asshole to jail, and lock him up. I sentence him to twenty years of prison time for extortion, amongst other things. Such as lying to the king!"

"Y-yes, sir," Miguel says. He signals for a few of the guards from the yard to come and get Ernest and take him away.

I follow them out, seeing Billy standing on the porch with tears in his eyes. I'm not sure if he's scared or upset about Ernest.

I walk alongside Miguel as he goes down the walkway. "You're the new Alpha," I tell him.

He stops in his tracks. "Sir? Oh… uh, thank you, but I don't think I'm qual-ified for that."

I stop and stare at him. "You've been Beta for fifteen years."

"Yes, I know," he says as the guards take Ernest on ahead of us. "But… Ernest never trained me to do anything. I've sort of figured out how to be Beta from my father and just doing what needs to be done. But Alpha? Sir, I'm not cut out for that. I can do it in the interim while you figure out what to do, but…."

"No, no, I understand," I say, dragging my hand through my hair. "I'll figure something out. In the meantime, keep things running smoothly here. Change the goddamn name back, look into all of the money Ernest was taking from the people, make sure the people at the hospital understand the free healthcare policy extends to everyone, not just people born here, and just… fix this place, Miguel."

He is nodding at me like he knows exactly what I'm talking about. "Yes, sir." He makes the sign of respect, and I thank him before returning to the car.

I should probably stay here and look into making sure this mess is cleaned up, but I don't have time. I want to go home now. I want to see Isla.

From the back seat, I tell Godfried, "Let's go home."

HIDDEN AND LOST

Isla

BACK IN MY ROOM, I sit on the bed and admire the cufflinks I've purchased for Maddox… with his own money… while Poppy is off fetching Mrs. Dixon.

I need to figure out what to do with them. I don't want to leave them lying around, but I'm not sure that locking them up will do any good either, not when there's someone like Mrs. Dixon around.

I remember something my mom did with my father's birthday present a few years ago. She had pinched and scraped and waved every penny she could find for months in order to buy him a new baseball glove so that he could play catch with my brothers. Afraid that Dad would find the gift in our small house, she ended up finding a loose floorboard and hiding it in there.

This is a castle, though. Would there be a place in the floor or wall that was loose enough for me to hide them?

Poking around on the floor, I don't notice anything like I did back at our house where the floor creaks with every step. For a moment, I think back to the house we used to live in, before my brother got so sick. It was such a nice house. I had loved it there, but then, my parents had to start spending all of their money on medical bills, and we had had to move to a small house that had a lot of problems.

Eventually, I get to a spot in the windowsill and realize that it lifts up a bit at the corner. I look inside and see that there's enough room for me to reach my hand in, which means I can drop the box inside but also will be able to retrieve it later. I place the box inside and put the wood back in place, just as I hear Poppy's voice in the antechamber.

"It'll only take a minute, Mrs. Dixon," she is saying. "And we do have a gift for you."

As the bedroom door opens, I grab the sweets we bought for the head of the staff so that when she comes in, I can present it to her.

Mrs. Dixon is a plump woman, older than my mom, and short. She barely comes to Poppy's shoulder. She has a scowl on her face that reminds me of the woman who was in her position before, Mrs. Worchestsiresauce, or whatever her name is.

"I'll do it this one time," Mrs. Dixon growls. "But from now on, you'll have to be more careful!" Then, under her breath, she says something I don't quite understand, something like, "These young ladies always needing me to pick locks!" I don't know who else she could be talking about, unless she means both Poppy and me.

"Here you go!" I say, offering her the chocolates. "We got these for you today. I hope you like them."

She looks at the box and then at me before she takes it and opens it. "Oh, my. These are good!" she says, a huge grin splitting her round face. "All right... but just this once. Next time, it'll cost you extra, hear?"

"Yes, thank you," I say. I offer to take the box while she picks the lock, but she puts it back inside of the bag and slings it around her wrist, as if she's afraid I might try to eat them while she's not looking.

Mrs. Dixon pulls a bobby pin out of her hair and sticks it into the lock on my armoire. In about two seconds, the lock pops, and the door swings open.

"There we go," she says. Then, turning to look at Poppy, she says, "Be more careful!"

"Of course," Poppy says, and I wonder if Poppy told her it was all her fault and not mine.

Mrs. Dixon walks out with her nose in the air, and Poppy pulls the key out of the armoire. "Maybe we should just keep it unlocked from now on. It's not like anyone is going to come in here and take any of your shoes."

She has a point. "That's fine with me."

Poppy makes sure the door is still unlocked and then puts the key in the top drawer of my dresser. "Now, what would you like to do with the rest of your afternoon?" she asks me with a big smile.

"Uh... I don't know," I tell her, but I do really know what I'd like to do. I'm just a little conflicted. "Any word from... the king yet?"

Poppy raises an eyebrow. "No, but he's out of town on business. Who knows what time he might be back?"

"Well, he said he'd be back soon when he left, so I was thinking it would only take a few hours." He'd already been gone for several.

She shrugs. "I could go ask Beta Seth, but he's been so busy running around, trying to handle everything King Maddox usually handles, I think he's a little overwhelmed. It's too bad. Beta Seth is so nice...."

The way she says that makes me arch an eyebrow. Does Poppy have a crush on the Beta? I wonder who his fated mate might be. He is old enough to have met her by now.

But then, Poppy should know who hers is as well....

Unless she also hasn't met her fated mate yet, which is possible. I know she's not that much older than I am.

Poppy doesn't seem too concerned about Maddox, but I am. I know it's silly. I'm sure he has plenty of guards with him, the best vehicles, and lots of places he could stop along the way, but I know there is some civil unrest at the moment, centering around his lack of an heir, and I can't help but wonder if something has happened.

In the pit of my stomach, I have a bad feeling, similar to the one I had a few days before we found out that my brother, Ben, had a rare form of cancer.

"Why don't we go out to the garden?" Poppy suggests.

I nod, and the two of us go back outside, this time to sit and relax, I hope, but still... I can't help but wonder if Maddox is all right.

As we walk, I say a silent prayer to the Moon Goddess. "Please, let Maddox be okay!"

~

MADDOX

GODFRIED'S HEAD is under the hood of the car, and he is poking around at things, trying to figure out what the problem is. At first, he said we probably just had some bad gas, but that made no sense to me because we had driven all the way to Willow pack with no noticeable problems. Then, on the way home, something happened, and the car made an awful noise. Now, it won't go at all, and we are a half an hour's drive from Willow and an hour and a half from home.

"I don't know," Godfried says, wiping his hands against one another. "I suppose we'll have to call a tow truck."

"A tow truck?" I repeat, looking around. We are in the middle of nowhere. There's not a lot on the drive from the castle to Willow pack, only a few sparse villages. Right now, we are in the midst of Green pack territory, and I've just received word a little while ago that their previous Alpha passed away —due to some accident. His son, Vincent, is assuming responsibilities as Alpha for now.

It wouldn't be very nice of me to try to bother them at the moment. Besides, my understanding is that Green pack is one of the worst packs when it comes to causing trouble regarding my lack of an heir. They are working closely with some of the packs that have been attacking smaller packs. I have to wonder if Willow pack will be at risk now that they don't have an Alpha.

I'll need to get that sorted out right away since Beta Miguel didn't feel up to it.

Why is my job always so complicated?

Godfried has a cell phone to his ear, but in a moment, I see him walking around with it stretched out. He is looking for a signal.

With a sigh, I think of all of the people I know in Green pack who might be loyal to me. I can't think of very many, but there is the former Beta, Austin, who was good friends with my dad.

I decide to try the mind-link. "Austin, this is Maddox. Can you hear me?"

I don't receive an answer, and I wonder if I'm too far away. Normally, the mind-link only works within a certain distance. If we are too far apart, it's too difficult to hear and gets scrambled some.

I keep trying for several minutes, but when he never responds, it's pretty clear to me he simply can't receive the message.

"What should we do?" Helena asks. "I can shift and run to the closest village for help."

"That's a decent idea," I tell her. "But we're sort of in hostile territory."

"Maybe I don't tell them who the help is for?" she suggests.

I chuckle. "They're even less likely to help a stranger than the king they should feel obligated to support. Maybe I should take a look at the engine."

"You?" Godfried asks, his eyes wide. "No offense, Your Majesty, but if I couldn't figure it out, how would you be able to? I've been your driver for years."

"You're my driver, Godfried," I remind him, "not my mechanic. I know a thing or two about cars."

I walk over to the car and take a look inside of the hood. I don't immediately see anything out of sorts, but then, upon closer inspection, I do see the problem. "We've thrown a belt," I tell him.

"What?" Godfried comes up behind me and looks over my shoulder. "Where?"

"There." I point to the belt in question. It's hanging loose, obviously the problem.

"Well, I'll be," Godfried says.

I reach out and touch it, seeing if I can work it back into place, but we will need tools for that. "Do you have a toolbox in the trunk?" I ask him.

"Yeah, I do," he tells me. "I'll get it."

I have no idea if I can fix this or not, but I have to try. I told Isla I'd be back soon, and I hate the fact that she might be worried about me.

I pull my hands away and take a glance down at them. They are covered in black grease. Well, I'm bound to get dirty if I'm going to be tinkering around with an engine, I suppose….

Godfried brings the toolbox, and the two of us get to work, seeing if we can fix the car. It's already afternoon, and I'd expected to be back by now. I think of Isla. If I can't get this car started soon, I'll have to shift and run back to the castle. It'll take hours for me to run there, but I'll do it because I want to make sure she's safe.

I have a bad feeling in my stomach that something is going on, and I have no idea what it might be… but it's unsettling.

And I don't think it's directly related to the fact that we're in the middle of Green pack where I am less than popular.

No, I think it revolves around Isla, and it makes me scared. Visions of Zabrina standing in the hallway covered with blood make my stomach turn, and I work faster on the car.

Thank goodness Isla has Private Parker and Private Wylie to keep her safe while I'm gone!

A WYLIE ONE

Isla

Something is wrong, and by the afternoon, I know it. I just don't know what to do about it.

I know in my heart that Maddox should've been back by now. He would've told me if he was going to be later, and if something came up, he would've sent a message to Beta Seth for me.

But when I go to the Beta's office, he is super busy, and he barely has time to look up at me with the phone resting on his shoulder as he tries to find something with one hand and write something with a pen with the other.

Feeling out of place and stupid for standing there, I start to back away, but he motions for me to stop. In a moment, he gets off the phone. "Hi, Isla," he says. "Sorry. I'm really busy now that Alpha Maddox is out of the office for the day."

"I understand," I tell him. "I just... wasn't Ma—uh, Alpha King Maddox supposed to be back by now?"

Beta Seth grins at me a bit for my slip up. I'm getting too familiar with the king, obviously.

"He said he'd be back a few hours ago, but you just never know with the king," he says with a shrug. "I'm sure he'll be home soon."

I nod, thinking I should let him get back to work. But I feel like he doesn't have all of the information that I have, that he doesn't understand how important this is.

Beta Seth looks away from me, his hands back on the papers in front of him, when I say, "It's only—"

He rolls his eyes a little and sighs and refocuses on me. "Listen, Isla, I know that King Maddox is important to you, but honestly, something probably just came up, some sort of business he has to take care of, and it probably didn't even cross his mind to let you know he'd be later than expected."

I feel my insides fall at his words. I don't know if he's meant to be so blatantly rude or if he even realizes what he's saying, but it hurts.

He must notice my face because he tries to fix it. "I mean… it's not that…. I'm just trying to say… he's the king. And you're… just his breeder. Not just his breeder. But you are… a breeder. So—"

"I understand," I say, swallowing hard. "Thank you for your help." I turn to walk away and get a few steps away from the door when I hear Beta Seth yelling after me.

"Isla, wait!" But then, the phone rings, and he answers that instead.

It doesn't matter. I can't expect the Beta to know why I feel the way I do. To him, I am just another woman that Maddox is fucking. I am not anything special.

And maybe that's the reality of the situation, and I'm nothing special to the king either. But I can't help but think that he really does care about me. Only he and I know what has transpired behind closed doors, and while I suppose it's true he might be able to make anyone feel the way he makes me feel, like I am the most important person in the world, but I don't think that's the case.

Maybe I am crazy for thinking that way.

As I am going back to my room, I see Zabrina walking toward me, and I remember the way that she first introduced herself to me, saying that she was the next Luna, and my stomach feels unsettled.

What if she is right, and she can somehow worm her way into Maddox's life through her father's influence? Or the threat of war? It makes my stomach twist into a thousand knots. I can't imagine him having to marry her. He could never love a selfish woman like her. She tried to poison him, didn't she? That's my understanding.

Alpha Jordan's daughter is dressed oddly for her. She's wearing jeans, a T-shirt, and tennis shoes. I've never seen her wear anything less elegant than a gown. Perhaps she's going for a run or a workout or something.

She sneers at me as she passes, but this time, she doesn't say anything like she did this morning when Private Wylie yelled at her. He really is a nice guy. Maybe the two of us can be friends….

He is standing outside of my room, but Private Parker isn't there, which is odd. "Hello," I say to him.

"Hello, Miss Isla," he says with a smile and a nod.

"Where's Private Parker?" I ask, looking at his empty spot.

"Just off to the restroom. He had too much coffee at the café earlier." Private Wylie snickers, and I smile at him. That's kind of odd, though. I don't remember him having more than one cup. Maybe whatever blend he had doesn't sit well with him. I bid Private Wylie goodbye and walk into my room.

As I enter the bed-chamber, I also think about something else I've heard is true about Maddox—that he never intends to take another Luna. He needs a breeder because he won't marry again. Not after what happened to his wife.

"Rebecca." I whisper her name into the stillness of my room. What happened to the former Luna? How did she die? People say that Maddox killed her, but I don't believe it. He's not capable of that.

He is capable of killing, I'm certain of that. He is a warrior, after all, and I have no doubt, given the chance, he would rip the heads off any opponents on the battlefield.

But killing a helpless woman, someone he loves—or did love at one point—I don't think that's possible. I don't presume to know how he felt about her in the days leading up to her death because, just like I can't expect Beta Seth to know the truth about my relationship with Maddox, I don't think anyone can know the truth of the king's relationship with his wife.

Still, he couldn't have killed her. Not on purpose anyway.

Poppy comes into the room, sighing under her breath. "Well, I have to go help Mrs. Dixon with a problem she's having now. Payback for her help earlier. I'll be gone for a couple of hours. Amanda just came to fetch me." She rolls her eyes. I'm seeing a lot of that today.

"Who is Amanda?" I ask.

"One of the other maids. At least I don't have her assigned duty. Since that other maid killed herself, she's been stuck taking care of that bitch, Zabrina. Gross!" She sticks her tongue out. I feel bad for Amanda, too.

"Okay. I don't need anything," I tell her, not that she's asked.

"Cool. I'll see you later." She rolls her eyes and takes off, and I sink down to sit on the bed. What really happened to Zabrina's maid? Why would she kill herself?

I am about to get up to go take a shower when there's a hard knock on my door.

"Yes?" I call, startled, I turn toward the urgent noise and stand.

"Miss Isla? It's Private Wylie. Are you decent? Can I come in?"

My nervous stomach twists into yet another knot as I say, "I am. You can." What is this about? Has he heard something about Maddox?

When he steps into the room, my own fear is written all over his face. "There's been an accident," he says in a tone that makes my blood run cold. "I'm to bring you to the king at once."

My eyes widen. "An accident? Has King Maddox been in an accident?"

He nods. "It's bad, Miss Isla, and he's asking to see you at once. He used the mind-link to contact me. He says… to hurry. We should go."

I look around the room, wondering if I should grab anything, but I'm terrified. All I can think about is getting to Maddox's side immediately. "Did you let Beta Seth know?" I ask. "Perhaps he should come with us."

"He knows," Private Wylie says with a nod.

I can't contact anyone in this pack with the mind-link because I am not a member. Though I should be able to reach the king. He is a member of all packs. Still, if he is too far away, I can't reach him. But Private Wylie has just said that he reached him. So I have to try. "Maddox? Are you all right?" I think, sending the message to him.

There's no response. What if he's injured so badly he's lost consciousness?

"This way!" he says, ushering me out of the room and down the hallway in a direction I've never gone before.

"Why do you think he didn't contact me himself?" I ask the private as we hurry along.

"He probably didn't want to upset you. He sounded bad, Miss Isla. Very bad."

My heart is breaking in two as I think about it. Tears cloud my vision as Private Wylie hurries me down halls I've never been to before.

"Where are we going?" I ask him as he tugs on my arm.

"There's a car waiting for you. I already sent for one," he explains.

It seems he's thought of everything. I should be grateful, but I'm too distraught.

We exit the palace to see a black sedan pulled up to the door. The windows are blacked out, but the engine is running.

Private Wylie rushes me to the back seat and opens the door for me, pushing me inside a little roughly. I bite back a scream as my shin connects with the metal frame of the door.

He doesn't apologize, just pushes me over and gets in behind me, shouting, "Go!"

I look up then, and all of the blood rushes out of my face.

"Zabrina?" I ask as I see her sitting on the other side of me.

"Hello, little bitch," she says, and we are off at breakneck speed, heading for the open gates in front of us.

"Where are we going?" I ask, but my only answer is a maniacal laugh from Zabrina and Private Wylie.

The driver, whose face I can't see, crushes the gas pedal, and we shoot through the gates. Fear mingles with my already nervous stomach, and I think I just might throw up all over the bitch next to me.

What the hell is happening? Where are they taking me? And where is Maddox?

ALPHA MADDOX GETS A DEAR JOHN LETTER

Maddox

MY WOLF'S paws tear up the ground as I run as fast as I can toward the castle. When I had seen that it was going to take a long time for us to get anyone to help us fix the car, I'd decided to take off for home in my wolf form, against my guards' and driver's better judgment.

But I just have a feeling in my gut that there is something wrong. It isn't something I can explain, not easily anyway.

I run all the way back to the castle. It takes hours, and by the time I get there, the sun is setting. I use the mind-link to call Beta Seth out to meet me in the courtyard with some clothes so that I can shift and get dressed. As soon as I see him coming toward me, using the mind-link, I ask him, "Is everything okay in the castle?"

I see Seth's forehead crinkle. "Yeah, everything's fine," he answers with his human voice. I can't talk because I'm still in my wolf form, but he sees no reason to use the mind-link, obviously. "Why do you ask? What's going on?"

We walk behind a tree so that I'm out of sight of the castle. Nudity doesn't really bother me for the most part, but if someone like Zabrina is watching, I see no reason to entice her.

I'm still breathing heavily as I shift into my human form and pull on the clothes that Seth has brought me. I shove my feet into the tennis shoes he's dropped on the ground for me and then turn to address him. "The car broke down about twenty miles out of Willow Village," I explain to him. "So I decided to run back here. I have a bad feeling, Seth."

He arches an eyebrow at me. "Everything is just fine, I'm telling you. I've been busy all day, but nothing has happened. No one has stabbed anyone or anything."

As we begin to walk back to the castle, I look up at the window where I swear I'd seen movement that morning as the car was pulling away.

Rebecca's room.

Rebecca's window.

Rebecca.

No, it couldn't have been her. Still, ever since I'd seen that form that morning, I'd had a feeling that something ominous was about to befall us.

I try not to let Seth know how concerned I am. But I have to ask. "Have you seen Isla recently?"

He makes a face at me. "Yeah, a few hours ago. She came to see if I'd heard from you."

I swallow hard and consider using the mind-link to call out to her now. I don't, though. It seems desperate, and I don't want her to know that I've been thinking of her all day.

We walk inside the castle, and Seth begins to tell me about all of the work I've missed. I don't want to hear it. I ignore him until he asks me a direct question. "What do you think about sending them forty-five cases instead of the usual forty?"

I have no idea what the fuck he's talking about. Cases of what to who? "Sure," I say. I don't give a damn what he does.

Heading down the hallway toward my room, not actually going there, I try to seem nonchalant, but Seth calls me out on it. "Are you going to shower and come to work? I've missed a lot today."

I turn and narrow my eyes at him. "I thought that's what I had a Beta for? To work for me in my absence."

He takes a step back. "Yeah, sure, but… there's a lot of stuff I'm not privy to, and I have no idea what you were doing. So it didn't get done."

I shrug. "It'll get done tomorrow, then."

"But… Green pack is still making threats."

"And I'm sure they'll still be making threats tomorrow." I turn around and walk away from him, hearing him let out an annoyed sigh.

I see Isla's room in the distance. I will get there before I get to my own, but I immediately notice that there are no guards outside of the door.

This is strange…. "Seth? Where are Private Wylie and Private Parker?" I ask, using the mind-link.

"I assume they're outside of Isla's door. Unless they switched out with another set of guards."

"No one is outside of Isla's door," I tell him.

He is quiet for a moment, but then he says, "Well, I'm sure it's nothing."

"Yeah," I say. But I am not so sure.

I push the door open. It's unlocked. Not a good sign....

Walking into her antechamber, I hear the sound of pacing footsteps on the other side of her bedroom door. I pray it's her, but I do not smell her.

I smell Poppy.

Without knocking, I push the door open to find the maid, wringing her hands, as she walks back and forth in front of the bed, wearing the carpet out.

"Your Majesty," she says, dropping her head.

I don't have time for that nonsense. "Where is Isla?" I ask her.

Poppy shakes her head. "I don't know for sure... but she left this note."

She hands me a piece of paper that is allegedly in Isla's handwriting. I've never seen it, but it's not as neat as I would've thought. All it says is, "Went out. Be back soon."

"Strange," I murmur. "When did you see her last?"

She shakes her head. "About... three hours ago, I think. I had to go help Amanda and Mrs. Dixon with something."

"With what?" I'm not sure it matters, but I ask anyway.

"Miss Zabrina's room was a mess," she explains. "They asked me to help pick it up. She'd thrown all of her gowns on the floor and wanted them rehung." She looks exasperated. I can feel that in my bones.

Nodding, I say, "Where are the guards?"

"That's the other thing," Poppy says. "They weren't here when I got back. I went to ask Beta Seth about it, about an hour ago, but he said he was too busy to help me. I tried to tell him I was worried about Isla, but he said she'd be fine."

"So... did you tell him you couldn't find her?" I ask.

She shakes her head. "I tried. But he wouldn't listen. Can you try the mind-link? Since you're the king, she'll have to let you into her mind."

Poppy was right—Isla could ignore anyone else's mind-link requests from her own pack, but not mine. I tried sending her a message. "Isla? Isla?" There was no response. That meant she had to be too far away from me to hear me. But how was that possible? Could she be that far away from the castle? No....

Unless she was asleep.

"Did you reach her?" Poppy asks.

"No," I tell her, trying to think of an alternative. "All right," I say, taking in a deep breath and blowing it out. "What did Isla do today?"

"We went to the village. We went shopping, and she bought you a gift, but I don't see that either. And then we came back here, and we sat around for a bit before I went to help Amanda, and she stayed here."

I ran a hand through my hair. None of this made any sense.

Was it possible that Isla thought that I'd be back already, so she went to my room to give me the gift?

I didn't know, but I was willing to go over there and find out. "Let me go check my room," I tell her. Perhaps she'd gone in there and fallen asleep. That would explain the lack of mind-link.

"I did that," she says, and I narrow my gaze at her. "I mean, I went and knocked on the door, but it's locked, and no one who has a key would check for me. And Mrs. Dixon was busy."

"Mrs. Dixon?" I repeated. "She shouldn't have a key to my room. Only my head maid, Agatha, my butler, Mr. Thompson, and Beta Seth have a key to my room." Mrs. Dixon is new to her post. Perhaps one day, I will give her a key, but not now.

"Right," Poppy says, and she makes a face that tells me there's something I don't know. But I'm not asking right now.

I head to my room, aware that I don't have a key with me either. I don't usually lock my door anyway, but if I'd taken one with me that morning, it was in the clothes I'd left behind at the car.

"Seth, meet me at my room," I tell him. I can practically hear him sighing in my head.

I go there, Poppy on my heels, and knock on the door, hoping that Isla will answer.

She doesn't.

A few moments later, Seth is there. "Yes, sir?" he asks in an annoyed tone.

"The key?" I say.

"It's locked?" Seth is confused.

"No. I just enjoy standing in the hallway staring at my chamber door," I explain, not able to help the sarcasm.

Seth fusses at me but then pulls the key out of his pocket. His keychain is massive, much like the one I'm supposed to carry around is. He unlocks the door, and I step inside. I do wonder if anyone has messed with my own special key, but that's back at the car on my keychain.

So whatever I saw this morning couldn't have possibly been due to someone sneaking in here before it was locked.

I walk inside, and it's clear that Isla isn't here.

"Can I go?" Seth asks.

I turn and glare at him. "No."

Looking around the room, I see nothing amiss. The room is perfectly tidied as it always is.

It's Poppy who makes the discovery, the squeal from her throat alerting me that something is the matter.

Walking over to where she is standing, by my nightstand, I look down.

A piece of paper sits on the little table. I can tell at first glance that it is the same color as the paper that Poppy had found in Isla's room.

With a deep breath, I pick it up and begin to read.

"Dear Maddox,

I am so sorry, but I had to go. I didn't think it was fair of my family to demand me to continue to stay here after they'd been paid by my Alpha, as I'm sure they have been by now. Since they care nothing about me and the fact that you are raping me on a nightly basis, I have decided to go. Don't try to find me. I don't love you. I think you are awful. Every word I've ever said that you might've taken as affectionate is a lie. I am not your property anymore as I have found my true fated mate, Private Parker, and the two of us have taken off together.

Isla."

I stare at the paper for a long time, reading it again before crumpling it and tossing it on the floor. None of it makes any sense! Raping her? Does she really feel that way? I sink down onto the bed. Had she just been waiting this whole time for me to leave so she could run?

"She couldn't have left this letter," Poppy says.

"Why not?" I can't even look up at her.

"Because… if she did, she'd still be in range of your mind-link, Alpha. She couldn't run fast enough in three hours to get over a hundred miles from here."

She had a point.

But then… something else occurred to me. "Unless she was in a vehicle."

"A vehicle?" Seth asks. "No, she wouldn't have access to a vehicle."

"Maybe they stole it," I say. "Maybe Private Parker is good at hot-wiring engines."

"Private Parker?" Seth repeats. His narrowed eyebrows come apart at about the same time I make another connection as well.

Standing up, I say, "We need to find Private Wylie."

THE BOAT IS COMING

Isla

THE SCENT of mildew overcame me as I struggle to stay sitting upright, my eyes straining in the dim light. I need to stay awake, but it's so hard, my head hurts so bad from the wolfsbane injected into my thigh earlier, but if I fall asleep, I may never wake up again, and then I have zero chance of ever getting out of here.

The stinging sensation from the chains around my wrists and ankles continues to bite into my flesh, a searing pain that refuses to dull, even though I'm pretty sure the silver has already eaten through my flesh. I know that Zabrina and her henchmen were hoping that I would just lay down here and die, but I can't do that—I won't.

The vision of King Maddox's face keeps flashing before my eyes. He's got to be back at the castle by now doesn't he? I know that Zabrina concocted a plan to make it seem like I'd run away, but I am praying he'll see through it. He's an intelligent man—he won't believe that, will he?

I'd like to think that Zabrina is a fool, that her plan has to fall apart, but when she stood at the bottom of the stairs, staring at my pitiful form hunched over in pain in the corner, she sounded convincing. She had it all worked out….

"The notes will convince them that the two of you left together, that you were in love, and I'll be there when he falls apart to help mend his wounded soul!" She'd laughed hysterically, one hand on her hip. Her driver, some man from her pack, had been at the top of the stairs, a nervous look on his face. Private Wylie, who was also from her pack, I'd learned, stood behind her, also laughing, his hand on Zabrina's shoulder. I knew the two of them were sleeping together now, but what he didn't realize was that she was just using him. Did he think that she just wanted Maddox for his name and title but that she really loved him? If so, Private Wylie was the biggest fool of them all.

They'd left a few hours ago, before the sun went down, leaving us here, in the cellar of an old abandoned house too far away from the palace for Maddox to use the mind-link to reach me—unless he happened to start searching in this direction. By then, I will probably be dead.

How long did it take wolfsbane to completely kill a shifter? I suppose it depends on how much one has been given. I heard the two of them standing at the top of the stairs debating about how much to give me so that I'd stay awake and feel the torture from the silver chains that were preventing me from shifting.

At least Private Wylie had had the decency to knock Private Parker out. I felt worse for him than I did myself. He'd looked so scared when they'd hauled him out of the trunk of the car, bound and gagged already. I didn't understand how they'd managed to get away with this. Were there no security cameras at the castle? I knew there was one on the gate leaving the palace because I'd seen it when we drove by.

But… that didn't mean that Maddox would put all of the clues together in enough time to find me and rescue me. Even if he reached me by mind-link, I wouldn't be able to tell him where we were. They'd blindfolded me pretty quickly once the car went through the gate so I wouldn't be able to help direct anyone to our location… if I am alive long enough for someone from my pack or King Maddox to get within mind-linking distance of me.

It is hard to believe everyone who might be looking for me is over a hundred miles away.

And Private Parker is breathing very slowly. His face is pale… I'm not sure how much time he has left.

It's no surprise that Zabrina so willingly sacrificed him. On the way here, she bragged about slicing that poor maid's throat. "It's not that hard, really," she said. "It's too bad I can't do the same to you. I'd love to watch your blood coat my palms the way hers did." Then she'd laughed, and Private Wylie had laughed, too.

My head is swimming. I lean back against the cold concrete, trying to concentrate on keeping air in my lungs. The stinging is enough to keep me awake for now, but it won't last forever.

I think of my mother. She will have no idea what happened to me. She'll be so upset. I can see her crying, on her knees, praying to the Moon Goddess that I'm found. My dad will comfort her, tears in his eyes as he tries to be brave.

And then there are my siblings. My brothers... Ben. He will miss me the most. My sweet brother who has already had such a hard life. I hope they have the money forgiven now so that they can afford any other procedures he needs. So that my mom doesn't have to worry about how she'll afford to make dinner every night.

Poppy is either fuming at me for pulling this stunt, or she's searching frantically for me, trying to convince the others that I wouldn't do something like this.

But most of all, my mind wanders to Maddox. Will he care that I'm not there? I would like to think he will care, but he probably won't give it too much thought, except, perhaps, for the loss of money. What if he goes to Alpha Ernest and says the deal is off? Alpha Ernest will demand my parents repay their debt as well.

Maddox... the thought of him has me longing for his touch. He wouldn't hesitate to break the silver chains from my body, though they would burn his flesh as well. He would scoop me into his arms and take me to the infirmary, have the pack healer administer the antidote to wolfsbane, something only invented in the last few decades. How many people died from this horrible plant being injected into them before that was created? Too many to count.

We read about it in school, how it causes the body to shut down. Slows breathing, heart rate, and then... thought. Next, a person's vital organs begin to shut down, and then... death.

The Moon Goddess might be preparing a place for me right now, and Private Parker as well. I think they gave him too much.

"Maddox?" I cry out with my mind. "If you can hear me, I didn't leave you. I was taken from you. I'm in a basement somewhere... far away. Please... look for me... find me... for Private Parker's sake."

My mind goes hazy again, and I am no longer in the basement. I'm on the beach. I see my sisters and my father ahead of me, waiting at the dock, and I am holding my mother's hand. It's nighttime or early morning. It's dark, and my mother says, "We must be quiet, Isla. If they hear us... we could be in trouble." In the distance, I see the boat coming in. It's tiny. That boat will take us all the way across the sea? But it's so small... just like me.

"Isla," I mutter under my breath, jarring myself awake. Isla... like the islands... where I was born. We don't speak of it. Thoughts of our former home make my parents too sad. They miss it. They miss our old house, our old friends, our old life. I don't remember any of it.

I was only two.... I didn't even know I remembered the beach and the boat.

But I do remember.

Maybe before I die, I will remember more, like what our life was like back there in our homeland before we came to Willow pack, but by then… it won't matter. I will remember for a few minutes before I die.

"Maddox!" I try again. "Please, if you can hear me, I'm sorry. I think… I think I could've loved you. I think… I think I might now. I never would've left you. Tell my mother I love her. And my dad. And my brothers. Ben…."

My head lolls to the side again. I jerk back upright, trying to stay awake, and it makes the chains move, finding new flesh to eat away. I grimace as I hear my flesh begin to sizzle. I try not to move again so that it doesn't bake my flesh further, but it's hard.

The scent of urine stings my nostrils, and I look across the room. A puddle of liquid is forming beneath Private Parker. His kidneys, his bladder, they've failed him. I can see he's breathing but only slightly.

It won't be long now.

I look at the stairs. I wish I could climb them, but I tried to stand up a few times when I heard the car drive away, and I wasn't strong enough, not to mention my ankles are chained to my wrists. No, I couldn't get away then when I was stronger, so I don't think I can now.

I'd even tried screaming aloud, but no one had come, and now, I can barely mumble. Zabrina had told me that we were in the middle of the woods with no other houses around, that she'd picked this place out specifically for me to die in. "Welcome to your coffin," she'd said. "But we'll come back and bury your corpse in a week or so, just in case someone comes across you. We don't want Maddox to know you didn't run away to marry your true love!" That had been so hilarious to her. Private Wylie had laughed, too.

Now, she is probably back at the castle, telling Maddox she's sorry I left him….

"Maddox…."

I am on the beach. My mother's hand is soft in mine. In the distance behind me, I hear howling.

"They're coming, Daniel!" she says, and my dad turns his head only slightly before he assures her that the boat is almost there.

"The boat is almost here." Did I say that aloud or only in my mind? "Maddox… the boat is almost here…." I am falling asleep, and this time, even the pain in my wrists doesn't make me jerk upright. "The boat is almost here… Maddox…."

I am standing on the beach, holding my mom's hand, watching the starlight twinkle in the water as the boat pulls up to the dock. We move forward. "It's okay, Isla. We'll be safe now."

"We'll be safe now." My mouth doesn't move. "I'll be safe now…." I step off the sand, onto the dock, but my feet don't hit the wooden planks. I am floating now, floating away….

"Isla!!"

JUST THREE WORDS

Maddox

"Find everyone in the castle who is from Willow pack, now!" I shout at Beta Seth as I personally go to find Private Wylie. I have every one of my guards, the ones I trust, searching the castle, looking for clues as to where Isla might be. My mind is going crazy with the possibilities.

"What can I do, sir?" Poppy asks me.

I shake my head, wishing she hadn't chased after me, but here she is. "Go check with the guards at the gate and see if any vehicles left the property in the timeframe when Isla first went missing."

"Yes, sir, Alpha," she says and takes off.

Ironically, I find Private Wylie exactly where I expect him to be… in front of Isla's door. But something is off. I can tell by the way he is looking at me. He seems a bit disheveled as well. "Private," I say, trying to keep my cool. For now.

"Yes, Alpha?" he says, his chin jutting out.

"Where is Private Parker?" I look to the vacant spot next to him.

"I don't know, sir. I left my post to another guard and just got back on duty. I assume that Private Parker also went off duty, but he was still here when I left, a few hours ago."

I study his face before I begin shaking my head. "You do know there are cameras everywhere in this castle, right?" That's true, but most of them don't actually record anything, and rarely are they monitored. Nevertheless, I point to a spot in the distance where a red light is flashing.

"Yes, sir," he says. "Though... I thought... doesn't that basically loop and not record anything?"

Again, I study him, seeing perspiration dot his forehead. "Why would you say that, Wylie?"

"Oh, uh... I was just thinking... we should install better cameras. That's all." He shifts on his feet.

"Well, the one on the gate works and will let me know if anyone has left the premises in a car recently. Also, Poppy knows you weren't here for many hours and that no one replaced you."

"Poppy?" he echoes, and I nod. "She wasn't here, sir. She was off helping some other maid. If she told you I wasn't here, she was lying."

I take a step closer to him. "Stop fucking around with me, Wylie," I say. "One of your confidants has already squealed. So... unless you wanna take the fall for this, tell me where the fuck Isla is, right now!"

He swallows so hard, I think he might choke on his own Adam's apple. "Sir... I don't know what—"

"Sir, Zabrina won't let me in her room," Beta Seth says in my head. "She says it's not necessary, and I don't need to go in."

"Force your way in," I tell him.

Back to Wylie, I narrow my gaze and grab his collar. "Zabrina doesn't have feelings for you, you know?" I am taking a gamble here. I see in the way his pupils dilate that I am on to something.

"Wh-who?" he stammers, and I cram him up against the door. "Listen, shithead, I'm not going to stand around and wait for you to decide to tell me what you know when Isla could be in danger!"

"Fine!" he shouts. "Parker told me not to say anything... but he left. With her. Earlier. They've been having an affair. He's snuck into her room several times!"

"That's bullshit!" I hit the wall hard, and my fist goes through the drywall, leaving a hole. I pull it out, bleeding, ignoring the pain that radiates up to my elbow. "Do you want that to be your fucking skull?"

"Sir, there's nothing here. We've searched every room in the castle, and we can't find anything that will give us a clue as to where she might be." Seth sounds a bit frantic.

I feel that in my soul. "Every room?" I ask him.

"Yes, every room, sir," he repeats. "Well, all but one...."

Rebecca's room. It's locked. No one has the key except for me and that key is back in the pocket of the pants I discarded when I left the car.

I'm getting nowhere with Wylie. Someone may need to torture him, but I don't have the time. I call one of my commanders who is nearby. "Commander Fife, take Wylie down to the dungeon and get him to tell me what he knows. He had motor oil on his hands this morning, right before my car broke down. He's not fooling me. Besides," I continue, staring at him, "Zabrina has already told me that he is involved in this mess."

"Yes, sir," my commander says, and I hope I can trust him. I thought I could trust Wylie up until a few minutes ago. In fact, when I saw that he wasn't there when I arrived at Isla's room the first time, I was even a little worried about him.

"No, wait!" Wylie shouts. "Please! I don't know anything!" but Fife is bigger than him and drags him away.

I need to get into Rebecca's room.

I head for the stairs that will take me up to it when Poppy tells me, "Sir! A car left here about four hours ago, and it hasn't returned, but some of the guards did notice three wolves coming in on the east side of the castle wall a bit later. They said they didn't recognize them but they didn't pose a threat, and they were assumed to be guests out for a run."

"Thank you, Poppy," I tell her. "Can you meet me at the Luna's room?" I don't know why I want her there, but she's the most trustworthy person I can think of, other than Seth, to help me find Isla.

"Of course, sir, but... do you mean Luna Rebecca's room?" She sounds as shocked as I was when I asked her to meet me there.

No one has been in there for years.

"That's right," I say. "I don't have the key, but I'll have to force my way in. It's the only room that hasn't been searched."

"No key?" she repeats.

"I left it in the car—"

She cuts me off. "Mrs. Dixon!" she shouts in my head.

I am taking the stairs two at a time, and I can't slow to go over this with her again. "Mrs. Dixon doesn't have a key to Rebecca's room. She just took over—"

"No! I know, Alpha, sir. It's just... Mrs. Dixon can pick any lock! And this afternoon, she was helping Isla and me get into her armoire. Mrs. Dixon made a comment about young ladies always needing for her to pick locks. What if she's opened that door before?"

I stop at the top of the stairs, frozen as I consider what that would mean. Has someone been infiltrating Rebeca's sacred space, against my commands?

"I'll find her," I say. Then, to Seth, I say, "Get Mrs. Dixon's fat ass up to Rebecca's room, right now, and tell her she'd better be ready to pick a fucking lock."

"Yes, Alpha." Seth sounds like he's got no clue what I'm talking about. I can't blame him.

I walk over to Rebecca's door. No one else is here. No one comes here. At least, they're not supposed to.

I walk to the door and take in a deep breath before I try the knob.

It's locked, just as it should be.

But that doesn't mean that it has been locked ever since the last time I walked out of it.

Standing there for what seems like hours, I stare at the door, listening to my own raspy breath. "Isla? Where are you?" I try again, but my mind can't reach her.

I have the forethought to tell the commander who lets me know that he's rounded up fourteen members of Willow pack from the staff that he needs to send them out running as fast as possible in fourteen different directions, reaching for Isla with their minds. They are her pack members. They might be able to find her with the mind-link.

"Sir?" Seth says behind me, making me jump.

I turn to see he has Mrs. Dixon with him. She is panting from climbing the stairs so quickly.

I step aside. "Open it."

She doesn't even begin to argue with me, only pulls a bobby pin out of her hair and shoves it into the lock. The door swings open almost effortlessly.

Before I go in, I ask her, "How many times have you opened that door recently?"

She swallows hard, her ruddy face turning redder. "Only three, sir, but the new Luna said that you had given her permission. She said she misplaced the key you gave her, and she didn't want to ask again."

"The new Luna?" I repeat, glaring at her.

"Y-yes… sir. Alpha Jordan's daughter. She's too mean for me to argue with."

I look at Seth, and before I even open my mouth, he turns to head back down the stairs.

"Stay here," I say to her.

Mrs. Dixon nods, and she looks like she might pass out.

I hear rushed footsteps coming up the stairs behind me and turn to see Poppy flying over to me. "Did you find anything?" she asks as she tries to catch her breath.

I haven't even looked in the room, so I don't answer her.

My eyes go to the window first, where I thought I'd seen Rebecca standing this morning. But it wasn't her. It wasn't my wife, the Luna.

The only Luna.

I walk inside and take a quick look around. It's quite clear that Zabrina has done nothing to try to hide the fact that she's been in here. All of Rebecca's items have been touched and moved. Her jewelry, her perfume, even her shoes. Rage boils up inside of me. How dare that fucking bitch touch my dead wife's belongings!

My eyes do not go to the bathroom. I have yet to see my wife's form in the castle since the night she died, but if I were going to see her, it would be in that bathroom.

Instead, I begin to open drawers, starting with the desk. Poppy does the same with the nightstand before moving to the dresser.

"Sir!"

I rush over. She has a paper in her hand, and her lips are quivering. "What is it?" I ask.

Poppy turns to look at me, her eyes wide, tears beginning to reach the brims. "It's a map—and a list."

I hold my breath and wait for her to show it to me.

Three words stand out to me as I take in the paper. "Silver chains."

And "wolfsbane."

THE TRUTH WILL NOT SET
YOU FREE

Maddox

BEFORE I SAY anything more to Poppy or Seth, who is standing in the doorway now, his hand grasping the wrist of the woman I believe is responsible for all of this, I tell the wolves I have sent out to look for Isla the address they should be running toward. Since they are all in wolf form, they will not have any sort of GPS, so I give them quick directions. What road they need to take, how to get to this cabin I see on the map marked as, "Secluded spot, perfect for death."

"What's going on?" Zabrina asks, trying to yank free of Beta Seth's grip, but he doesn't release her.

I need to hurry. I don't have time for her bullshit right now, not when Isla is in a cabin some two hours away, dying of poisoning from wolfsbane and being tortured by silver chains.

Still, I have to ask this bitch some questions because she may know information important to me finding Isla in time. Is she really at this location? Or is this another one of her fucking tricks?

"What is this?" I ask Zabrina, holding the map out in front of me.

"How the fuck am I supposed to know?" she replies. "I've never been in this room before."

"Liar!" Mrs. Dixon says, and Zabrina turns toward the woman in the hallway. "Who the hell are you, bitch?" she asks, but it's clear that she knows exactly who the woman is.

183

"Alpha, I let her in here three times. She said she was the Luna to be, and you gave her permission to enter. She said you didn't have a spare key yet!"

"She's a lying fat cow!" Zabrina says, looking at me again. "I've never been in here before, and I have no idea what that fucking map is! I've already told my father that you're harassing me! He has powerful friends, you know?"

My hand closes into a fist at my side. I want to slap the fuck out of her, but I don't. "Zabrina, I know you've been in here! You were in here earlier today!"

"No, I wasn't!" she argues. "I don't know what you're talking about!"

I take another step closer to her. "I saw you, Zabrina! How do you think I knew where to go?"

Her eyes enlarge, but then she blinks a few times, and says, "You're just trying to blame your whore running away on me. You didn't see me in here this morning. You have no idea who was in here."

I tilt my head to the side. "This morning?" I repeat.

"Yeah," she says. "You just told me you saw me in here this morning. But I was having breakfast with my entourage. They'll vouch for me! Even your own fucking maids saw me in the dining room."

I can't help the smile that creeps onto my face as once again I've caught her in a lie. It's surprising to me that someone so fucking stupid thinks she is such a mastermind. "Zabrina, I never said when it was I saw you in here. By telling me that you weren't in here this morning, you're only pointing more guilt at yourself."

Her eyes widen, and her mouth drops open for a second before she says, "Uh, you did, too, say that."

"No, he didn't, you stupid bitch!" Poppy chimes in. I give her a look, but she doesn't back down. "Fucking bitch!"

"Yes, you did!" Zabrina says. "Besides, even if you didn't, and I know you did, that's the only time you could've seen me because you've been gone all day!"

"How do you know that I didn't think I saw you when I came back home?" I ask her.

She shrugs. "Because… I wasn't in here then so you couldn't have."

I can only stare at her. She knows then that her idiocy has incriminated her.

Taking rapid steps toward her, I back her up as Seth stares her against the wall. "Now, you listen to me, and you listen good. If you want to keep your head on your shoulders, you're going to tell me right now where the fuck Isla is. Is she in this house?" I ask her, holding up the map.

"Y-yes," she stammers. "But it wasn't me. It was Private Wylie! He's a spy! He made me do it!" she says, her eyes wild as she realizes she can't get out of this now.

"And how much wolfsbane did you give her?" I ask.

She shakes her head. "I'm not sure. Quite a bit!"

Again, my hand is a fist. I have never wanted to punch a woman as desperately as I want to cram my fist into her stomach.

"Did you assholes mess with any of my other cars or just the one that broke down on me today? I swear to the Moon Goddess above, if I have car trouble going to find her, I will sever your head from your neck with my own bare hands!"

"Only the one!" she yells, and I know that Seth is already getting my car for me as I speak.

I don't think there's anything else I need from this bitch, so I say, "I need you to come with me, Seth. Call someone to meet us downstairs to take care of her."

"Yes, sir," he says, and we start moving out the door.

"Mrs. Dixon," I say, "come along. You're in trouble, too."

"Yes, Alpha." She is weeping, as she should be.

Poppy follows. "Do you want me to summon Mystic?" she asks me.

"Yes, please do." Our pack healer will need to come with us. "Make sure she brings the antidote, plenty of it. I assume Private Parker is with Isla?" I ask the woman Seth is dragging toward the stairs behind us.

"He is," she says. "But you'll be wasting supplies taking them with you for him. He's already dead."

I turn and look at her, wondering if I could make her trip and fall down the stairs and call it an accident—and a day.

Before we even reach the staircase, I see Alpha Jordan coming up, along with several of the guards he has brought with him. "What is the meaning of this?" he demands. "Unhand my daughter, this instant!"

"Your daughter has just confessed to being a coconspirator in the kidnapping of my Breeder and the murder of one of my guards!" I tell him.

"That's preposterous!" Alpha Jordan says, making himself as big as possible as he blocks my way. "My Zabrina would never!"

"She did," I tell him. "There's no need to try to lie for someone who's already confessed!"

"Daddy!" she says, beginning to sob, "Private Wylie forced me to! He said he'd rape me if I didn't go along with it!"

"You hear that?" Alpha Jordan says. "My daughter is the victim here!"

"Get the fuck out of my way," I warn him. I'm not afraid of him or the three guards he has with him.

"You can't seriously think—"

Alpha Jordan's words are cut short when my fist meets his jaw and knocks him backward. He stumbles into his guards, and then the four of them fall down the stairs, landing in a heap on the first landing.

Shaking my hand out, I ignore Zabrina's shouts, not of, "Daddy are you okay?" but of "Daddy, get up and save me!"

We step over them, and then I make my descent as quickly as possible, headed for the garage. Commander Weston is there to take Zabrina away, along with a few of my guards. "Lock her up, and make sure that you don't leave her, Weston. I trust you not to give in to her beguiling ways, but no one else!"

"Yes, sir," the middle-aged, happily married commander says to me, and I hear Alpha Jordan's voice booming behind me, threatening that this means war.

I don't care at the moment. He can call in all of his allies, I'll call mine, and we'll rip each other's throats out on the battlefield. But that's for another day. For now, I need to get to Isla.

"He doesn't leave," I tell Weston, and he nods in understanding. More of my guards are already streaming down the hall toward the scene.

We make our way to the garage door, and I see Mystica standing there, a concerned look on her face. She is old enough to be my mother, and sometimes, she acts like she is. "I'm so sorry, Alpha," she says in her soothing voice.

"No need for that, yet," I assure her, and Seth and I head out the door with her.

We are about fifteen yards away from the garage, a large building near the south side of the castle, when I realize Poppy is with us. I turn and look at her, and she says, "You need me."

I have no response to that, so I keep walking.

"Where do you think the car they drove out there is?" Seth asks me.

"They probably ditched it, thinking it would be easier to sneak back in as wolves." We move to an SUV near the back of the garage, one I am fairly certain no one will have messed with. I grab the keys off the hook near it and toss them to Seth. I'm in no state to drive.

Climbing into the passenger seat, I wait for him to start the vehicle and then punch the address into the GPS.

"You will arrive in two hours and twenty-seven minutes," the robotic female voice tells us.

"The fuck we will," I say. "Seth… drive like your life depends on it."

My Beta doesn't need to be told twice. He peels out of the garage and tears down the road driving so fast, the guards barely have a chance to get the gate fully open even though I'm certain he's warned them that they need to open up.

As we drive through the night, I can't help but send messages to Isla, even though I know she can't hear me yet. We aren't close enough at the moment. But with Seth driving twice the speed limit, pushing the car, and the road, to their limits, we will be there soon enough.

"I'm coming, baby," I tell her using a mind-link that is currently useless. "I'm coming, baby, and I'll be there soon. Hold on, Isla. Please. I know it hurts, but hold on. I'm bringing help. I'll be there soon!"

I keep repeating that over and over and over again. Soon enough, the GPS ticks off that we have ninety-nine miles to go.

"Isla," I say, "can you hear me, baby?"

In my head, I hear a weak voice say, "Maddox… the boat's here…. I'll be safe now."

I have no idea what that means, but it makes my blood run cold. All I can do is scream, "Isla!!"

WHY DID SHE TRY TO KILL ME?

Isla

"WHERE ARE WE GOING?"

I ask the person who is grasping my hand now, but there's no answer. It's not my mother. I know that much. The grip is tight and painful, and Mom would never hold onto my hand so tightly.

In response, I hear a voice that sounds like it's coming from beneath the waves say, "You have to stay with me, Isla."

"But why?" I ask. Glancing down, I see that my feet are not on the ground anymore. When I stepped onto the wood of the dock, going out onto the boat, my feet never made contact with the ground again, and now, I am floating away, up into the sky.

The only thing that seems to be tethering me to the ground is this person whose face I cannot see, whose grip is so strong, I can't break away from it.

"Because... you must," is all the person says.

I can't tell if it is a male or a female, young or old, or even where the voice is originating from. I can't see them at all. When I try to look down to see the grasp on my arm, all I can see is a band of silver that reminds me of a snake.

Silver—is that why it hurts so badly?

Why does it hurt so badly?

I'm only walking to the boat with my parents. We are leaving our home-land behind because of the war. My father doesn't want to go, but he knows it will no longer be safe for us there—my sisters, my mother... and most especially him. I remember now, the conversation he had with my mother just the other night. I am too small for him to know I am eavesdropping. My parents often think that because I am only three, I cannot comprehend what they're speaking about.

But I remember now.

"Constance, if we stay, they will most definitely break through the defenses any day now, and we will be killed. I can't take that risk, not with the girls. You know I don't want to abandon the pack, but what choice do I have? All of our allies have already been killed or imprisoned."

"I understand that, Daniel, I do." My mom is crying. It's hard to understand her through the tears. "I want the girls to be safe, too, I just feel like maybe I should stay behind. If anyone can speak reason to Tony, it's me. He's my cousin, after all."

"No, Constance. The girls need you. We should've known better than to listen to his advice. Ever since your father died, he's been scheming. It doesn't matter now. The decision has been made. I only wish we could've prevented this war from ever happening. If I'd gone when the hostilities first started, tens of thousands of innocent lives would've been spared."

"Daniel, don't talk that way!" My mother seems more angry than sad now as she shouts at my dad, and I think she is mad at him. But she's not really, is she? She's mad at Tony—Uncle Tony, that's what we used to call him, but not anymore. Not since he got mean.

"Constance, it's true," my father says. "I should've let him have it to begin with. I'm not fit for this sort of work. I don't even know how I became your mate."

"You're my mate by the Moon Goddess's divine power!" My mother sounds angry at my father now, not just in general. "Your grandfather was a mighty—"

My father cuts her off. "I know who my grandfather was! But that was ages ago, and he gave that up for my grandmother. You know that."

"I do know that," my mom says. "Which is how you got to be here... so I could fall in love with you."

"So I could be the cause of a war that's destroying our pack." Now, my father sounds sad. I want to run to him and hug him tight, but they don't know I'm listening in.

"It'll be all right," Mom says. "We'll start over where no one knows who we are. I've heard that the Alpha King of Crescent Falls is very welcoming."

"Yes, but he's also quite old and not liable to be king much longer. If his son finds out who we are, he may banish us back here."

"Well, then, we'll have to find a pack that is small and unassuming, far away from the castle, where we can blend in. We'll get normal jobs and be normal people."

"But what about the girls?" my dad asks. "I know that Isla's too young to remember any of this, but Kenna and Brandy will remember. They will know the truth."

"We will make them understand that they can't tell anyone," Mom says.

"What are the chances of that?" My father sounds cynical. "Two growing girls, not ever going to tell anyone, not even their best friends, that their father was once—"

"Isla!!"

I feel a sharp pain in my wrist and my eyes fly open. I stare at several faces, but I have no idea who any of these people are or what I'm doing here.

I'm lying on a cold, damp concrete floor, darkness all around except for the light from one swaying, naked bulb above their heads. The man leaning over me has blond hair and brown eyes. He's shirtless, mostly naked except for a pair of old shorts, and he looks concerned.

Next to him is a woman I don't know who is also nearly naked. She is holding a rag against my arm. Her red hair is messy, and her eyes are wide with fear.

"Are you awake?" she whispers.

I nod. "Y-yes." My voice sounds foreign to me. "Wh-where am I?" I try to sit up, but she gently pushes me back down, and then I realize that there is another man at my feet, and he is doing something with a tool of some sort.

"This is going to hurt a bit," he says, and then I feel the same sharp, burning sensation in both of my ankles for a moment before it dissipates.

"There," he says, "I got them."

"We need the antidote," the woman says. "She's going to end up like the other one without it."

"He's ten minutes out," the blond man says. The other man has dark hair, and he is now holding something against both of my ankles. It's soft, but it doesn't make the lingering stinging pain go away.

"Who are you?" I whisper, or at least, I try to. I'm not sure all of the words come out right. I'm starting to fade away again, my head swimming. For a moment, I think I see a boat across the room, bobbing up and down on imaginary waves. I'm starting to fade away.

"We're friends," the woman says. "We are members of Willow pack. We got here as quickly as we could."

"We ran for hours," the dark-haired man at my feet says. "Don't worry. Mystica will be here in a few minutes."

All I can force out is, "Wh-who?"

"She probably hasn't met her yet," the woman says. "She's only been at the castle a few weeks."

"Wouldn't she go there first? She's a Breeder, isn't she?" the dark-haired man says.

"Maybe he hasn't… done anything," the woman reasons.

"My name is Greg," the blond says. "This is Holly, and that's Rob. We work at the castle. Mystica is our royal healer. She's on her way."

I relax a little since I can see now that these people are here to help me.

But I don't remember why I need helping.

"Wh-what happened to me?" My voice doesn't sound stronger now that I am more aware. It sounds weaker than ever.

"You were kidnapped," Holly explains to me. "Given wolfsbane and bound with silver chains. Mystica has the antidote to the wolfsbane, just keep breathing. We'll get it in you."

"Kidnapped?" I repeat. Why would anyone want to kidnap me? I am nothing. I am….

Wait—that's not true! I know who I am now. I just heard my parents talking about it, only a few moments ago.

But then… that can't be right. I'm not three anymore. I am a full-grown woman. I'm twenty years old.

So… that must've just been a dream….

And yet, I remember it all like it just happened in real life.

"I'm going to go up and watch for the car," Greg says. "Use the mind-link if you need me."

"All right," Holly tells him, and she watches him leave before she returns her attention to me. I try to smile at her, but I can't keep looking at her. My head lulls to the side, and I fight to keep my eyes open.

Then… I see him.

Lying on the ground about five feet from me, still chained, still unconscious. I try to sit up again as shock hits my system. "Parker!" It takes all of my strength to say his name.

"I'm sorry, honey." I feel the brush of Holly's hand along my forehead as she pushes my hair back. "We didn't make it in time for him."

"Dead?" I can only ask my question with one word.

"I'm afraid so. Were you friends?"

"No," I say. "But… he died for me." I remember going to the market that morning with Parker.

And… Poppy… and….

"Wylie."

"Who?" Rob asks.

"The other guard," Holly tells him. "The one they locked up."

I want to tell them that Zabrina had a hand in this, too, but I can't say all of that, and the mind-link will not work because I am too tired.

"He's here!" Rob and Holly both say at the same time, and I suppose they've gotten a mind-link message from Greg.

But I thought we were waiting on a woman. Mystica. The healer.

So when they say "he" is here... who do they mean?

I close my eyes. They are too heavy. I can't keep looking at Parker's body anyway. I know he is dead because of me. Because of who I am.

But it doesn't make any sense.

How did they find out?

No one knows who he is.... No one knows that my dad is the—

"Isla? Oh, thank the Goddess!"

I look up into the most handsome face I've ever seen, and everything comes back to me. That's why they want me. It has nothing to do with my parents. It has to do with him!

"Maddox!" It's all I get out before everything goes black.

I am not on the dock anymore. I am floating above it.

In an inky black sky full of stars, and in front of me, I see the full moon.

In front of the moon, is a beautiful woman with long flowing golden locks, floating along with me, her arms outstretched as she beckons me.

"Isla, come home!"

I go to her.

ISLA ISN'T BREATHING

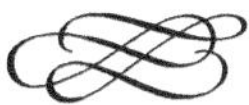

Maddox

"Isla!" I shout as I see her lying on the floor, her eyelashes flickering like a butterfly's wings as her eyes roll back in her head. Mystica finally catches up to me, her middle-aged legs not quite as quick as mine, and I see she has a shot in her hand, ready to inject it into Isla's body.

Rob, Holly, and Greg, three of the wolves I sent out from the castle ahead of me, are kneeling by Isla's body, and I can tell by their expressions that they are concerned.

"What's happening?" I ask, not caring who answers. I stay back out of the way as Mystica forces her way in between them to get access, and the others, still a bit dazed it seems, back away.

"Is she breathing?" The question comes out of my mouth before anyone has even gotten a chance to answer my last one.

"Not at the moment," Mystica says.

"She was talking a moment ago!" Holly sounds panicked as she looks at Isla's face. Her skin is turning a bit blue, and I have to wonder if that's the lack of oxygen or the wolfsbane.

I fully expect Mystica to inject the antidote into Isla's arm or thigh, maybe her buttocks, but she doesn't. Instead, she pulls her top down slightly and injects it into her chest, right over her heart, pushing the needle in as far as she can before she deploys the plunger.

I remind myself that Isla can't feel it at the moment, not if she's... not breathing.

"Please," I say, looking up at the crumbling basement ceiling as if I might catch a glimpse of the Moon Goddess herself. "Please, don't take her, too." I can't bear to think of losing another woman who means so much to me.

Isla is not my wife. She is not the love of my life, my mate, like Rebecca was. At least, she isn't yet. But I do know that sometimes the Moon Goddess is kind enough to bestow a second mate on those of us who are not lucky enough to grow old with the first, and I have wondered over the last few days if the reason I have been so drawn to this beautiful young woman is because she is my second mate.

She might not know it yet because she is so young, or she might not know it because I am the king, and she could mistake her own fascination with someone of my status with the mate bond.

But as I stare at her, tears beginning to form in my eyes, I can't help but wonder if we could grow old together.

Could we marry, have children, raise a family, rule together, and then die within a few months of one another at a ripe old age?

She's not royalty. Many of the Alphas would have a fit if I were to marry her, a commoner. My breeder. She does not carry the blood of an Alpha or a king, but she is an amazing person from good stock, and that is enough for me to want to make an heir with her.

So... why shouldn't it be enough for her to sit next to me on the throne?

At the moment, none of that matters, though, because she is not breathing.

Mystica is doing something I've never seen before, pounding on Isla's chest. "What are you doing?" I ask the healer.

"Pumping her heart for her," she says. "Trying to get the antidote to circulate." Mystica is older and not that strong.

"Can I help?" I should be able to pump her heart more efficiently.

"Yes," she says, and I drop down, Rob scooting away. She shows me how to position my hands and then tells me, "You might break her ribs if you're not careful. Pump her heart, but don't crush her."

At the moment, I have to think it is more important to pump than to try not to break a bone, but I will attempt to do one without the other.

I stare at her face as I continue to pump, praying she will open her eyes, but she doesn't, and I cannot feel the warmth of her breath on my hands near her face. I cannot hear her heart beating, but I can hear the swoosh of blood as I force it through.

I can smell her, though. I can smell that sweet scent I always smell when I'm around her, vanilla, flowers, all things happy and joyous. I can also smell perspiration—the scent of fear.

What has happened to her makes me so angry, I want to crush something but I refrain because Isla's body is the only thing I can crush at this moment, and that would make me as bad as those bastards who put her in this position.

Zabrina, Private Wylie, their driver… who else was involved? Who would dare go behind my back and steal this precious soul from beneath my wing? Behind me lies the corpse of a man who had given his life to protect her. I hadn't known Private Parker long, but I knew he deserved a hero's funeral. His family would be greatly compensated for what he had done for Isla, or what he had tried to do anyway.

"Sir, it doesn't seem to be working," Beta Seth says from across the room, back by the stairs. "Should we try something else?"

"Not yet," Mystica says. "Give her a few more minutes. It can still work."

"Is there anything else we can try?" Poppy is crying, and it is hard to understand her through her tears.

"No," Mystica says. "If this doesn't work, I'm afraid the Moon Goddess has beckoned the poor dear home."

I can't even think of that. I continue to pump. The longer I do so, the more I hear the people around me beginning to sob, the women particularly, though I think either Rob or Greg is also crying.

"Do you want me to try for a bit?" Seth asks. "So that you can rest?"

All I can do is shake my head.

"How long does it usually take?" Holly asks Mystica as she swipes at her nose.

"Usually a minute or so," the healer answers.

"How long has it been?" Greg's voice reveals he is the one that is crying.

"Four," Mystica says.

The chances that I can save her now are slim. I will keep trying, though. I will keep trying until my hands fall off or someone drags me away. I can't imagine getting up and leaving this place without Isla with me.

She'd called my name. I'd heard her say it right as I came into the room. Were we only seconds late?

No, I wouldn't accept it.

"Alpha?" Seth says again. "Perhaps—"

"No!" I shout at him. "I'm not quitting. Not yet."

As I continue to pump, I stare at her face. She's so beautiful. It's hard to believe that she's not here. It's unimaginable to think that this is just the shell of her, that the sweet soul I've fallen in love with over the last week or so is gone. No, it just… can't be.

"Isla," I whisper. "Please, come back to me. Open your eyes." She doesn't.

"Alpha, I think it's time," Seth says, and his hand is on my shoulder now.

"No," I say to him. "Go ahead and take care of Parker, but I'm not leaving. Not yet."

I see an exchange of glances between my Beta and the other men in the room. Greg and Rob both get up, still sniffling, and move to where Parker lay. They'll wrap him up in something, perhaps sheets from the old bed we passed on the way down here, and we'll take him back with us so that he can have that hero's burial that he deserves.

"Alpha, I've never seen one come back after this amount of time," Mystica says, her voice solemn. "I'm afraid we were too late."

I say nothing, only continue to pump the heart I am willing to restart on its own.

One by one, the others get up and leave, or at the very least, back toward the stairs where I can no longer see them.

Now, it is just me, and Isla, and the Moon Goddess who I am continuing to barter with. I list off for her all of the charities I will help, all the good deeds I will do. She says nothing.

And neither does Isla.

Is this really it? Am I going to have to leave here without her? I can't fathom it.

I lean down, my hands still working over her chest, and I press my lips to hers. They are still warm, but only just barely. I want to blow into her mouth, to give my breath to her. If I could, I would blow my own life into her body, let her live while I fade away. I know she'd be sad without me, but I would gladly give my life for her so that she could live.

She deserves that.

She deserves a long happy life with lots of love, and children, and laughter.

A tear slides down my cheek and lands on hers, near her mouth.

Finally, I break down. My head sags, and I drop it to her chest as wave after wave of bitter emotion overcomes me. I can't believe this is it, that the Moon Goddess would bring me such a beautiful, gentle creature if I could only have her for a few days. Rage boils up as I imagine what I will do to Zabrina and her insipid followers. I can't handle it. I want to rip them apart and then climb to the top of the castle and jump from the highest turret.

As my mind goes wild with all of the thoughts of things I'd like to do to those bastards, I begin to realize I'm hearing a new sound. It is faint at first, but I can hear it. At first, it is just a swoosh, swoosh, swoosh, along with a shallow rasp of air. I sit up and turn my head.

Isla's eyelashes are fluttering again!

"Isla!" I say. "Isla, sweetheart, can you hear me?"

I brush her hair back away from her face, and I can hear that her breathing is getting stronger, as is her heartbeat.

She's alive!

"Isla!" I shout as I hear footsteps on the stairs. "Isla, look at me!"

As if she can't refuse my command, her eyes open, and she looks directly into mine. I want to kiss her, to leap up into the air and sing the praises of the Moon Goddess, but I have to know first if she's okay.

"Are you all right, Isla?"

She stares at me for a long moment before she asks, "Wh-who are you?"

WHO YOU ARE

Isla

"Go back, Isla," the Moon Goddess says to me. "Go back."

"But I want to come with you," I argue as I continue to float toward her.

She shakes her golden curls and says, "It's not time yet. I brought you here only to remind you of two things, dear child. One, you are loved, and two… it is time that you remembered who you are."

I stare at her in confusion. My mind is foggy anyway. I can't remember how I came to be here, floating through the sky with her, and I can't remember where I'm meant to be.

So how am I supposed to remember who I am?

But she doesn't give me a chance to ask that question. She just says the same words to me again. "Go back, Isla. Go back."

I open my mouth to attempt another protest. The sky is full of stars—I am floating on air! It's all so perfect, and in my heart, I feel nothing but light and love.

But then… pain begins to set in. It starts as a dull ache in my limbs, but then it becomes a throbbing, biting sting that doesn't stop. Not only are my limbs set ablaze, but the inside of me also hurts as well, and when I try to suck in air, I feel like my lungs are coated in oil.

My eyes widen as I stare at the Moon Goddess, wanting to ask her what is happening to me, but she only smiles reassuringly. "Go back."

With her final words, I am launched backward through the air so quickly, the stars become beams of light, and the Moon Goddess fades from view so that I cannot even see her outline against the orb she's named for.

I slam back into my body, and all of the aches and pains I felt before are magnified a hundredfold. I can't even open my eyes, the pain is so all-consuming.

But I can breathe. I can feel my lungs moving up and down now. It's laborious, but it's happening, and then… a fuzzy light fills my line of sight from the top down, and I realize I've opened my eyes.

The world around me begins to come into view, but I can't really see anything. Only the form of a man who seems to be weeping from the sounds he is making.

All at once, he seems aware that I am breathing and that I am looking at him, and he reaches to touch my face. "Isla!" he shouts. "Are you all right, Isla?"

I can't see him. I can't make out who he is, but I know it's not my father or one of my brothers. His voice is familiar in a way, but I can't quite place him, and as I attempt to gather my thoughts, all I can think to say is, "Wh-who are you?"

It's not a question I expect him to answer because I am truly only trying to take inventory of myself, but when he says, "Isla, darling, it's me—Maddox," a rush of memories come back to me, and suddenly, tears have filled my eyes. I want to sit up. I want to press myself against his chest and for him to assure me this has all been nothing but a horrible dream, that we are safe back in his bed, or mine, and that none of what I've just remembered is real.

But I can see now. My eyes have adjusted to the dim bulb hanging overhead and the fuzziness brought on by the wolfsbane I remember being given now, and beyond Maddox's broad shoulders, I can see someone else.

"P-Parker," I manage to force out.

Maddox nods. "Yes, Parker didn't make it, baby. I'm so sorry."

My uncontrollable tears are forced into overdrive as I process what he's saying.

Private Parker died because Zabrina hates me.

It wasn't fair! He was completely innocent in all of this. I had done nothing wrong either, but at the very least, it should've been me who was dead.

Others are here now, standing behind Maddox, a couple of them holding sheets. I wonder, were they about to wrap one of them around me?

I remember them now, the two men and the woman who were with me before. They'd removed the silver chains from my wrists and ankles, but they couldn't stop the wolfsbane.

So how did Maddox stop it?

I try to sit up, and his arms reach around me, guiding me to sit, leaning against him. He pulls me to him, as I have longed for him to do since I realized who he is. "What happened?" I ask, but then, I think he might try to retell the entire story, and I am not interested in hearing how I got here. I can remember. "I mean, how did you save me?"

"Mystica brought the antidote," he whispers, and then he gestures to a woman standing near the stairs. She is older, with streaks of gray in her hair, but she looks kind, and I want to thank her, but my voice is so weak, I'm not sure she'll hear me from here.

"I'm so glad that it worked, child," she says. "How are you feeling?" She approaches, carrying a black bag, and kneels down on the floor next to me.

"Awful," I tell her. It's an understatement.

She nods. "You will continue to ache and have a fuzzy head until the wolfsbane completely leaves your system, but in a few days, you will feel better."

"Th-thank you." It's not enough, but it will have to do for now.

She pats my arm. "I am so glad we made it on time, dear."

Maddox lets go of me with one arm to reach out to her. Resting his large palm on her slender shoulder he says, "Mystica, I can never repay you for what you've done, but I will try."

She pats his hand. "Your Majesty, you have always taken care of me and mine. You know that. This is part of my job, a job I am honored to perform. Now, when you're ready, carry our sweet girl up the stairs, and let's go home."

She patted him again, as if he were her grandson, and then got up off the floor, her knee popping as she stood. One of the men from before rushed over to help her. I couldn't remember their names. I did see Beta Seth and the other one wrapping Private Parker in the sheets, using both of them for him now that I didn't need one.

I saw someone else as well. It was the quietest I'd ever seen her.

I smiled at Poppy, and she came over. "I'm so glad you're okay." She bent down and hugged me, sobbing, and then moved aside, as if she couldn't handle being so upset in front of everyone. I would have plenty of time to talk to her later, but there was someone else looking at me, someone I needed to speak to.

Behind Maddox, the woman who'd been with me before stood with tears in her eyes. I smiled at her and eked out, "Thank you."

She nodded. "I'm so glad you're all right, Your Highness."

I raised an eyebrow. "Oh, just Isla," I told her.

She shrugged. "After what I've seen tonight, I'm not so sure about that." She winked at King Maddox and then headed up the stairs.

Now that everyone was gone, Maddox and I were sitting alone in the basement, the place I'd been trying to free myself of for hours. I wanted nothing more than for him to lift me into his strong arms and carry me out.

But he didn't, not right away anyhow.

"Do you remember now, what happened?" he asks me.

"I remember. Private Wylie said there was an emergency and I had to leave the castle right away. I left with him, and when I got in the car, Zabrina was there. They had Private Parker in the trunk. I guess they needed him in order to formulate their lie," I say.

He nods. "That's right. And the driver? You would recognize him if you saw him?"

My head rocks back and forth "They called him Bernard."

"That's right," he says. "That's Alpha Jordan's driver's name." He sighs and shakes his head. "All right, at least you remember what happened to you. When you first opened your eyes, I thought...." His voice fades, and he looks off at nothing, his eyes staring at a spot on the concrete wall. "I thought you didn't remember me. It was terrifying."

"I couldn't see you," I tell him. I don't want to tell him the truth, that it took a moment for me to remember who he was. I didn't want to see his expression go back to the morose absence of light I'd seen a moment ago.

As his eyes focus on my face, I see his smile broaden. "I'm glad that's all it was. I don't know what I'd do if... if you couldn't remember me, Isla. When I thought you might not ever open yours again, it scared me to death." He holds me tighter, and I am at a loss for words again.

He is the king. He is the most powerful man in the world—my world, anyway—and he cares enough about me that I feel a tear slide down his cheek and land on my face.

He is said to be cruel, unkind, relentless, unmerciful, but when I am resting with my cheek pressed to his heart, all I hear is the sound of love thumping against his chest.

"Let's go home, darling," he says, and I think for the first time that the castle is my home, too.

He lifts me up as he stands, as if I weigh nothing, and I wrap my arms around his neck, burying my face in his shoulder. I don't want to see this place anymore. I don't want to smell the mildew or the stench of bodily fluid left behind when Private Parker lost his battle. I don't want to feel the fear or face the anguish that burrowed its way deep inside of me when I was lying on that cold concrete floor.

I don't ever want to experience this again, but I know I will.

I know it will sneak up on me when I least expect it, that I will be doing something completely normal, and the memory of this place will burst out of the shadows from nowhere and send me to my knees, trembling with fear.

Because that's how these sort of experiences creep into our minds and make us who we are, for better or worse.

And that's why, even though it's been sixteen years, I remember still the terror I felt that night with the wolves howling behind us as my family boarded that boat and left our homeland to come to Willow pack.

I hadn't thought about it in forever, but it's still in my head.

Now, I've just got to remember why we were running from the war.

Why did those other wolves want us dead?

Forcing myself to remember would be as painful as reliving what had just happened to me, but it was important for me to remember. The Moon Goddess had told me so.

"It's time that you remembered who you are."

WHAT HAPPENS NEXT?

Maddox

I sit in the backseat with Isla on the way back to the castle, holding her as close against me as the seatbelts will allow. She is exhausted and dozes off. Mystica, who is sitting on her other side, assures me that she's fine, she's just sleeping, but I worry anyway. Seeing her so still again makes my heart rate increase. The idea that she might not open her eyes again is terrifying.

My eyes focus out the window as I try to decide what to do when I get back to the castle. We clearly have enemies that need to be dealt with, but I also need to be careful.

Alpha Jordan is a powerful man. I knew that before he even arrived at the castle, but in the last few weeks since he's been there, the information I have received from my contacts in other regions have confirmed that he is influential to the Alphas who are already at odds with my plans for the kingdom.

While the outcry against me allegedly stem around the fact that I am not planning to produce an heir, that isn't their true problem with me, and now that I am in a position where an heir could be imminent, their fear has begun to take over. They've started to calculate moves against me that will reveal their true intentions—to take the kingdom from me by force.

What these rival Alphas fail to realize that there would only be room for one of them at the top of the food chain when this is all over, and that means that they will end up battling each other after they eliminate me.

Perhaps they'd rather duke it out amongst each other than accept the status quo. But I have to make sure I am in a position to fight them all off.

I should be. Assuming that the Alphas who have pledge their loyalty to me are true to their word, I should have greater numbers than they do. But the only way to know for sure is to test that loyalty, and that's something I've been hoping to avoid.

It will take an act of war.

In my opinion, what Zabrina has done qualifies as just that. Even if I don't think of Isla as the potential mother of the heir to the throne, someone who is protected by pack laws, Zabrina and her coconspirators have killed a royal guard. That by itself is reason enough for me to have her and everyone acting with her executed for treason. Whether or not her father is part of the plan remains to be seen, but he clearly supported her when I was trying to leave the castle and he stood up against me.

"What are we going to do when we get back?" Seth asks me, his voice quiet.

"We'll have to get to the bottom of who all is involved," I say, trying to also be quiet so as not to wake Isla. I could use the mind-link, but I am certain that Poppy wants to know the situation. She has been unusually quiet since Isla awoke, and though I normally wouldn't involve a housemaid in the affairs of the crown, she has proven herself loyal beyond question in the last few hours, and I appreciate anyone who is willing to go to so much trouble to show their support to me and the woman I love.

Love.

I never thought I'd say that word about anyone again, but when I saw her lying on that damp, dirty floor, there was no question in my mind that I love her. My heart couldn't ache uncontrollably the way that it did if I wasn't in love with her.

Now, have to decide what to do about it.

I vowed long ago that I would never take another Luna, and I am quite certain that the Moon Goddess heard those words. Up until now, she has honored my wishes and kept anyone and everyone within my reach of little interest to me.

But now, I have Isla, and even if she was just intended to be a Breeder, even if she hasn't got a drop of royal blood, or even Alpha blood, within her, I am drawn to her in a way only a moth that is hearing its own wings sizzle from the lick of the flames before it is consumed by the heat can understand.

Even though deciding I wanted her to be the mother of my child was a difficult decision, but once I allowed myself to be with her, the landslide set in, and I quickly found myself buried beyond all hope of resurrection.

At this point, I have no choice but to accept the fact that the promise I made myself after Rebecca died has to be broken. I can't live without Isla. The events of the last few hours have proven that, and while that doesn't mean I am ready to call her my queen, it does mean I have to take the time to reevaluate what this means for both of us and our potential child.

I feared proclaiming her my Luna for fear that she would be hurt, like Rebecca was, but we are beyond that now. We are in a situation where she has already almost lost her life because of my affection for her. So what could possibly be worse?

From now on, she will have a target on her back because of me, and if I were to attempt to return her to her family, I would still have to provide her with guards.

My mind reverts to images of Willow pack and how simple her life would be there compared to how it will be at the palace. Perhaps I should give the idea of taking her home more thought. I have removed Ernest from power, and I don't have another Alpha in place yet. But maybe she would be safer there.

Without the attention I bring.

Without me.

I will need to think this through. While it would be exceptionally painful for me to let her go, if it is what's best for her, wouldn't it be better for me to love her from afar?

Especially if she becomes pregnant with my child and we go to war.

No, I'm not sure I can protect her if she is with me, not when I'm unable to demonstrate with one hundred percent certainty who my friends are—and who my enemies are....

"Sir," Beta Seth says, "we'll be at the castle in five minutes. What would you have me do?"

He is looking at me in the rear view mirror, and I can see in his eyes that he regrets the part he played in this. While I do not blame him for what's happened, he was supposed to be keeping an eye on Isla while I was gone, and she was taken under his watch.

"I'll take Isla to her room," I tell him. "I want Commander Weston with her at all times. We need to get a report from Commander Taylor on the current situation in Duster, and I need an account of Green pack's activities as well." Those are the most solid threats I have outside of the situation in the castle.

"Yes, sir," he says. "And what would you have me do once I give those orders?"

"Accompany me to the prison to find out as much as possible from our guests," I say. It is a bit ironic that they were our guests at the castle until they betrayed me. Now, I suppose there's a different word that would fit them better. Captives, perhaps. Prisoners.

My plan is to carry Isla to her room myself. Then, once she is settled, and

I'm sure she is safe, I will report to the dungeon to oversee the collection of information.

We pull through the gate, and I am thankful to be home with this woman at my side, but I am also irritated. None of this should've ever happened. She should've been safe her. This is my home.

How in the world did something like this happen right beneath my nose?

I can't let myself dwell on how I should've been able to prevent it. All I can do now is focus on what I can do to make sure she is safe moving forward.

Seth pulls up to the external door that is closest to her room, and I get out of the car, careful not to let her slump over. I slide her into my arms, and she whispers, "Where are we?"

"We're back at the castle," I tell her, settling her against my chest. "You're safe, baby." I hope that she believes me. I'm not sure why she should feel safe here. This is the place she was kidnapped from, after all.

But she doesn't even open her eyes, just rests against me as I carry her inside and take her to her room.

She needs a shower and a change of clothes, but I don't think she can handle the former at the moment. Instead of taking her to the bathroom, I lay her in her bed, accepting Poppy's help to pull the blankets down. "Can you get her washed up a bit and changed?" I ask the maid.

"Of course, sir," Poppy says, her tone so different than her usual chipper self.

Mystica has come with us as well, and I see the pack healer checking Isla's vitals as Poppy prepares to do what I've asked. "Her heartbeat is stronger now," Mystica tells me. "I do think she will be just fine."

"Thank you," I tell the woman whom I rely on for so much.

I hear a knock on the door and go to see who it is, though I already know. It's Commander Weston.

I step out into the antechamber and see that he has five guards with him. I look into their eyes and see nothing but loyalty there. I know all of these people, three men and two women. They have worked for me for many years, and I trust them.

Perhaps that will end up being my downfall, but I have to be able to trust someone or else I will go mad.

"No one comes in here except for me or Seth, got it?" I say to Commander Weston.

He is older than me, almost old enough to be my father, and I see in his face that he completely understands. "Of course, sir," he says, as is expected of him.

I give him a nod of thanks and then head out the door, hoping that Isla is fine while I am away. Even as I take a few steps down the hallway, I feel an ache in my heart that compels me to go back to her. It seems stronger than any mate pull I've ever experienced, even when Rebecca lay dying in the bathroom.

I can't be with her at the moment, though. I have other matters to attend to. So I force myself to keep walking.

When I reach the dungeon, I see Seth there, speaking to Commander Fife. My Beta is shouting, his hands in fists, as he narrows in on the commander who is about our age but highly experienced and someone I trust.

Or someone I trusted up until the moment I see this interaction.

"What is it?" I ask Seth and Commander Fife as I reach them.

Seth shakes his head, his anger not allowing words to come out of his mouth.

"Seth?"

"They're gone," he tells me, looking into my eyes. "Both of them are gone."

REMEMBERING HOME

Isla

Poppy gently washes me down the best she can while I sit in my bed, my head still swimming. Mystica is here, too, but she's not washing my body. She's checking my vitals and insisting that I try to swallow down some broth, saying, "You'll feel better once you have some food in your stomach. It'll help dilute the wolfsbane."

Maybe she is right, but I can't seem to choke it down. I don't know how long I was lying there without breathing, but it seems like it must've been a while. It's like my body forgot how to do it, and now, with every breath I suck in, my lungs almost refuse to do anything with the oxygen, just letting it sit there and build, and build, and build until I feel like I might burst.

When Poppy is finished with all of her washing, she helps me into a night-gown. Mystica is kind enough to turn away, though, at the moment, I don't really care who sees me naked. I don't feel like this is my body anymore anyway, so it really doesn't matter who sees it.

Once I am changed, they slide me beneath the sheets, and Mystica continues to spoon-feed me broth and force water down my throat.

"Can you just put one of those things in her arm?" Poppy asks. "With the fluid and stuff?"

"We could use an IV," Mystica says with a shrug. "But I think she'd feel better if she just got it into her stomach directly.

Poppy is studying my face, like a mother hen watching over her eggs to see if they are really hatching or if it is a false alarm. Like she's not sure if I am really alive or not. But I am. I just need some time to remember how to be alive.

"Did you die?" Poppy finally asks me. She pulls a chair from the window closer to my bedside, and I know she has to be exhausted. She's been under a lot of stress. I want to thank her properly for helping to find me, but I can't talk that much right now.

Besides, I am still pondering her question.

Did I die?

"I don't know," I tell her. "Maybe a little."

"You can't die a little," Poppy says. "Can you?"

I'm not sure if she's asking me or Mystica, so I turn my head slightly to look at the older woman who is setting the spoon down to reach for my cup of water. It's ice-cold and should be refreshing, but my throat is as stubborn as my lungs and does not want to cooperate.

"Oh, I think you might be able to die a little," Mystica says. I finish with the water and she sets that aside to pick up the spoon out of the bowl of broth. "Over the years, I've treated a lot of patients who have been near death, especially back during the rebellion, about twenty years ago. That was a time when our kingdom saw a lot of death and destruction. So... yes, I think you maybe can die a little."

I didn't know much about the rebellions she spoke of. I hadn't been born yet—and apparently, I didn't live in the kingdom then either. My mind wandered back to what I'd seen when I'd been unconscious.

My family... a boat... water... howling wolves behind us.

"The rebellion against King Maximillian," Poppy said to Mystica. It wasn't a question, but the healer nodded. "I was just a little girl then, and I lived in a distant area of the kingdom."

Poppy was from Bridges pack. She'd mentioned it to me before. She lived in an area with lots of beautiful lakes and rivers—near Lake pack and River pack—but since those names were already taken by other packs, when her pack came into existence, they chose to name themselves after the construction projects they'd done around them. They were created from a group of hard workers who were tired of doing the work of others.

In those days, in order to become a pack, a group of people had to petition the king and pledge their allegiance to him first and then the new Alpha. Bridges pack had done that over a hundred and fifty years ago.

And some of the groups that were having trouble now in distant lands were having them because they wanted to form new packs, but Alpha Maddox wouldn't acknowledge them. He was faithful to the Alphas who had already been put in charge in those areas.

Most of them were loyal back, but I had heard rumors that a few were not.

That's what had happened when his father, King Maximillian was in charge. Packs had risen up against him because he didn't want to recognize new packs, and there'd been a huge war over it—the rebellion Mystica was talking about. I knew about it from the history books, not because I'd lived it.

But Mystica had.

"Did you see anything?" Poppy asked me. "When you were a little dead?"

I ran my tongue along my dry, swollen bottom lip. I wasn't sure why my entire body felt so swollen, but it probably had to do with the poison. My wrists and ankles had been slathered in ointment and bandaged. Mystica was taking care of me. The pain medication she'd given me was also helping a lot. But I was still so tired and out of it. I wasn't sure I wanted to try to answer Poppy's question.

I might sound like a crazy person.

Still, I didn't want to lie. "I saw a boat," I told her. "And an ocean."

Her eyebrows arched. "Did you recognize it?"

I nodded. "Yes. I believe it was the boat I got on to come here when I was a little girl."

"You came here by boat?" Mystica asks me.

"That's right," I tell her. "When I was three. We came to Willow pack, to start over."

"Why did you leave your homeland?" Poppy asks. We have never talked about this before. It has never been important to me before. I have spent almost all of my years in Willow pack lands, so I haven't really thought too much about my time before that.

"I don't remember exactly," I say, but the more I think about it, the more I remember the conversation that had taken place on the beach when I was little. I don't remember it from when it had initially happened; I remember it from when I was out of it because of the wolfsbane.

I sit up a little as I think about it, trying to draw the memories out. "My parents were scared," I tell them. "They were afraid that we might die."

"Die?" Poppy repeats. "From what?"

"From… enemies." I shake my head, trying to get the thoughts to make sense to me. All I'm seeing are flashes of my parents' faces, my sisters, the beach, the boat, the sky… the Moon Goddess.

But that part wasn't real, was it? I had imagined that. Because if I had actually seen the Moon Goddess, that would mean I really was dead for a bit, and I didn't think people could come back from that, no matter how much medicine they were given.

"What's the matter, dear?" Mystica asks me. She seems done trying to get the food down my throat. This time, when she reaches for the water bottle, she puts the entire bowl down and not just the spoon.

"I was just remembering… my uncle," I say. I hadn't thought about him in years, but I remember now that my parents were speaking of him while we were on the beach. We hadn't brought him with us. Why not? He had always been a part of my family….

"Your uncle? What about him? Is he dead? Did you see him while you were dead?" Poppy asks me.

"No," I tell her. "I didn't see him. I have no idea if he's dead or not. But, my parents were talking about him while we were on the beach, coming here. I saw the boat in the water, and I heard the wolves howling in the background. They were afraid we were going to be killed… because of my uncle."

It is all slowly coming back to me now.

"Why?" Poppy is clearly intrigued, like my life was a book or a play. "Why did they think you'd be killed because of him?"

I shake my head. "I don't remember the details. My mom said something about my grandfather making it so that my parents could be together, but they were afraid because of my uncle…. And then we got on the boat. We were on the water for a long time, then we arrived on land but had to walk for so long. My father and mother shifted, and us girls rode on their backs for a bit, but it was hard for us to keep hold of our bags that way…. Eventually, a nice man gave us a ride to Willow pack, and that's where we settled."

"Did you ever go back to visit your uncle?" Poppy asks me.

"No," I tell her. "We never even spoke of him again. In fact, we never spoke of home again." Other memories come to mind. "Except… a few times… my older sisters mentioned it, but my mom would always tell them they had to forget and pretend it never existed. Because we could never go back."

"Because there was a war?" Poppy asks.

I don't get a chance to answer her. Mystica stands and pats Poppy's knee. "I think our patient has spoken enough and needs to get her rest," she tells my maid—my friend.

But I want to keep pushing my memories. "I think there might've been a war," I tell her. "But I don't know for sure."

"And… where was this?" Poppy asks.

Mystica sighs. "You listen so well, child."

What is the name of the island I'd lived on? The kingdom I'd left behind?

"M… M…M—a? Matin? Matton? I can't remember."

I look over at Mystica to see her mouth hanging open just a bit. "You're from the islands?"

I nod. "Yes, but I can't remember which one."

She cleared her throat. "I am also from the islands. I fled many years before you were born, but that is why my name is Mystica, because where I come from, healers are revered for their closeness to the Moon Goddess. It is said that our people are directly descended from her, though I don't think that's true of all of us, but certainly the leaders."

"What island are you from?" Poppy asks.

Mystica doesn't answer her. Instead, she looks at me. "What is your last name, dear?"

I know that answer. "Moon," I tell her immediately.

She gasps and shakes her head. "No, honey, it's not. You're from Maatua, aren't you?"

I tip my head to the side and stare at her. "Maatua?" I repeat. It comes back to me now. "Yes, I am. That's how we say it in my language." I had once spoken another language?

"And your last name isn't really Moon, dear, is it?" she continues.

I swallow hard, letting her words soak in. Then, as the word comes to my mind, I shake my head and look into her eyes. "No, it isn't. It's... Masina."

"Masina means moon in Maatuatian," Mystica explains. "And you, dear, are a descendent of the Moon Goddess, Masina Atuafafine."

A DEADLY COMBINATION

Maddox

MY MOUTH DROPS open as I stare at my Beta, unable to comprehend what I've just heard.

"Gone?" I repeat. "What do you mean they're gone?"

With a loud sigh, Commander Fife says, "Sir, I'm so sorry. I stepped away for a few moments. Alpha Jordan was causing a ruckus. When I came back, my two soldiers whom I'd left in command were knocked out on the ground, and the keys were gone."

"But… how?" I don't even know how to ask the questions in my mind.

"It appeared that Zabrina must've lured them in close to her, and when they were standing next to her, she managed to knock their heads together hard enough to knock them out then took the keys." Commander Fife is a smart man, a logical man, and all of the words coming out of his mouth are laced with doubt.

How could anyone be that stupid?

I am having a hard time believing him. Once I've been betrayed by one member of my staff, I find it very hard to trust anyone else.

I look to Seth, probably trying to gauge his reaction since he's about the only one left in the castle I know I can trust for sure, other than Isla and Poppy. "Does that make sense to you, Beta?"

"Not really," he says. "After all, Zabrina is not that strong."

"She is beguiling, though," Commander Fife insists, swallowing hard, and I almost have to wonder if she hadn't pulled something over on him. Had she managed to trick this man I'd specifically chosen to put in charge to keep an eye on her because of his morals and dedication to his family?

I didn't have a lot of time to stand around and think about that at the moment. "I assume Wylie is missing as well?" I ask.

Fife's head rocks back and forth. "That's right. And Alpha Jordan and his wife escaped, too."

My eyebrows arch. "How is that possible? He is an elderly man who had just fallen down the stairs!"

"They were able to overpower the healers—the guards. Alpha Jordan's guards." Fife was sputtering now. "They all shifted and managed to escape through the windows. Their driver met them outside, or so it appears by the look of the video I saw from the perimeter. They hopped into a car and took off."

Running a hand through my hair, I mumbled, "Son of a bitch!"

"We can catch up to them," Seth suggested. "We can send alerts ahead of them so that any pack they cross through, the Alphas can be on the lookout. If they show back up in Maple pack, we'll have them arrested."

"I appreciate your enthusiasm," I tell my Beta. "But that won't happen. Short of us sending a military presence directly to Maple pack, Alpha Jordan won't be detained upon his arrival. He's too powerful, too influential among his own pack members."

"But you're the king!" Seth declares, as if I may have forgotten.

"I know, but they're more loyal to him than me," I tell him. It's not something I'm proud of, but it's true. Alpha Jordan has been their pack Alpha for many decades, and over that time, he has convinced his pack members that he is an indestructible leader and all of them are superior to nearly all of the other packs.

He has allies, though, and I can't forget that. He likely won't go home anyway. "We need to see if we can stop them before they get to Duster or Green pack," I tell Seth. "Send out messages ahead of them to all of the packs whose territories they'll have to cross through in order to escape. I want patrols on every major road stopping every car. I want our wolves in pursuit in vehicles and on foot. I want a line of defenders from Hailstone pack blockading the border into Maple pack, and more soldiers between us and Duster and Green, got it?"

Seth nods. "I understand, sir. I'm on it."

Turning to Fife, I say, "I want you to round up anyone who is left here from Maple pack. It sounds like not all of Zabrina's friends got out, maybe some of the guards? Find them." He nods, and I continue. "Is Mrs. Dixon still in her cell or did she manage to beguile the soldiers into letting her out as well?"

His face turns red. "She's in her cell, sir," he tells me.

I nod and head down the hallway toward where I assume Mrs. Dixon is being held.

She is in a cell, sitting on a bench, staring across the small space at nothing. When I approach, she doesn't turn to look at me, but I can tell she's been crying.

Mary Dixon has worked in the castle for decades. She is a hard worker and had served as the second in command for many years. When Mrs. Worsthingshorethinshire was let go, Mrs. Dixon was the logical choice to replace her. Now, however, I see that someone who was easily manipulated was put in that position, someone without the sort of savvy and common sense that had made Mrs. Worsthingshorethinshire so good at her job—even if she was a raging bitch.

"Mary," I say, and she slowly turns her head, an absent look in her eyes. "What happened?"

"Your Majesty!" she says, as if she has just recognized me. "I'm so sorry, sir. I thought I was helping." Tears spring into her eyes again. "That woman, she told me she was meant to be the next Luna, and you had given her permission to go into the Luna's suite so that she could start planning remodels."

I sigh and rest my head against the bars, thinking Mrs. Dixon probably isn't going to come and bash my head against anything to knock me out…. "Why didn't you come to me or Beta Seth and ask if that was true, Mary? After all, you've worked here long enough to know my feelings on taking another Luna."

"Yes, sir, I know," she says. "I'm sorry. I should have. But I wanted to prove that I was a good choice for my new job. That woman threatened me, saying she would have me fired if I questioned her. So… I just did it, sir. I'm very sorry. I didn't know she was going to hurt anyone. The other girl, the little blonde, is she all right?"

It was clear to me that she was genuinely remorseful for what had happened. I don't think she meant to hurt anyone. I think she just got caught up in the lies of a very manipulative, psychotic bitch.

I should've done something more to stop Zabrina before, when she tried to poison me, and when she obviously slit the throat of her own maid. I thought that Isla and my other friends were safe because we were in my own home.

But obviously, I was wrong.

"Guards!" I shout, and the closest guard rushes over. "Release Mrs. Dixon."

"Yes, sir," he says, pulling his keys from his pocket and hastily following my direction.

When the gate swings open, she slowly walks toward me. "Thank you, Alpha King Maddox."

I nod. "Now, have you heard any discussion about where they were going once they left? Or what their plans were at all?"

She shakes her head. "No, Alpha Maddox. I'm sorry. They never said anything in front of me. All I did was unlock the door for them. Then… they'd go in there for a few hours and come out laughing."

"And… did you ever unlock any other doors for them?" I ask.

She shakes her head, but I can tell by her face that that's not exactly true.

"Mrs. Dixon?" I ask, sternly.

She sighs. "Well, I did unlock the healer's supply closet for her yesterday." She drops her head and stares at the ground.

"You let her into Mystica and the other healers' supply closet?" I clarify.

She says, "Yes, she said she needed some medicine for an injury."

"What injury?" I ask.

She shakes her head. "I don't know. I didn't ask."

I can't believe anyone would do something so reckless and irresponsible.

But I have a feeling it wasn't just the wolfsbane that was stolen from the healers' closet. I'm just glad Mystica is wise enough to keep the antidote to wolfsbane somewhere else—at least, I assume she is, since she had some to treat Isla with.

I rush to the closet and realize the door is locked. I don't have my keys. My master keys are still in the broken-down car.

Using the mind-link, I call for Mrs. Dixon, whom I had just left standing there in the dungeon. It takes her a while to get there, but when she does, she is breathing heavily.

"You sure about this, sir?" she asks, pulling a bobby pin from her hair. I have to think the guards were stupid not to have taken those from her.

"I'm sure." As she unlocks the door, I realize I won't know what I'm looking for. I call for one of the secondary healers, Chester, and he hurries over from the infirmary.

The door opens, and I step inside, turning on the light, still waiting for Chester. My eyes scan the shelves, and I immediately realize there are two spaces that are completely empty.

When Chester gets there, I ask him, "What goes here and here?" pointing at the two spots.

"Oh, no," he mumbles, shaking his head. "This isn't good at all."

I turn to look at him, my heart racing.

"Well, this shelf contained red wolf's blood, and that one contained… wolf shadow."

My eyes widen as I realize what this means.

Zabrina and her friends have stolen the same aphrodisiac they poisoned me with the first time and a powerful sedative.

"What the hell do they have in mind?"

"I have no idea, sir," Mrs. Dixon tells me, but when I look at the healer, he has a grim look on his face.

"Sir, when you mix those two concoctions together, you get a very deadly drug called red wolf's shadow—I'm sure you heard of it. Some of the enemy forces used it against us in the last war."

I take a deep breath. I know exactly what he's talking about. I have heard the stories about what happened to people who were inflicted with that particular drug, and I can't even imagine the pain they must've suffered.

I need to find Zabrina and those drugs—and I need to find them now.

THE GIFT THAT DOESN'T KEEP ON GIVING

Isla

"Masina Atuafafine?" I repeat as I try to process everything that Mystica has just said to me.

"Yes, that's what we call the Moon Goddess in our ancient language. Most people speak the same language there as is spoken here, but some of us remember the ancient terms for the Moon Goddess and for royalty."

I nod, wishing I had some inkling of what she is speaking about, but I am lost. "How do you know that my last name is Masina, though?" I ask her.

"Because... the scene you described let me know who you are, dear." Mystica sits on the side of my bed, and my eyes wander to Poppy. She looks just as confused as I feel. "You probably spoke both languages at one time, honey, assuming you were old enough to speak when you left. How old were you, three? Are you the youngest child?"

I shake my head. "No. I have two older sisters, but I have five younger brothers. They were born after we moved to Willow pack."

She nods. "So you are the youngest of the girls who fled with Tupu Daniel and Masiofo Constance. You are Tama'ita'i Isla."

"What does that mean?" I ask her, but rather than answering me, she reaches into the top of her shirt and pulls out a locket.

Opening the locket, she shows me that each side has a golden wolf in it. One has a red eye and the other a green one. My eyebrows furrow together as I realize I've seen those wolves before.

"Do you recognize this?" she asks me.

"Yes," I tell her, nodding as she takes it off and hands it to me. In my palm, the wolves look small, but I would recognize their form anyway.

"This is the royal seal of our kingdom, Maatua, which has two translations. One means 'parents' because we think of our kingdom as our family, but the other means 'stone back' or gems. Our island was full of beautiful gems like these. For centuries, they were used to adorn our palace, as well as common homes. Then, the kings and queens began to trade the gems for other necessities. Eventually, greed set in, and when the royal family refused to continue to trade away what made us special, there was a great war, a revolt."

I stare at her, wanting to hear the history of my homeland but also feeling nervous. Obviously, this story does not have a happy ending.

"The royal family, and other important leaders who had a conscious were forced to flee. Otherwise, the greedy powers taking over would've killed all of those people. Many of the citizens fled as well."

"Where did they go?" I ask.

She sighs and looks down, "To all ends of the earth. No one kingdom could've absorbed all of them, though Maatua was a small kingdom, only about ten thousand people."

"That is small," Poppy agrees. "We have millions of people here in Crescent Falls."

Mystica nods and then continues. "So... my family came to join me here, though I was already a part of the royal healing group here. My powers were recognized by King Maddox's father during a visit he paid to Maatua, and he told me he felt that I could benefit many people if a revolution came about. At the time, I had no idea Maatua would also have a rebellion soon enough."

"So you came here?" I clarify, and she nods.

"I did. And then, when war broke out in Maatua, I couldn't make it back there in time to help, so I welcomed as many people into Crescent Falls pack as I could. No one knew what happened to the king and queen and their daughters."

I feel a fluttering in my gut as I try to process what she is saying to me. "The king and queen... and their daughters?"

She nods and reaches out to smooth back my hair. "That's right, dear. I believe, I now know where they are."

"Wh-where?" I ask her. My mind will not allow me to fill in the blanks on my own. It's all too much for me to accept.

Mystica opens her mouth to respond, but she is interrupted when my door swings open and Maddox rushes in.

I start to get up, alarmed at his hasty entrance. "No, don't get up," he insists. "I've just come to tell you I'm leaving the castle for a bit."

"Why?" I ask, the idea of him going out now, when it's late, and he's been through so much, makes my heart hurt.

He comes to stand next to me, and Mystica moves so that he can have a moment. Poppy holds her seat, her eyes wide as she listens in.

"We have some issues that need resolved immediately," he tells me. That's his way of saying that he doesn't want to tell me the truth.

"Did something happen?" I want to know.

Maddox sighs and drags a hand down his face. He sits down next to me. "Zabrina got away."

"What!" Poppy exclaims. We both turn and look at her, and she sinks back into her chair, realizing she is a terrible eavesdropper.

"She got away?" I repeat.

He nods. "She escaped and took Wylie with her. Both of her parents are gone as well. We've rounded up her remaining soldiers and are interrogating them now because we are afraid they might hurt people."

"Hurt them how?" I ask.

"It's a long story," he says. "I will explain when I get back."

"Are you going to look for her?" I ask him. "You don't know where she's at yet?"

"We don't know, but we have posts on all of the roads so that we can find her easily. Don't worry. I'm certain she'll be located soon. Hopefully, we will catch up with her before she's able to harm anyone else."

"All right," I say. "I understand."

"I feel that you'll be safe this time, now that she is gone. I've assigned Commander Taylor to watch over you, and he is very trustworthy, but if you want me to have Seth stay you—"

I cut him off. "No, it's fine. I'll be all right."

"Okay." He has a hint of sadness in his voice, and I understand why. I was hoping he could hold me all night. But now, he'll be out chasing around that witch.

"I have to go," he says. He leans in and presses his lips gently to mine, like he is afraid I'm made of glass and might shatter.

When he pulls away, he starts to stand, but I grab hold of him "Hold on a minute," I say. "I got something for you at the village this morning, and I want to give it to you." Was that this morning? It seems like a million years ago.

"You got something? For me?" he asks, and I can tell he's shocked. "You didn't have to do that."

"Well, technically, it was your money," I tell him, "but I did pick it out for you."

He chuckles at me. "My money is your money, Isla," he tells me.

"If that's true," Poppy chimes in, "I think I need a raise!"

Maddox turns and stares at her. "Perhaps you should be let go for poking your nose in where it doesn't belong." He cracks a smile at her, and she blows out a hot breath.

"I guess my moments of appreciation for helping earlier are over." She waggles her eyebrows at him, and I can tell they are both teasing, though I also wish that Poppy would've given us some space, like Mystica did.

"Let me get them," I say, starting to get up, but all three of them protest.

"No! I'll get the gift," Poppy says. "Where did you put it?"

I don't want her to know about my secret hiding spot because then I won't be able to use it again, but I have no choice. Even if I got up to fetch them, she would see. "In the window sill," I tell her. She stands, forehead wrinkled in confusion, and walks to the window. "The board pops up on the left side," I tell her.

Eventually, she discovers what I am talking about and brings me the box. She hands it to me, and then, miraculously, she backs away, going to stand by the door near Mystica.

I clear my throat. "I hope you like these." I realize what I am holding in my hand now before I even explain to him why I chose them. "When I saw them, I thought of you immediately. They look so regal. But then… the man at the store said that they were found in an abandoned palace in the islands."

My eyes go to Mystica, and she is listening, though she doesn't come closer.

Maddox opens the box and sees the cufflinks that perfectly match the wolves in the locket I am still holding . Rubies, emeralds, golden wolves….

But Maddox doesn't look happy. "Uh, thank you, darling," he says. "These are… nice."

"You don't like them?" I ask him.

"No, I like them," he says, but I can tell he's lying. "I like them a lot. And I love that you thought of me." He leans down and kisses me. "I have to go now, though, okay?"

"Okay," I say, not convinced that he hasn't hated my gift. I wonder what it is about them he doesn't like.

Maybe he doesn't know they are from Maatua.

He certainly doesn't know that I am from there.

"Be careful," I tell him.

"I will be. And I'll be back as soon as I can be."

I know he means he'll come back not just to the palace, but to me. As he approaches the door, he says to Poppy, "Can you give these to Teressa, for safekeeping?"

Teressa is one of his maids.

"Yes, sir," she says, taking them from him. I can tell by her face that she is also confused that he didn't like the cufflinks.

Maddox waves at me, smiling, before he leaves, but I feel even worse to see him go now.

He didn't like my gift, and I have no idea why.

Mystica has a strange look on her face before she says, "I can't blame him for not wanting those."

"Why is that?" Poppy asks her, holding the box in her hand.

"There's a reason they were left behind in the palace in Maatua." Mystica has an uneasy expression.

"Why did they leave them behind?" I ask her, feeling my heart beginning to thump against my rib cage. Maybe I don't want to know.

Turning to look at me, she says, "Because they are cursed."

TANGLED MEMORIES

Maddox

I HAVE HURT Isla's feelings, and I feel terrible about it, but I don't have time to ponder what to do about it at the moment. I have got to track down Zabrina. I imagine she is a good hour ahead of us at least. Without footage of the vehicle once it left the palace, it's hard to say. And none of my guards outside seem to have seen anything to help provide a lot of information about where she might be headed.

All of the pack Alphas that are close enough to my location for the mind-link have let me know they have barricades up on every major road and as many of the minor ones they can get to leading into and out of their packs. Every single car will be stopped. I've given them a description of the vehicle Zabrina's family is driving, but I wouldn't put it past her to steal another car along the way.

Rushing out to the garage, I get into my own sports car and head out to where the vehicle they drove Isla in was spotted. I decide to start there and see if I can track Zabrina's scent. That will be nearly impossible. I have already sent teams out from that spot in all directions to look for signs of which way they went, but it's not likely they will catch up with Zabrina unless she is delayed by a roadblock or stops somewhere for the night.

Who knows what other hidden cabins she may have located when she was deciding to use that one for Isla. She might have plenty of places to hide.

I pull the car to a stop along the ditch near where their car was spotted and get out. It's within a few miles of the castle wall, so they didn't have far to run as wolves coming or going. I should've had someone take care of the car while I was out looking for Isla, but it didn't occur to me.

Now, I look around for clues as to where they went. It's dark, and even with my keen wolf eyes, in my human form, I cannot see anything that truly lets me know where they went. The road runs east and west, but within a mile in each direction are junctions with roads that go north and south. It's not an all-terrain vehicle, so they will have to stick to the roads. That's something at least.

The freshest tracks appear to be headed west, which doesn't surprise me. That's the direction I expected them to go. Zabrina's father's pack lands lie in that direction. I doubt they are stupid enough to go directly back there, but I do think they will try to get to an allied pack and then sneak back into their own.

I've made it clear that no one is to help them, but that doesn't mean that Duster pack or Green pack will listen to my directives. Anymore, their Alphas sort of do what they want. After all, Green pack has a new Alpha, and if they cared what I thought, that wouldn't have happened, not without my approval anyway.

I head off to the west, driving recklessly, on the edge of control, as I think about the damage that could be done if Zabrina has the opportunity to drop any of those chemicals into the water supply.

People will die from the wolf's shadow on its own and be exceptionally aroused by the red wolf's blood. But put together, they will die long, agonizing deaths caused by their sexual drives making them go mad. They will become sexual deviants while their bodies are slowly being deprived of oxygen via the wolf's shadow.

"The water supply…." I've already told people at the castle to turn off the water and not to let people drink it two hours after I left. We have bottled water in great quantities as a reserve, just in case of war. But… where would Zabrina take the chemicals to poison the water.

She won't know that I am aware that she's stolen them. So she'd probably go to the lake. But then… she might assume that the water treatment facility would remove enough of the chemicals that it would be safe to drink after it was treated, though I wouldn't want to take the chance.

Would she pour it into the water towers?

Using the mind-link, I contact as many people in charge of water towers and the water treatment facility as possible. She might also try to poison our food with it, so I send out a bulletin to the farmers, including those that raise cows. She could poison the milk…. Who knows what she intends to do!

We need to find her, and we need to do it fast.

I come to an intersection and have to decide which way to go. To my right,

I will be headed toward Duster pack. To my left, I will be headed toward the water treatment facility.

I turn left.

~

Isla

Cursed....

Mystica had said that the cufflinks I gifted to Maddox were cursed, and that's why they were left behind in the palace on Maatua. I've never believed in curses before, but now, I have to wonder.

She didn't say much more to me, only that the cufflinks had been a gift from one brother to another, and when they were given, everything went wrong. Could those two brothers be my Uncle Tony and my dad?

I want to talk to my parents, but they don't have a phone. I can't call Alpha Ernest at this hour and expect the Alpha to send someone to fetch them. I wish I could just pay them a visit, but I know that King Maddox won't allow me to leave the castle while all of this madness with Zabrina is going on. So I'll just have to stay there.

I hope that my family will be all right.

Sleeping will be difficult, even though I am exhausted from everything that has transpired with the kidnapping. I want to bury my face in Maddox's chest and let his strong arms lull me to sleep, but I can't do that because he is out there chasing that monster.

"Please, Moon Goddess," I prayed. "Let him find her."

She is the epitome of evil, and I know the Moon Goddess is real because I've seen her with my own eyes.

Well, perhaps I had been hallucinating. Or just dreaming. But it seemed real.

I roll onto my side and close my eyes, hoping that the Moon Goddess will hear my prayers and answer them. Whatever Zabrina and her sinister allies are up to, they need to be stopped.

I stare at the wall in the distance, unable to keep my eyes closed.

Princess. I was a princess?

Was that true?

It doesn't seem like it could be true. I need some sort of proof about the entire situation other than the fact that I had left an island around the time that the Alpha king had been displaced. Mystica had said lots of people had left the island then. How did she know it was my father who was the king?

"She'd said his name, hadn't she?" Tupu Daniel and Masiofo Constance.

Yes, she had. King Daniel and Queen Constance. Those are my parents' names. I don't think I said them to her first, and I doubt she could've looked that up before she came in here.

So… it sounds like she might be right. But Daniel is a common name, right? Maybe it's a coincidence?

Constance is not a common name.

I try to remember back to those moments I'd been dreaming about when I was in the basement, when we were leaving on that boat. What had they been saying? Did my mom ever call my dad Tupu? I don't think so.

What about before that? Why can't I remember a palace? Or guards? Or any of the fine things we must've had if my parents were royals.

"Because I was only three," I remind myself.

How awful is it that my parents had to give all of that up and become common workers because of something my father's own brother did?

I want to find my Uncle Tony and figure out what had happened. Why had he betrayed my father?

It is all too much, and my head is pounding and swirling. I want to go to sleep! I decide to get up for a glass of water and go into the bathroom to fill a glass I keep in a drawer by my bed.

Padding across the floor, I try to keep my eyes focused, but I am tired. I turn the tap on, but nothing happens. No water comes out. There's just a gurgling noise and some air.

"That's weird," I mutter. I try the other tap, the hot water, but nothing happens. So I try the bathtub and then the shower.

No water.

Frustrated, I go to the door between my room and Poppy's and knock. "Just a minute," I hear her say in a groggy voice. She opens the door, and it's clear I woke her. "Yes, Miss Isla?" She is trying to be respectful but is clearly annoyed.

"Hi. No water is coming out in my bathroom. Do you know why?"

She nods. "Yes, we received a bulletin about it. Sorry, I guess you wouldn't get it since you don't have the mind-link with the castle authorities. The water has been shut off while the king investigates tampering with the water supply."

My eyebrows knit together. "Tampering?"

"That's right. They think that Zabrina might try to poison all of us."

I wouldn't put anything past her.

"All right," I say with a sigh, not bothering to ask when it will be turned back on. I wonder if Zabrina said anything about her plans while I was in her presence but drugged up. I can't remember that she did.

"I'll get you a bottle of water from my stash," Poppy suggests.

"Thank you," I say and wait for her to do so. A moment later, she comes back with a bottle of water.

"It's room temperature," she says apologetically.

"That's okay," I tell her. "It'll work. Thank you." I take the bottle over to my bed as Poppy goes back to hers, and take the lid off, sipping it down and hoping it's enough to help me fall asleep.

I have never seen this kind of water before. It says, "Bottled at Wolf Springs," and has the king's seal on the label. Back home, we couldn't afford bottled water. We only drank from the tap.

I set the bottle down and try to go back to sleep, pulling the blanket up to my chin.

"What are you up to now, Zabrina?" I ask myself aloud. I get no answer, though, and soon enough, my dry throat quenched, I find myself dozing off.

WHERE DID SHE GO?

Maddox

THE WATER TREATMENT facility looms in the distance, and nothing seems to be stirring within the giant chain-link fence that guards the perimeter. As I slowly drive around, looking for any indication that this place has been tampered with, my eyes are met with not a single sign of distress

I pull my car to a stop in front of the guard's building and get out. "Facility is closed!" he barks at me, clearly not recognizing me in the dark. I have made sure that the proper authorities that are in charge of this facility know the threat, but that must not mean that the guards at the gate are aware that I might be coming by.

"I'm aware of that," I tell him. "I just wanted to make sure that you haven't seen anything suspicious. No strange vehicles. No wolves carrying bags that could potentially contain chemicals?"

He studies me for a moment before he says, "Nope, nothing of the kind. Everything is fine here, mister. So you can head back to the palace, and let the king know. Ol' Virgil and the others is takin' care of this place."

From his tone, I get the impression he must be Ol' Virgil. Another guard saunters up behind him, an odd expression on his face. I smile at him, and he immediately goes into a submissive, respective stance with his right fist over his heart.

Ol' Virgil is confused. "What you doin' Jimmy?"

"Th-th-the king!" Jimmy manages to get out.

"This here ain't the king!" Ol' Virgil insists. "The king wouldn't be out in the middle of the night checkin' on the water treatment facility!"

"He would be if he thought there was a possibility that the entire pack could be poisoned," I tell him.

Ol' Virgil finds this humorous and begins to chuckle. "Well, like I said, everything's just fine out here. So you can go tell the king, we's got it under control."

I decide I'd rather talk to Jimmy. "At ease, there, Jimmy," I say to him. "You haven't seen anything suspicious?"

"N-n-no, sir," he stammers. "Mr. Folk sent us out on patrol, though, just to make sure. We got a keen eye on everything. I don't believe anyone will be able to break into the facility, sir."

"Good," I tell him with a nod. "That's what I wanted to hear. All right then. Thank you for your time." I give Jimmy a nod of appreciation and try not to roll my eyes at Ol' Virgil.

As I turn to walk away, I hear the older guard say, "Why you got your panties in a wad? That weren't the damn king!"

Jimmy only says, "Ol' Virgil, you're lucky his reputation isn't true or else he might've ended you."

I can't help but chuckle despite myself as I get into the car and turn around. "Where the hell did you go, Zabrina?" I ask myself.

Of course, that gets me nowhere, so I use the mind-link to check with everyone I can think of who is also out looking for her. I am going through the list of commanders, checking in with them, and no one has seen anything when I hear a frantic voice in my head.

"Alpha King Maddox, this is Captain Thomas. I'm stationed out by the edge of Crescent City, and it looks like something funny is going on out here in the industrial region of the town. One of my privates just saw a car go flying by really quickly down one of the side streets. He tried to follow it, but he couldn't keep up."

"Crescent City?" I repeat aloud, not using the mind-link. "All right, Captain Thomas," I say. "What facilities are you closest to, how many wolves do you have with you, and what's their fighting capability?"

I head in that direction. Crescent City is about an hour's drive from the castle, and I've gone the right direction to reach it, so I'm only about twenty minutes from there now, but I have to turn the car around and head back in the other direction. It's to the southwest of the water treatment facility, which sits along the same river that runs through Crescent City, Great Wolf River.

"I have thirty soldiers with me, sir, and we are spread out all over the town on various roads, watching for the car. I believe that my private saw that car, and it's headed toward the edge of town where several factories are stationed."

"Which factories?" I feel like I have already asked him this question. He's nervous and doesn't want to fuck up.

"Uh… there's a packaging factory there that makes plastic and paper bags and bins. A bakery that makes bread and other grain products, a glue factory…."

I think through those choices. None of them make sense. She could try to poison the food supply, but it wouldn't work too well. If the chemicals were baked into bread or another food product, they would lose their effectiveness.

No, if Zabrina really wants to kill a bunch of people, she'll need to get that chemical into the water supply.

But she's not at the water treatment facility.

Where is she going?

My mind catches up to her at about the same time that Captain Thomas adds, "Oh, and Wolf Springs."

"Wolf Springs!" I shout at him. "Of course! The water bottling company—she knows that we'll all assume she's poisoning the water in the treatment facility, so she's going to the place we'll all turn to, assuming it's safe! Captain, get your asses to the water bottling facility as quickly as possible, got it?"

"Yes, sir," he says, and I let the mind-link go as I mash the pedal to the floor. I know that Seth and most of my other higher-ups are nowhere near Crescent City at the moment. It's not located close to Zabrina's pack or her allied packs, so it wouldn't make sense for her to go there—for any reason other than to tamper with water that's already been packaged.

Nevertheless, I tell Seth what's happening. "Close in the circle so that if she slips through my fingers, we can find her and cut her off!" I tell him.

"Yes sir, Alpha," my Beta says, and I know that we are tightening the noose on her.

I only hope she doesn't slip through our paws. Duster pack isn't too far from Crescent City, if she can get over the river, and while I've already ordered all of the bridges to be shut down, she could find another way.

Going around isn't likely—that would be a long shot. But swimming across in her wolf form might just work. I doubt that Alpha Jordan is in any shape to swim after his tumble down the stairs.

Zabrina will abandon her injured father and make a break for it. I just know it.

Crescent City is a large industrial town with lots of factories and apartment buildings where the factory workers live. I try to make sure that everyone within my kingdom is able to make a nice living, and while it's not possible for me to micromanage all of the packs—like Willow pack—I do make sure that the workers within my own pack lands, the ones directly around the castle, are taken care of.

So even though it's a big city, it is clean, with roads that are well taken care of, very little crime, and not a lot going on this late at night, especially since I asked the city manager to send out a mind-link bulletin to all of the citizens to stay at home, out of the way.

The last thing I need is for someone to get run over while we hunt Zabrina down in a high-speed chase.

Knowing that the roads are likely pretty clear, I do not slow down entering the city. I see very little traffic as I speed toward the factory in question, and as it looms in front of me, I have a feeling Zabrina is here.

"We don't see anything at the facility, Alpha," Captain Thomas says in my head.

"Keep a tight perimeter and keep looking," I order. "She's got to be there somewhere. No sign of the car?"

"No, sir," Captain Thomas tells me.

"Where would she park if she was going to sneak into this facility?" I ask myself.

And then it occurs to me.

The water that they use for the bottled water comes through a large pipe from beneath the ground that taps directly into the spring that feeds the river. The water treatment facility also uses water from this river, but the bottled water is cleaned at this facility—it's a privately owned business, after all. They don't need to bottle and sell the public water, though it comes from a public source.

I try to remember where that pipe originates. I reach out to the company owner, Bill Bixby, but I can't get him on mind-link. I ask Captain Thomas, "Where the hell is Bill Bixby?"

He hesitates. "I don't know, sir."

"Send someone over to his house and see if he's asleep!" I insist. I may need Bixby's help before this is all over with.

In the meantime, I don't drive directly to the water bottling facility. I drive to the river, and as I make my way down the shoreline, I am looking for Alpha Jordan's car.

As I near the older of the two bridges that cross the river, I slow down. A feeling deep inside of me tells me that Zabrina is nearby. It's like I can smell her, though it's not my nose that tells me she's here.

"Sir, this is Bill Bixby. I'm sorry, I was asleep. What's going on, King Maddox?" says the voice in my head.

"The pipe where you collect your water from the spring, is it by the old bridge?" I ask him, slowing down.

"Yes, sir," he says. "About a quarter-mile south of there."

"Thanks, Bill. Get to your factory. We may need you yet."

I cut off the mind-link as I bring the car to a stop.

Tire tracks, to my right, near the river. But no car.

I get out and walk over, and I understand why the car isn't there now.

She knew we'd see the car, but she had no idea I'd see the tracks—shooting through the grass, right up to the two-foot concrete rise that goes around the river's edge here.

The driver would've had to have a running start to take the car up and over that barrier, but it's clear to me by the chips in the top of the concrete that's exactly what's been done.

"So… Alpha Jordan's car is at the bottom of the river," I say, scratching my chin. "Where the hell is Alpha Jordan—and his daughter?"

I look around, following the tracks back across the open field. If I can find their origin, I might be able to pick up her scent. Because I know Zabrina well enough to know one thing—she didn't just plummet to her death in that river.

No, just because the car is gone, that doesn't mean my problems have gone away. In all likelihood, the trouble is just beginning.

BREATHING UNDERWATER

Isla

I AM UNDERWATER.

How I got here, I don't understand, but that's where I am.

It's odd, though. It's like I can breathe just fine under the water, like I have shifted, but not into the wolf I'm meant to have. No, I have shifted into something aquatic, like a fish.

I can't see my own form as I press along underneath this rapidly moving body of water. Rather, I am only aware of what is around me—the green algae growing up from the rocky muddy depths beneath my feet, the large rocks that lay in piles strewn all around me, the occasional fish that shoots by in front of me.

Water—lots and lots of murky greenish-brown water.

"Where am I?" I ask, but not aloud. If I open my mouth, this dirty water will fill me up until I am sputtering. No, it is an internal question. I don't know the answer, but I don't think this is the ocean.

I think it must be a river of some sort because of how quickly the current is moving and how it is flowing from right to left in a nearly straight line like it is being carried by gravity and not the wind.

I also don't think I am too far from the shore because the water doesn't appear to be too high over my head. When I tip my head up to look, I can see the reflection of lights on the waving surface, and beyond that, the sky.

And bubbles. Lots of bubbles. Why are there so many tiny bubbles directly above me?

I don't have any idea, but I know I need to hurry before I run out of air, so I rush forward looking for… something.

What is it? I have no idea, but I move anyway.

And then… in front of me, I see what looks like a circular entryway cut into the ground at an odd angle. Quickly, I walk around it so that I am facing back the way I came, and I see that it has a grate over the top of it, like a door. I reach behind me and grab something from somewhere, some kind of tool, and then I take the grate off, tossing it aside. A cloud of debris flies up around it, momentarily prohibiting me from seeing what lies in front of me.

When it dissipates, I see that this is a tube of some sort. A pipe, perhaps? A few words are written in faded white paint on the side of it. My eyes don't linger there as I make sure this is my objective. And even though I am terrified to do so, I begin to move inside of it, flowing along with the current, pushing off the sides with my hands as I glide further and further through the narrow space.

I have no idea how long I will even fit in this tube, but I keep moving forward because I am compelled to do so. I have to. I've been commanded to. Beyond that, I would do anything for her. I love her so much.

"Who?" I ask myself, but I don't know the answer to that question.

Nor do I have any idea what I am doing or why I feel so out of touch with my own body, but the further I go through the pipe, the more I begin to panic.

What if they turn it on? What if I can't get out? What if this goes wrong?

It doesn't seem like a foolproof plan, now that I am here, and for a moment, I consider turning around and going back the other direction.

But I don't. Even if I die, I've done it for her.

A loud whirring noise sounds, all around me, and suddenly, my heart begins to pound. "No!" I shout, moving my lips this time. She promised she wouldn't let this happen! I am being sucked forward now at an impossible rate. Everything around me blurs, and then, all that remains is unbearable, all-consuming pain.…

I jolt upright in bed, a scream leaving my lips as the ripples of pain wash through me, the energy leaving me as soon as I realize that I am in bed—that it was just a dream.

But it wasn't just a dream, was it?

Have I ever had such a lucid dream before?

I reach for the lamp to turn it on just as Poppy comes flying into the room, her hair a mess, and her nightgown crooked. "Miss Isla?" she calls. "Are you all right?"

I can't answer her at first because I'm out of breath from the nightmare and the screaming, but I nod to her.

She reaches for the bottle of water she gave me earlier and takes the lid off for me, handing it to me, and I thank her with a nod before a sip of the luke-warm water refreshes me.

Poppy drops down next to me on the bed, her hip by my knee. "Do you want to talk about it?" she asks, laying her hand on my leg.

I put the lid back on the water and set the bottle on my nightstand. "It was a strange dream," I tell her. "I've never dreamed anything like it before." I am still shaken, and she can see that, so she gives me a few moments before she asks me anything else.

Eventually, Poppy asks, "Was it about the kidnapping?"

I shake my head. "No, it wasn't." I take a deep breath, my mind running back over the dream. "I was underwater," I begin. "In a river or something. And I didn't want to be there, but I knew I had to be. I had a job I had to do."

"What sort of job?" Poppy asks, her eyes knitting together as she studies my face. It is as if she thinks there might be some sort of mystery to unravel in my dream.

"It was just a silly dream," I say with a shrug.

"You never know," she tells me. "Princesses might have fancy dreams."

I roll my eyes at her. "We don't know that I'm a princess." In fact, Mystica telling me she thinks I am a princess seems less real than the dream I've just had.

"So you were underwater?" Poppy repeats, and I nod. "What were you doing?"

Flashes of what I'd seen in my dream came back to me. "I had to go in this pipe," I explain. "Underwater. I had… something I had to do. I just remember thinking that this woman I loved had asked me to do it, and even though I was really scared to do it, I did it anyway. For her."

"Was it your mother or something?" she asked me.

Shaking my head, I say, "No, I don't think so. It didn't seem like that sort of love."

"Hmmm," Poppy says. "Well, how long were you under there? Did you drown? Is that why you screamed?"

"I don't know how long I was down there, but it was a few minutes. I didn't drown. Somehow… I was able to breathe. But…." The memory of what had happened at the end of the dream comes back to me, and for a moment I remember the intense pain I felt being sucked through the pipe and colliding with whatever was at the other end—another grid or a door or a propeller or something…. I didn't last long enough to know for sure. "It sucked me in, the pipe. And then, everything hurt… and I woke up."

Poppy studies my face for a long moment before she says, "Thank good-ness it was just a dream and you're safe in bed." She pats my knee again.

I agree. I am very thankful that it was just a dream. Still, I have to wonder, when I lay back down and close my eyes, will I end up right back in that same dream.

I can't think about that. Instead, I ask her, "Do you know if King Maddox has found Zabrina or the others yet?"

"Let me see," she says, and for a moment she is quiet while she uses her mind-link. Poppy shakes her head. "Not yet. They've chased her to Crescent City, though. My friend Wynn who works as a maid in the military department is trying to keep on top of everything."

"Crescent City?" I repeat. I have never been there before, but it seems like an odd place for her to go to. "Why would Zabrina go there?"

"Who the hell knows. She's nuts. Maybe she has allies there or something?" Poppy guesses.

"Maybe so," I say. "But it's nowhere near her pack."

"No, you're right, it's not." Offhandedly, she says, "Maybe they'll trap her against Great Wolf."

"Yeah, maybe so." I reach for my water as Poppy begins to head back to her room. But when I see the label, I stop. "Great Wolf?" I repeat.

"Yeah, you know," she says. "The river?"

"No, I know," I tell her. "The river… Poppy. In my dream, I was in a river." I lift the bottle again, but this time, I'm not removing the lid. I'm looking at the label. "Wolf Springs! Where do they get their water from?"

"I don't know, but I hope it's not the river." She makes a face.

"Is the river spring-fed?" Could it be that the pipe I saw in the ground in the riverbed actually draws the water up from the spring, before it gets to the river?

Poppy studies my face for a moment and then asks, "You think Zabrina went through a pipe in the river to poison the bottled water?"

"No," I tell her, and I watch her relax and laugh for a second at the silly notion before I say, "I think Private Wylie did."

CATCHING THE AQUATIC GOPHER

Maddox

Bill Bixby is standing near me, staring at the pipe, wearing a robe over his pajamas, his hair disheveled, and is eyes barely focusing.

"This is the drain pipe," he says. "It lets the unusable water back out into the river."

I stare at him for a moment. "So this doesn't reach the spring where the water that's used for the bottling comes from?" I have to clarify.

"No, no, no," he says. "We can turn this pipe in reverse to make the water flow the other direction. We do that from time to time to bring in more water to run the machinery and keep it cool, but for the most part, this pipe flows into the river, not the other way around."

"Where does the water come into the plant?" I ask.

"Over there." He points into the distance where I can see a large pipe that actually goes into the ground. "The spring isn't under the river. It's under the ground there, and it flows into the location of the river through an underground tributary. So we catch the spring water before it goes out into the river. It makes it easier to clean. Drinking river water is possible, but the cleaning is a lot more difficult."

What he is saying makes a lot of sense to me. But I am still confused. "Is it possible to get into the pipe that goes into the spring to pull the water out?"

He shakes his head. "No, not without pulling the pipe out of the ground, which would take a lot of work. And the water would have to be shut off to do that, too. We never shut the water off, not through that pipe."

I nod. "Okay, so... what is she up to?"

"I'm not sure," he admits. But then, he's obviously tired and not thinking straight. I need to sort this out....

"Alpha Maddox?" I hear a familiar female voice in my head.

My forehead scrunches as my heart begins to race a bit. Why is Poppy mind-linking me? She should be asleep. I immediately assume that something is wrong with Isla. "What's the matter?" I ask her. "Is everything okay?"

"Yes, yes, everything is okay," she says. "It's just... Isla just had a strange dream, and she wanted me to tell you about it. She is a little shook up and didn't want to try to mind-link at the moment."

My pulse doesn't slow. I haven't even thought about mind-linking Isla, now that she's within range of me again, because I was hoping she was asleep. To hear that she's shaken up again makes me unsettled. "What is it?"

"Well, she said that she had a dream where she was underwater, and she walked into a long pipe. It was red and said, 'Great Wolf,' on the side of it. She thinks maybe Private Wylie went into a pipe to poison the water supply."

I am not sure what to say at first as I stare at the giant red pipe in front of me. Why would Private Wylie go up this way?

Maybe because it's the only pipe he can access?

"All right, Poppy, tell her thank you, and I'll look into it."

"She's trying to go back to sleep, but she's worried about you and every-thing that has to do with this situation," Poppy continues.

"Right. Tell her I'm fine, and I'll be home soon." I have to cut the mind-link then because Poppy will just keep talking. I turn to Bixby. "Is it possible to get into the facility through this pipe?"

His eyes widen. "I mean... there's a grate on either end. And the person would be swimming against the current if the water is on."

"Is the water on?" It seems like an obvious question.

"Well, no, not at the moment," he admits.

I remember something he said earlier about the water also running in the other direction.

"What would happen if a person was inside of that pipe when you turn the water on in the other direction?" I ask him.

A ghastly expression hits his face as he scrunches his face up. "The force of the water rushing through the pipe would crush a person against the grate in the building where the water comes into the machines."

"Is it possible to get through that grate, into the machine, and out into the facility?" I ask him.

"It would be difficult. If one could get the grate off, then yes, they could get into the vat and then swim to the top," he tells me.

I weigh that information against everything else I know. "Do you have workers in the plant right now?"

"A few," he says. "We have a small night crew that works on bottling and labels, but we don't clean the water at night. I have some security guards. They said that you had sent some soldiers in there, too, Alpha."

I nod at him. That's true. I did. Captain Thomas's people should be in there if someone shows up. But they might not see them until it's too late.

Without another thought, I tell Bixby what we need to do. "Have them throw the switch to run the water backward in this pipe, so that it's sucking water into the facility."

His eyes widen. "Are you sure, sir?"

I nod. "Yeah, if there's anyone in that pipe, I wanna know." Then, I rush off toward the facility.

"Where are you going, sir?" he shouts after me.

"To see if we catch anything."

I make the run to the water treatment facility in my human form, even though it would be faster to shift. But I don't want to try to lead this team naked, so I just do it as a human.

When I get to the facility, I mentally shout at Thomas to send someone to let me in, which he did.

I run through the door, shouting at them to tell me where the vat Bixby had told me about was located. I thought the business owner was on his way, but he hasn't arrived yet. I assume I am much faster than him, and he's barely awake.

"It's that way," a man dressed in a custodian's uniform tells me as he points down the hall.

I run in that direction and listen for the whirring of machinery. I can hear it in the distance. Since Bixby told me they don't bottle water at night, it has to be the machine I've asked him to flip on.

I hear shouting as I reach a large room full of machinery. Soldiers near a large metal vat are yelling at workers who are rushing to a control panel across the room.

"Turn it off! Turn it off!" I hear, and then, one of the men leaps over the side of the vat with a pair of bolt cutters in his hand. I have no idea where those came from at first, but then I see a row of tools on the wall with a sign over it that reads, "Safety Utensils," above it.

A few moments later, as I reach the edge of the vat, the soldier who leaped over the edge emerges, bolt cutters in one hand, and in the other, a limp, bloodied body.

It's Private Wylie

"We need a healer!" the soldier shouts.

"No, we don't," I tell him.

He stares at me for a moment, like he thinks he might need to talk some sense into me, but I'm not bringing a healer for this scumbag, not after what he did to Isla.

"Get him out," I say, and the soldiers, who have suddenly realized who I am, act quickly to yank the bastard out of the water.

They deposit him on the ground, and I can see that he's not breathing. He's bloodied and battered, his face bruised and mangled. I have no idea how forcefully he hit that grate, but I can see the imprint of it on his face.

He's wearing a wet suit with a small oxygen tank that's half off him. Zabrina put a lot of thought into this plan. She had to have in order to have oxygen available.

It made me wonder—did the rest of them use similar tanks to cross under the river? If so, they could be anywhere by now.

The oxygen tank is not the only thing Wylie has, though. He has a water-proof backpack as well.

I unzip it and look inside.

It's the two missing medications.

At least we have those now, even if we don't have Zabrina.

I pick up the two plastic jars and see that they haven't cracked or broken, and they look to be full, so she didn't divide them into different containers, and she probably didn't use any of it since they're full.

The soldier who had risked his life to try to save Wylie kneels beside him now and starts doing CPR, breathing into his mangled mouth and pressing on his chest. Another comes to help. They can knock themselves out trying to save the asshole, but I'm not going to do anything to help the man who tricked the woman I love and kidnapped her.

He was trying to kill Isla, so fuck him if he dies.

It does cross my mind that bringing him back could allow us to torture him enough to tell us where the hell Zabrina is, but I figure he probably has damage to his brain from being out of oxygen for so long. It seems pretty clear that the mouthpiece wasn't in his face when it hit that grate.

"Nice plan, Zabrina, you stupid bitch," I mumble as I walk back the way that I came.

I run into Bixby, who is panting slightly from the strain of making it to the factory. "What happened, sir?" he asks.

"We caught a gopher," I tell him. "An aquatic gopher."

He stares at me for a moment. "Is he alive?"

"Nope," I tell him. "But they're working on it." I walk past him and then tell him, "You probably need to wash the blood out of your vat." I'm not sure I'll be drinking any bottled water for a while.

I run into Thomas on my way out. "We're still looking for Zabrina and Alpha Jordan," I tell him.

He nods. "Yes, sir." He makes the sign of respect.

I head out to my car, using the mind-link to tell Beta Seth what's going on.

Zabrina still needs to be found, and while I can say I won't mentally rest until she is found, I am going to rest.

I'm going to go home and lay down with my Isla, hold her against my chest, and make sure she knows she's safe.

And then, tomorrow, I'll resume my search for the Alpha's daughter.

In the meantime, I have another mystery to solve.

How the hell did Isla know where Wylie was?

WAKING IN HIS ARMS

Isla

I FALL BACK INTO A DREAMLESS, restless sleep after Poppy assures me that she has spoken to Maddox and relayed the information I had given her.

I don't know why I am suddenly dreaming about what's happening with other people, people I am not related to and have no connection to, but I am certain that what I saw was real, not just a regular dream spurred on by everything that has happened to me today.

A few hours after my conversation with Poppy, I feel a shift in the bed and slit my eyes to see what is happening. Part of me wants to react with panicked fear that I am being attacked again, but I am too tired for that.

Thankfully, that is not the case.

It is Maddox.

He is slipping into bed next to me, and while I am too tired, and it is too dark, for me to see exactly what he has on, when I rest my hand on his chest, it is bare.

"I'm sorry I woke you, beautiful," he whispers, his warm lips pressing against my forehead.

"It's okay," I manage to get out before I roll onto his chest. He holds me tight, and I inhale him, so glad to be back with him. I don't ever want him to leave me again.

But I also want to know what happened.

I am slightly more awake as I ask him, "Did you get Wylie?"

"Wylie is dead," he tells me, his hand running the length of my hair. It feels soothing, to have his fingers running through my curls over and over again.

I contemplate what he has told me. Wylie is dead.

The man who tried to kill me, who was supposed to keep me safe, but tricked me instead, led me from my room, kidnapped me, tortured me, and injected me with poison, was dead.

Why did that make my heart feel heavy?

"How?" I force out.

"He went through that pipe at the water bottling factory, and when we turned the machine on, it smashed him against the grate," he says, his tone matter-of-fact, as if it is all a matter of business to him.

Perhaps it is. Perhaps, to Maddox, this is all just what happens in war or whatever the hell this is.

"How did you know, baby?" he asks me, his tone still gentle, though his voice is slightly louder than before. "How did you know that Wylie was in that pipe at the water bottling factory?"

I shake my head slightly. "I don't know. I dreamed about it," I tell him. "It was like I was in there with him, though I didn't know who he was." I look up at him, and my eyes have adjusted slightly to the dark. "What about Zabrina?"

He sighs, and before he even answers, I know what he's going to say. "We are still looking for her. We think they all must have had wet suits with oxygen tanks, like Wylie did. I have no idea where they might've gotten them."

I think for a moment. "There's a shop in the village that sells diving equipment. Wylie was in the village with me earlier today. Maybe he saw it and went back later to buy it. Or sent one of Zabrina's guards."

"That's possible," he says. "We have some of her ladies and Alpha Jordan's guards here. Her mother is missing, too, and we don't know if she went with them or if she left ahead of all of this."

I can't imagine the Luna being involved in such a dastardly scheme. It seems beneath a lady, but then, I don't know the woman.

All I want at the moment is to go to sleep, and now that Maddox is here, I know I will sleep well.

But something else is bothering me. "Promise me you won't leave without waking me?" I ask him.

His face pulls up into a smile as he asks, "Why is that, gorgeous?"

I don't know why this question amuses him, but I answer him honestly. "Because I don't want to be without you unless I know that you're gone." I'm not sure that makes sense; I'm so tired. But he seems to get the meaning. He lowers his head to my lips and grazes them over my mouth, softly.

"All right," he tells me. "I will stay until you wake, or I'll wake you myself if I have to."

That's all I need to hear. I trust him, and with that promise, I doze off with my head resting over his heart.

When I open my eyes again, I'm lying in the same position, but the sun is streaming between the curtains, and from the brightness and angle, I have to think it's late morning.

I don't want to lift my head off Maddox's chest to look at the clock, but I think he might be uncomfortable since he hasn't moved for hours.

Lifting myself, I roll off him, keeping my eyes on his face. His eyes are open, and he is smiling at me.

"I'm sorry," I say to him. "Did I delay you from going on about your work?"

His smile widens as he drags his thumb across my cheek, shaking his head. "Work isn't important right now, Isla. You are. Did you get some rest?"

I nod. He has been awake for a while and probably knows that I've been sleeping on him for hours.

"That's good to hear," he tells me. "Do you feel any better?"

"I feel a lot better," I tell him, and I mean it. Last night, I felt like my body was underwater as much when I was awake as I did when I was dreaming. I felt like I could hardly move. But the medicine that Mystica gave me, the shot that was meant to reverse the wolf's bane, must've taken full effect now, because even though I am still a little groggy from having just woken up, I am feeling significantly less tired and achy than I had the night before.

He continues to rub my cheek, and I see that look in his eyes that lets me know that he wants me. I think he is probably hesitant because he is afraid he might hurt me. Or perhaps I am not cognizant enough of the situation to make the best decision.

But I want him, too, and as I lean toward him, my mouth reaching for his, he responds to me, his lips meeting mine halfway.

All he is wearing are his boxers. I have on a nightgown and panties, but he will make short work of those. He is gentle, taking his time, touching me carefully, as if he believes I am made of glass and might break.

His hand glides down my neck as he continues to kiss me, settling on my breast where he works my nipple through the material of nightgown. I lift a leg and throw it over his hip, wanting to get closer to him.

Maddox takes hold of my hips and pulls me to him, and I can feel his erection against my belly as he trails kisses down my neck. When he reaches for the hem of my nightgown, I help him get it off me, and then his hands are both on my breasts. I toss my head back and enjoy the feel of his thumbs and fingers pulling and tweaking me to life. When his lips close around my hardened peak, I nearly come undone. My hand flies to his crotch, and I realize these boxers have a slit.

I work his massive cock out of the open fly and run my hand up and down his shaft while he groans against my breast. I feel myself growing wetter by the second as I need him inside of me desperately. It hasn't been that long since we've been together, but it seems like a lifetime, especially considering how close I came to dying.

I thought I would never feel him again.

He slides his hand around the back of me, along my bottom to my sopping pussy, from behind, which makes me moan even louder, the thought of him taking me that way awakening my body even more than it already was. I arch my back, and he understands exactly what I want.

He turns me around, but he doesn't position me so that I'm on my knees like we've done it before. No, instead, he works my panties off and then shoves his fingers deep inside of me while holding me against his chest. His other hand continues to caress my breasts. I have no idea how this will work exactly, but I trust him completely.

His fingers slide through my outer folds and then deep inside of me, his thumb working against my clit as he grinds into my ass with his massive penis. He directs me gently to lie down, bent only slightly at the waist, and then, he is on top of me, his boxers removed, and I feel him slide inside of me from behind but at an angle I was not expecting.

It doesn't seem like this should work, but Maddox has found a way to command my body in a way I never would've imagined.

And it feels so good. His hands work my hair as he continues to push into me, deep, slow strokes that light me on fire but don't risk what he considers to be my fragile circumstances. I take him in, my mouth open, buried in the pillow as I cry out, moans of pleasure rippling between my open lips like the waves that consume me from my core all the way through my body.

He feels so good inside of me, like that's where he belongs, and with each grinding thrust, I feel he is penetrating more than my wet pussy; he is working his way into my very soul.

I can't help but gasp for air as he keeps me at my peak for so long, my throat begins to feel raw.

When he finally joins me, I find myself grateful to get a bit of a rest but also saddened that he will remove himself from me physically, and then, I will feel empty inside without him.

His warmth spreads through me, and then he is done, and he lies next to me, pulling me around to face him as I am tangled in his arms again.

"I didn't hurt you, did I?" he asks, and I shake my head, incapable of words.

His mouth is slightly salty when he kisses me, from the perspiration he's built up in taking me, but I don't mind at all.

"Maddox," I whisper, not sure if it's appropriate or not, "I love you." I want him to know. After I've almost died, I see no reason to keep that from him.

He says nothing for a long moment, and I think I have messed up in telling him the truth at this moment. When he finally speaks, I hear notes of haunted sadness in his voice. "You're precious to me, Isla. I hope that love doesn't destroy you."

257

A NEW PLAN OF ACTION

Maddox

I SHOULD HAVE TOLD Isla I love her, too, but I didn't.

A million reasons why that isn't a good idea flock my mind as I hold her in my arms, looking down at her beautiful face.

I want her to know that I love her more than anything, that I will do whatever I can to protect her, but I know that she is in a dangerous position because she loves me. Clearly, that has been demonstrated in the past few days when Zabrina and her minions tried to kill her.

Promising her that she is completely safe now would be foolish and dishonest of me. I want to do everything I can to protect her, and I will, but having just failed her, I find it impossible to know for certain I can do that.

I couldn't even protect Rebecca from herself.

Isla isn't sure how to respond to my statement, and I can't blame her. I lean down and kiss the top of her head and then slide from the bed. "I need to go," I tell her. I find my boxers and put them back on.

"Are you going to look for Zabrina some more?" she asks me as I pull my boxers up and bend down to grab my pants.

"That's right," I tell her, shoving one leg in and then the other.

"Do you think you'll find her today?" Isla leans back against the pillows, and I imagine she is still exhausted. After what her body has been through, she should sleep more. I shouldn't have made love to her, but it's so hard to keep my hands from her. It wasn't as if she was telling me no, after all.

"I have no idea if we'll find her today," I admit. "But I will keep looking until she's found so she can be brought to justice." It kills me to think that the wormy little bitch was able to get out of her cell. Didn't we learn anything from how easily Larry was manipulated?

"Be careful," Isla says, reaching for me as I sit down on the bed to put my socks and shoes on. My shirt is on but very wrinkled. I am just going to my room to shower and change, but still, I hate looking so messy even for a few moments.

I reach for her and take her hand in mine. "I will be careful," I assure her.

A small smile graces her lips, but she seems unsure.

An idea comes to my mind. "While I am gone today, why don't you call your parents?"

Her eyebrows arch as her eyes meet mine. "Uh… they don't have a phone," she reminds me.

My head rocks back and forth. "I know, but you can call the Alpha's number and ask for them to come to the phone."

She bites down on her bottom lip, and I can see that she's frightened. "I don't think I want to speak to Alpha Ernest. He's not exactly kind to me."

"Oh, Ernest isn't the Alpha of Willow pack anymore," he explains. "I removed him. There isn't an Alpha right now, but the Beta has taken over. For now, anyway. Miguel said he doesn't want to stay the Alpha, but he'll handle it for the time being."

Isla adjusts where she's sitting on the bed, pushing herself up slightly. "I don't understand, King Maddox." I grunt a little at her formality, but she doesn't go back and try to change it. "Uhm, why would you remove Alpha Ernest from his position?"

"For lots of reasons," I tell her. "First of all, he failed to tell your parents where you were. He didn't forgive their debt either. He also lied and told the hospitals to collect the medical debt from people who were not born in our kingdom, which is why your parents owed so much money to begin with. I took care of it, baby. I went there and made sure that he was punished for what he'd done. Your parents will be getting that money back, and I made sure they had enough money in the meantime as well. Who knows? Maybe they actually have a phone in their home by now."

She continues to stare at me for a long moment. I smile at her and rub her hand. "That's where you went?" she asks me. "When you left here, yesterday? It was to see Alpha Ernest?"

"That's right," I tell her. "My car broke down when I was coming back. I believe Private Wylie tampered with it. I saw grease on his hands earlier yesterday morning, but I didn't have any suspicions about him because he had seemed to be loyal."

"Yes, he always seemed loyal to me, too," she agrees with a heavy sigh. "I wish I would've known you were going there. I would've loved to have seen my parents."

"I'm sorry." I mean it. "I just didn't think it was a good idea until after I got to the bottom of what was happening with Alpha Ernest. Now that he's out of the picture, you can go there whenever you'd like. I told your mother that you were working in the castle, but I didn't tell her what your job is. I thought she would be upset if she knew the truth."

She drops her eyes, and I wonder if she is ashamed of being my breeder. If she is, it's my fault. I am the one who just made her feel like that's all she is to me. That's not the case, but I was too scared to tell her that I love her right now, so she'll likely just assume this is just a job again.

I don't have time right now to go through the intricate differences between what she is doing to me as my breeder and what separates her from someone who is doing just another job.

"Anyway," I continue, "your family should be doing well now. You should call them. I know they'll want to speak to you, and Beta Miguel will help you get in touch with them. Just… tell them whatever you'd like about your job. But I believe your mother thinks you're a maid."

Isla scoffs. "I thought that's what I would be, too, even after Beta Seth told me I was your breeder. I didn't even know what it meant until Poppy explained it to me. I guess… I've never heard of anyone using someone just to have a baby."

"I'm not using you just to have a baby, Isla," I try to assure her, but she looks unconvinced. "I'm serious. You mean so much more to me than just that." I lift her hand and kiss the back of it.

In my head, Seth asks me if I'm up yet, and if so, what my orders are.

This will never end…. Not until that bitch is found. I hate it. We may as well be at war. It feels the same way with this immediate sense of urgency. I tell him to give me thirty minutes and return my attention to Isla.

"I've got to go," I tell her. "But I will talk to you about it later. You should get as much rest as possible and then go call your mother, all right? Don't worry about me. I'm not afraid of Zabrina or her awful father."

"I will try not to," she says, but I know she will worry about me because she is a worrier.

I lean down and press my lips against her, noting that her skin is a bit cold. I pull the blankets up to her chest and run a hand along her cheek.

"I'll check in with you later, okay?" I tell her. "And if you need to use the mind-link with me, don't hesitate, baby. I'm always here for you. I shouldn't be going out of range, but if I have to for some reason, I'll let you know before I do so."

"All right." That's all she says.

It makes a sigh escape my lips. I should tell her. I should say those three words that would set her mind at ease.

But now doesn't seem like the time.

"Goodbye, Isla," I say.

"Goodbye, Alpha King Maddox."

That's even more formal than before. I tip my head at her and say, "Just Maddox from you, babe."

She smiles, but it looks forced. When she says my name, I feel my heart tighten in my chest and my pants grow snugger. "Maddox."

I think I'd rather be her lover than anyone's king, but I have a responsibility to everyone, and that means I can't just step aside for this woman.

I'll have to find a way to keep her safe while maintaining my station.

With one more look at her beautiful face, I head out, going to my room to take a shower. I let the water run slightly cold so that I'm not going off to find that murderous bitch with a hard-on. It doesn't matter that I've just taken Isla from behind; already, I am growing hard for her.

But she needs a break, and I don't have time to take care of myself, not at the moment.

After my coldish shower, I get dressed and go out to meet Seth.

"Any word?" I ask him as I take the protein shake he's offering me.

He shakes his head. "No. I've got wolves out on the far shore of the river, trying to sniff her out. So far, they haven't found a trace of her."

I swear under my breath. I was hoping she'd emerge on the other side of the river. "All right. Widen the search. We need to go to the village."

"What village?" Seth asks, confused, as I walk toward the door that leads to the garage and my car.

"The local village. I've heard there's a diving shop there. I want to see if they happened to sell any oxygen tanks yesterday. If they did, I want to know to whom, how large, and how long they'll last underwater."

My Beta seems to be on the same wavelength as me now. "All right then. Let's go. But if you expect me to go diving, you're crazy."

I smile at him, knowing he's not even a fan of swimming in his human form, and think that might be necessary. We can determine where the car entered the water. Perhaps, if the mud near that part of the river bottom is deep enough, we'll be able to find her tracks. "I promise nothing," I tell Seth and he groans as we get in my car, me behind the steering wheel, him in the passenger seat, glowering at me.

He'll live.

TRACKING THEM DOWN

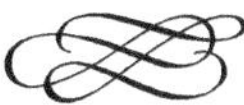

Maddox

We arrive in the village less than twenty minutes after we left the castle. I see the dive shop I've been told about pretty quickly and pull into a parking spot not far from the front door. It's still fairly early in the morning, and most of the activity around the shops is centered around the coffeehouse and the bakery—not the dive shop, which doesn't even look to be open.

I will not let that deter me.

Hopping out of the car, I make my way to the door and try it. I'm relieved that it is unlocked, despite the fact that the lights are not on, and there being no sign in the window that says, "Open."

In fairness, and in my defense, there's no "Closed" sign either.

When the chime above the door dings, I hear an aggravated sigh from the back of the shop and have to assume that whoever is working this morning would prefer not to have any customers.

That makes me glad I'm not intending to give them any money.

Despite the humor I would find in making Beta Seth dive down into the river to have a look around, I wasn't planning on doing that to him or anyone else from the castle when he'd declared it wasn't going to happen.

My theory is, they aren't still down there with the same oxygen tanks, and while I'd considered seeing if there were any tracks down there, I figure it would have to be pretty specialized divers who would be capable of finding any tracks that might be left behind.

That isn't Seth....

And if I need the help of specialized divers, well, I have to assume they will have their own equipment.

This shop doesn't seem to have much for diving anyway, which makes sense to me since the river is the only major body of water anywhere near here, and most people go diving in the ocean, I imagine. That is several hours' drive away from us.

The walls are lined with surfboards, many of them covered with dust. A few wetsuits hang on racks throughout the store, but mostly I see bathing suits and boogie boards, the sorts of things people might use in a lake or in a pool.

If people go diving in a lake, they probably aren't doing it recreationally.

As Seth and I look around, an older man with a scowl on his face comes from the back. His tan skin tells me that he seems to like the beach himself. His mostly gray hair is in sharp contrast to his dark, lined skin, and the frown he wears makes him look a bit ruthless.

Not that I am scared.

"Oh, great, more suits," he mumbled under his breath as he approached us. "My shop keep ain't here yet, so if you need something, it's best you come back later. I ain't got the time or the patience to answer a bunch of stupid-ass questions."

Beta Seth and I exchange a questioning glance. I can tell my friend is about to put this guy in his place, but I am amused and decide to let this go on for a bit. Obviously, he doesn't recognize me, and that is twice in less than twenty-four hours someone older than me has decided to try to put me in my place.

I sort of enjoy it.

"We're not actually here to buy anything," I begin.

He cuts me off really quickly. "Well, then get the hell out. I don't have a public restroom, I don't give directions, and if you want advice about how to dive, look it up in a book!"

He waves his hand at us dismissively, but when he sees we aren't leaving, he only gets angrier.

Before he could open his mouth again, I say, "We're here on official business from the crown."

His eyebrows arch for a second before he says, "What? The wetsuits your friends bought the king didn't work out so well? That ain't my fault. Take it up with the manufacturer."

"What wetsuits for the king?" Seth asks before I can say anything at all.

"The ones I sold those guys in suits yesterday afternoon, right around closing. Some guard from the palace came in yesterday morning, sent his friends back yesterday afternoon to get the suits. Three of 'em. Three tanks, and a waterproof bag. Isn't that what you're here to ask about?" He rubs his chin thoughtfully.

"Yes, that is what we're here to ask about," I confirm, "but we weren't part of the party that bought them yesterday. We are following up to see exactly what they bought and if you know what they look like."

"Yeah. You deaf or somethin'? I just told you what they bought, dumbass," he says to me.

Seth is angry again, wanting to step forward and punch the guy. I stifle a laugh. It's funny to me to have this man call me names, though I'm not sure why.

"I heard that," I tell him. "But I was explaining to you why we had come here to begin with. Now, we have half of the information we need. I know what they bought, but I still don't know exactly who bought it. Can you describe them for me? How many of them were there?"

"Hell, I don't know. Three guys in suits. Said they need them for a date the king was taking some stupid bitch on last night. I hear he has a breeder now, so maybe it was her. Fuck if I know. Anyway, that's what they bought. Paid me extra for it, so I didn't give 'em a hard time, but they were all a bunch of stuck-up assholes, just like you guys. Pretty boys with their nails buffed and their hair styled, nice sunglasses, shiny shoes."

I look at Seth again. He has to be talking about three of Alpha Jordan's guards because my soldiers don't wear suits. They wear uniforms in the color of the crown.

"All right," I say. "Thank you."

"Whatever," he says, waving his hand at us again. "Now, get the hell out of here."

"Of course," I tell him, but then I give Seth the gesture I always make whenever I secretly want him to pay someone off

Seth's eyes widen as he scoffs. "You want me to do what?" he asks using the mind-link.

"Give the guy a couple hundred. We may need him again. He's been helpful."

"He's been a downright fucking asshole!" Seth tells me, but as I move toward the door, I see Seth is doing what I said.

"Gee, what's this," the guy says. "Couple bucks?"

"Why don't you look at it before you make snide remarks?" I hear Seth say.

"Holy shit!" the guy exclaims. "Anything else you two need to know?"

"We're good for now." I look back at him from the door.

"Well, if you do need anything, let me know. If I'm not here when you come, ask for Bud. Don't be paying those asshole kids who work here who are always late, now. They don't deserve one fucking dime!"

"I'll keep that in mind," I tell him. "Oh, one more thing. How many gallons of oxygen did those tanks they bought hold?"

"Uh, eleven liters," he tells us.

"So.. in the river, how long would that last?" I want to know.

"Great Wolf River? Probably about an hour, maybe an hour and a half. You got folks diving in that river? There's a real choppy undercurrent. It'll take you right downstream, real quick, especially if you don't know how to handle it." He looks concerned.

"Yeah, I do have divers in there. Where do you think they'd end up if they left Crescent City, near the water bottling facility?" Maybe he is more help than I thought he would be.

"Fuck, I think they'd end up about twenty miles downstream," he tells me. "Probably near Hill Country pack."

"Hill Country pack?" I repeat. That's one of the packs that Alpha Jordan considers his ally. Won't that be convenient for him? "Thanks," I say again.

He nods and wishes us a good day, and I tell him the same before we are out on the sidewalk, heading toward the car.

"You never tell them who you are," Seth mutters. "You need to get that mug of yours out there more. Put your face on the currency or something so they know who you are and don't act like such assholes."

I laugh a little as I get into the car, but I am lost in my thoughts. I'm definitely not putting my face on the currency.

"Where am I going?" Seth asks as he backs out of the parking spot.

"Uh… Hill Country pack, I guess," I tell him.

"How did I know you were going to say that?" Seth mumbles. "Did you finish your protein shake? We should stop at the bakery and get some real food."

"I'm good," I tell him. "But if you insist, run on in like a good little boy, and be quick about it."

He grumbles at me and pulls in next to the bakery, leaving me to finish my half-consumed protein shake and think about what Alpha Bryant of Hill Country pack will do if he has a turd wash up on his shores. Will he help Alpha Jordan out or let me know he's there? By now, every pack in my kingdom should know I'm looking for Alpha Jordan, his wife, and his daughter, though I'm not too worried about the Luna. I'm guessing she's on her way home in a vehicle. I don't have the manpower to look for her right now, and I'm guessing she won't be of any help. I'm not going to torture her….

A few minutes later, Seth returns with a coffee in his hand and a glazed donut hanging out of his mouth. He gets in, puts his coffee in the cupholder, and removes the donut saying, "I really wish you would've gone with me. I wouldn't have had to pay."

"Why didn't you tell them you were the Beta?" I ask him as he is heading back onto the road again.

"I did, but they said they didn't care. They said if I was an Alpha, they'd care." He looks injured, like they've wounded his sensitive soul, and I have to try not to laugh.

"Well, they probably wouldn't have recognized me anyway," I remind him.

We sit in silence as Seth eats his donut and sips his coffee, and I think about Isla. I hope she's all right, and I didn't offend her with my hasty comment about falling for me being dangerous.

We are nearly to Hill Country pack when I hear a voice in my head. "Alpha King Maddox, this is Alpha Bryant. I hear you're on your way to see me."

"How the hell do you know that?" I ask him.

He chuckles. "I have my ways. Listen, I think I know what this is about, and I think I can help you."

My gut clenches at both of his remarks. Does he have spies around my castle? In the village? A connection with the shop owner I just paid for his help? And… how could he possibly be able to help me?

"I'm listening," I tell him. "What is it?"

He is quiet for a moment before he says, in a measured voice, "I think I have something you want."

I feel my heart start to race as I imagine what he's about to tell me. "What is it?" I ask him.

"Not what," he begins. "But who."

CALLING HOME

MY HEAD IS a little fuzzy when I open my eyes later that morning after Maddox has left. I run a hand through my hair and stretch my other hand over to the bed where his body had been. It's not even warm anymore.

I sit up, slowly. I still don't feel completely right after everything I went through yesterday, but I feel a little better than I did before I went back to sleep.

I remember what he said about calling my parents. Should I even bother to do that? Alpha King Maddox has explained to me why he thinks it's worth it, but I'm not sure he really understands how Willow pack works. If it's true that Alpha Ernest is no longer in power, that doesn't mean that he won't find someone to let him out of prison. He's a little worm, and he has people working for him that Maddox would've never suspected wouldn't be loyal to him.

I have to wonder, as I sit there pondering everything that's happened recently, how many people truly are loyal to Maddox?

It's not something that's ever crossed my mind before. When I was in Willow pack, I was busy trying to help my family and survive. I didn't have time to give much thought to the Alpha King. Whether or not there was about to be a civil uprising never occurred to me. I didn't even remember the first one I'd gone through, and I just assumed everyone was loyal to the king.

That might not be the case, though, and if Alpha Jordan and his daughter were willing to go to these lengths to stir things up, what were others who were supposed to be loyal to Maddox doing?

I can't say....

I decide to go ahead and call my parents, but I need a shower first. Poppy scrubbed me down last night, but I still feel disgusting. I head to the bathroom, not wanting to bother the maid. I can get my own outfit together.

While I'm standing beneath the hot water, hoping that every last minuscule amount of residue from the basement, from Private Wylie, from Zabrina, from everyone involved off my body, down the drain, and as far away from me as possible.

I also think about what Maddox said to me when I told him that I love him.

Picking up a bar of soap, I rub it over my body, not for the first time. I can't get clean enough...

It wasn't like I expected him to say that he loves me, too. Of course, not. I mean, he is the Alpha King, after all, and I'm just his breeder.

The shampoo I'm using is vanilla-scented, and I breathe it in deeply as I lather up my hair for the second time. At this rate, I'll be in the shower longer than the water will stay warm.

"He's the Alpha King. You're his breeder," I remind myself. "Why would he love you?"

No answer for that pops into my mind. While I do think there's a chance he cares about me, I'm not vain enough to think it's love. After all, I haven't even fulfilled my duties as a breeder yet. Maybe if I was the mother of his child it would be easy for him to fall in love with me, but I'm not.

Not yet.

I am a woman whom he seems to prefer to spend his time with, though, so maybe that means he has feelings for me.

Perhaps he sees me as a friend, maybe even a close friend.

But he'd said that it was dangerous for me to have feelings for him. While I can see now why that would be true, I've survived this attack. Who's to say I won't survive another?

I don't want there to be another, but if I have to choose between staying close to Maddox and being safe, I choose Maddox.

No one ever said being in love is easy—and I know, despite his response, I mean what I said.

I love him.

I finish rinsing my hair, apply the conditioner, and let it sit for a few minutes while I think about calling my parents. I rinse it out, get out, dry off, get myself cleaned up, and go into my room to see Poppy there.

"Hi, how are you?" she asks. "How are you feeling?"

"Okay," is about all I can say. She's brought some brunch foods—bagels, muffins, ham and cheese to put on the bagels I suppose.

"Get dressed, have a seat, eat something," she tells me.

I do as she says, taking the yellow sundress and underclothing into the bathroom with me to get dressed. When I'm finished, I come back out and eat a little bit, but I'm not hungry.

"What are your plans for today?" Poppy asks me.

"Uh, I am going to go try to call my parents," I tell her.

Her eyes widen. "Wow. Okay. To tell them what happened to you yesterday?"

Shaking my head, I tell her, "No, I don't want to worry them. I'm just going to tell them I'm doing well, that sort of thing."

Poppy stares at me from across the room where she had been straightening things that were already straight. "And... what about the information Mystica gave you yesterday? Are you going to ask about that?"

I take a deep breath, hold it, and let it out slowly. "Uhm, I don't know. I've been thinking about that, but I'm not sure."

"I think you should," she says. "You know. Ask them. Feel them out."

I nod. "Maybe. It just doesn't seem that important at the moment."

"You don't think being a princess is that important?" she asks me.

My stomach feels unsettled. Maybe it's from this conversation. Maybe it's from all of the stress of the last few days. "I don't know," I say. I set the muffin I had been eating down. I don't want my parents to feel like I'm upset about not knowing the truth or that I feel like anything is different because I know the truth now.

If it is even the truth....

When I am done eating, I realize that I have something I need to say to Poppy. "I'm not sure I properly thanked you," I tell her. "You did so much to help me yesterday. I feel bad even asking you to continue to be my maid after all of that."

She smiles at me. "You're welcome. I was glad to help. For a little while, It was like the king and I were good friends and not just the king and a lady who works for him, you know?" She chuckles under her breath. "I think we're back to normal now."

"Well, we're not," I say. "You're a dear friend to me, Poppy. You always have been, and yesterday, you just further proved it."

Her smile widens. "You're welcome," she says again. Then she comes a bit closer to me and says, "Maybe when you're queen, you'll remember me and make me a duchess or something?"

I can't help the laugh that escapes my lips. "I won't ever be queen, Poppy. King Maddox has already said he will never take another wife, right?"

She shrugs like what I'm saying is inconsequential. "When a man falls in love—"

I shake my head and interrupt her. "He doesn't love, Poppy."

She stares at me, her eyes still wide, before she asks, "What makes you say that?"

It's my turn to shrug. "He just doesn't. I told him I love him, and he didn't say the same. He doesn't. Why would he?"

She laughs for a long moment, and I stare at her like she's lost her mind. She finally says, "Well, no, he's not gonna just say it. Dudes don't do that, Isla. Especially not dudes that are king. But, trust me, since I saw him yesterday, the way he was frantically looking for you... I'm certain, Isla. Regardless of what he's said, that man loves you."

I want to believe her, but I don't even know what to say to her. I mean... what can I say in response? "Okay," is all I can get out.

Pushing back from the table, I tell her, "I'm going to go make a phone call. Where do I go for that?"

"Oh, uh, you can probably use King Maddox's office. He won't mind."

"Won't it be locked?" I ask her. "I don't want to pick anymore locks."

"No, probably not. He doesn't have much to hide. Come on." She waves for me to come with her, so I do.

I can't imagine King Maddox has nothing to hide, but I'll go see if his office is unlocked.

Lost in my thoughts, I go over what I'll say to my parents as I follow Poppy to his office, and when we get there, we find the door is unlocked. I look around the hall to make sure that no one is looking, and we duck inside.

His office is immaculate, just as I expect it to be. No papers piled up, nothing out of place, not even a speck of dust.

I know he has people to clean his office, but I'm impressed that everything is so nice and neat.

Poppy picks up the receiver on the table and looks in a Rolodex next to it. I've only ever seen one of those on Alpha Ernest's desk the few times I've been in his office.

"Willow pack?" she asks, and I nod.

She dials and then hands me the phone.

I take it, staring at it for a second, before I hold it to my ear. I haven't ever talked on one of these much.

"I'll wait outside," she says, and Poppy leaves.

I sit down in a seat across from the desk and wait. After several rings, a voice I think I recognize answers. "Willow pack. Beta Miguel."

"Uh... hi, Beta Miguel," I stammer. "This is... Isla Moon. King Maddox said it would be possible for me to speak to my parents. Is that... is that true?"

"Oh, hi, Isla." He sounds like he remembers me, which is surprising because I've never spent much time around the Beta. "Yeah, sure. Hold on. I'll send someone to your house. What's the address?"

I tell him, and he says to hold on again, so I do.

About five minutes later, I hear my mother's voice. "Isla? Is it really you?"

I can hear she's been crying, and knowing that makes me burst into tears, too "Yes, hi, Mom!"

"Oh, thank goodness you're safe!" she says. "Are you at the castle?"

"I am," I tell her. "Where's Dad?"

"He's at work. Oh, tell me how things are there."

I don't want to tell her what happened to me the day before, so I don't. I tell her a lot of other things, though, that I'm getting to know King Maddox, that I work directly for him. I tell her about Poppy and how she's such a good friend, and I tell her that I miss all of them so much.

"We miss you, too, but we love you so much, Isla. What you've done for our family is… indescribable. I went to the grocery store yesterday, and for the first time in many years… I didn't have to worry about money. Thank you so much, honey."

"I'm glad to hear that, Mom," I tell her. "I hope it stays that way."

"As long as you keep doing a good job for the king, I'm sure it will."

I hesitate for a moment, thinking about what I wanted to tell her about what Mystica told me the day before. I don't want to upset her, but I have to know. "Mom, have you ever heard of an island called… Maatua?"

My mom is quiet for a moment before she repeats the word. "Maatua? Uh… why do you ask?"

"Well, I met this woman named Mystica, and she was telling me all about this war that happened there. She says that the displaced king and queen were named Daniel and Constance. Mom, she seems to think I'm a lost princess. Isn't that… wild?" I pause, hoping she'll confirm what Mystica has told her is true.

She continues to be quiet for a long moment before she says, "Uh, yeah, baby. That is… wild. Maatua? I've never even heard of it."

MORE SURPRISES

Maddox

I GET out of the car in front of Alpha Bryant Logan of Hill Country packs mansion. It's huge, though it's no castle. Still, it looks a lot more modern than the place I live in, a lot homier.

As I make my way up the long path to the door, I daydream about down-sizing a bit but getting something where the electrical wires are actually in the walls instead of along them since my castle was built about four hundred years ago before electricity was even an idea.

Beta Seth clears his throat behind me, and I know he's nervous. He always does that when he's uncomfortable. I turn and look at him, and he adjusts his tie like maybe it's choking him a little.

"It's just Alpha Bryant," I remind him. "He's on our side."

Seth nods, but I know he doesn't quite believe that. I don't either, but we're here. We may as well see what the fuck he wants.

Besides, I have to think he's not choosing to side with Maple pack over me. If he was, he never would've let me know what he'd found along the river early that morning.

I raise my hand to knock on the door, but it swings open before I can lower my fist, and the Beta for Hill Country pack, Vinny, is standing there with a look on his face that says he thinks he's got something on me.

And I don't like it.

"Vincent," I say, using his full name though no one ever calls him that. "Alpha Bryant says he's got someone for me?"

Vinny cackles at me. "Yeah, yeah, he sure does, Alpha King Boss Man."

I don't think I've ever been called that particular title before.

I follow Vinny through the foyer, around a large marble table with a huge vase full of flowers in it, to the back of the house where he shows me to an office.

I already know who I'm going to see in that room with Alpha Bryant. He didn't tell me through the mind-link, but I know just the same.

I walk in and see the Alpha behind his desk. To the left of him are four large Omega guards… and one tied up, gagged, doubled-over-in-pain Alpha.

Or should I say former Alpha?

"Alpha King Maddox. Welcome to my home," Alpha Bryant says, standing to offer me his hand.

I shake it. He greets Beta Seth as well. Then, we turn our attention to Alpha Jordan.

Or should I just say Jordan?

"Where'd you find him?" I ask the Alpha.

He laughs and rocks back and forth from his heels to his toes with his hands in his pockets. He isn't in a hurry to enlighten me about the situation, so I pretend like I'm not in a hurry either.

Alpha Bryant is not quite as old as Alpha Jordan, but he is probably old enough to be my father. He has gray streaks at his temples, and the rest of his hair is mostly brown, though it's hard to tell the way that he has it slicked back whether that's his natural color or if he just uses some kind of greasy, almost black product in his hair.

"Listen, Maddox," he begins, and I raise an eyebrow at him. It's a warning. We are not on a first-name basis—he's not privileged enough to call me Maddox, anyway. He clears his throat. "King Maddox. Here's the deal. You know I'm on your side, right?" He comes from around his desk and stands next to me, gripping my upper arm for a moment, but then, when I give him a similar look to the one I had given him before, he lets go. "I hear the bullshit lots of the other Alphas is always spewin' about you bein' easy to knock off because you don't have an heir. I get it. They think that they can come in, take the throne, get rid of you, and not many folks is even gonna say boo because you don't have anyone to replace you anyway. Right?"

I stare at him for a long moment, daring him to continue down this path. If he's trying to make me nervous, it's not working. I know everything he just said is bullshit. While it's true there are a few packs that are talking about trying to take the throne, a handful of stupid ass Alphas who think they're bigger than they are isn't going to scare me.

Besides… I'm working on that heir thing right now, aren't I?

"Where did you find him?" I ask again.

Bryant removes his hand, clears his throat, and walks over to where Jordan is slumped in the chair. It's clear the Alpha of Maple pack isn't doing so well. He looks to be in excruciating pain. He's hunched over, his eyes are slits, and a stain on the chair tells me that it's not just water that has his pants all wet.

"On the shore, down a ways from my industrial complex," Bryant tells me. "He was layin' there, half-dead already. We picked him up, brought him here, and now we're holdin' him for you." He gives me a crooked grin, and I think that's probably not all he has to say to me.

"Did you interrogate him?" I ask.

Bryant nods. "Yep. Squealed like a little piggy with his head caught in the electric fence."

"So you know where his daughter went?" I ask, not wanting to continue to fuck around with these assholes.

"Oh, yeah. He told us the plan. Said he couldn't make it that far. Doesn't surprise me. Think the poor bastard's back is broken."

"Well, it might be," I say rubbing my chin. "He did take an awful fall down the stairs."

Jordan tries to glare at me, but he can't. His face is too swollen.

"So where the fuck is she?" I ask Alpha Bryant.

"Well, you see, King Maddox. That's the thing...."

And there it is. He is going to try to bargain with me. "Alpha Bryant, don't you even start," I say, giving him a warning.

"Now, now, hear me out," he says, holding up his hands between us. "Seems to me, you have a couple of problems you need to have taken care of. And it also seems to me, that good old Alpha Bryant is just the man to help you out with both of them." He lays a hand on his chest like he's saluting himself.

I'm already shaking my head. "The only problem I have is that you have this asshole, and I want him. Don't think I can't just take him from you. And anything that he's told you, he'll tell me. My guys are a hell of a lot rougher on traitorous assholes than yours." I look Bryant in the eyes. "And don't you forget it, Alpha."

Again, Bryant's hands are up in mock surrender. "Sure, sure. I know you can get the information I have. But here's the thing, Maddox—King Maddox, you're in my pack right now, and there's just the two of youin's right? So...."

I step really close to him, and he backs up a few steps. "Are you threatening me, Bryant?" I ask him in a low rumble. "Because if you are, you'd better be fucking sure of yourself. My guards will have this entire pack surrounded in less than thirty minutes, and your ass isn't going anywhere before I shut the highways down. You sure these guards of yours are going to have your back and not mine, their king?" I look over at the guards who are standing around Alpha Jordan, and most of them look undecided, like they can go either way.

I don't have to tell Seth anything to know what he's already doing, calling for backup, closing down the highways, getting ready to bar the door behind me. I can take these assholes by myself while Seth keeps anyone else from coming in. It may have been a while since I've been in a fight, but I can handle my shit.

Bryant shakes his head, a crooked grin spreading across his face as he, once again, holds his hands up. "No, no, of course I'm not threatening you, sir. But it would be easier if you'd just... hear me out. I have two things you want. One, Alpha Jordan and the location of his daughter, and two... someone who can give you an heir."

I arch an eyebrow at him, not sure what the fuck he's talking about now. I'm only interested in the first thing he mentioned, which was really two. Alpha Jordan is on his last limb. He could be dead before nightfall without me touching him. All I wanna know is where is his daughter?

"Someone who can give me an heir?" I repeat, scowling at him. "I don't remember asking for help with that, Bryant." My words come out full of venom.

"No, I know you didn't," he admits. "But... I have a little problem you can help me with, and you get your major problem solved with no fuss. Hell, you don't even have to fuck her. Just... take her off my hands. Have your baby. Tell them the mother is whoever the hell you want her to be, and I'll go along with all of it. No one'll hear a peep from me."

I can't figure him out, not to save my life. I stare at him as he begins to sweat. He's obviously nervous about what he's just proposed to me, though I have no idea why.

Alpha Bryant is married. He has children who are in their mid to late twenties, almost my age, but as far as I know, he and his wife have issues. Major issues. They're not exactly fated mates, and I believe he married her for prestige. She was the daughter of another Alpha. Her sister is married to the Alpha of the next pack over, and that marriage isn't exactly solid either. In fact, it's my understanding that Alpha Ronald Rogers and Luna Elise of Mountain Range pack fight so frequently, one of their kids recently came to live here in Hill Country pack with Alpha Bryant and his wife.

That's one messed-up family.

"I don't need your help getting an heir, Bryant," I tell him. "Perhaps you're unaware of the reason Alpha Jordan and his daughter went running to begin with? They tried to kill my breeder."

He arches his eyebrows. "Oh, no, well I didn't know that. But, hey, you won't need a breeder after this. Just take a look okay?"

He whistles and gestures with his hand, and from a side door, a guard comes in, tugging along a small woman with dark brown hair... and a large abdomen.

She has huge eyes, overflowing with tears and fear, and I can tell immediately that whatever is going on here, it's not on the up and up.

"What the fuck, Bryant?" I ask him.

"Yeah, so she's eight months along. So far, we've been able to hide it, but I figure, you take her, you know? Say you visited last year, and uh... you know? Enjoyed her. It's your kid. Right? Save us both some trouble."

She is sobbing, but she doesn't even try to pull away from the guards.

Confusion washes over me as I look at her face. I can't quite sort out what the issue is. Obviously, he knocked up a young girl, and he's trying to hide it—but from whom? Just his wife? His whole pack?

I have no fucking idea.

"Who is she?" I ask him, using a tone that tells him he'd better not lie to me.

"Uh... this is... Sydney," he tells me.

I look at her, still not sure why it matters so much to him that I take her. "Sydney who?"

Alpha Bryant clears his throat. "Sydney... Rogers."

My eyes widen as I realize what he is telling me, and all I can say is, "Holy fuck."

BIG LITTLE SECRETS

Isla

I TRY to process what my mom is saying to me, but something about her words isn't computing. I'm not sure why. What did I expect her to say? Yes, she did use to be the queen of an island kingdom called Maatua, and yes, I used to be a princess?

I mean, it's not as if I really expected what Mystica said to be true. What are the chances, really, that my family is from royalty? For most of my life, I've required safety pins to keep my socks up. That doesn't exactly sound like the princess life.

Still… there's something about my mother's tone that makes me think she's not being completely straightforward with me. Her voice has that little quiver to it like it did when she told Ben that his cat went to live on a farm outside of the city. I had seen the cat's body lying by the side of the road earlier that day, so I knew that Otis wasn't going to live out a peaceful life chasing mice in a barn. Otis was dead.

Mom wasn't a good liar.

"Oh, you've never heard of the place at all?" I ask her.

"Uh… nope. Not that I can think of," she says. "Oh, your father is going to be so glad that you called, honey."

She is trying to change the subject.

I'm not quite ready to abandon ship completely yet. "Mom, what was the name of the island that we came from?"

"That was a long time ago, sweetie. It's probably best if we just let those days go from our memory altogether. There was a lot of death and destruction back then in that part of the world." She is trying to get me to let it go again.

"Mom, now that I'm at the castle, a lot of people ask me questions about my family and where I came from. It's sort of important for people who are working closely with the king to be able to tell him their background so that he knows he can trust them. The last thing I need is for the king to think I'm a spy from some other kingdom." Perhaps I can guilt her into telling me something.

"Would that really happen?" she asks.

"Uh, yeah. It could. I mean, you do know that he's currently looking for some fugitives who were plotting a murder assassination against someone close to him, right?" She definitely doesn't need to know that that someone was me.

"No! Are you okay, honey?"

And now, I've totally lost her again....

"Yes, Mom. I'm fine. I'm perfectly safe. That's not the point. If there's an interrogation, I need to be able to tell Mad—uh—mad people who are yelling at me the truth." I suppose I shouldn't call the king by his first name to my mother. That would really get her off the subject at hand.

"Well, I certainly don't want that. Okay, dear. We came from Tushti. Do you know where that is?" Mom says.

I think for a second, not sure how to respond. Yes, I know where Tushti is. It's far away from here, south, across a different ocean than the one I always thought we traveled over.

And as far as I know, there haven't been any wars there for many centuries.

"Why did we come?" I ask her.

"Because... of the... economic hardships," she says. "Your father needed work."

"And what did he do before, when we were in Tushti?" I want to see how much further my mother is willing to take this lie.

"Uh... he was a factory worker there, too. A foreman. So... he wanted to have a similar job in Willow pack, but they only had regular worker packs. We made do."

"What about the others who fled Tushti? Where did they go?" I ask her.

"Oh, all over," she says. "But they don't like to talk about it, you know? It's a bad memory for most of us. So we try not to speak of it. If you were to ask someone if they were from Tushti, they would probably lie and say they were from somewhere else. Or if they did say they were from there, they'd probably pretend everything had been just fine." She clears her throat. It is still wavering.

I don't understand. I want to know the truth, but she's unwilling to tell me.

So I have one last question for her.

"What about Uncle Tony?"

Mom is silent for so long, I look at the phone to see if it is still connected. I see that I have a signal.

"Mom?"

"Wh-what do you mean?" she stammers. "You remember your father's brother?"

"I remember him," I say, confidently. "I remember a lot, Mom. I remember the boat the night we left, with the howling in the background. I remember the sea and the waves. I remember my sisters and dad being in front of us, and you were so scared. Dad didn't want to go. I remember… I remember a lot."

She makes a whimpering sound but chokes it off. "I think… you may have dreamed some of that, Isla," she says. "I think… you might be remembering something from a book that you've got all mixed up in your head. We left with a large group of people on a boat in the middle of the day. No wolves, nothing like that. Your father was happy to go. Your sisters were ready for an adventure. But now, well, you probably shouldn't ask either of them about it. Your sisters are happy in their current lives. They don't want to talk about any of that either."

It's clear she doesn't want me asking questions or remembering who I am or where I'm from. "Okay," I say. "I understand." I don't tell her what she wants to hear, though, not directly.

I'm not going to promise her I won't say anything to my sisters.

"So what kind of work are you doing?" she asks, changing the subject once more. I let her.

"Oh, uh… mostly… bedchamber work," I say. It isn't a lie.

"Oh, like changing the sheets and cleaning up? That sort of thing?" she asks.

I can't tell my mom the truth, so I say, "Sure, sure. Something like that."

We talk for a few more minutes before I hear two men talking in the background and figure Beta Miguel wants his phone back eventually.

"Well, I should go," Mom says. "I need to get back home. We should get our own phone now, though, so we can talk more often. What number should I call you on at the palace? Aren't there lots of different lines?"

"Oh, yeah, there are," I say. I look at the list of phone numbers in front of me and decide to give her Beta Seth's number. It seems silly to give her the king's number to call me. "I love you, Mom," I say as we prepare to hang up.

"I love you, too, dear. So much. And I'm so proud of you. I hope you're not too disappointed that you're not a real princess, but you'll always be a princess to me."

It's a sweet thing for her to say, and I thank her, even though I'm still a little wounded that she's not being completely honest with me.

I hang up and sit in Maddox's chair for a few minutes. None of what my mom said makes any sense.

Across the room, I see a book that says Atlas on the outside, so I go and pull it off the shelf, taking it to his conference table and setting it down. It's heavy and thick, but there's a good table of contents, and I quickly find what I'm looking for.

Tushti. Nope, there's no way that's right. I can remember seeing the sun rise and set on that boat, and I know we had to be sailing east. If we were coming from Tushti, it would've been different.

I look for Maatua. It's hard to find, but eventually, I see it.

The island is small, and it's near another continent, one covered with large mountains and jungles.

It's to the west of Crescent Falls pack lands. If we came from there… the sun would've been setting behind us, rising before us.

"Just like I remember it," I say.

I sigh and pick the book up, putting it back on the shelf. Maybe I'll just have to go to Maatua and see for myself.

I do think about what my mother has said, though, and even though I know it's not what she'd want me to do, I cross back over to Maddox's desk.

I pick up the phone and look at Maddox's list of extensions. I've never done anything like this before, and my heart is racing. I dial a few numbers and wait.

A kind female voice answers. "Eclipsed Plateau pack. This is Ginger. How can I help you?"

"Hello. This is… Isla, from King Maddox's office." She has to have caller ID. "I'm trying to get in touch with Brandy Moon… Brandy Bear," I remember she is married now. "Do you happen to have a number for her?"

"Certainly, miss. One moment, please."

I wait for the receptionist, Ginger, to find my sister's number. She reads it off to me, and I write it down on a scrap piece of paper before I thank her and hang up.

Taking more deep breaths, I dial Brandy's number, hoping she answers and will talk to me. It's been a long time since I've spoken to either one of my sisters. Mom's right about one thing—they don't like to remember stuff. Like their siblings.

"Hello?" a distracted voice says on the other end of the line.

"Brandy?" I ask.

"Yeah? Who is this?"

"It's Isla…. Your sister."

She's quiet for a minute before she asks, "What's wrong?"

"Nothing," I tell her. "It's just… I need to ask you a question."

"Listen, sis," she says, "whatever it is, you should ask Mom. She doesn't want me talking to you about—stuff."

"Brandy, I work for King Maddox now," I begin. "I live in the castle. I'm around guards and soldiers all day long. They want to know where I'm from. I can't lie to them."

"Tell them you're from Willow pack," she says dismissively.

"I can't!" I say. "They know that's not true. Mom told the king herself that we moved here. So… where from, Brandy? And don't tell me Tushti because I know that's bullshit."

"Tushti?" She says the word like that's the stupidest thing she's ever heard. "Who the hell told you we were from Tushti?"

"Mom did. But I know she's lying."

"Oh, uh… no… that's right." She tries to cover up the fact that she's just disagreed with Mom.

"Brandy… are we from Maatua?"

The phone is silent for a long moment before she says, "Don't ever say that word again."

JUST A FRIEND

Maddox

I STARE at the young woman in front of me for a long moment before I return my attention to Alpha Bryant. Rage washes over me as I figure out what is going on here. "Is this your niece?" I ask him.

He shrugs. "Not by blood."

The young woman is sniffling, and I can't help but think she has to be... seventeen? Maybe eighteen at most.

"What the fuck?" I ask Bryant, turning on him. "What did you do to her?"

"Hey, King Maddox," he says, holding his hands up between us again. "I didn't give her nothin' she didn't want. She's a little tramp. I wasn't even sure the baby was mine until I did a DNA test on the little bastard. Pretty much every guy in my pack has gotten some of her."

With that, the little girl starts crying even harder.

I am furious. It looks like I'm about to have a second pack without an Alpha.

But I have to be more careful with this one. I can't just force Alpha Bryant out the way that I did Alpha Ernest because there are forces here that will fight back. Unlike Ernest, Alpha Bryant is a powerful leader.

"The girl and Alpha Jordan are coming with me," I tell him. "But that does not mean that your problems are over, Bryant." I snarl at him, and a smirk forms on his face as if he disagrees with me. "I'm taking her for her own protection, not because I plan on passing this baby off as my own. Trust me, I don't need your fucking help with that."

"Well, you might need my help with other stuff," he says with a shrug, as if he knows something that I don't know. "You know, there are some pretty strong Alphas out there who think it's a weakness that you don't have a kid yet, and you're almost thirty. How much longer you got before they're going to be knocking down your door, huh?"

I grab him by the collar and shove him against the wall, my grip on his shirt ripping the material as I change tactics and wrap my hand around his neck. I squeeze until his face starts to turn red, and he is clawing at my hand.

I hear his thugs coming toward me, but I put up a hand, and they stop. A sign to him that he's not as fucking strong as he thinks he is.

As close to his face as I can get, I say, "If you ever even think about threatening me again, Bryant, I will rip your balls off and shove them down your throat. I am your king, and you will respect me. Do you fucking understand me?" Some of my spit lands on his face, hangs there for a moment, and then drips down to his shoulder.

His eyes are rolling back in his head, and I know there's no way he can answer me. He can't even breathe. I don't need him to say the words to know that he gets it.

Pushing him backward into the wall, I let him go and turn to face Vinny and the others. Their eyes are wide, and they look like they might be about to shit their pants.

"Do any of the rest of you feel like tough guys today?" I ask.

Vinny shakes his head. "N-no, sir," he says. "Alpha King Maddox."

I'm about to tell Seth to get Jordan when I see movement out of the corner of my eye and realize Bryant is actually going to go there. He's lunging at me with something sharp and shiny in his hand.

I throw my elbow into his throat and bring my forearm up and catch him in the face before I whirl around, wrap my arm around his neck and hold him in a half-nelson with one arm as I pluck a blade from his flailing hand with the other.

With very little effort, I drag his body to his desk and then slam his head into the corner of the desk. Blood gushes everywhere. Sydney screams, and that flailing arm goes still

I drop him on the floor, not interested in whether or not the motherfucker is dead.

"Seth," I say, motioning to my Beta to get Jordan. "Come with me, sweetheart," I say to the girl who's crying and trembling now. I take her by the arm, careful not to squeeze too tight, and lead her to the door.

"Alpha King Maddox!" Vinny calls after me, and I see he's following me out.

"What, Vinny?" I ask.

"If... uh... Bryant's dead, am I the Alpha?"

I shake my head and whisper a curse word under my breath. "Vinny, if I could trust that you're loyal to me, I wouldn't have a problem with that, but I don't think you are."

"Yes, I am!" he insists, making the sign of respect.

I shake my head. "Prove it. Do something about this shit he was threatening me with. Find out where the hell Zabrina is and get her back. Then, we'll talk."

"Yes, sir, Alpha King Maddox," the idiot Beta says, saluting again. I want to tell him to go fuck himself, but I have an hysterical teenage pregnant girl with me who needs to get home.

I decide that the girl doesn't need to ride in the back seat with Jordan, so I put him in the trunk. He'll live long enough for us to make it back to the castle. Then, Seth opens the door for Sydney, and she gets in. But as we are starting to pull away, she asks, "Can I get my stuff?"

I curse again. "What stuff?" I ask her.

"My clothes... shoes... my phone." It's hard to understand her when she's crying.

"Where is it?" Beta Seth asks her.

"In my room, upstairs." She gestures back at the Alpha's mansion.

I look at Seth. "Ten minutes. Don't get blindsided."

"Yes, Alpha," he says with a sarcastic tone, and then he shoots out of the car, back up to the porch, and inside.

I wait for him, not sure what to say to Sydney. Finally, I ask her, "Do you want to go back to your parents' pack?"

She shakes her head. "No, my dad would kill me."

"All right. To the castle it is, then."

Beta Seth comes back a few minutes later with what looks like hastily packed bags. He tosses them into the back seat beside Sydney and then hands her an older model cell phone.

As he gets in behind the steering wheel, he says, "Alpha Bryant is dead."

I say, "We should stop in Crescent City on the way back."

He arches an eyebrow. "What? Why?"

"There's a restaurant there I like. I'm starving."

~

Isla

. . .

"WHAT DO you mean never say that word again?" I don't understand why my sister is being hostile. "Is that where we're from or not? Mom wouldn't tell me the truth. She said we were from Tushti. But that's not true."

"Isla, you're asking questions that are going to get you into trouble," Brandy says, her voice sounding borderline angry. "Can't you just leave it be?"

"No!" I shout at her. "Listen, I almost died yesterday, and now that I'm alive, I'd like to know who the hell I am. Where did I come from? Was Dad really an Alpha? A king? Or is it just a coincidence that the king of Ma—that place—happened to be named Daniel and the queen was Constance? Tell me, Brandy. What do you know?"

She sighs loudly, and I hear the sound of a baby crying. "Your nephew is hungry," she tells me.

"I have a nephew?" I didn't even know she was pregnant again. "Brandy, you've completely cut yourself off from the family. So has Kenna. Why?"

"Why?" she shouts at me. "For exactly this reason! Why are you even calling me, Isla? I don't want to fucking talk about our past, okay? It was a long time ago, and it doesn't matter now. Where are you even calling me from?"

"I'm calling you from King Maddox's office," I tell her, unable to keep the anger out of my voice anymore either. "I work at the castle now."

"And you're calling from the king's phone? Someone has grown a pair of balls! Won't he be pissed if he finds you in there?"

I laugh. I can't help it. "I'll make it up to him," I say.

"What?" Brandy is confused.

"Nothing. Just answer my questions, please."

"No!" she says. "I'm not going to tell you anything, Isla. For whatever reason, Mom and Dad don't want us to ever talk about the past, and they certainly don't want you saying that word. No one needs to know where we came from or who they were. So please, just drop it. All right?"

"I can't just drop it, Brandy!" I think maybe I should call Kenna, but then I realize she will probably say the same thing to me.

"Drop it. That place is cursed. Anyone will tell you that. If this person who told you the king and queen's names didn't tell you that, too, they're no friend. Just let it be," she says. "And don't ever call me again."

She hangs up the phone, and I stare at the wall for a good five minutes before I say, "Well, that didn't go as planned."

I push up from Maddox's desk and start to walk out the door when he walks in. His eyes widen at seeing me, and then I realize he's not alone.

He's got a girl with him, and she doesn't even look like she's my age. She's beautiful, with dark hair and large eyes.

And she's very, very pregnant.

"Isla?" he says, staring at me. "What the hell are you doing in my office?"

I can't figure out why he's mad at me. "You said I could call my parents," I remind him.

"We have phones in other offices," he says, though his tone isn't quite as angry right now.

"I'm sorry," I say. I look at the girl again. She is just staring at me, confused.

"Who is she?" she whispers to Maddox, her voice barely a whisper.

"Isla is… uh…" Maddox stammers. "She's… a friend."

I stare into his eyes for a moment, wondering why he would describe me that way.

Who is this woman?

Is that his baby?

Maybe he doesn't need me to be his breeder anymore, so I can be just a friend.

"Yep, I'm just a friend," I say, trying to contain my tears until I'm out of the room. "And I was just leaving."

I push past both of them and head to my room, swiping away at tears as they fall down my cheeks.

"Isla!" I hear him call, but I don't stop.

It turns out my position at the castle has been filled by someone else, and I'm no longer needed by Alpha King Maddox.

Or anyone.

Maybe everyone is right, and people from Maatua are cursed….

If that's the case, then I'm definitely from there.

I may as well be the fucking queen.

End of book one

Keep reading to enjoy chapter 1 of *Loved by the Alpha: The Alpha King's Breeder Book 2*

Bella Moondragon
LOVED
BY THE
ALPHA
THE ALPHA KING'S BREEDER
BOOK TWO

LOVED BY THE ALPHA CHAPTER 1: WHAT NOW?

Isla

I am ashamed of the fact that I am crying when I get back to my room. I want to scream and break something. I think about how it was when I first arrived at the castle and that old witch, Mrs. Whateverthehellhernamewas got mad at me for accidentally running into something. Now, I want to pick up an antique and toss it across the room.

I can't believe what's happening! Not only did my own sister refuse to answer my questions about where we came from, King Maddox just described me as a friend to a very, very pregnant little girl.

I lay down on my bed and pull a pillow over my head, angry sobs coming out. What in the world have I gotten myself into?

How the hell did I think I could actually stroll into the castle and mean something to the king?

He's the KING, after all, and I'm nothing. I've never been anyone.

Even if my parents truly were once the king and queen of Maatua, they certainly aren't now. That island has been described as cursed by everyone who has ever heard of it.

It seems to me like my entire family is cursed at this point. My parents, having to leave their homeland, my brother's illness, my kidnapping and near-death experience.

And falling in love with the cruel king who obviously doesn't mind making little weaklings like me think that he has feelings for us when he really doesn't at all.

Hearing footsteps behind me, I flip around, pulling the pillow off of my face far enough to see who is in my room.

Thankfully, it's not Maddox. It's Poppy, and she looks concerned. She sits down next to me, and when I roll back over and put the pillow back in place, she rubs my back.

"Didn't go well, huh?" she asks me after a few minutes, which actually makes me laugh.

"You can say that again," I reply. I'm not bawling and crying anymore, but I am still upset. Her hand is soothing in a motherly way, though.

"I'm so sorry," she says, still smoothing her hand down my back. "Did you speak to your sister?"

I sit up, pulling away from Poppy as I move my pillow aside and lean back against the headboard. I try not to think about the times I've actually hit my head on this headboard while making love to Maddox.

Poppy hands me a wad of tissue, and I swipe at my eyes. "I spoke to her. She wouldn't tell me anything. It seems pretty clear to me, though, that we are from Ma–that place. Everyone says it's best not to even say the word."

Poppy snickers. "I didn't take you as the superstitious sort, Isla."

I shrug. "Yeah, well, I need to be more careful. Things aren't exactly going well right now."

Her smile becomes even more sympathetic. "You're alive. That's something."

"I guess that's true. Goddess, my emotions are all over the place, though." I sniffle a few more times and wipe my nose.

"Well, dear, you were poisoned. Your body is probably trying to adjust."

I nod. Maybe she's right. "Anyway, King Maddox came back as I was leaving his office. And he was pissed that I was in there."

Poppy's eyes almost bulge out of her head. "Seriously? Why? He said you could use his phone. As far as I can tell, he has no business being mad that you were in there if he wants to keep getting in there." She gestures with the top of her head at my lower body, and I want to laugh.

But it's too much of a sore subject for me to laugh at the moment.

Instead, I sigh. "I'm not sure that he does," I say. "He had some… girl with him."

"What?" Her eyes are so big now, they look like cereal bowls with pupils, and her mouth hangs open after she's said the word.

"Yeah. She was young, too. Way younger than me. And… super-duper pregnant. So it seems I've been relieved of my services. In fact, considering her baby was about to pop right out of her, I guess I wasn't ever needed in the first place."

"Shut up!" Poppy insists, dropping her hand on my leg, hard. I know she didn't mean to smack me, not that hard anyway, but it stings a little. "No fucking way!"

I can only shrug again. "I'm just telling you what I saw, Poppy."

She is shaking her head. "I can't believe he would do such a thing! I mean, it's not like he has been a saint since the Luna passed, but I can't imagine that he would sleep with someone who isn't even old enough to be his… sister."

I don't know what that means. I think she's just so flabbergasted she doesn't know what to say, and I am right there with her.

"Anyway," I say, "I may as well figure out what to do now. I have no reason to stay here. I guess I can go home, but I'm not sure my mom wants to see me right now."

"You can't leave!" Poppy blurts. "I don't want to be the maid to just any old whore!"

I raise an eyebrow at her. "As opposed to me? An extra-special whore?"

She bursts out laughing, but I'm not sure what's so freaking funny. "That's not what I meant. You're not a whore. You've only been with one man."

I am glad I can amuse her. I slowly shake my head. I didn't intend to be with any other man either, but now… well, if I'm ever going to have a family or anything, I'll need to find someone who will love me.

And here I was thinking perhaps King Maddox was my fated mate! Maybe the Moon Goddess had it in her heart to give him a second chance mate, and that could be me.

The idea almost makes me laugh aloud.

But I bit my tongue. There wasn't anything funny going on here, except for whatever the hell Maddox was up to with that little girl.

"Don't decide anything now," Poppy says, patting me on the leg where she smacked me a little while ago. "You have plenty of time to decide what you want to do."

I hope she's right because I don't want to leave right this very minute, but I also have to wonder what I will do if Maddox comes storming into my room and demands that I leave in the same tone he used when he found me in his office.

"I'll go get you something to eat," Poppy says. "You've got to be tired after everything you've been through."

"Thank you," I tell her, feeling bad that she's even waiting on me. I don't think I need a maid when I am likely no longer the Alpha King's Breeder.

I'm just a glorified guest in the castle who might be asked to leave at any moment, and honestly, I don't want to give Maddox the satisfaction of tossing me out on my ass.

And if he does tell me to leave, I guarantee he'll take back the credit card he's given me, as he should, as well as the little amount of cash I have.

Why would he pay me for having sex with him? That wasn't what I was supposed to do here. I was supposed to have his baby, and he doesn't need me for that anymore.

Poppy gives me another sympathetic look and then leaves the room, leaving me lost in my thoughts.

Eating something fattening and going to sleep sounds tempting. But I'm not sure that's what's in my best interest now. If I have to leave the castle, I need a plan in place….

I'll have to go somewhere.

I think of the cufflinks. I think of the mystery surrounding my homeland. I think of the curse….

Maybe I know where I'll go after all….

Maddox

Sydney is sitting in the chair behind my desk, sobbing, as she speaks to her mother on my phone. I am angry. At a lot of people. Including her.

I'm not mad that she was in an awful position and got herself knocked up by her aunt's husband. I don't think that was the girl's fault, even though I can tell by the one-sided conversation I'm overhearing that she wasn't taken against her will by Alpha Bryant. He wasn't her first. This was the problem that had sent her to her aunt and uncle's house to begin with.

Little Miss Sydney had spreaders disease–the inability to keep her knees together.

But she was only nineteen–a little older than I had thought–and she clearly didn't feel like she was loved at home.

I'll let her stay in the castle until her child is born, and then, after that, we'll reevaluate the situation. Perhaps she can work here as a maid or something.

Beta Seth comes in and says, "Her room is ready. It's on the bottom floor, like you asked, so she won't have to climb stairs, but in the opposite wing as your room, so no one will assume anything is going on."

"Thank you," I tell him, glad I have a Beta who is reliable. "Did you assign her a maid and tell Mystica to come and check her out?"

He nods. "She's on her way, so Sydney might need to get off of the phone."

The girl looks up at his words, and it's clear she's heard him as she manages to tell her mother goodbye. It seems like Sydney loves her mama even if she's disappointed her time and time again.

I will need to have my phone de-snotified before I use it again with all of those tears and mucus flowing out of the girl. She plucks a tissue from my desk and heads toward us.

"Beta Seth will take you to your room," I tell her.

"Thank you, King Maddox," she says, and I think she's actually batting her eyelashes at me. I recoil in disgust.

I want to say she's too young for me, but that's not true since she's basically the same age as Isla, but the fact is, Sydney is far too pregnant for me to even consider what she might look like not pregnant, and she's obviously wild and immature.

Besides that, I'm not interested in anyone other than Isla.

Isla.

I've fucked up.

Again.

After Seth and Sydney leave the room, I sigh and wonder what I should do.

I shouldn't have yelled at her. Thinking back, I'm pretty sure I told her, or at least gave her the impression, that it was fine for her to use my phone. I was just angry when I walked in.

And I honestly didn't want her to see me with Sydney. I didn't want to explain something that had no explanation because I hadn't done anything wrong.

I know what I need to do. With a deep breath, I head down the hallway toward Isla's room.

When I arrive, I stop and stare at the closed door for a moment, gathering my thoughts.

The door to her antechamber is unlocked, so I walk in, but when I reach her bedroom door, I pause again before knocking.

She doesn't answer.

"Isla?" I call.

Again, it's quiet.

"Isla, it's Maddox." Like she wouldn't know that. "Can I come in?"

She says nothing, and I notice I don't smell her like I usually do. I don't sense her.

A bit of panic wells up inside of me as I remember how terrified I was when I discovered she was gone before.

I try the door, and it's locked, but I am better prepared this time. I pull the keys out of my pocket and unlock the door.

My heart stops.

Her room is empty.

Click here to read *Loved by the Alpha: The Alpha King's Breeder Book 2*

Bella Moondragon
LOVED
BY THE
ALPHA
THE ALPHA KING'S BREEDER
BOOK TWO

www.ingramcontent.com/pod-product-compliance
Lightning Source LLC
Chambersburg PA
CBHW070412310726
48977CB00003B/650